Conten

M000040468

Acknowledgments

In regard to this book I am mostly indebted to my darling wife LaBreeska, one of the greatest ladies I have ever known. She has had a remarkable life - long hunger to know who the God of the Bible is. Her prayers, faith and wisdom have been priceless and I am eternally grateful.

Thanks to all of my wonderful family for your love and prayers. A special thanks to our secretary, Dawn Mansfield for her diligent labor in typing and perfecting the manuscript. Thanks also for your insight and encouragement. Thanks to Lou Crowder for her technical help with polishing the writing. Lynsae Harkins of Lynsae Design did a great job with the cover and I thank you.

Thanks to some twelve ministers *(pastors and evangelists)*, with whom I shared Chapters of this book, and who examined it closely and had the courage to say, "This is the truth." You know who you are and to you I am extremely grateful. Much thanks to several of these who gave special help and encouragement. Thanks also to a very few with whom I shared portions, who disagreed with the premise. Your input helped me as well.

A very special thank you to Elbert and Allison Lumley and Nancy Carter at Digital Imaging for their help with the printing.

May you all be blessed!

Dedication

To my parents, Mrs. Beatrice Hemphill and the late Elder W.T. Hemphill who taught me many things in many ways, but mostly through love and Godly example.

Introduction

In the spring of 1986 I had an awesome encounter with the God of Abraham, Isaac and Jacob. Along with many other things that He told me *(see Appendix A)*, He said for me to study the Scripture, as He was going to reveal Himself to me in His word. This seemed strange as I was forty-six years old, had been saved since I was ten, had been a minister of the Gospel since the age of nineteen, and thought I had a pretty good grasp on who He was. I was mistaken! He also said that I would one day "write a book or books" about His glory. Regarding this I knew my understanding was lacking, as God's glory was not something on which I had really focused. I knew that the Shekinah glory was seen on Mt. Sinai, in the Tabernacle and Temple, and by the shepherds when the angel announced Jesus' birth, all of which I could perhaps have written on one page.

I did begin to search the Bible, still focused mostly on the Shekinah (the radiance of His seldom seen presence), but soon came to see that if I was to write a book about God's glory, He would have to "reveal" more to me. I also understood that it was about His timing, so I stayed aware but ceased to struggle with it.

Through the years I have said to close friends, "Someday I'm going to write a book about God's glory." Around the first of November 2005, I felt stirred to put some thoughts on paper, thinking that it might turn out to be a gospel tract for our ministry, as I have done from time to time. My wife LaBreeska, seeing the zeal with which I was writing said to me one day, "Honey, I think this may be the book that the Lord talked to you about," but at that time I could not see the connection. That happened about a week later. Now, over 500 hand written pages later I believe that I have delivered my heart. I have not done justice to this awesome subject, but I have done my best.

Though this book is completely Bible based, it is not for everybody, especially two types of people. Those who are willing to take the word of theologians, Bible school teachers and church creeds over "thus saith the word of God." Also those who say in their hearts, "I know what I believe about God, so don't confuse me with what the Bible says about Him." Hopefully these will be few. I have not dealt with every scripture that might shed light on the subject of this book. That would be impossible. Obviously, I do not know every scripture that may apply. Also, that would be unnecessary. I have tried to give overwhelming Bible proof for every statement of doctrine that I have made, and every other scripture must agree with the ones quoted herein. Paul does not contradict Paul. Neither does he contradict, Peter, John, Moses or Jesus. They all agree.

Now some words regarding my writing style. I have written and published several hundred Gospel songs, some fifty magazine articles and a few Gospel tracts but I have never before written a book. It has been a learning experience for me. I have purposely used some repetition as I think it is necessary for clear understanding. King David said 26 times in *Psalm 136, "For his mercy endureth for ever."* What was he wanting us to see? That *"his mercy endureth for ever."* I have **bolded** some words and phrases for effect. This emphasis is mine throughout. Since the Supreme God is the absolute focus of this book, I have made the choice to capitalize all nouns and pronouns that refer to Him, except when quoting from the Holy Bible. For the sake of clarity, even when scripture quotes are indented, I have chosen to put them in italics with quotation marks.

Some things dealt with in this book are of a historical nature, especially in Chapters 2, 13, 14 and 15. I am not a historian so I have relied on the best sources I could find, and on what is commonly understood to be historical fact. Paul says in *I Cor. 5:1, "It is reported commonly that there is fornication among you,"* and then he proceeded to deal with it on that basis.

This book does not seek to diminish Jesus in any way. God forbid! Neither should it ever be used to try and do so. He is everything the Holy Bible says he is, the virgin born, righteous, anointed, appointed, approved Son of God, Messiah of Israel. He is our loving Savior, Redeemer and soon coming King. But here is the problem, he is not everything that some of

10

Christianity says he is, and I have been called to help sort it out. This is not about denomination. I have pastored Southern Baptist and Pentecostal churches but I am not trying to make Baptists or Pentecostals, however I am highly concerned that people have a divine encounter with God our Father, through our Lord Jesus Christ. *"This is life eternal"* (*John 17:3*).

Now, a note to ministers and Bible teachers. If you see and embrace the truths found herein you must speak out. But please pray and ask God to give you wisdom regarding when and how to present it. *(Consider giving a copy of this book)* This is God's message, and there is nothing as powerful as a truth whose time has come. It calls for some fundamental adjustments in our thinking, but it must be dealt with on an emotional level as well. This takes more time for some than for others. The best teacher is a good example, so just begin to walk in the light from henceforth, as you see the light, and trust the work of the Holy Spirit.

> *"When he, the Spirit of truth is come, he will guide you*
> *into all truth: and he will show you things to come"*
> (Jesus speaking) (*John 16:13*).

Finally, I have approached the subject of this writing carefully and prayerfully as its importance is too great to get it wrong. I have also kept in mind Jesus' words to Peter, *"Feed my sheep"* and *"feed my lambs."* These are of different maturity and need different food. Perhaps there are even a few goats. The challenge is to awaken the goats without harming the sheep and lambs. Only time will tell if I have succeeded. I love you all.*

To God Be The Glory!

* Note: The use of any person's name in this book is not meant to imply that they agree with its conclusions. *"To God Be The Glory"* represents the sincere beliefs of the author, and he is solely responsible for its contents.

God The Creator's Glory

*"Thus said the Lord, the Holy **One** of Israel, and his Maker. **I have made the earth**, and **created man** upon it: I, even **my hands**, have stretched out the heavens, and all their host have I commanded....and there is **no God else beside me**; a just God and a Saviour; **there is none beside me**. Look unto me, and be ye saved, all the ends of the earth: for **I am God, and there is none else**"* (Isaiah 45:11-12, 21-22).

*"I am the Lord: that is my name; and **my glory will I not give to another**"* *(Isaiah 42:8).*

*"**I will not give my glory unto another**" (Isaiah 48:11).*

*"And I saw another angel fly in the midst of heaven, having the everlasting gospel to preach unto them that dwell on the earth, and to every nation, and kindred, and tongue, and people, Saying with a loud voice, **Fear God**, and **give glory to him**; for the hour of his judgement is come: and **worship him** that made heaven , and the earth, and the sea, and the fountains of waters"* *(Revelation 14:6-7).*

Jesus' Glory

*"The Son of Man...shall come in **his own glory**"* (Jesus speaking) *(Luke 9:26).*

*"The Son of man shall sit in the throne of **his glory*** (Jesus speaking) *(Matt. 19:28).*

*"Father...the **glory which thou gavest me**...that they may behold **my glory which thou hast given me**"* (Jesus speaking) *(John 17:21, 22, 24).*

(Christ) *"verily was **foreordained** before the foundation of the world, but was manifest in these last times for you, Who by him do believe in **God**, that raised him up from the dead, and **gave him glory**; that your faith and hope might be in **God**"* *(I Peter 1:20-21).*

12

Chapter 1

"Ye Shall Know The Truth"

*"God is a Spirit; and they that worship him **must worship him** in spirit and **in truth**"* (Jesus speaking) *John 4:24.*

*"**And ye shall know the truth, and the truth shall make you free**"* (Jesus speaking) *John 8:32.*

*J*esus, the virgin born, sinless son of God, was teaching in the temple in Jerusalem, when the scribes and Pharisees interrupted him, bringing in a woman caught in the act of adultery. After giving them a lesson in forgiveness, he continued his powerful teaching regarding his light, his truth, his mission, his Father and the danger they faced of dying in their sins. *John 8:30 - 31* says, *"As he spake these words, many believed on him."* Then he said to the believers, *"If ye continue in my word, then ye are my disciples indeed."* Jesus gave the new believers a wonderful promise that, as they continued to follow him, they would **"know the truth"** and be made free by it. This promise was and is of utmost importance, for they lived as we do, in a world in which many people believed and taught that truth was unknowable. They believed there was no absolute truth as set down by a Creator, but that knowledge could only be arrived at by *experience.* Jesus faced one who held this philosophy some months later, Pontius Pilate, and said, *"To this **end was I born, and for this cause came I into the world**, that I should **bear witness unto the truth**. Every one that is of the truth heareth my voice."* Pilate's response seems to have in it a note of sarcasm, *"**What is truth?"** (John 18:37-38).* Of course Jesus had already answered that question for all of time and eternity one Chapter prior, in his prayer to his

13

Heavenly Father, saying, *"Sanctify them through thy truth:* **thy word is truth.**" God's word is **truth**, eternal, pure, powerful, unshakable, life-giving truth!

Deut. 32:4 says:

> *"He is the Rock, his work is perfect: for all his ways are judgment:* **a God of truth** *and without iniquity, just and right is he."*

Ps. 100:5 says:

> *"For the Lord is good; his mercy is everlasting; and* **his truth** *endureth to all generations."*

The great apostle Paul states it strongly in *Romans 3:3-4*:

> *"For what if some did not believe? Shall their unbelief make the faith of God without effect? God forbid: yea,* **let God be true, but every man a liar.**"

God's written word, the Holy Bible is true. Let's look at some examples of its accuracy.

About 513 years ago Christopher Columbus and his companions sailed from Palos, Spain, in three ships looking for a new trade route to the East. Many feared for their safety, as the best scientists of his day believed that the world was flat, and thought that they might "sail off the edge." But God's Bible had proclaimed some 2200 years before Columbus sailed that *"It is He* (God) *that sitteth on the* **circle of the earth,** *and the inhabitants thereof are as grasshoppers" (Isa. 40:22).* Columbus proved what the Bible said, the earth is **a circle**!

Around the year 1799, George Washington, the aging father of our country, became ill and the best doctors were called in to treat him. Because it was commonly believed by the elite of the medical profession of that time that sickness was caused by "bad blood," he was drained of considerable amounts of his precious life's blood on several occasions. This was, as we know now, ill-advised treatment and no doubt helped to hasten his death. Had these sincere doctors only read and believed the Scripture, he might have lived longer, for God had said some 3300 years before:

*"**For the life of the flesh is in the blood**: For it is the life of all flesh; the blood of it is for the life thereof: therefore I said unto the children of Israel, Ye shall eat the blood of no manner of flesh: for **the life of all flesh is the blood thereof**" (Lev. 17:11, 14).* Now Doctors give patients blood.

It is widely accepted among the scientists of today, that the continents of the earth once fit together as one land mass and separated at sometime in the past. Of course the earth as one land mass, and the seas together as one, is exactly what was pictured by Moses, the author of Genesis approximately **3500** years ago *(Gen. 1:9-10).* No scientist can tell you when the continents separated but the Holy Bible does, in *Genesis 10:25* and *I Chronicles 1:19.* These verses say that a man by the name of Eber named his first son Peleg, which means *division," for in his days was the earth divided."* One more example of the absolute accuracy of God's Holy Word.

God told Job, as recorded in the book of *Job 38:7,* written some 3520 years ago, that at the time of creation *"the morning stars sang together."* Modern scientists say that at the time of the "big bang," the planets vibrated and rang like bells. They "sang together." Recently an earthquake produced a tsunami that struck Asia and killed over 200,000 people. Scientists say the shock of it moved the earth off its normal axis about one inch and caused the earth to "vibrate like a bell" every 17 minutes for weeks afterward. God's word is true!

Why is knowing the truth so important? Jesus said to the woman at the well in *John 4:24,* *"God is a Spirit: and they that worship him **must worship** him in spirit and **in truth**."* **Our worship of God is not accepted by Him unless it is done according to His truth**. His truth regarding who He is, His divine nature, mercy, grace, readiness to receive and forgive sinners. In *Mark 7:7* Jesus quotes from Isaiah where God says, *"Howbeit **in vain do they worship me,** teaching for doctrines the commandments of men."* God's truth is revealed by the Holy Spirit, *"the Spirit of truth" (John 14:17, 15:26, 16:13)* in His son Jesus, who said in *John 14:6 "I am the way,*

15

the truth, *and the life: no man cometh unto the Father,* **but by me.**"

What is the truth regarding Almighty God and his son Jesus Christ? *1 Tim. 2:3-5* says:

> *"For this is good and acceptable in the sight of God our*
> *Saviour; Who will have all men to* **be saved**, *and to*
> *come unto the* **knowledge of the truth**. (What truth?)
> *For there is* **one God**, *and* **one mediator** *between God*
> *and men,* **the man Christ Jesus**."

Do you understand this truth? Or what Jesus said in *Rev. 3:14*:

> *"And unto the angel of the church of the Laodiceans*
> *write; These things saith the Amen, the* **faithful and**
> **true witness**, *the* **beginning of the creation of God**."

Do you understand that foundational truth? Do you believe and receive it? And again when Jesus says in *John 8:17-18*:

> *"It is also written in your law, that the testimony of* **two**
> *men is true. I am* **one that bear witness of myself**, *and*
> *the* **Father that sent me** *beareth witness of me*."

Jesus is saying "I and my Father are two, two witnesses." Do you understand that truth? Do you love it? My point is that we have leaned on our creeds, dogmas, and denominational doctrines for so long that we sometime seem to love them more than we love *"thus saith the word of God."* It matters not what traditions, orthodoxy, theologians, early church fathers or councils say, **the Bible is right!** The only authority on which to base any doctrine that we hold and declare, is the inerrant and infallible word of God, the Holy Bible. David said in *Psalm 119:128*:

> *"Therefore I esteem* **all thy precepts** *concerning all*
> *things to be right; and* **I hate every false way**."

The Bible

God is the custodian of His word. It was not written **by** theologians nor **for** theologians but to be read and understood by the common man, "a wayfaring man tho a fool." By a series of wonderful acts He has given it to us in English, that we might understand it as we would any other book

16

written in that language. Some of it is parable, some of it is allegory, but the overwhelming majority of it is to be taken literally. God is not trying to hide the truth. A reader can tell when it is parable or allegory, and when He says "it was," it was! *(Even that part which is parable or allegory, refers to something that is literal).*

We must love the truth. Let me remind you that to play carelessly with the truth is both immoral and dangerous. We must love the truth to be saved. Those who do not receive a **love for the truth** will one day soon receive from God a strong delusion and be damned. Paul says in *II Thess. 2:9-12* regarding the antichrist:

> *"Even him, whose coming is after the working of Satan with all power and signs and lying wonders, And with all deceivableness of unrighteousness in them that perish;* ***because they received not the love of the truth,*** *that they might be saved. And for this cause God shall send them strong delusion, that they should believe a lie: That they all might be damned who* ***believed not the truth.***"

I was saddened as I read the words of a noted Jewish Rabbi recently as reported in the media, "I would not believe that Jesus is the Messiah if Moses himself told me so." And of course Moses did tell him in *Deut. 18:15*:

> *"The Lord thy God will raise up unto thee* ***a Prophet from the midst of thee, of thy brethren,*** *like unto me; unto him ye shall hearken."*

Then God said to Moses:

> *"I will raise them up* ***a Prophet from among their brethren, like unto thee,*** *and will put* ***my words in his mouth;*** *and* ***he shall speak unto them all that I shall command him.*** *And it shall come to pass, that whosoever will not hearken unto my words* ***which he shall speak in my name,*** *I will require it of him" (Deut.*

17

18:18-19).

I know the rabbi and most other Jews do not understand these verses, but do you? This is not another *"God"* that the Lord God promised Israel, but a *"Prophet," "from the midst of thee," "from among their brethren, like unto thee"* (Moses). This is none other than Jesus Christ Messiah *(John 1:45; Acts 3:22 and 7:37).* He was to act as God's exclusive agent in truth, salvation, and judgement; but there was no promise that he would be God. Jesus said to God the Father, *"And this is life eternal, that they might know thee, **the only true God,** "* and **that** is the truth.

Understand this truth as well. God said of this Prophet Messiah, *"My words which he shall **speak in my name.** "* Jesus said in *John 5:43, "I am come in **my Father's name.** "* And again in *John 10:25, "The works that I do in **my Father's name.** "* The Father's name is not "Jesus." **God's name is His authority**. God said to Moses regarding the **angel** that was leading Israel to the promised land:

> *"Beware of him...provoke him not: **for my name is in him"** (Ex. 23:21).*

Notice that God told Moses this Prophet *(Jesus)* would be *"from among their brethren" (Deut. 18:18).* *Hebrews 2:17* says of Jesus, *"Wherefore **in all things** it behooved him to be made **like unto his brethren.** "* Jesus did not come in the "God family," he came in the "man family." He is our brother, "the **man** Christ Jesus."

The unbelieving rabbi has very little chance of being saved, short of a Damascus road experience like the Apostle Paul, and that is unlikely to happen. He and we must receive and believe God's written word or be lost. God has made His written word of paramount importance. Peter said in *Acts 3:23* of Jesus, the promised Prophet, *"And it shall come to pass, that every soul, which will not hear that prophet, shall be destroyed from among the people. "* How do we know what Jesus said? **Faithful men wrote it down!**

Listen to David in *Psalm 138:2 : "For thou hast **magnified thy word above all thy name.** "* God has magnified His word above His name;

therefore we know for sure that He has exalted it above our **creeds** and **denominational doctrines**. Notice what Peter says in *II Peter 1:17-21*:

> *"For he received from God the Father honor and glory,* when *there came such a voice to him from the excellent glory, This is my beloved Son, in whom I am well pleased.* And *this voice* which came from heaven *we heard,* when we were with him *in the holy mount. We have also a more sure word of prophecy; whereunto ye do well that ye take heed,* as unto a light that shineth in a dark place, until the day dawn, and the day star arise in your hearts: Knowing this first, *that no prophecy of the scripture* is of any private interpretation. For *the prophecy came not in old time by the will of man:* but *holy men of God spake* as they were moved *by the Holy Ghost."*

You may need to read these verses over several times to receive what Peter is saying. "We heard God's voice speak from heaven concerning Jesus, but we have **a more sure word of prophecy** than a voice from heaven." We have the "prophecy of the Scripture," to which we had better "take heed." I did not write this, but **I am called to declare it**.

Even we, who call ourselves fundamental Christians and pride ourselves in our stance of "solo scriptura" *(solely Scripture)*, have allowed tradition to cloud our understanding of what the Bible says about God and the Godhead.

In *John 16:13* Jesus refers to the Holy Spirit as *"the Spirit of Truth"* and promises that *"he will guide you into all truth."* Surely with His help sincere seekers can find the truth regarding who God is. This is foundational. Erroneous teachings and doctrines are not **truth**. Truth is pure! It is the truth that makes us free, Jesus said to the Father in *John 17:17, "thy word is truth."* **When truth is mixed with error, truth is destroyed!**

Bible believers will all agree that the Bible does not contradict itself. It has one author, God the Father, though He used some 40 writers to write it down under the inspiration of the Holy Spirit *(II Peter 1:21, II Tim. 3:16)*. Since God cannot contradict Himself, anytime one Scripture **seems** to contradict another, it means only that our understanding is deficient; therefore we must study and pray that our understanding will be opened in that area. In *Luke 24:45*, Jesus opened *"their understanding, that they might understand the scriptures."* This is what we must seek for.

Paul wrote to the young minister Timothy some words of good advice:

> *"**Study** to show thyself **approved unto** God, a workman*
> *that needeth **not to be ashamed, rightly dividing** the*
> *word of truth" (II Tim. 2:15).*

The Bible is the best commentary on itself. The context often explains the text. I am sorry to have to say it, but we have too many men and women in the pulpit and on radio and T.V. today who are "wrongly dividing" the word of truth. A man said to my grandfather in derision many years ago, "you can prove anything by the Bible. The Bible says, Judas went out and hanged himself, go thou and do likewise, and what thou doest, do quickly." This is **"wrongly dividing."** We must quit taking single verses out of context and pieces of verses to establish profound foundational truths. We should ask ourselves this question, do our beliefs fit the **whole** of Scripture?

John Chapters 6 and 7 tell the story of a time in Jesus' early ministry when the area called Galilee was in an uproar over the question, *"Who is he?"* Some believed on him and some didn't. Because he spoke with authority and performed miracles, many said he must be the Prophet or the Messiah. The unbelieving Pharisees said he was neither. Multitudes followed him from place to place, even by ship *(6:24)*, and some would have taken him by force and made him a king, had Jesus not disappeared *(6:15)*. They finally summed it all up with this question:

> *"Shall Christ come out of Galilee?* (Jesus was born in
> Bethlehem but grew up in Nazareth of Galilee). *Hath*
> *not the scripture said, That Christ cometh of the seed of*
> *David, and out of the town of Bethlehem, where David*

20

> *was? So there was a division among the people*
> *because of him" (John 7:41-43).*

When Nicodemus spoke up on his behalf they answered him:

> *"Art thou also of Galilee? Search, and look: for out of*
> *Galilee ariseth no prophet. And **every man** went unto*
> *his own house" (John 7:52-53).*

Please understand what happened: In the midst of the turmoil and discussion someone quoted a verse of Scripture, *Micah 5:2 "But thou Bethlehem...."* and that settled it! Messiah was to come from Bethlehem and Jesus was from Galilee; therefore, they reasoned, he could not be the Messiah. So with their cherished Bible verse firmly in mind, they rejected Jesus and went home to sleep that night in their own beds and never gave him another serious thought. Anytime he was mentioned thereafter, they just brushed it aside, because they had written him off with one Bible verse.

But Jesus said,

> ***"Search the scriptures**; for in them ye think ye have*
> *eternal life; and they are they which **testify of me"***
> *(John 5:39).*

He said again in *Matthew 22:29*:

> *"Ye do err, not knowing the **scriptures**."*

When the apostle Paul preached to the Bereans, in *Acts 17:11*, a doctrine which they had not previously been taught:

> ***"These were more noble** than those in Thessalonica, in*
> *that they received the word with all readiness of mind,*
> ***and searched the scriptures daily,** whether those things*
> *were so."*

To say, "This is what I have always believed" is not a good argument for doctrine. You may be sincere but wrong. Those who crucified Christ and persecuted the apostles were sincere, "but not according to knowledge." The Bible is a spiritual book and it must be spiritually discerned. The carnal mind cannot receive the things of God. What is the intent of the verse? What is the Spirit saying? Does your interpretation do violence to the text?

21

Jesus knew the multitudes "heard" what he was saying, but they did not truly "hear."

"He (Jesus) *said unto his disciples, Let these sayings* **sink down into your ears"** *(Luke 9:43-44).*

Hearing was a problem in Jesus' day.

"Their ears are dull of hearing" (Matt. 13:15).

"And having ears, hear ye not?" (Mark 8:18).

Eight times in the Gospels Jesus says, *"He that hath* **ears** *to* **hear** *let him* **hear.** *"*

For me, writing this book is a sincere effort to submit to and embrace the truth concerning what Holy Writ says regarding the Godhead. I am seeing that this truth goes counter to what I had previously believed and taught. I grew up in what is known as a Oneness Pentecostal Church. I pastored a church of that faith for ten years and defended it strongly. I now see and admit that I was mistaken. Jesus said to the Father in *John 17:3,* *"And this is* **life eternal***, that they might know thee* **the only true God***, and* (in addition to) *Jesus Christ, whom thou hast sent."*

I would like to say also to my Trinitarian brethren, God is not three persons, **God is one.** Paul says in I Corinthians 8:4 & 6, *"There is none other God but one...to us* **there is but one God, the Father***, of whom are all things,...and one Lord Jesus Christ."*

The Old and New Testaments contain over 10 thousand **singular** pronouns and verbs referring to the one God *(I, Me, He, Him, His -* **not** *"they", "them", or "we").* [1] If this great number of singular pronouns used of God, will not convince someone that **He is one person**, it is unlikely that there is anything else **in the use of language** that will.

Truth is not determined by majority vote. Many people who never take time to search out Bible truth for themselves, take comfort in the fact that they are part of a large group or denomination, and that millions of others believe as they do. This is called "herd mentality" and in religion is dangerous. Please consider this fact: Truth is not diminished if the whole world denies it, and error is not strengthened though millions proclaim it!

How many people believed that a flood was coming in Noah's day? How many people understood and believed that Jesus was the promised Messiah of Israel in 32 A.D.? How many people believed that God was about to pour out the Holy Spirit on Gentiles about 41 A.D.? Dare to be different for the sake of truth!

Let me say regarding the question of the Godhead that many fine men, smarter and better educated than me have struggled with this awesome subject and gotten it wrong, so with this in mind I approach it with fear and trembling. But I have studied it and feel that I have some things to say. *"Nevertheless, what saith the scriptures" (Gal. 4:30)?*

My friend, if you do not love the truth more than all else you may not want to proceed further with this book. I agree with the late Dr. J. Vernon McGee that likely the reason Jesus spoke to the scribes and Pharisees in parables, rather than more plainly, was he knew **in any case** they were going to **reject** and **crucify** him; and they would only be judged by God for their rejection of **additional** truth. **What we hear we are responsible for**; and in our hearts we must say yes or no, and then speak it. **To love the truth is to hate error!** Some have asked, "If you believe this, why not just keep it to yourself?" There is a good answer for this in Scripture.

> *"As it is written, I believed, and therefore have I spoken; **we also believe, and therefore speak**" (II Cor. 4:13).*

For a Christian and especially a minister of Jesus Christ to see a truth is to speak it. **I believe, therefore I speak!**

This book is a search for truth. Those who are on a search for **truth** need never be afraid of the facts. If there is one verse in Scripture that causes pain to your doctrine, do not avoid it, but approach it head on, and ask God to open your understanding.

> *"Then opened he their understanding **that they might understand the scriptures**" (Luke 24:45).*

As Brother McGee said also, there is more than one kind of pride. There is pride of **"race,"** pride of **"face,"** pride of **"place,"** and pride of "**faith**." It was **pride of "faith"** that caused the Pharisees to miss their Messiah. Approach God's word humbly lest pride of "faith," past creeds and denominational doctrines cause you to miss the **true Jesus**.

Chapter 2

The Godhead 101

"Thou art God alone" (Psalm 86:10).

*"And this is life eternal, that they might know thee **the only true God**, and Jesus Christ, whom thou hast sent"* (Jesus speaking) *(John 17:3).*

*"There is **none other God but one**...to us **there is but one God, the Father**, of whom are all things, and we in him; **and one Lord Jesus Christ**.... Howbeit there is not in every man that knowledge"* (The Apostle Paul) *(I Cor. 8:4, 6-7).*

$\mathcal{W}$hy have we made the understanding of who God is in relation to his son Jesus so hard when the Bible has stated it so clearly. The prophet Daniel and John the Revelator were told by God to seal up certain things regarding prophecy that were to be revealed at a later time, but I have never found one Scripture where God sealed up the understanding of the Godhead. In fact, He said the very opposite in *Isa. 43:10-11*:

*"Ye are my witnesses, saith the Lord, and my servant whom I have chosen: that you may **know and believe me**, and **understand** that I am he: **before me there was no God formed, neither shall there be after me. I, even I am the Lord; and beside me there is no savior.**"*

God Almighty said through the prophet Jeremiah:

*"Thus saith the Lord, Let not the wise man glory in his wisdom, neither let the mighty man glory in his might; let not the rich man glory in his riches: But let him that glorieth glory in this, **that he understandeth and**"*

25

> **knoweth me**, *that I am the Lord which exercise loving-*
> *kindness, judgement, and righteousness, in the earth"*
> *(Jer. 9:23-24).*

The apostle Paul says in *Romans 1:19-20*:

> *"Because that which may be known of God is manifest*
> *in them; for God hath* **shown it** *unto them.* ***For the***
> ***invisible things of him*** *from the creation of the world*
> ***are clearly seen, being understood*** *by the things that*
> *are made,* ***even his eternal power and Godhead;*** *so*
> *that they are without excuse. "*

Do we need further proof that God is knowable and the Godhead understandable than is found in these statements by the Holy One of Israel and His great apostle Paul? Look again at the words that are used, "**know, believe,** and **understand**," "**understandeth** and **knoweth**," "**known, manifest, shewed, clearly seen, being understood**, even his Godhead." Then why do so many Christian ministers preach and teach that the Godhead is too difficult to understand? May I say that I believe we, Trinitarians and Oneness alike, have long ago left behind the biblical view of who God is, and have tried to force the Holy Scriptures into the mold of our pre-conceived ideas.

There are reasons for our lack of understanding. One, when we look back on what the Bible says regarding this most important subject, we look at it through glasses tinted by the mistaken teachings of some post-Apostolic church fathers and the non-biblical conclusions and creeds of the Nicene *(325 A.D.),* and Chalcedon *(451 A.D.)* church councils. Regarding the early church fathers, it should be said that evidence cannot be found showing that even one of them taught the doctrine of the triune God, as stated by the councils, before 200 A.D. [1] This was long after the death of the apostles of Christ, and all those men who knew them personally. It is well known that much Apostolic teaching went awry after the deaths of these chosen men. In fact, Jude, the half brother of Jesus, could see it coming when he wrote his small but powerful epistle around A.D. 66, and made a heartfelt plea, *"that* *ye should earnestly contend for the **faith which was once delivered** unto the saints" (Jude 1:3).*

Regarding the council of 325 A.D., it was convened by the Emperor Constantine, who had supposedly converted to Christianity. A serious division had developed in his empire between the Christian theologians of two very important cities, Antioch and Alexandria, regarding the person of Jesus Christ and his relationship to God the Father. Those in Alexandria believed that Jesus had eternally preexisted as a divine being and only **seemed to be** a real human being, **"man"** but not **"a man."** Those from Antioch, a city mentioned numerous times in the N.T. and said in *Acts 11:26* to be the place where believers in Christ were "first called Christians," held a more traditional view. They based their view on Jewish monotheism, of the **oneness of God**, and of Jesus, though son of God, **not** coequal and coeternal with the Father. In an effort to settle this troubling dispute and steady his empire, Constantine wrote letters to each faction urging that they reconcile their differences. The identical letters read in part:

> "How deep a wound has not only my ears but my heart
> received from the report that divisions exist among
> yourselves. Having inquired carefully into the origin
> and foundation of these differences, I find their cause
> to be of a **truly insignificant nature**, quite unworthy
> of such bitter contention." [2]

When this effort failed, Constantine called a council of 300 bishops at his palace in Nicea, a town in Turkey. These differences in understanding of who Jesus is **are not** "insignificant," and he could not have known what a profound effect this council of Nicea, which he presided over, would have on the foundational teachings and beliefs of hundreds of millions of professing Christians for centuries to come. Constantine, a professional soldier, was a man of violence and had many murders, executions, and much slaughter to his account. He had killed his relatives to ensure that his three sons would be his successors. [3] Though he professed a conversion to Christianity, it is doubtful that he ever really became a Christian at heart.

Jesus said *"By their fruits you shall know them" (Matt. 7:20).* Paul Johnson says in his work *"A History of Christianity"* that "Constantine appears to have been a sun-worshiper, one of a number of late pagan cults which had observances in common with Christians. Worship of such gods was not a novel idea. Every Greek or Roman expected that political success followed from religious piety. Christianity was the religion of Constantine's father. Although Constantine claimed that he was the thirteenth Apostle, his was no sudden Damascus conversion. Indeed it is highly doubtful that he ever truly abandoned sun-worship. After his professed acceptance of Christianity, he built a triumphal arch to the sun god and in Constantinople set up a statue of the same sun god bearing his own features. He was finally deified after his death by official edict in the Empire, as were many Roman rulers." [4]

Constantine, who presided over the debates from his place on a wrought-gold chair, did not fully understand the issues at hand but favored the minority view of the Alexandria delegates. His entrance is described thus by the historian Schaff, quoting Eusebius of Caesarea;

> "The moment the approach of the emperor was announced by a given signal, they all rose from their seats, and the emperor appeared like a heavenly messenger of God, covered with gold and gems, a glorious presence, very tall and slender, full of beauty, strength and majesty." [5]

It was in this setting that the church of Jesus Christ took a sharp turn from the monotheism of the Bible to the non biblical doctrine of the Trinity, with the decision that Jesus is coequal and coeternal with God, "very God of very God," of "one essence with the Father." This is the belief that is held by the majority of Christians to this day, nearly seventeen centuries later. The church had been taken over by the thinking of the theologians of Alexandria, thinking strongly influenced by Greek philosophy. Millions of sincere Christians today unwittingly bow at the wrought - gold throne of Constantine in their understanding of who God is. The God of the Bible is **one**!

The *Creed of Nicea* reads in part:

28

"We believe in one God, Almighty Father, Maker of all things seen and unseen and in one Lord Jesus Christ, the Son of God, eternally begotten of the Father and only begotten. That is, from the essence of the Father, God from God, Light from Light, True God from True God, Begotten, not made, of one substance with the Father."

Those who opposed this Creed taught that the Son is not God in the same way as the Father is God. To be divine means above all to be unoriginated, or to have no origin. The Son and the Father could not both be **unoriginated**, since there is only one God. Thus, only the Father is unoriginated and truly God; the Son originates from the Father. Although the Son exceeds all other creatures in perfection, nevertheless, the Son has the status of a creature in relation to the Father.

The Council in saying that the Son was "of one substance with the Father" *(Gk., homoousios)*, ascribed **divinity** to the Son. In other words, "The Son is truly God, just as the Father is truly God." [6]

At the end of the Creed, the Council attached a written condemnation of anyone denying its conclusion, especially those who believed that Christ did not exist in all eternity. The fourth century Church father Athanasius summed it up with these words, **"God was made man that we might be made gods."** [7] This is not Bible doctrine, but Greek and Roman thinking.

With Constantine's approval the Creed was accepted and a decree of banishment was issued against all dissenters. Christians who had been the victims of Roman power a few years before were now using Roman power to persecute one another. We should not think it strange that Constantine would preside over a Council that accepted a Deity consisting of two persons, for the Roman and Greek world was saturated with many gods *(Acts 17:16-23)*. Nor that **a man** *(Jesus is called a "man" some 20 times in the N.T.)* would be declared as being God. Constantine had ordered that his own father be deified and he himself would be granted that same honor after his death. Upon his death he was declared to be the 13th Apostle.

According to Eusebius of Nicomedia, some of the delegates from

Antioch who had signed the parchment later protested in writing to Constantine that they had **"committed an impious act, Oh Prince, by subscribing to a blasphemy from fear of you."** [8]

In their work, *"A Summary of Christian History,"* Robert Baker and John Roberts state:

> "Everyone knew that the decision of the council had been **arbitrary**. Constantine had determined what the Council should decide, yet the decrees of the Council were recognized as **authoritative Christian pronouncements**. Thoughtful leaders pondered this new development. They began to believe Christian **motives and conduct were secondary**; their goal was to attain authoritative decisions. Many of the later universal councils reached their decisions through **physical coercion** and rough-and-tumble tactics. It is difficult to see what part genuine Christianity had in some of these councils." [9] They say also, "the development that began with the first world council at Nicea in 325 led **directly to the Roman Catholic Church**. Such a development would have been impossible without the friendly attitude and **strong arm of the secular power**."
> *(Emphasis mine throughout).*

Constantine succeeded in bringing harmony to his empire, but it was at the cost of a devastating blow to the truth!

The doctrine of the Trinity as we know it today was further advanced at the Council of Constantinople in A.D. 381, which added the Holy Ghost as the third person with this decree:

> "I believe in one God, the Father Almighty, maker of heaven and earth, and of all things visible and invisible. And in one Lord Jesus Christ, the only begotten Son of God, Light from Light, true God from true God...**and in the Holy Ghost**, the Lord and Giver of Life... ."

This became the dogma of the Christian church; and for centuries thereafter, to descent from its teaching was punishable by death. And many died rather than embrace its error. In fact, history records that in the following two centuries after its inception, thousands upon thousands of "Christians" slaughtered other Christians over the doctrine of the Trinity.

The Encyclopedia of Catholicism calls the doctrine of the Trinity "a late-fourth century Christian doctrine:"

> "Today, scholars generally agree that **there is no doctrine of the Trinity** as such in either the O.T. or the N.T. It would go far beyond the intention and thought-forms of the O.T. to suppose that **a late-fourth century Christian doctrine** can be found there. Likewise the N.T. does not contain an explicit doctrine of the Trinity." [10]

Concerning the beliefs of the "early Church fathers" *(after 100 A.D.)*, a word of warning is certainly in order. The statements of these men are quoted in Christian pulpits and books as if they were junior apostles whose word is to be taken as Bible doctrine when, in fact, the historical record shows that many of them, though perhaps well intentioned, were seriously in error on two main points.

The first one, their rabid anti-Semitism *(hatred of Jews)*, is addressed by John Hagee in his book, *"Jerusalem Countdown"*, where he says:

> "Anti-Semitism in Christianity began with the statements of the early Church fathers, including Eusebius, Cyril, Chrysostom, Augustine, Origen, Justin and Jerome." He says, "They labeled the Jews as 'the Christ killers, plague carriers, demons, children of the devil, bloodthirsty pagans...money hungry Shylocks, who were as deceitful as Judas was relentless." [11]

The attitudes of these, **and others** who should be added to the list, taken up by the Roman Catholic Church in the form of "Replacement Theology," helped bring about the wanton slaughter of hundreds of thousands of innocent Jews during the Crusades, the Spanish Inquisition and other violent events in the Dark Ages. From the time of the Reformation, Martin Luther,

John Calvin and other Protestants continued to speak this heresy "without serious examination." Every doctrine bears fruit and this one bears bitter fruit. It is a matter of record that Adolf Hitler quoted some of the vile statements made by Luther as justification for his hatred of the Jews, which led to the slaughter of six million in the Holocaust.

The second erroneous doctrine that these post-Apostolic Church fathers gave to Christianity is **the doctrine of the Trinity**. The same council of Nicea that decided that Jesus is "of one substance with the Father," *(that the Son is God, just as the Father is God)* decided that Christians should celebrate Easter on Sunday instead of on the 14th of Nisan when the Jews celebrated Passover. They wrote a letter to this effect which stated in part:

> "It seemed to everyone a most unworthy thing that we
> should follow the custom of the Jews in the celebration
> of this most holy solemnity, who, **polluted wretches!**
> Having stained their hands with a **nefarious crime**, are
> justly blinded in their minds. Let us then have nothing
> in common with the **most hostile rabble** of the
> Jews...let us withdraw ourselves...from that **most
> odious** *("deserving hatred")* **fellowship**...carried away
> by an unrestrained impulse wherever their **inborn
> madness** may impel them" [12] *(emphasis mine)*.

With this hostility toward the Jews, they were more than willing to leave behind **the Jewish view of God** as one person.

And what was the "nefarious crime" with which this Council charged the Jews? **Deicide**, the killing of God. As Chrysostom was to write later:

> "For **killing God** there is no expiation *(atonement)* possible,
> no indulgence or pardon. Christians may never cease
> vengeance, and the Jews must live in servitude forever. God
> always hated the Jews. It is incumbent upon all Christians to
> hate the Jews" [13] *(end of quote)*.

Many of the Jews did insist that Rome crucify Jesus, God's Son, but they certainly did not "kill God,"as **that is impossible!** No N.T. writer ever

32

hinted that the Jews "killed God," or that they should be despised or mistreated for their part in the crucifixion of Jesus. Listen to Paul who suffered much from the Jew's opposition to his Gospel message:

> *"For I could wish that myself were accursed from Christ for* (if it would save) *my brethren, my kinsmen according to the flesh" (Rom. 9:3).*
>
> *"Hath God cast away his people* (Israel)? *God forbid "(Rom. 11:1).*

The "early Church fathers" were **seriously in error** on both counts!

If Jesus Messiah is "co-equal" or "co-eternal" with God Almighty, **Peter did not know it**.

> *"Jesus of Nazareth, **a man** approved of God" (Acts 2:22).*
>
> *"Him hath **God exalted** with his right hand to be **a Prince** and **a Savior**" (Acts 5:31).*

Paul didn't know it.

> (Jesus) *"Who is the image of the invisible God, the firstborn of every **creature**" (Col. 1:15).*
>
> *"The head of Christ is God" (I Cor. 11:3).*
>
> *"Ye are Christ's, and **Christ is God's**" (I Cor. 3:23).*

And Jesus did not know it.

> *"My Father is **greater than I**" (John 14:28).*
>
> *"These things saith the Amen, the beginning of the **creation of God**" (Rev. 3:14).*

If God's Holy Bible, Old or New Testament, does not teach a doctrine of the Trinity, then **what does it teach** about God? **We must know for sure!** Constantine, with his heavy hand of authority, determined the conclusions of the Nicene Council, but this does not satisfy hearts hungry to know our God. We must have the truth. **God's Bible has the answer!**

GOD IS ONE IN THE OLD TESTAMENT

Deuteronomy 6:4-5:

> *"Hear, O Israel: The Lord our God is* **one Lord***: And thou shalt love the Lord thy God with all thine heart, and with all thy soul, and with all thy might."*

Deuteronomy 4:39:

> *"Know therefore this day, and consider it in thine heart, that* **the Lord he is God** *in heaven above, and upon the earth beneath:* **there is none else.***"*

Deuteronomy 5:4-7, 9:

> *"The Lord talked with you face to face in the mount* **out of the midst of the fire***, saying,* **I am the Lord thy God***, which brought thee out of the land of Egypt, from the house of bondage. Thou shalt have* **none other gods** *before me. For I the Lord thy God am* **a jealous God.***"*

Deuteronomy 32:39:

> *"See now that I, even I, am he, and* **there is no god with me.***"*

Nehemiah 9:5-6:

> *"Stand up and bless the Lord your God...* **Thou even thou art Lord alone***; thou hast made heaven, the heaven of heavens, with all their host; and the host of heaven* **worshipeth thee.***"*

I Samuel 2:2:

> *"There is none holy as the Lord;* **for there is none beside thee***; neither is there any rock like our God."*

Psalm 86:10:

> *"***Thou art God alone.***"* Please ask yourself this question, What does **"alone"** mean?

Isaiah 37:15-16:

> *"And Hezekiah prayed unto the Lord, saying, O Lord of*

> *hosts, God of Israel, that dwellest between the cherubims, **thou art the God, even thou alone,** of all the kingdoms of the earth: thou hast made heaven and earth."*

Isaiah 37:23: (God says)

> *"Whom hast thou reproached and blasphemed? And against whom hast thou exalted thy voice, and lifted up thine eyes on high? Even against the **Holy One** of Israel."*

Isaiah 43:10-11:

> *"Ye are my witnesses, saith the Lord, and my servant whom I have chosen: that ye may know and believe me, and understand that I am he: **before me there was no God formed, neither shall there be after me.** I, even I, am the Lord; **and beside me there is no saviour."***

Isaiah 44:6:

> *"Thus saith the Lord the King of Israel, and his redeemer the Lord of hosts; I am the first, and I am the last; and **beside me there is no God."***

Isaiah 44:8:

> *"Fear ye not, neither be afraid: have not I told thee from that time, and have declared it? Ye are even my witnesses. **Is there a God beside me?** Yea, **there is no God; I know not any."***

Isaiah 44:24:

> *"Thus saith the Lord, thy redeemer, and he that formed thee from the womb, **I am the Lord** that maketh all things; **that stretcheth forth the heavens alone; that spreadeth abroad the earth by myself."***

Isaiah 45:5-6:

> ***"I am the Lord, and there is none else, there is no God beside me:** That they may know from the rising of the*

sun, and from the west, that there is **none beside me. I am the Lord, and there is none else.**"

Isaiah 45:11-12:

"Thus saith the Lord, **the Holy One of Israel, and his Maker. I have made the earth,** and created man upon it: I, even **my hands, have stretched out the heavens,** and all their host have I commanded."

Isaiah 45:18:

"For thus saith the Lord that created the heavens; God himself that formed the earth and made it; he hath established it, he created it not in vain, he formed it to be inhabited: **I am the Lord; and there is none else.**"

Isaiah 45:21-22:

"Tell ye, and bring them near; yea, let them take counsel together: who hath declared this from ancient time? Who hath told it from that time? Have not I the Lord? and **there is no God else beside me;** a just God and a Saviour; **there is none beside me.** Look unto me, and be ye saved, all the ends of the earth: for **I am God, and there is none else.**"

Isaiah 46:9:

"Remember the former things of old: **for I am God, and there is none else;** I am God, and there is **none like me.**"

Isaiah 47:4:

"As for our redeemer, the Lord of hosts in his name, the **Holy One** of Israel."

Jeremiah 10:10, 12, 16:

"But the Lord is the true God, he is the living God, and everlasting king: He hath made the earth by his power, he hath established the world by his wisdom, and hath stretched out the heavens by his discretion. **The Lord**

36

> *of hosts is his name.*"

Hosea 13:4:

> "*Yet I am the Lord thy God from the land of Egypt, and*
> **thou shalt know no god but me: for there is no saviour**
> **besides me.**"

Joel 2:27:

> "*And ye shall know that I am in the midst of Israel, and*
> *that **I am the Lord your God, and none else.**"

Malachi 2:10:

> "*Have we not all **one father?** Hath not **one God**
> **created us**?*"

Could anything be clearer? Could God have said it any plainer? Let me ask you a question. What part of "one," "alone," "none else," "by myself," or "none beside me," don't we understand? **"I am God the Creator, I am one, I am alone.**" This truth has been ground into every little Jewish child from the time of Moses until now. *Deuteronomy 6:4*, repeated by Jesus in *Mark 12:29*, is the **Shema** (Creed) of Israel, *"Hear, O Israel the Lord our God is one Lord."* They sing it in their songs, they say it in times of danger and distress, and repeat it at the time of death. That's why its so hard to convince a Jew that God is three persons, or three of anything. The Hebrew word for one is **"echad"** and that is exactly what it means, "one." Not a compound one, a plural one, or a multiple one. **There is no such thing!** *(Neither is there a triune one or a triad "one".)* It is one, singular, not two or three and carries no plural connotations. It is used as a numerical adjective, as is our English word "one," and may be used with nouns such as bunch, group, troupe, or family but this does not change the meaning of the word "*echad*," **it is still one**. If you divide "one" you lose it, you have fractions. If you multiply "one" you lose it; **it ceases to be one. One is one** under all of the laws of grammar and reason, and you cannot make anything else out of it.

Israel learned from their prophets that **God is one**, able to be approached and to be loved. *Exodus 33:11* says, *"The Lord spake unto*

*Moses face to face, as **a man** speaketh unto his friend."* At the time of the Exodus, the Jewish people as a nation were brought into intimate contact with their one true creator God, awesome in power, and yet personal. This experience was imprinted in their national consciousness forever, and this is what they have given to the world, **monotheism**, the belief in one God and from that **they have not wavered**.

> *"Did ever people hear the voice of God speaking out of the midst of the fire, as thou hast heard, and live? **Unto thee it was shown, that thou mightest know** that the Lord he is God; **there is none else beside him. Out of heaven he made thee to hear his voice,** that he might instruct thee; and **upon earth he showed thee his great fire; and thou heardest his words out of the midst of the fire"** (Moses speaking) (Deut. 4:33, 35-36).*

Today, the Jewish people are very divided, mainly into three groups, Orthodox, Conservative, and Reform; but the common thread that runs through all their teachings and the glue that holds them together as a people is this belief in one God, stated so clearly in *Deut. 6:4, "Hear, O Israel, the Lord our God is **one** Lord."* We look at the Jews with dismay because they cannot see that Jesus is their Messiah, and they look at us with dismay because we have taken "a man" and made him "God."

ONE GOD IN THE NEW TESTAMENT

In the N.T. as well as the old there are numerous, very plain statements that God is one *(entity, being, person).* Here are a few:

Matthew 19:17:

> *"And he said unto him, Why callest thou me good? There is none good but **one, that is, God"*** (Jesus speaking).

Matthew 23:9-10:

> *"And call no man your father upon the earth: for **one is your Father, which is in heaven.** Neither be ye called masters: for one is your **Master**, even Christ."*

Mark 12:29-32 & 34:

> *"And Jesus answered him, The first of all the commandments is, Hear, O Israel; **The Lord our God is one Lord**: And thou shalt love the Lord thy God with all thy heart, and with all thy soul, and with all thy mind, and with all thy strength: **this is the first commandment**. And the second is like, namely this, Thou shalt love thy neighbor as thyself. There is none other commandment greater than these. And the scribe said unto him, Well, Master, thou has said the truth: **for there is one God; and there is none other but he**: And when **Jesus saw that he answered discreetly, he said unto him, Thou are not far from the kingdom of God**."* (Where does that put those who do not believe that **God is "one?"**)

In *John 5:44*, Jesus says to his critics:

> *"How can ye believe, which receive honor one of another, and seek not the honor that cometh from **God only**."* Who is this that Jesus says is "God only" *(the one and only God)?* Verse 45 *"The Father."*

In *John 17:3*, Jesus says in his great prayer to the Father:

> *"And this is life eternal, that they might know **thee the only true God**, and Jesus Christ, whom thou has sent."*

In *Romans 3:29-30*, Paul says:

> *"Is he the God of the Jews only? is he not also of the Gentiles? Yes, of the Gentiles also: **Seeing it is one God**, which shall justify the circumcision by faith, and uncircumcision through faith."*

In *I Corinthians 8:4-7*, Paul says:

> *"**There is none other God but one**. For though there be that are called gods, whether in heaven or in earth, (as there be gods many, and lords many,) But to us*

39

*there is but **one God, the Father**, of whom are all things, and we in him; and **one Lord Jesus Christ**, by whom are all things, and we by him. **Howbeit there is not in every man that knowledge**."*

In *Galatians 3:20*, Paul says:

*"Now a mediator is not a mediator of one, **but God is one**."*

In *Ephesians 4:5-6*, Paul says there "is":

*"One Lord, one faith, one baptism, **One God and Father of all, who is above all**, and through all, and in you all."*

In *I Timothy 1:17*, Paul says:

*"Now unto the King **eternal, immortal, invisible, the only wise God**, be honour and glory for ever and ever. Amen."* (The God who is invisible is the only God).

In *I Timothy 2:3-5*, Paul says:

*"For this is good and acceptable in the sight of God our Saviour; Who will have all men to be saved, and to come unto the knowledge of the truth. **For there is one God, and one mediator between God and men, the man Christ Jesus**."*

In *James 2:19*, James the half brother of Jesus makes this strong statement:

*"Thou believest that there is **one God**; thou doest well: the devils also believe, and tremble."*

In *Revelation 4:2 & 8*, John saw God the Creator on His throne and described the scene thus:

*"Behold, **a throne** was set in heaven, and **one sat on the throne**.... and they* (the beasts) *rest not day and night, saying, Holy, holy, holy, **Lord God Almighty**, which was, and is and is to come."*

Now, look back at *I Cor. 8:6*. If there is **only one** who is God, "**the**

40

Father," then who is the person whom Paul calls "Lord Jesus Christ?" Please turn with me to the next chapter to see the answer that God's word gives to this important question.

"Know then, my friend, that the Trinity was born above three hundred years after the ancient Gospel was declared; it was conceived in ignorance, brought forth and maintained by cruelty."

William Penn (1644-1718)

English Christian preacher and statesman,

founder of Pennsylvania. [14]

(He was imprisoned in the Tower of London for his anti-Trinitarian beliefs. When informed that he would be freed if he would recant, he replied: "My prison shall be my grave before I will budge a jot, for I owe my conscience to no mortal man"). [15]

God Has A Son

*"And Simon Peter answered and said, Thou art **the
Christ, the Son of the living God**. And Jesus answered
and said unto him, Blessed art thou, Simon Barjona; for
flesh and blood hath not revealed it unto thee, but **my
Father** which is in heaven" (Matt. 16:16-17).*

ccording to a proper understanding of Scripture, before the foundation
of the world, the first creative thought in the mind of God the Creator was
something like this, "I am going to have a son." He spoke that thought, and
from that event forward Jesus has existed as reality in God's plan and
purpose. God's word **is reality**; in fact, it is the only reality. No power can
change or annul it - **it is reality!** Everything else is temporal; His word is
eternal. That's why the apostle John says in *John 1:1*:

> *"In the beginning was the Word and the Word was with
> God and the Word was God."* (This is the beginning of
> Creation, God has no "beginning").

The "Word" *(Greek-logos)* is not another person, but it means "thought,
intention or motive." The King James translators gave "Word" a capital "W"
as if it were a person; but many translators, Tyndale, Coverdale and others,
did not do this. We have already learned in the previous chapter that God is
one, and He created all things by Himself. According to *Job 38:7* the angels
were there and "shouted for joy," thus the **"us"** in *Genesis 1:26*.

Jesus says in *Revelation 3:14, "These things saith the Amen...**the
beginning of the creation of God."*** Paul says in *Colossians 1:15* that Jesus
is "the **firstborn of every creature**." Since Jesus is the expression of God's
first creative thought (the logos), *Revelation 19:13* says, *"And his name is
called the Word of God."* God the Father spoke Jesus **before time**, but he

43

appeared **in time**. *Galatians 4:4* says, *"But when the **fullness of the time** was come, God sent forth His Son, **made of a woman**, made under the law."* *I Peter 1:20* says, *"(Christ) Who verily was **foreordained** before the foundation of the world, but was **manifest in these last times** for you."* Not pre-existent but "foreordained" before time, for a certain day in Bethlehem.

The writer of Hebrews agrees when he says in chapter 9 verse 26:

> **"But now once in the end of the world** *hath he appeared to put away sin by the sacrifice of himself."*

Look at what the angel said to Mary in *Luke 1:35*:

> *"The Holy Ghost shall come upon thee, and the power of the Highest shall overshadow thee: Therefore* (**for this reason**) *also that holy thing which shall be born of thee shall be called the Son of God."*

Study this verse closely, as it is very important in understanding who Jesus is. The **angel did not say** Jesus "shall be called the Son of God" because he is "God the Son," "the eternal Son," that he is "in fact the Lord God," or that he "is God Incarnate," but **because** *"the Holy Ghost shall come upon thee, and the power of the Highest shall overshadow thee."* Jesus was generated by the Holy Ghost in the womb of Mary. *(**What God said became flesh**, John 1:14).* God, or God the Son did not move into her womb to come forth **only appearing to be a man**, God Incarnate. The incarnation as taught in modern theology is an invention of men, a fable, and is not a doctrine taught in God's Holy Bible. Jesus as a person did not preexist his mother and is not as old as his Father. Such a thing has never happened in the history of creation and did not happen in Jesus. Paul said the things of God are *"clearly seen and understood by the things that are made* (nature), *even his eternal power and Godhead"* *(Rom. 1:20).* This is what nature, along with Scripture teaches us regarding the birth of Jesus, who *"was made of a woman."*(**"Made"** *Gk. ginomai "generate - to cause to come into being".)*

WHO IS JESUS?

Not who do you think he is, but who does the Bible say he is? Pre-

44

conceived ideas can cause you to miss the **true Jesus**. The Jews rejected their true Messiah because he did not fit their notion of who he was to be. They looked for a mighty king to deliver them from Rome, and to restore Israel as a powerful nation. But he came as *"a **man** of sorrows and acquainted with grief,"* the suffering servant of Isaiah Chapter 53 and Psalm 22.

- Jesus is the promised seed (posterity) of "the woman," Abraham and David *(Gen. 3:15, John 7:42, Rom. 1:3, Gal. 3:16)*.
- Jesus is the promised Messiah *(Gk. Christus - anointed one)* of Israel *(Dan. 9:25-26, John 1:41, 4:25-26)*.
- Jesus is the virgin born Son of God *(Isa. 7:14, Matt. 1:23, Luke 1:27)*.
- Jesus is the sinless and righteous Son of God *(II Cor. 5:21, I Peter 2:22, I John 3:5)*.

Jesus was definitely promised, described, and anticipated in the Old Testament; but he was generated *(his genesis, Matt. 1:18 "birth" - Gk. "genesis")* by the Holy Ghost in the New, the Son of God.

WHAT DOES IT MEAN TO BE CALLED THE SON OF GOD?

We have already learned from many Scriptures that **God is one**, therefore **unique** *(one and only; single; sole "a unique specimen," having no like or equal; unparalleled)* and the only one in the God family. As the only one in the God family, He has no relatives, **no one is kin to God**. Every Scripture in the Bible **will**, and every doctrine taught from the Bible **must,** agree with that. Truth is not negotiable, and it will not vary.

But the one God, most High God, the Lord God, the Holy **one** of Israel has called angels, some men, Israel as a nation collectively, and we as Christians, "Sons" of God. What does the phrase "Son of God" mean? Since God has no relatives, it is not kinship; it is **"position."** It is a relationship position. God created the angels and they are called "the sons of God" *(Gen. 6:2, Job 1:6, 2:1, 38:7)*. Please note that when you see in your Bible the word "Son" with a capital "S" as referring to Jesus, this does not mean it was so written in the original manuscripts. This is a choice made by

45

the editor or publisher and does not affect the meaning of the word "son." God created Adam and breathed His breath into him, so he is called "*the son of God*" *(Luke 3:38)*. God said of David's son Solomon, whom God **adopted** as His own, *"And he shall be my son"* *(II Sam. 7:14)*. Israel collectively, as a nation is called God's son.

> *"And thou shalt say unto Pharaoh, **Thus saith the Lord, Israel is my son, even my firstborn**: And I say unto thee, **Let my son go**, that he may serve me: and if thou refuse to let him go, behold, **I will slay thy son**, even thy firstborn"* (*Ex. 4:22-23*).

God is saying to Pharaoh, "I have a son *(Israel)*, and you have a son. If you do not let my son, 'my firstborn' go I will slay your firstborn." God called Israel "Ephraim" in *Jeremiah 31:9* and said, *"I am a father to Israel, and **Ephraim is my firstborn**."* In fact, God saw His bringing forth of Israel as a nation, with Jerusalem as its capital, as a birth.

> *"Thy birth and thy nativity is of the land of Canaan; in the day that thou wast born thy naval was not cut, ...and when I passed by thee, and saw thee polluted in thine own blood...I said unto thee, Live "* *(Ezek. 16:3-4, 6)*.

Look at *Hosea 11:1*:

> *"When **Israel** was a child, then I loved him, and **called my son** out of Egypt."*

This refers to Israel, God's son. But *Matthew 2:15* says prophetically it spoke of Jesus, God's son as well.

> *"And was there until the death of Herod: that it might be fulfilled which was spoken of the Lord by the prophet, saying, **Out of Egypt have I called my son**."*

This is very enlightening. Matthew is telling us that Jesus is God's son, similar to the way in which Israel is God's son. The terminology is the same. God **birthed Israel** "my son" in Exodus, and **birthed Jesus**, "my son" from the womb of the virgin Mary.

Yes, Jesus is the virgin born, sinless Son of God, the "only begotten of the Father" *(John 1:14)*. Only once has God "begotten," *(brought forth)* from the womb of a woman, without the aid of a man, a child whom He calls the Son of God. Therefore Jesus is unique, the only one of his kind, "the only begotten," but he is nevertheless **a man**, of the species "mankind." He is called "son of God" 28 times in the four Gospels, which is one third as many times as he is called "son of man" (84), **a human being**. Of these 28 references to "Son of God," only five of these are spoken by Jesus himself, in John, and none in Matthew, Mark, or Luke. Of course, if he only spoke it once, it is established as truth, but we must put his title "Son of God" in perspective. We must not make him less than the Bible says he is, the **highly exalted, appointed, anointed, approved, Son of God**. He is the **way**, the **truth**, the **life**, the **door**, the **prince of life**, our **Savior, redeemer**, our **Lord** *(master)* the *"one mediator between God and men, **the man Christ Jesus.**"* We **dare not** make him more than the Bible says he is, using non-biblical terms such as "God the Son," "the eternal Son," "the preexistent Son," "God" *(as in Lord God - Jehovah Eloheim)*, "King of Heaven" and "the second person of the triune God." The Bible does not apply these terms to the Son and for us to do so borders on idolatry. There is one Lord God in the Old and New Testaments and He is not Jesus Christ *(Messiah)*, the Son of God. God has been patient with our lack of understanding and self-will in this area. This is **important to God** and He is ready for it to be **understood**. The judgement that is soon coming on the world will begin at the house of God. If we rebel against the truth, we will be judged!

> *"For the time is come that **judgement must begin at the**
> **house of God**; and if it first begin at **us**, what shall the
> end be of them that obey not **the gospel of God**" (I Peter
> 4:17)?*

Nearly two billion people in the world today who are called "Christians" do not have a clear understanding as to who their God is. We can no longer allow the fourth century pagan ruler Constantine to define the answer for us. *The New International Encyclopedia*, under the topic heading "The Trinity Doctrine" says:

47

"The Catholic Faith is this: We worship one in trinity, but there is one person of the Father, another of the Son and another of the Holy Ghost. The Glory equal; the Majesty coeternal. The doctrine is not found in its fully developed form in the Scriptures. Modern theology **does not seek to find it** in the Old Testament. At the time of the Reformation **the Protestant Church took over the doctrine** of the Trinity **without serious examination.**" [1]

The Encyclopedia of Catholicism says:

"Today, however, scholars generally agree that there is no doctrine of the Trinity as such in either the O.T. or the N.T." *It goes on to say,* "It would go far beyond the intention and thought-forms of the O.T. to suppose that a late-forth, century....Christian doctrine can be found there," *And again,* "Likewise, the N.T. does not contain an explicit doctrine of the Trinity." [2]

The Encyclopedia International says:

"The doctrine of the Trinity did not form part of the apostles' preaching, as this *(preaching)* is reported in the New Testament." [3]

Do you understand this? God is speaking to us not only in the Bible but also through these encyclopedias! Seek Him for guidance and to open your understanding, and go back to the Bible to see who God is, **who your God is!** *(God is not a committee, He is one).* What does the Bible mean when it says Jesus is the "Son of God?"

PETER'S REVELATION

Simon Peter had been with Jesus for perhaps two years when Jesus asked him and the other disciples, *"Whom do men say that I the Son of man am"* *(Matt. 16:13)?* Their answers varied from John the Baptist to Elijah, to Jeremiah, or "one of the prophets." Then he asked *"But whom say ye that I am?"* And Peter answered and said, *"Thou art **the Christ**, the Son of the living God."* Did Jesus humor Peter, holding back in his own mind and thinking, "His understanding is incomplete, but later he will realize who I

48

really am, God Incarnate, the preexistent eternal Son, second person of the Triune God?" **No!** Jesus rejoiced at Peter's insightful understanding and said, *"Blessed art thou, Simon Barjona: for flesh and blood hath not revealed it unto thee, but my Father which is in heaven."* And what was Peter's divine revelation? That Jesus was the promised Messiah of Israel, **not God**, but the **one anointed** of God. Notice verse 20:

> *"Then charged he his disciples that they should tell no*
> *man that he was Jesus **the Christ**" (Matt. 16:20).*

He did not caution them, ***"Tell no man that I am God,"*** for they would never have thought of such a thing. They were Israelites and knew that when God spoke it shook the world *(see chapter 2)*. When Mark gave his account of Peter's confession, he quotes him as simply saying, *"Thou art **the** Christ" (Mark 8:29).* This was the **important part** of Peter's revelation, that **Jesus was Messiah**, not God. Luke's account of this event has Peter saying, *"Thou art the **Christ of God.**"* There is a great difference between "God" and "Messiah of God." How did we arrive at the place in Christianity where "Christ" equals "God," or "Son of God" equals "God?" These things are not taught in Scripture! A few months later at Pentecost, in Acts chapter 2, Peter's opinion had not changed. Jesus was still *"a man approved of God"* *(v. 22)*, *"Whom God hath raised up"* from the dead *(v. 24)*, whose *"soul"* God had not left *"in hell" (v. 27)*, raised up to sit on David's throne *(v. 30)*, sitting at *"the right hand of God exalted" (vs. 33-34)*, and still Christ the Messiah.

Some 25 years later when Peter wrote his epistle of First Peter, had his perception changed as to who Jesus is?

> *"Blessed be the **God and Father** of our Lord Jesus*
> *Christ" (I Peter 1:3).* (The Lord God was still Jesus'
> **God** and his **Father**).
> *"The precious blood of Christ, as of **a lamb** without*
> *blemish" (1:19)*
> *"God, who raised him up from the dead, and **gave him***
> ***glory**" (1:21).*

Peter knew Jesus' glory was **derived** from God the Father. God is self-consistent, the **"I am,"** and not derived from anyone. God's glory is underived and therefore is much greater than Christ's, which is a "given" glory.

> *"Who is gone into heaven, and is on the right hand of God; angels and authorities **being made** subject unto him" (I Peter 3:22).*
>
> *"That **God** in all things may be **glorified** through Jesus Christ" (4:11).*

It is not Jesus who has taken the Father's glory unto himself, but we who have given God's glory *(honor - esteem)* in our hearts and worship, to His Son, a human being, to our shame. God the Father says in Malachi chapter one:

> *"A son honoreth his father and a servant his master: **if then I be a father, where is mine honor?**...for I am a **great King**, saith the Lord of hosts, and my name is dreadful among the heathern" (vs. 6 & 14).*

NATHANAEL'S REVELATION

Jesus was walking in Galilee and chose Philip to be one of the twelve. Then:

> *"Philip findeth Nathanael, and saith unto him, **We have found him, of whom Moses in the law**, and the prophets, **did write,** Jesus of Nazareth, the son of Joseph" (John 1:45).*

Philip knew that Jesus was the "Prophet like Moses" that God had promised to raise up "from among their brethren," with God's words in his mouth and speaking what God commanded him *(Deut. 18:18).*

> *"Jesus saw Nathanael coming to him, and saith of him, Behold an Israelite indeed, in whom is no guile! Nathanael saith unto him, **Whence knowest thou me?** Jesus answered and said unto him, Before that Philip called thee, when thou wast under the fig tree, I saw*

50

> *thee. Nathanael answered and saith unto him,* **Rabbi,**
> **thou art the Son of God; thou art the King of Israel"**
> *(John 1:47-49).*

Nathanael, being "an Israelite indeed," knew the prophecies concerning the coming Messiah, the **prophet - king of Israel**. When Philip gave his witness to Nathanael in verse 45, faith began to arise in his heart. Then Jesus' knowledge of their conversation under the fig tree completed his realization that this was the Christ, King of Israel, **and therefore the Son of God**. "Son of God" was **a messianic title**. Look at Psalm chapter 2, where David prophesied of the coming Messiah. Remember Peter called David a prophet in *Acts 2:29-31*, and said he saw the resurrection of Christ some 1000 years before it happened, and knew that of the fruit of his loins God *"would raise up Christ to sit on his throne."*

> *"Why do the heathen rage, and the people imagine a*
> *vain thing? The kings of the earth set themselves, and*
> *the rulers take counsel together, against the Lord, and*
> ***against his anointed,*** *saying, Let us break their bands*
> *asunder, and cast away their cords from us. He that*
> *sitteth in the heavens shall laugh: the Lord shall have*
> *them in derision....Yet have I set my king upon my holy*
> *hill of Zion. I will declare the decree: the Lord hath*
> *said unto me,* ***Thou art my Son; this day have I***
> ***begotten thee....Kiss the Son,*** *lest he be angry, and ye*
> *perish from the way, when his wrath is kindled but a*
> *little. Blessed are all they that put their trust in him"*
> *(Ps. 2:1-4, 7, 12).*

David had a "great" son Solomon, who was called God's son, but this pictures David's "greater" son Jesus, also called Son of God. Notice God's son *(Messiah)* in *Ps. 2:7* is **"begotten"** on a certain **"day,"** from the womb of a virgin. ***"This day have I begotten thee."*** As Messiah, King of Israel, Jesus is the Son of God. Notice, that when the King Messiah was enthroned "upon my holy hill of Zion" in Jerusalem, the Lord God was sitting in the heavens, laughing at His enemies (*When God laughs, it's not funny*). Please consider one other thing. Although Jesus saw Nathanael miles away under the fig tree, this did not mean that he was omniscient *(knowing all things)* and therefore God. At that moment he did not know when he would return to earth *(Mark 13:32)*, nor did he know the future events of the book of Revelation *(Rev. 1:1)*. The supernatural knowledge that Jesus displayed on this occasion is a prophetic gift of the Spirit, which was also used by Samuel, Elisha and others *(I Sam. 10:2-6, II Kings 6:8-12 & 32, 7:1-2)*.

WHAT JESUS KNEW ABOUT WHO HE WAS.

Jesus knew the truth regarding who he was and never varied from it in word or deed:

> *"The Son can do nothing of himself...I can of mine own self do nothing...If I bear witness of myself, my witness is not true" (John 5:19, 30-31).*
> *"For I have not spoken of myself; but the Father which sent me, he gave me a commandment, what I should say, and what I should speak...so I speak" (John 12:49-50).*

Jesus knew that he was not God. He never one time used the terms, "God," "eternal Son," or "God the Son" in speaking of himself. Again and again, when one reads the writings of those who teach the doctrine of the Trinity, they admit that Jesus is not "explicitly" called "God," but that it is "inferred." Jesus told Pilate *"for this cause came I into the world, that I should bear witness unto the truth" (John 18:37)*. If Jesus had in fact been "God," he loves us enough to have told us **plainly**. It would not have been by **inference**. If Jesus, the "witness unto the truth" never said he is God, we need to quit saying it! This is too serious to be wrong about!

Jesus denied being God. In *Matthew 19:16-17 "**one** came and said*

52

*unto him, Good Master, what good thing shall I do, that I may have eternal life? and he said unto him, Why callest thou me good? there is none good but **one**, that is God."* Jesus is not playing word games here. He is saying, "I am not God." As the man was "one," God was "one," and Jesus was not He.

Earlier in this same chapter, regarding the question of divorce, Jesus had said, *"Have ye not read, that **he** which made them at the beginning made them male and female (Matt. 19:4).* He did not think nor say, "I really made them." He says in verse six it was "God." As the Word *(logos)*, Jesus was the "motive" for all that God made, but he was not the Creator. There are verses in the writings of the apostle Paul which would seem to indicate that Jesus had a part in the original creation, notably *Colossians 1:13-18*, but these must be put in context and properly understood. Paul knew nothing of a trinity, and the councils that formulated such an idea occurred centuries after his death.

> *"Who hath delivered us from the power of darkness, and hath translated us **into the kingdom of his dear Son**: In whom we have redemption through his blood, even the forgiveness of sins: Who is the image of the invisible God, **the firstborn of every creature**: For by him were all things created, that are in heaven, and that are in earth, visible and invisible, whether they be thrones, or dominions, or principalities, or powers: all things were created by him, and for him: And he is before all things, and by him all things consist. And he is the head of the body, the church: who is the beginning, the firstborn from the dead; that in all things he might have the preeminence"* (Col. 1:13-18).

Let's notice three things about these verses: (1) Jesus is the instrument of Creation; (2) He sustains all; (3) All moves toward him as goal. Paul's words *"by him were all things created"* must be taken in relation to his statements, *"by him all things consist,"* and *"he is the head of the body, the*

53

church." When taken together, we see that Paul considered Jesus **creator** in his capacity as **redeemer** of all. God the Father would not have created all things, seen and unseen, without a future planned redeemer, who is Christ. His function as creator is viewed **on condition** of his subsequent work as redeemer. In other words, the Creatorship of Christ is never dwelt upon alone, **but always** in relation to his Saviorhood. Look at *I Corinthians 8:6* for further understanding of this concept from Paul.

*"But to us there is but one God, the Father, **of whom are all things**, and we in*
    *him; and one Lord Jesus Christ, **by whom are all things**, and we **by** him."*
*"God...***created all things by** Jesus Christ" (Eph. 3:9).

So Jesus' part in creation was by redeeming all things from the fall, by his death on the cross. Look at this statement by James Hastings, a noted theologian and recognized authority on the Bible, and himself a Trinitarian:

"We must avoid every kind of language which suggests that to St.
Paul the ascension of Christ was a **deification**. To **a Jew** the idea
that **a man might come to be God** would have been **an intolerable
blasphemy**. It is to be noted that the increased glory which St. Paul
and all the N.T. writers regard as pertaining to Christ after his
resurrection, has only to do with His dignity, His 'theocratic
position,' not with His essential personality." [4]

THE LORD GOD CREATED THE WORLDS ALONE.

"Thus saith the Lord, the Holy One of Israel, and his
*Maker. **I have** made the earth...**my hands** have*
stretched out the heavens" (Isa. 45:11-12).

"Thus saith the Lord, thy redeemer, and he that formed
*thee from the womb, **I am the Lord** that maketh all*
*things; **that stretcheth forth the heavens alone; that***
***spreadeth abroad the earth by myself**" (Isa. 44:24).*

*"See now that I, even I, am he, and there is **no god with***
***me**" (Deut. 32:39).*

*"Have we not all **one father**? Hath not **one God***
***created us**" (Mal. 2:10)?*

The Creator, the eternal God, needed no help in the God department, but He did need **a sinless man**, a lamb, to die for fallen **men:** a man whose righteous blood was untainted by the original sin of Adam.

JESUS DENIED CALLING HIMSELF GOD.

Jesus said in *John 6:46, "Not any man hath seen the Father."*

Now look at chapter 10.

> *"And Jesus walked in the temple in Solomon's porch. Then came the Jews round about him, and said unto him, How long dost thou make us to doubt? If thou be the Christ, tell us plainly" (vs. 23-24).*

The question at hand, from these Jews seeking occasion against Jesus **was not**, "Are you God?" for he and they knew that no man could be God. The question was "Are you the Messiah?"

> *"Jesus answered them, I told you, and ye believed not; the works that I do in my Father's name, they bear witness of me. But ye believe not, because ye are not of my sheep, as I said unto you....My Father, which gave them me, is greater than all; and no man is able to pluck them out of my Father's hand. I and my Father are one" (vs. 25-26, 29-30).*

Jesus never one time claimed to be God or God the Father or that he and the Father were **one person**. They are **one**, just as he desires **Christians to be one**: one in love, unity, purpose, and fellowship, *("That they may be one, as we are one" John 17:11).*

> *"Then the Jews took up stones again to stone him. Jesus answered them, Many good works have I shewed you from my Father; for which of those works do ye stone me? The Jews answered him, saying, For a good work we stone thee not; but for blasphemy; and because that thou, being a man, makest thyself God" (John 10:31-33).*

To which Jesus replied:

*"Say ye of him, whom the Father hath sanctified, and sent into the world, Thou blasphemest; because **I said, I am the Son of God**" (John 10:36)?*

The Jews tried to twist Jesus' words and have him saying he was God, which he was not, but he set them straight with these words, *"I said, I am the Son of God,"* **and he is.** Would Jesus not correct those today who twist his words, and have him saying he is God?

Jesus' rebuttal to his enemies regarding this matter was so strong, there is no Bible record that they ever brought it up again. Even at the time of his trial and Crucifixion he was not charged with saying he was God *(which he did not)*, but rather he was accused of saying he was Messiah *(Christ)*, Son of God *(which he did)*.

*"But Jesus held his peace. And the High priest answered and said unto him, I adjure thee by the living God, that thou tell us whether thou be **the Christ, the Son of God**. Jesus saith unto him, Thou hast said...Then the high priest rent his clothes, saying, he hath spoken blasphemy...What think ye? They answered and said, he is guilty of death" (Matt. 26:63-66).*

*"When the chief priests therefore and officers saw him, they cried out, saying, crucify him, crucify him. Pilate saith unto them, take ye him, and crucify him: for I find no fault in him. The Jews answered him, We have a law, and by our law he ought to die, because he made himself **the Son of God** (not God)" (John 19:6-7).*
Messiah or Christ are not synonyms for God but mean "the anointed one," Israel's promised deliverer and our Savior, "Son of God."

*"The Lord (God) said unto me, Thou art **my Son; this day** have I begotten thee" (Ps. 2:7).*

*"I will be his father, and he shall be **my son**" (II Sam.*

56

7:14).

WHEN JESUS IS CALLED GOD.

In this discussion with the Jews , Jesus brings up a subject which we should explore further in order to better understand who he is. That is, that others beside the Lord God are, at times in the Scripture, called "god" or "gods." Look at Jesus' argument in verses 34-36 that he had not blasphemed when he said God was his "Father," that they were "one" in unity, or that he was the "Son of God."

> *"Jesus answered them, Is it not written in your law, I said, Ye are **gods**? **If he** (God) **called them gods**, unto whom the word of God came, and the scripture cannot be broken. Say ye of him, whom the Father hath sanctified* (set apart), *and sent into the world, Thou blasphemest; because I said, I am the Son of God"* (John 10:34-36)?

Jesus is referring to *Psalm 82*, where God called the elders of Israel "gods."

> *"I have said, **Ye are gods**; and all of you are children of the most High" (v. 6).*

The casual Bible reader may not be aware of this fact, and it may seem offensive to our western minds; but in Scripture angels, elders, rulers, kings, the Messiah and those acting under God's authority are legitimately called "gods." This is even said by the Lord God himself and generally means "mighty ones."

> *"And the Lord said unto Moses, See, I have made thee a **god** to Pharaoh: and Aaron thy brother shall be thy prophet. Thou shalt speak all that I command thee"* (Ex. 7:1).

Moses was ordained, empowered and sent by God to Pharaoh with God's authority to turn the water to blood, the dust to lice, and was for a time the "**god**" of Egypt. Moses was the "god" of **that deliverance**, and all who were saved had to hear and heed **his** voice. Some of the Egyptians believed

Moses and came and bowed down to him, and some went with Israel out of the land. *(Ex. 9:20, 11:8, 12:38, Num. 11:4)* He is a type of Jesus, the "god" of **our deliverance**, who saves both Jew and Gentile. Moses acted in place of God, as God's agent and even had himself a prophet, his brother Aaron. God said to Moses regarding his brother:

> *"And thou shalt speak unto him and put words in his mouth....and thou shalt be to him instead of **God**" (Ex. 4:15-16).*

Please understand this fact. The Bible usage of the word "god" is similar to our use of the word "president." If you said, "I saw the President today," you would likely mean the man who sits in the Oval Office *(I did see President Bush today in Nashville on February 1, 2006 as he gave an address).* But you could mean the president of the Chamber of Commerce, whom I also saw today, or some other president. The context of your statement would help to determine your meaning. So it is with the Bible word "God." It is the Hebrew word "Elohim," and some 2700 times in Scripture it refers to the Lord God *(Jehovah Elohim)*; but on occasion it is used of others.

> *"Thou shalt not revile the gods, nor curse the ruler of thy people" (Ex. 22:28).*
> *"Worship him, all ye gods" (Ps. 97:7).* These are "mighty ones." Images cannot hear nor worship.
> *"God standeth in the congregation of the mighty: **he judgeth among the gods**. How long will ye judge unjustly, and accept the persons of the wicked" (Ps. 82:1-2)?*
> *"For the Lord your God is God of gods, and Lord of lords" (Deut. 10:17).*

With this in mind, let's look at *Psalm 45*, a psalm regarding the kings of Israel and ultimately fulfilled in the coming king Messiah.

> *"My heart is inditing a good matter: I speak of the things which I have made **touching the king**: my*

*tongue is the pen of a ready writer. Thou art fairer than the children of men: grace is poured into thy lips: therefore **God hath blessed thee** for ever. Gird thy sword upon thy thigh, O most mighty, with thy glory and thy majesty" (Ps. 45:1-3).*

Beware of the word "most" in verse 3, as it is in **italics** and was not in the original. The Davidic kings and Messiah are "mighty" but not "most mighty." The translators were Trinitarians.

*"Thy throne, O **God**, is for ever and ever; the sceptre of thy kingdom is a right sceptre. **Thou lovest righteousness,** and **hatest wickedness: therefore God thy God**, hath anointed thee with the oil of gladness above thy fellows" (Ps. 45:6-7).*

Please note, the throne of Israel in Jerusalem is called "the throne of the Lord."

*"Then **Solomon sat on the throne of the Lord** as King instead of David his father, and prospered; and all Israel obeyed him" (I Chron. 29:23).*

The kings were God's appointed regents. The Davidic ruler was "the Lords anointed" *(II Sam. 19:21)*, and because of his special relationship with God, was called at his enthronement the "son" of God *(Ps. 2:7, II Sam 7:14, I Chron. 28:6).* He was called "god" as a title of honor. We see that Psalm 45, though Messianic, was spoken first to a Davidic king. Notice in verses 9 and 13 that he has daughters; in verse 16 that he has "children; whom thou mayest make princes"; and a name that will be remembered in all generations *(v. 17).*

Notice **who** called the king, "God." **"Thy God,** "who "hath anointed thee with the oil of gladness **above thy fellows."**

There is no doubt that this Psalm is ultimately fulfilled in Christ. Look at *Hebrews 1:8-9*:

*"**But unto the Son he saith,** Thy throne, O God, is forever and ever: a sceptre of righteousness is the*

*sceptre of thy kingdom. Thou hast loved righteousness,
and hated iniquity; **therefore God, even thy God**, hath
anointed thee with the oil of gladness above thy
fellows."*

The writer of Hebrews did not mean for us to understand that Jesus was divinity, a part of the Godhead. Notice in verse 9, *"above thy fellows."* We are Christ's fellows, his brethren. He says in chapter 2 verse 17, *"Wherefore **in all things** it behooved him* (Christ) ***to be made like unto his brethren.***" We are not **divinity*,** and he was "made in all things like" us. The writer of Hebrews, with clear understanding, goes on to call Jesus **"this man"** four times in his book *(Heb. 3:3, 7:24, 8:3, 10:12).*   **see note page 65*

With over 2700 occurrences of the word "God" *(Elohim)* in the Bible it is spoken of Jesus for sure only four times, once more in the O.T. and once more in the New. God is spoken of over 1300 times in the N.T. where it is **not referring to Jesus,** and 500 times in Paul's writings, where he **always** makes a separation between the Lord Jesus and the Lord God. James Hastings, a Trinitarian, in his work *Hastings' Dictionary of the Bible*, says regarding Paul's view of Jesus:

"It may be that St. Paul **nowhere names Christ** "God," and that verses that seem to him (Hastings) to infer it, "must all be otherwise explained." Hastings calls this "one of the most **baffling problems** of N.T. theology." He states that "No candid exegete *("an expert in explaining scriptures")* will deny that over and over again Christ is somehow given a **place inferior to God**, His entire redeeming work and position being traced back directly to the Father. We have such expressions as 'God sent forth his Son' *(Gal. 4[4]),* 'He that spared not his own Son' *(Rom. 8[32]),* 'God hath highly exalted him' (Ph. 2[9]) in which either the gift of Christ to the world, or the bestowal of exalted glory on Christ Himself, **is declared to be God's act. All is accepted, endured, achieved 'to the glory of God the Father.'"** Hastings continues, "Still more explicit is *I Co. 11*[3]

'The head of the woman is **the man, and the head of Christ is God'; and** in *I Co. 15*[28] Christ is portrayed as **delivering up the Kingdom to God**, and as finally submitting even **Himself to a higher**, that God may be all in all'. **St. Paul does not give us much help, perhaps, in solving this antinomy** *(inconsistency)*." [5] (Paul is not **inconsistent**, it is we who have been inconsistent in our interpretation of Paul, in our effort to make Jesus "God!")

Look at *Isaiah 9:6.*

> *"For unto us **a child** is born, unto us **a son** is given: and the government shall be upon his shoulder: and his name shall be called Wonderful, Counselor, The mighty God, The everlasting Father, The Prince of Peace."*

This is a great prophecy concerning Jesus, "a child," "a son." We must see in it **all** that Isaiah is saying, but we must not read into it **more** than Isaiah is saying. Yes, he is "The mighty God" over all that **his God**, The Most High God has put him over. He is "mighty" but not **Almighty**. Yes, he is the everlasting Father of everything that **his Father** has given him. **The son is definitely not his own father.** The word "everlasting" in this verse is the Hebrew word "Ad" *(#5703 Strongs concordance)* and means "terminus" or "duration." It is taken from the primary root word "Adah" *(#5710 Strongs)* which means to "**advance or continue**." *(From this point on)*. The only **other** time this word "ad" is used in the O.T. is Habakkuk 3:6 *'The **everlasting** mountains were scattered."* Neither the "son" nor the mountains were in eternity past, but they shall "**continue**." When Isaiah, Habakkuk, and all O.T. writers speak of the "**everlasting** God," it is the Hebrew word "Olam" *(#5769 Strongs);* and it means "to the vanishing point," "time out of mind **past or future**," "eternity" *(Gen. 21:33, Ps. 90:2, Isa. 40:28, Jer. 10:10, Hab. 3:6).*

> Do you see the difference? Remember Paul's words *'To us there is but one God, the Father...Howbeit there is not in every man that knowledge" (I Cor. 8:6-7).* One

note of caution. Some will try to apply the word *"everlasting (Olam)"* to the Messiah *in Micah 5:2* but this is a mistake.

> *"But thou, Bethlehem...out of thee shall he **come forth** unto **me** that is to be ruler in Israel; **whose goings** forth have been from of old, from everlasting."*

The word *"everlasting"* in this verse is *Olam* but it does not refer to the Messiah but to **"me,"** the eternal God. Notice the phrase *"shall he come forth **unto me**."* The Messiah's *"coming forth"* was to be in Bethlehem but the eternal God's *"going forth"* had been *"from of old,"* from eternity. To see for sure that *"from of old"* speaks of God and not the future Messiah look at Chapter 7, verse 20:

> *"Thou* (God) *wilt perform the truth...which thou hast sworn unto our fathers **from the days of old**."* (This is the same terminology and Micah is referring to the eternal God).

Jesus' declaration to Mary Magdalene at the tomb.

> *"Jesus saith unto her, Touch me not: for I am not yet ascended to my Father: but go to **my brethren**, and say unto them, I ascend unto **my Father**, and **your Father**: and to **my God**, and **your God**" (John 20:17).*

This was the resurrected Christ speaking to Mary; and if he were Almighty God, God the Son, or the **eternal** Father, this would have been an ideal time to say it.

> *"For though there be that are called gods, **whether in heaven or in earth** (as there be gods many, and lords many,) But to us there is but **one God, the Father**"* (Paul speaking) *(I Cor. 8:5-6).*

Now to the only other time in the N.T. that we can be sure Jesus is called "God."

> *"And Thomas answered and said unto him, My Lord and my God" (John 20:28).*

The resurrected Jesus appeared to the disciples for the first time in a room in Jerusalem and Thomas was not there. Jesus showed them his hands and his side and said, *"Peace be unto you: as my Father hath sent me, even so send I you" (John 20:20-21)*. The disciples were glad and told Thomas they had seen the Lord, but he did not believe and remained in serious doubt for eight days. What was he doubting? **That Jesus had risen,** and therefore he must not be the Messiah, Son of God. Paul said in Romans 1:4 that Jesus was *"declared to be the Son of God....by the resurrection from the dead,"* **and Thomas did not believe it!**

> *"But he said unto them, Except I shall see in his hands the print of the nails, and put my finger into the print of the nails, and thrust my hand into his side, **I will not believe**. And after eight days again his disciples were within, and Thomas with them: then came Jesus, the doors being shut, and stood in the midst, and said, Peace be unto you. Then saith he to Thomas, Reach hither thy finger, and behold my hands; and reach hither thy hand, and thrust it into my side: and be not **faithless**, but believing" (John 20:25-27).*

Then Thomas' declaration, *"My Lord and My God."* Did he go from **"faithless,"** not believing that Jesus was the Messiah of Israel to the sudden realization that he was not only the Christ of God, but was in fact God Almighty or the eternal Son? **No!** Thomas used the word "theos" *(Gk.) (#2316 Strongs)* which means "a deity," a "magistrate," "god." Only with the Greek word "ho" *(#3588 Strongs)* the definite article "the," is it for sure **"the supreme Divinity."** Thomas did not mean, **and we must not take his statement to mean**, that Jesus whom he thought a few moments before was **not even the Messiah**, is now the supreme Deity, the most High God. **It did not happen!** Jesus is "God" *(Hebrew Elohim)* as God's agent in delivering all those *(his brethren)* who receive him, from sin, death, and hell, as Moses was "God," the God of Israel's agent in delivering the Hebrews *(his brethren)* from the bondage of Egypt.

*"Thou shalt be to him **instead of God"** (Ex. 4:16).*

"The Lord thy God will raise up unto thee a Prophet
*from the midst of thee, **of thy brethren, like unto me"***
(Moses speaking) *(Deut. 18:15).*

To make Jesus more than the Scriptures make him, especially to put him in place of his "God and Father" or equal in glory *(honor-esteem)* with the Lord God *(Jehovah Elohim)* is to flirt with idolatry. *("Thou shalt have no other gods before me,"* the Lord God, Holy **one** of Israel speaking; *Ex. 20:3).* Yes, he is the Messiah *(anointed one)* of God, a "highly exalted" **man**, now seated at the right hand of God, second in authority to God himself, but he is not the one and only Lord God Almighty!

Please consider with me this fact of Scripture. No O.T. writer ever stated that the Messiah of Israel who was to come, would in fact be the Almighty *(El Shaddai)*, the Lord God *(Jehovah Elohim)*, Most High *(El Elyon)*, or the Holy One of Israel. No O.T. prophet gave a prophecy to that effect. No. N.T. writer puts forth an argument anywhere that Jesus the Christ is indeed the Most High God. Jesus himself is nowhere recorded as saying that he is God the Creator. If such a revolutionary idea had been presented to those steeped in the Jewish Monotheism of the Torah, there would have been no limit to the **discussions** that such a thought would have caused, and no end to the **councils** that it would have provoked. It was stated repeatedly and strongly that he was to be and is the Son of God, the son of David, the **Messiah** *(Christ)* of Israel, the **deliverer**, the **redeemer** but **not God Almighty**.

Just think of the opposition Jesus and his apostles received to their claims that he is the Son of God, the Messiah, and imagine what the reaction would have been if **he or they** had proclaimed that he was in fact Almighty God. Councils were held to discuss circumcision, the eating of previously prohibited meats, and the inclusion of the Gentiles in their missionary effort; **but not one** to discuss and debate the revolutionary idea that the "man Christ Jesus" was God Almighty, or God the Son, preexistent member of the Blessed Trinity. This was nowhere stated and no council was called in Bible

64

times to debate it. This silence in the Scripture record speaks loudly! [6]

JESUS IS THE SON OF GOD, BUT HE IS NOT IN THE GODHEAD.
It is said by those who hold to the doctrine of the Trinity that the word Abba *(father)* defines the intimate relationship between Jesus and his Father, and it does. But it also defines **our** intimate relationship with God our Father. Of the three times it is used in Scripture, one is Jesus speaking to God:

> *"And he said, Abba, Father, all things are possible unto thee" (Mark 14:36).*

And two pertain to us as Christians:

> *"Whereby we cry, Abba Father" (Rom. 8:15).*
>
> *"Into your hearts crying, Abba Father" (Gal. 4:6).* We too are Sons of God.
>
> *"Behold, what manner of love the Father hath **bestowed upon us**, that **we** should be called the **sons of God**.....Beloved, now are **we** the **sons of God**" (I John 3:1-2).*

The next time you read in the gospel of John things that seem to "infer" that "Son of God" means "God," just remember that John wrote his **entire gospel** so that we *"might believe that Jesus is the Christ (Messiah), the Son of God" (John 20:31).* Christ is a synonym for "Son of God." Look at Martha's statement in *John 11:27, "I believe that thou art the Christ, the Son of God."* John says in Christ **we also** are "Sons of God."

With that understanding, please go with me to the next chapter to learn more about whom Jesus our Savior is.

*Note – The word "divine" can mean "Deity – God", or "given or inspired by God; holy; sacred". Jesus is divine as he is given by God, holy, sacred; but he is not divine as part of the Godhead. (See II Peter 1:3-4 and Heb. 9:1).

"Today, however, scholars generally agree that there is no doctrine of the Trinity as such in either the Old Testament or the New Testament...It would go far beyond the intention and thought-forms of the Old Testament to suppose that a late-forth century...Christian doctrine can be found there...Likewise, the New Testament does not contain an explicit doctrine of the Trinity."

The Harper Collins Encyclopedia of Catholicism;
1995 Edition; p. 564-565

Chapter 4

The Man Christ Jesus

*"But now ye seek to kill me, **a man** that hath told you the truth"* (Jesus speaking) *(John 8:40).*

*"For this is good and acceptable in the sight of God our Saviour; Who will have all men to be saved, and to come unto the knowledge of the truth. **For there is one God, and one mediator** between God and men, **the man Christ Jesus**; Who gave himself a ransom for all, to be testified in due time"* (I Timothy 2:3-6).

We must adjust our thinking in regard to the person of Jesus Christ. For over 1700 years theologians, under the influence of Greek and Roman thinking, have been telling us that Jesus was **not a man** but, in fact, "God the Son," the "eternal Son," second person of the Godhead, "Very God of Very God," and "coeternal with the Father." For nearly 100 years the Oneness *(Jesus only)* believers have taught that Jesus was in fact the God-man, God Almighty, the Father in flesh. They teach that he had a dual nature, "the God part of him was all God, and the man part of him was all man." To quote from some of their literature which I have in my possession, "In Jesus Christ, two wills or natures are portrayed: a human will and a divine will. He was man *(flesh)* and He was God *(Spirit)*. So as man, Jesus Christ prayed in His **human nature** to His **divine nature**." [1]

The problem with both of these views of Jesus is that they do not fit what is said of him in God's Holy Bible. Neither view is sound doctrine! What does the Bible teach regarding the true nature and person of the Son of God, Jesus Christ our Savior?

WHO DID THE OLD TESTAMENT PROPHETS SAY HE WOULD BE?
Isaiah Chapter 53 is one of the greatest O.T. prophecies regarding the life and

67

death of Jesus, and of the purpose of his first coming. It was written some 700 years before Christ and was definitely inspired, along with all Scripture, by the Holy Spirit. Verses 5 and 6 could not be more meaningful.

> *"But he was wounded for our transgressions, he was bruised for our iniquities: the chastisement of our peace was upon him; and with his stripes we are healed. All we like sheep have gone astray; we have turned every one to his own way; and the Lord hath laid on him the iniquity of us all."*

Now look back at verse 3:

> *"He is despised and rejected of men; **a man of sorrows**, and acquainted with grief: and we hid as it were our faces from him; he was despised, and we esteemed him not."*

Did Isaiah say he would be a man, live as a man, suffer as a man, and die as a man? Yes, that is the awesome truth as stated in God's word.

See *Jeremiah 33:15-17*:

> *"In those days, and at that time, will I cause the **Branch** of righteousness to grow up unto David; and he shall execute judgment and righteousness in the land. For thus saith the LORD; **David shall never want a man** to sit upon the throne of the house of Israel."*

So God said through the prophet Jeremiah that it would be "**a man**" who would sit upon the throne of Israel as David's heir. Messiah, **a man!**

The prophet Zechariah said in Chapter 13 verses 6 and 7 that Israel's "shepherd" would be a "man."

> *"And one shall say unto him, What are these wounds in thine hands? Then he shall answer, Those with which I was wounded in the house of my friends. Awake, O sword, against my **shepherd**, and against **the man** that is my fellow, saith the LORD of hosts: smite the shepherd, and the sheep shall be scattered."* Jesus confirmed that he was speaking of him *(Matt. 26:31,*

        Mark 14:27).

The prophet Micah agrees with his fellow prophets when he speaks of Jesus' coming birth, and ministry in *Micah Chapter 5*. Verse 2 says his birth will be in *"Bethlehem Ephratah, "* and verse 5 says *"And **this man** shall be the peace, when the Assyrian shall come into our land. "* I can find no O.T. prophet who said that Jesus would be the "Lord God" or "God the Son," but these mentioned clearly said he would be a **"man."** The doctrine of the Trinity could only have developed in the centuries after the O.T. had lost its relevance for the Christian Church.

JOHN THE BAPTIST BELIEVED JESUS WAS A MAN.

The N.T. prophet and forerunner of Jesus, John the baptizer, believed and taught that Jesus was **a man**. The gospel of John, Chapter 1 verses 29 and 30 says, *"The next day John seeth Jesus coming unto him, and saith, Behold the Lamb of God, which taketh away the sin of the world. This is he of whom I said, After me cometh **a man** which is preferred before me: for he was before me. "* Don't be confused by John's statement that Jesus "was before me," which simply means that, although in the flesh John was 6 months older than his cousin Jesus, in the foreordained plan of God, Jesus was the *"beginning of the creation of God" (Rev. 3:14)* and *"the firstborn of every creature" (Col. 1:15).* John taught of Jesus' **manhood** clearly; for much later when John's followers saw Jesus' miracles and heard his teachings, they said, *"All things that John spake of **this man** were true. And many believed on him there" (John 10:41-42).*

THE CONTEMPORARIES OF JESUS VIEWED HIM AS A MAN.

Although their opinions do not carry nearly as much weight as the statements of God's holy prophets and apostles regarding the person of Jesus, it is nevertheless informative to see how they viewed him.

The woman at the well to whom Jesus told the secrets of her heart said:

> *"Come, see **a man**, which told me all things that ever I did: is not this the Christ"* (Messiah) *(John 4:29)?*

A blind man who was healed by Jesus said:

69

*"**A man** that is called Jesus made clay, and anointed*
mine eyes, and said unto me, Go to the pool of Siloam
and wash: And I went and washed, and I received
sight" (John 9:11).

The officers who were sent by the chief priests and Pharisees to arrest Jesus came back without him and explained why, *"Never a man spake like* ***this man*** *"(John 7:46).*

Pontius Pilate said of Jesus:

"Behold, I bring him forth to you that ye may know that
I find no fault in him*. Then came Jesus forth wearing*
the crown of thorns, and the purple robe. And Pilate
saith unto them, ***Behold the man****" (John 19:4-5)!*

The Roman Centurion, who oversaw Jesus' crucifixion and witnessed God's power demonstrated at that event, said, *"Truly **this man** was the Son of God"(Mark 15:39).*

The disciples who traveled with Jesus, ate and slept with him, saw that he grew tired, weary, hungry, and had bodily functions as they did, **knew he was a man**. But on the Sea of Galilee when Jesus calmed the storm with words from his lips, they asked a question with which you and I are still faced today. *"The **men** marveled saying, What manner of **man** is this, that even the winds and the sea obey him"(Matt. 8:27, Mark 4:41, Luke 8:25)?* The writers of the inspired N.T. can help us with the answer.

THE APOSTLE PETER, A CLOSE COMPANION OF JESUS, SAW HIM AS A MAN.

In Peter's **great sermon** on the day of Pentecost he says:

"Ye men of Israel, hear these words; Jesus of Nazareth,
a man approved of God*, among you by miracles and*
wonders and signs, which God did by him in the midst
of you, as ye yourselves also know: Him, being
*delivered by the determinate counsel **and***
foreknowledge of God, ye have taken*, and by wicked*

> hands have **crucified and slain: Whom God hath**
> **raised up,** *having loosed the **pains of death***: *because it*
> *was **not possible** that he should be holden of it.   For*
> ***David speaketh concerning him.*** *I foresaw the Lord*
> *always before my face, for he is on my right hand, that I*
> *should not be moved: Therefore did my heart rejoice,*
> *and my tongue was glad; moreover also **my flesh shall***
> ***rest in hope:** Because **thou wilt not leave my soul in***
> ***hell,** neither wilt thou **suffer thine Holy One** to see*
> ***corruption"** (Acts 2:22-27).*

Peter continues speaking regarding Jesus, whom they had recently slain, and King David from whose lineage he came:

> *"Therefore, **being a prophet** and knowing that God had*
> *sworn with an oath to him* (David) *that of the fruit of*
> *his loins, according to the flesh, he* (God) *would raise*
> *up Christ* (Messiah) *to sit on his* (David's) *throne; He*
> (David), ***seeing this before,*** *spoke of the **resurrection of***
> ***Christ** that his* (Jesus') *soul was not left in hell, neither*
> *his flesh did see corruption"* (decay in the grave) *(vs. 30*
> *and 31).*

David is one of the greatest prophets in the O.T., and Peter quotes him extensively in his sermon about Jesus. Let's see what we can learn from Peter *(and David).*

Jesus was a **man** *(v. 22). "A man approved of God."*

Jesus was tried, crucified, and slain in the *"foreknowledge of God" (v. 23): "the Lamb slain from the foundation of the world"(Rev. 13:8).* This is **not preexistence**; it is "the foreknowledge of God." **Please get hold of this truth.**

For a better understanding of the *"foreknowledge of God, "*look at verse 31. Peter says, *"He* (David) ***seeing this before,*** *spoke of the **resurrection of Christ. "*** How could David see the resurrection of Christ and write about it in

Psalm 16, some **1000 years before it happened**? Because it was very real in the unchangeable purpose and plan of God. In God's mind, it was done; although in history it was not done until around 32 A.D.

Jesus was raised up by God, *"having loosed the pains of death from him"* *(v. 24)*. Jesus himself raised up his body *("this temple" John 2:19)*, but he did it acting as God's **agent in resurrection**. *"I have power to lay it down, and I have power to take it again. This* **commandment have I received** of *my Father" (John 10:18)*. Please understand this power of Jesus' "**agency**," **acting as God's appointed and empowered agent**, *"A man approved of God" (v. 22)*. Jesus' resurrection did not prove that he was the second person of the "triune God"; it proved that he was the Son of God, Messiah, Son of David.

> *"Declared to be the Son of God...by the resurrection*
> *from the dead" (Rom. 1:4).*

Prophetically, David under the anointing of the Holy Spirit quotes Jesus speaking in vs. 25 thru 27, and pictures him as **taking comfort**, **rejoicing**, **being glad**, and **resting** in the knowledge that God the Father was with him and would not leave his **"soul in hell**." This does not picture a "God-man" but "**a man,** "confident in the love of **his God**, the Father *(see John 20:17)*. *"Thou wilt not leave my soul in hell"* (Jesus to God) *(Acts 2:27)*.

Jesus had a soul *(v. 27, 31)*! Does a man have a soul? Yes. Did Jesus have a soul? Yes! *"My soul is exceeding sorrowful, even unto death: tarry ye here and watch with me"* (he needed his friends) *(Matt. 26:38, Mark 14:34)*. The day before his arrest Jesus said, "**Now is my soul troubled**; *and what shall I say? Father, save me from this hour: but for this cause came I unto this hour" (John 12:27)*. Listen to what Isaiah has to say about Jesus' soul in *Isaiah 53:10-12*:

> *"Yet it pleased the LORD* (God) *to bruise him; he hath*
> *put him to grief: when thou shalt make **his soul** an*
> *offering for sin, he shall see his seed...he* (God) *shall see*
> *the travail of **his soul**, and shall be satisfied...Therefore,*

will I (God) *divide him* (Jesus) *a portion with the great...because he hath poured out his soul unto death...and he bare the sin of many, and made intercession for the transgressors. "* (And *"he ever liveth to make intercession* for us." *Heb. 7:25)*

Jesus' soul went to hell! **Peter said so, David said so, God's Word says so** *(v. 27, 31).* Thank God, Jesus went in my place so I will not have to go!

This fact was still on Peter's mind several years later when he wrote his epistle called First Peter *(I Peter 3:18-22):*

"For Christ also hath once suffered for sins, *the just for the unjust, that he might bring us to God,* **being put to death in the flesh,** *but quickened by the Spirit:* **By which also he went and preached unto the spirits in prison; Which sometime were disobedient, when once the long-suffering of God waited in the days of Noah, while the ark was a-preparing,** *wherein few, that is, eight souls were saved by water. The like figure whereunto even baptism doth also now save us (not the putting away of the filth of the flesh, but the answer of a good conscience toward God)* **by the resurrection of Jesus Christ: Who is gone into heaven, and is on the right hand of God; angels and authorities and powers being made subject unto him.**"

Dear reader, God is not playing word games in the Bible. Jesus was "**a man**" who died and went to hell *(Heb. Sheol),* and preached to the captive "spirits" in prison. He arose three days later victorious, *"having the keys of hell and of death" (Rev. 1:18).* We are not "gods" but men, so we did not need "God the Son" to die for us but "a man," *"the man Christ Jesus "(I Tim. 2:5).* He is our **hero**, our **champion**, our **advocate, and because he lives, we shall live forever!**

73

THE GREAT APOSTLE PAUL BELIEVED JESUS WAS A MAN.
In 13 epistles written by Paul, he mentions "God" over 500 times and not one time can it be proven that he was speaking of Jesus. If Jesus is "God," Paul did not know it. He said the one and only God is the Father. *"But to us there is but one God, the Father."* (You can argue with Paul.)

> *"If in this life only we have hope in Christ, we are of all men most miserable. But now is Christ risen from the dead, and become the firstfruits of them that slept. For since by man* (Adam) *came death, by man came also the resurrection of the dead. For as in Adam all die, even so in Christ shall all be made alive. But every man in his own order: Christ the firstfruits; afterward they that are Christ's at his coming"* (I Cor. 15:19-23).

Listen to the apostle Paul, *"by man came also the resurrection of the dead. For as in Adam* (a man) *all die, even so in Christ* (a man) *shall all be made alive. But "every man"* - *"every man in his own order: Christ* (a man) *the firstfruits; afterward they that are Christs' at his coming."* Jesus lived as a man, died as a man, and arose from the grave as a man.

See *Luke 24:36-43*:

> *"Jesus himself stood in the midst of them, and saith unto them, Peace be unto you. But they were terrified and affrighted, and supposed that they had seen a spirit. And he said unto them, Why are ye troubled? And why do thoughts arise in your hearts? Behold my hands and my feet, that it is I myself: handle me, and see; for a spirit hath not flesh and bones; as ye see me have. And when he had thus spoken, he shewed them his hands and his feet. And while they yet believed not for joy, and wondered, he said unto them, Have ye here any meat? And they gave him a piece of a broiled fish,*

74

and of an honeycomb. And he took it, and did eat
before them" (Luke 24:36-43).

My friend, Jesus is not putting on a charade here. This is a man, resurrected from the dead with a glorified body, who is not a spirit but "flesh and bones," who can be handled and who eats food. This does not answer all questions, but it tells us **all we need to know**. Did he grow hungry? We don't know, but he did eat and we are left to believe that the food that was eaten digested in the body of a man. Paul says in *Philippians 3:20-21*:

"Heaven, from whence also we look for the Savior, the
Lord Jesus Christ: Who shall change our vile body,
that it may be fashioned like unto his glorious body."

After our resurrection or change at his coming we shall be like him, men and women with glorified bodies, and we shall **feast with him** at the marriage supper of the Lamb *(Rev. 19:9, Luke 14:17, 22:16).*

Paul says in *Acts 13:38*:

"Through this man is preached unto you the
forgiveness of sins."

Paul says in *Acts 17:31*:

"Because He (God) *hath appointed a day, in the which*
*he will judge the world in righteousness **by that man***
whom he hath ordained; (appointed or specified)
*whereof he hath given assurance **unto all men**, in that*
he hath raised him from the dead."

Paul says in *Romans 5:15*:

*"For if through the **offense of one** (Adam) many be*
dead, much more the grace of God, and the gift by
*grace, which is by **one man, Jesus Christ**, hath*
abounded unto many."

Paul says in *Philippians 2:8*:

*"And being found in fashion as **a man**, he humbled*
himself and became obedient unto death, even the death

75

of the cross."

Look at what Paul tells us in Colossians. Chapter 1 verse 15 says:

> *"Who* (Jesus) *is the **image** of the **invisible God**, the firstborn of every **creature**."*

Now look at Chapter 3 verse 3:

> *"For ye are dead, and your life is hid **with Christ in God**."*

Now see verses 9 and 10:

> *"Lie not one to another, seeing that ye have put off the old man* (Adam nature) *with his deeds; and have put on the **new man** (**Christ**), which is renewed in knowledge after the **image of him** (God) **that created him** (Jesus)."*

These are awesome verses in understanding our Lord Jesus' place in God and our place in him. Look at the context to see for sure what Paul is saying.

> *"As ye have therefore received **Christ Jesus** the Lord, so walk ye **in him**" (2:6).*
>
> *"**Putting off the body of the sins of the flesh** by the circumcision of Christ" (2:11).*
>
> *"**Buried with him** (Christ) in baptism, wherein also ye are **risen with him** through the faith of the operation of God, who hath raised him from the dead" (2:12).*
>
> *"If ye then be **risen with Christ**, seek those things which are above, where Christ sitteth on the right hand of God" (3:1).*

Now please look again at verse 10, *"Put on the **new man**."* Christ Jesus is the **new man**. And **God created him!** *(Jesus is a **created being**)* *"Put on the **new man*** (Christ)" agrees with other writings of Paul.

> *"But **put ye on** the Lord Jesus Christ" (Rom. 13:14).*
>
> *"For as many of you as have been baptized into Christ **have put on Christ**" (Gal. 3:27).*
>
> *"Do all in the name of the Lord Jesus, giving thanks to*

76

    God and the Father by him" (Col. 3:17).

THE INSPIRED WRITER OF HEBREWS TEACHES US THAT JESUS IS A MAN.

Hebrews 2:9 says:

> *"...that he by the grace of God should taste death for **every man**."*

Hebrews 3:3 says:

> *"For **this man** (Jesus) was counted worthy of more glory than Moses."*

Hebrews 7:24 says:

> *"But **this man** (Jesus)...hath an unchangeable priesthood."*

Hebrews 8:3 says:

> *"...it is of necessity that **this man** (Jesus) have somewhat also to offer"* (his blood).

Hebrews 10:12 says:

> *"But **this man**, after he had offered one sacrifice for sins, forever, sat down on the right hand of God."*

James 1:13-14 says:

> *"Let no man say when he is tempted, I am tempted of God: for **God cannot be tempted with evil**, neither tempteth he any man: **But every man is tempted**, when he is drawn away of his own lust and enticed."* Jesus, **as a man**, was enticed; but he did not yield and sin.

Hebrews 2:18 says:

> *"For in that he (Jesus) himself hath **suffered** being tempted"* (Heb. 2:18).

Hebrews 4:15 says:

> *"But (Jesus) **was** in all points **tempted** like as we are, yet **without sin**."*

Why so many Scriptures telling us that Jesus was **a man**? God the

Father wanted us to know for sure that all of the eternal riches in glory that Jesus Messiah attained for us through his sinless life, his sacrificial death and his glorious resurrection, he won for us not as **a God** but as **a man**! **And we still got it wrong**! We made him "God" in our minds, hearts, and worship. So what should we do? Repent and start to reprogram your mind as I have. God the Father is loving, patient, and forgiving. We know by studying His Word and by looking at His Son Jesus, who is the mirror "image" of the Father *(II Cor. 3:18)*, and *"the express image of his person" (Heb. 1:3)*.

MORE ABOUT JESUS' HUMANITY.

Since we have missed the point so badly in the past, let us look a little further into what the Bible says about Jesus' humanity. The Scriptures teach that Jesus had a **human spirit**, as do all "men." Look briefly at what the Bible says about the human spirit. *"And God formed man of the dust of the ground and **breathed into his nostrils the breath of life**; and man became a **living soul" (Gen. 2:7)**. Job 34:14-15 says, "If he* (God) *gather unto himself his spirit and his breath; **all flesh shall perish** together, and **man shall turn again unto dust**. "* So man's spirit is the breath of life from God. *(The word "spirit" in Hebrew means "breath")*. Death is the separation of the body from the spirit. *Genesis 49:33* says that when Jacob died he *"yielded up the ghost* (his human spirit) *and was gathered unto his people. " Acts 5:10* says Sapphira *"fell down...and yielded up the ghost. "* Thus, we understand *Matthew 27:50* when it says that when Jesus *"cried again with a loud voice, he yielded up the ghost. "* His human spirit departed from him.

The spirit lives on after departing the body. *"And **the spirit** shall return to God who gave it" (Eccl. 12:7). "And they stoned Stephen calling upon God, and saying, Lord Jesus, receive **my spirit" (Acts 7:59)**.* He prayed to God and commended **his spirit** to Jesus.

> *"He that is slow to anger is better than the mighty; and he that ruleth **his spirit** than he that taketh a city" (Prov. 16:32).*

78

> *"**The spirit** of man is the candle of the Lord, searching all the inward parts of the belly" (Prov. 20:27).*

Mark 8:11-12 says:

> *"And the Pharisees came forth and began to question with him, seeking of him a sign from heaven, tempting (testing) him. And he sighed deeply in **his spirit** and saith, Why doth this generation seek after a sign?"*

This says plainly that Jesus sighed "in **his spirit**." *Luke 2:40 says, "And the child* (Jesus) *grew, and waxed **strong in spirit**, filled with **wisdom**; and the **grace** of God was upon him. "* The wisdom he was filled with came from God the Father; the "grace upon him" was God's, but the **spirit** in which he grew "strong" seems to be his human spirit. In verse 80 of the previous Chapter, it says also of John the Baptist, that *"the child grew and waxed strong in **spirit**. " Luke 4:1 says, "And Jesus, being full of the Holy Ghost, returned from Jordan, and was led by the Spirit into the wilderness. "* This speaks of Jesus now *"being full of the Holy Ghost" that had **sired** him ("that which is conceived in her is of the Holy Ghost" Matt. 1:20),* and led by the "Spirit" *(the same Spirit – notice the capital S).* Do not be confused by the fact that Jesus was **sired** in Mary's womb "of the Holy Ghost," yet God is his Father. God is a Spirit; He is the "Holy Spirit," the "Holy Ghost." They are **one** and **the same**. The Holy Ghost was manifest at Pentecost in another form and filled the believers, but He is the same Spirit. I will discuss this later.

BACK TO JESUS' HUMAN SPIRIT.

Luke 10:21 says:

> *"In that hour Jesus rejoiced **in spirit**, and said, I thank thee, **O Father, Lord of heaven and earth**, that thou hast hid these things from the wise and prudent, and hast revealed them unto babes: even so, Father; for so it seemed good in thy sight."*

Jesus is rejoicing in his spirit *(notice the small s)* because of his Father's wisdom and goodness. (Notice also Jesus' words *"Lord of heaven and earth."* We have given that honor and position to Jesus, but he said it belongs to his **Father**).

John 11:33-35 says when Jesus met Mary at the tomb of her brother Lazarus, she was weeping and fell down at his feet.

> *"When Jesus therefore saw her weeping, and the Jews also weeping which came with her, **he groaned in the spirit, and was troubled**, And said, Where have ye laid him? They said unto him, Lord, come and see. **Jesus wept**."*

These are clearly human reactions from Jesus' human spirit.

John Chapter 13 tells of the events of the last supper, of Jesus washing the disciples feet and talking to them of his coming death. Verse 21 says:

> *"When Jesus had thus said, he **was troubled in spirit**, and testified, and said, Verily, verily, I say unto you, that one of you shall betray me."*

Jesus seems to be troubled, not in the Holy Ghost, but in his **human "spirit."**

THE HOLY GHOST IS THE SPIRIT OF GOD (NOT ANOTHER PERSON).

Let's establish from the Scriptures at this point that the Holy Ghost is none other than God, the Holy Spirit. Look at Matthew 1:18, *"Now the birth of Jesus Christ was on this wise: When as his mother Mary was espoused to Joseph, before they came together, she was found with child **of the Holy Ghost**."* Verse 20 says that the angel of the Lord said to Joseph, *"..fear not to take unto thee Mary thy wife: for that which is conceived in her is **of the Holy Ghost**."* Now, it is for sure that **by whom** a woman conceives, **he is the father of the child**. The Holy Ghost is none other than the Holy Spirit of the Lord God, who is Jesus' Father. He is also called the Comforter, whom Jesus said would be manifest after he went to the Father *(John 14:16, 26; 16:7)*. The Holy Ghost **was in** the O.T., though **not** called **by that**

80

name. *"They departed, after that Paul had spoken one word, Well spake the* **Holy Ghost** *by Esaias (Isaiah) the prophet unto our fathers" (Acts 28:25).* *"For the prophecy came not in old time* (the O.T.) *by the will of man: but holy men of God spoke, as they were moved by the* **Holy Ghost**" *(II Peter 1:21).* Acts 1:16 says, *"The Holy Ghost by the mouth of David spake concerning Judas, "* 1000 years before.

Look at the Gospel accounts of Jesus' water baptism. Mark 1:10 says that at that time, *"he* (John) *saw the heavens opened, and the Spirit like a dove descending upon him"* (Jesus). Matthew 3:16 says, *"he saw the Spirit of God descending like a dove and lighting upon him, "* and Luke 3:22 says, *"and the Holy Ghost descended in a bodily shape like a dove upon him."* Now, here is a question for those who hold the doctrine of the Trinity. Was it the **"Spirit of God"** *(the first person of the Trinity)* or the **"Holy Ghost"** *(the third person of the Trinity)* who descended like a dove on Jesus? Of course, they are one and the same person not two separate Spirits! God is a Spirit and He is the Holy Spirit.

> *"For by* **one Spirit** *are we all baptized into one body...and have been made to drink into* **one Spirit**" *(I Cor. 12:13).*

> *"The Spirit of God dwelleth in you" (I Cor. 3:16).*

Jesus teaches us in Matt. 12:32 that **he** and the Holy Ghost are not the same person. *"And whosoever speaketh a word against the Son of man, it shall be forgiven him: but whosoever speaketh against the Holy Ghost, it shall not be forgiven him, neither in this world, neither in the world to come. "* (A serious warning!) He was certainly **filled with the Holy Ghost**. *"And Jesus being* **full of the Holy Ghost** *returned from Jordan, and was led by the Spirit into the wilderness" (Luke 4:1).* Others had been filled with the Holy Ghost prior to this. Elizabeth was filled with the Holy Ghost *(Luke 1:41).* Her husband *"Zacharias was filled with the Holy Ghost" (v. 67).*

Jesus was filled with the Holy Ghost without measure. John the Baptist, who himself was filled with the Holy Ghost from his mother Elizabeth's womb, said of Jesus, *"For he whom God hath sent speaketh the words of*

81

God: for God giveth not the Spirit by measure unto him" (not a limited portion) *(John 3:34).*

Jesus was anointed by the Holy Ghost.

> *"The Spirit of the Lord is upon me, **because he hath anointed me** to preach the gospel to the poor; he hath sent me to heal the brokenhearted, to preach deliverance to the captives, and recovering of sight to the blind, to set at liberty them that are bruised" (Luke 4:18).*

Peter says in Acts 10:38:

> *"**How God anointed Jesus** of Nazareth **with the Holy Ghost** and with power: who went about doing good, and healing all that were oppressed of the devil; for **God was with him**."*

Notice that Peter did not say that "he was God," but rather that "**God was with him**." We have already seen from Scripture that when Jesus died on the cross, he went in his human spirit to the place of the dead and preached to the captive spirits in prison. Paul says in Ephesians 4:8-10 that Jesus took "captives" with him to heaven when he arose from the grave and ascended.

> *"Wherefore he saith, When he ascended up on high, he led captivity captive* (a multitude of captives) *and gave gifts unto men. (Now that he ascended, what is it but that he also **descended first into the lower parts of the earth?** He that descended is the same also that ascended up far above all heavens, that he might fill all things.)"* (His soul descended to Hades. The tomb where his body lay was not in "the lower parts of the earth.")

Jesus was still a man, "the Son of man" *(a human),* **when he arose from the grave with his glorified body.**

> *"And as they came down from the mountain, Jesus charged them,*

82

saying, *Tell the vision to no man,* **until the Son of man be risen again from the dead"** *(Matt. 17:9).* "Son of man" is a Messianic title taken from Psalm 8, a Psalm of David while he was in wonderment over God's **name**, His **glory**, and His **works as seen in creation**.

> *"O Lord our Lord, how excellent is* ***thy name*** *in all the earth! Who hast set* ***thy glory*** *above the heavens. When I consider thy heavens, the work of thy fingers, the moon and the stars, which thou hast ordained;* ***What is man that thou art mindful of him?*** ***And the son of man****, that thou visitest him? For thou hast made* ***him a little lower than the angels****, and hast crowned him with glory and honour. Thou madest him to have dominion over the works of thy hands;* ***thou hast put all things under his feet****: All sheep and oxen, yea, and the beast of the field; the fowl of the air, and the fish of the sea, and whatsoever passeth through the paths of the seas. O Lord our Lord, how excellent is* ***thy name*** *in all the earth" (Ps. 8:1, 3-9)!*

UNDERSTANDING JESUS' MANHOOD FROM HEBREWS CHAPTER 2.

Hebrews Chapter 2 very clearly puts Jesus in this Psalm, and it is amazing and enlightening to see **where**. He is not in the first three verses, **that is the Lord God**, with a **name** that is excellent in all of the earth, with **glory**, that is set above the heavens, and who is **creator of all**. Then the writer of Hebrews quotes verse 4 of the psalm, *"But what is man that thou art mindful of him" (Heb. 2:6).* Why would such an awesome God even think about **lowly, sinful man**? When God said to the angels in Genesis 1:26, "Let us make **man**," He evidently spoke in Hebrew, for that is the language of the O.T., of the Hebrew people, and the language in which the Lord Jesus spoke to Saul *(Paul)* from heaven at the time of his Damascus road encounter. The word "man" in Hebrew is **"adam"** which pertains to

83

showing blood in the face *(red-ruddy)* and means **"a human being,"** an individual or the species, **"mankind."** A secondary meaning is, **"of low degree"**. King David and the writer of the book of Hebrews wondered at the fact that the Most High God, Creator of all would be mindful of man (adam).

The second thing that David and the writer of Hebrews wondered about was, what is **"the son of man, that thou visitest him"***(Ps. 8:4, Heb. 2:6).* Please look closely, God is mindful of **man** *(adam)*, the first generation, and visits the **"son of man,"** the next or second generation of man *(adam).* The word "Son" in Hebrew is "ben" and means **"child, one born."** The secondary meaning of man *(adam)*, **"of low degree"** is seen in Ps. 8:4 and Heb. 2:6. *"Thou madest him* (man) *a little lower than the angels; thou crownest him with glory and honour, and **didst set him over the works of thy hands.** "*

Now look at Hebrews 2:8:

"Thou (God) *hast put all things in subjection under his* (man's) *feet. For in that he* (God) *put all in subjection under him* (man), *he* (God) *left nothing that is not put under him"* (man).

This speaks of the dominion that God gave Adam and Eve, as seen in Gen. 1:26-31:

"And God said, Let us make man in our image, after our likeness: **and let them have dominion** *over the fish of the sea, and over the fowl of the air, and over the cattle, and over all the earth, and over every creeping thing that creepeth upon the earth.* **So God created man in his own image,** *in the image of God created he him; male and female created he them.* **And God blessed** *them, and God said unto them,* **Be fruitful,** *and* **multiply,** *and* **replenish the earth, and subdue it: and have dominion over the fish of the sea, and over the fowl of the air, and over every living thing that moveth upon the earth.** *And God said,* **Behold I have given**

84

> *you every herb bearing seed, which is upon the face of*
> *all the earth, and every tree, in the which is the fruit of*
> *a tree yielding seed; to you it shall be for meat. And to*
> *every beast of the earth, and to every fowl of the air,*
> *and to everything that creepeth upon the earth,*
> *wherein there is life, I have given every green herb for*
> *meat: and it was so. And God saw every thing that he*
> *had made, and, behold, it was very good. And the*
> *evening and the morning were the sixth day."*

God is not just speaking words. God saw everything that He had made pertaining to "earth" *(v. 28)*, and gave to man, and to woman who was taken out of man *(adam)*, **dominion** over it, to **rule** over it, **populate** and **subdue** it! But sadly man and woman sinned in the Garden of Eden; and the serpent, Satan, the devil, usurped *(took)* their God given authority and became, "**god of this world**" *(II Cor. 4:4)*. For further proof of Satan's usurped dominion see Luke 4:5-7:

> *"And the devil, taking him* (Jesus) *up into an high*
> *mountain, shewed unto him all the kingdoms of the*
> *world in a moment of time. And the devil said unto*
> *him, all this power will I give thee, and the glory of*
> *them: for that is delivered unto me; and to whomsoever*
> *I will I give it. If thou wilt worship me, all shall be*
> *thine."*

Jesus did not dispute Satan's claim that all this dominion was his, but simply said, "*Get thee behind me, Satan: for it is written, Thou shalt worship the Lord thy God, and him only shalt thou serve" (v. 8)*. One day very soon Satan will bestow this usurped authority upon the anti-christ. *"And the dragon gave him his power, and his seat, and great authority" (Rev. 13:2, 12:9)*.

To understand the present limits of Satan's "great authority," turn to Job 1:6, *"Now there was a day* (in time) *when the sons of God came to present themselves before the Lord, and Satan came also among them."* These

85

"sons of God" are angels, **created sons of God**.

Now to Job 1:7:

> *"And the Lord said unto **Satan, whence comest thou?***
> *Then Satan answered the Lord, and said, **from going***
> *to and fro in the earth**, and from **walking** up and down*
> *in it."*

God calls Satan's attention to a God fearing man by the name of Job, and gives him power over all Job had, with **one** limitation.

> *"And the Lord said unto Satan, Behold, **all that he hath***
> *is in thy power; only upon himself** put not forth thine*
> *hand. So Satan went forth from the presence of the*
> *Lord" (Job 1:12).*

So with permission from God, Satan went out and created havoc with Job's family and possessions *(vs. 13-19)*. But Job, with faith in his God, faced the bad news with worship and praise *(vs. 20-21)* and *"sinned not, nor charged God foolishly" (v. 22).*

> *"**Again there was a day** when the **sons of God** came to*
> *present themselves before the Lord, and Satan came*
> *also among them to present himself before the Lord.*
> *And the Lord said unto Satan, from whence comest*
> *thou? And Satan answered the Lord, and said, from*
> *going to and fro in the earth, and from walking up and*
> *down in it" (Job 2:1-2).*

Remember that these angels, with whom Satan came to report to God, are created "sons of God," are **not related to God**, as in **kin** to God. They are **not of God's substance**, but were, along with all the rest of creation, created *"by the breath of His mouth" (Ps. 33:6)*. This time God gives Satan permission to go further.

> *"And the Lord said unto Satan, **Behold, he is in thine***
> *hand; but save his life**. So went Satan forth from the*
> *presence of the Lord, and smote Job with sore boils*
> *from the sole of his foot unto his crown" (Job 2:6-7).*

When man sinned in the garden and lost **his** God given authority, **God lost none of His power** and **authority!** He is still Almighty and will do according to His pleasure. **He is God!** Nebuchadnezzar learned this lesson well.

> *"And at the end of the days* (7 years of insanity) *I Nebuchadnezzar lifted up mine eyes to heaven, and mine understanding returned unto me, and I blessed the **most High**, and I praised and honoured him that liveth for ever, whose dominion is an everlasting dominion, and his kingdom is from generation to generation: And **all the inhabitants of the earth are reputed as nothing**: and **he doeth according to his will** in the army of heaven, and among the inhabitants of the earth: **and none can stay his hand, or say unto him, what doest thou"** (Dan. 4:34-35)?*

Daniel 5:21 says:

> *"His body was wet with the dew of heaven: till he knew that the **most high God** ruled in the **kingdom** of men, and that he **appointeth** over it whomsoever he will."*

Compare this with what Jesus said in Luke 22:29:

> *"I appoint unto you a **kingdom, as my father hath appointed unto me."***

The writer of Hebrews says:

> *"Christ Jesus; who was faithful to him that **appointed** him "(Heb. 3:1-2).* (Jesus is **a man** that God "appointed").

Job held firmly to his integrity and his God, and God healed and restored him gloriously. *(Job 42:10-16) "So Job died, being old and full of days" (v. 17),* but he died with the hope of resurrection and of seeing God.

> *"For I know that my redeemer liveth, and that he* (God) *shall stand at the latter day upon the earth: And though after my skin worms destroy this body, yet in my*

*flesh **shall I see God"** (Job 19:25-26).*

This is the hope that Jesus **gave us** of seeing **God the Father**, though he said in John 5:37, *"Ye have neither heard His voice at any time, nor seen His shape." **"Blessed are the pure in heart: for they shall see God"*** *(Matt. 5:8).* If you must run ahead as I do sometime, turn to Rev. 22:3-4 and see that the **throne of God** is in the new Jerusalem, *"**And they shall see His** (God's) **face."***

MORE ABOUT JESUS FROM HEBREWS CHAPTER TWO.

Now with that understanding of Scripture, let's go back to Hebrews Chapter 2 and see **where God put Jesus into this picture**. The writer of Hebrews started this Chapter with a strong warning *(v. 1):*

> *"Therefore we ought to **give the more earnest** heed to the things which we have heard, lest at any time we should **let them slip."***

We must get hold of this!

> *"But **we see Jesus**, who was **made a little lower than the angels for the suffering of death**, crowned with glory and honor, that he by the grace of God should taste death for **every man"** (v. 9).*

How was Jesus made? A little lower than the angels, **a man,** *"for the suffering of death."* **God cannot die**, a **"God-man" cannot die**, an **"eternal Son" could not die**, but Jesus Christ *(a man)* the sinless son of God **did die**. Look at the prophecy of Caiaphas:

> *"And one of them, named Caiaphas, being the high priest that same year, said unto them, **Ye know nothing at all, Nor consider that it is expedient for us, that one man should die for the people**, and that the whole nation perish not. And this spake he not of himself; but being high priest that year, **he prophesied that Jesus** ("one man") **should die for that nation;** And not for that nation only, but **that also he should gather***

> *together in one the children of God that were scattered*
> *abroad" (John 11:49-52).*

Paul agrees:

> *"For if through the offense of **one** (Adam) many be*
> *dead, much more the **grace of God**, and the gift by*
> *grace, which is by **one man**, Jesus Christ, hath*
> *abounded **unto many" (Rom. 5:15).***

***"Crowned with glory and honor"** (v. 9).* Jesus was given "glory." The Gospel of John says, *"We beheld **his glory**, the glory as of the only begotten of the Father" (John 1:14).* We dare not give Jesus his **Father's glory**! **God the Father said some 700 years before Jesus came** *(Isa. 42:8),* "*I am the Lord* (God)*; that is my name: and **my glory will I not give to another**."* God says in Isaiah 43:10-11:

> *"Ye are my witnesses, saith the Lord, and my servant*
> *whom I have chosen: that ye may know and believe me,*
> ***and understand that I am he**: before me there was no*
> *God formed, **neither shall there be after me**. I, even I,*
> *am the Lord* (God); *and beside me there is **no Savior**."*

Then He said it again, *"I will not give **my glory** unto another" (Isa. 48:11).* God gave Jesus his **own** glory, **not the Father's**! It is we who have done that, **to our shame**.

> *"And Jesus said unto them, Verily* (truly) *I say unto you,*
> *that ye which have followed me, in the regeneration*
> *when the Son of man shall sit in the throne of **his glory**,*
> *ye also shall sit upon twelve thrones, judging the twelve*
> *tribes of Israel" (Matt. 19:28).*

> *"For whosoever shall be ashamed of me and of my*
> *words, of him shall the Son of man be ashamed, when*
> *he shall come in **his own glory**, and (in his) Father's,*
> *and of the holy angels" (Luke 9:26).*

Jesus is coming **"in his own glory"** which was given to him by the Father *(John 17:22);* and it is a reflection of God the Father's glory, as the moon reflects the sun *(I Cor. 15:41).* *"The light of the knowledge of the glory of God in the face of Jesus Christ" (II Cor. 4:6).* **At Jesus' birth** the angels were praising **God**, and saying, *"Glory to God in the highest" (Luke 2:13-14).*

Please do not misunderstand me, Jesus our Lord and Savior has **great glory**.

> *"And then shall appear the sign of the Son of man in heaven: and then shall all the tribes of the earth mourn, and they shall see **the Son of man** coming in the clouds of heaven with power and **great glory**" (Matt. 24:30, Mark 13:26, Luke 21:27).*

It is not our precious Savior's fault that for 1700 years the Christian Church has tried to confer on him *(Jesus)* the glory that is **due only to the creator**, God the Father. **Jesus always pointed us to the Father!**

- *"My Father is greater than all" (John 10:29).*
- *"My Father is greater than I" (John 14:28).*
- *"Jesus answered, I have not a devil; but **I honor my Father**, and ye do dishonor me. And I seek **not mine own glory**, there is **one** that seeketh and judgeth" (John 8:49-50).*

GOD AND JESUS IN REVELATION CHAPTERS FOUR AND FIVE.
Oh, dear reader, please get a vision in your mind of what the apostle John saw in Revelation Chapters 4 and 5:

> *"And immediately I was in the Spirit: and behold **a throne** was set in heaven, and **one sat on the throne"** (4:2)*
>
> *"And the four beasts had each of them six wings about him; And they were full of eyes within: and they rest not day and night, saying **Holy, holy, holy, Lord God Almighty**, which was, and is, and is to come. And when those beasts give **glory** and **honor** and **thanks** to him that sat on the throne...and **worship him that liveth forever and ever**, and cast their crowns before the*

90

> *throne, saying, Thou art worthy, **O Lord**, to receive*
> ***glory** and **honor** and **power**: for thou hast created all*
> *things, and for thy pleasure they are and were created*
> *"(Rev. 4:8-11)!*

This is worship before the throne of God, "**Lord God Almighty,**" as they cast their crowns before Him saying, *"Thou art worthy, O Lord to receive **glory** and **honor** and **power**,"* to the Creator. Now the scene changes.

> *"And he* (the Lamb) *came and took the book out of the right hand of him* (God) *that sat upon the throne. And when he had taken the book, the four beasts and four and twenty elders fell down before the Lamb, having every one of them harps, and golden vials full of odors, which are the prayers of saints. And they sung a new song, saying, Thou art worthy to take the book, and to open the seals thereof: **for thou wast slain, and hast redeemed us to God by thy blood** out of every kindred, and tongue, and people, and nation; And hast made us **unto our God kings and priests: and we shall reign on the earth.** And I beheld, and I heard the voice of many angels round about the throne and the beasts and the elders: and the number of them was **ten thousand times ten thousand, and thousands of thousands;** Saying with a loud voice, **Worthy is the Lamb that was slain to receive power,** and **riches**, and **wisdom**, and **strength**, and **honor**, and **glory**, and **blessing**" (Rev. 5:7-12).*

This is Jesus, the Lamb of God, who was slain for our salvation, who *"stood" (v. 6)* and took the 7 sealed book from the hand of God the Father who *"sat on the throne."* When he took the book, the four beasts and four and twenty elders fell down before the Lamb and played harps and sang. Then 10,000 times 10,000 and thousands of thousands of Angels saying,

*"Worthy is the Lamb that was slain to receive **power**, and **riches**, and **wisdom**, and **strength**, and **honor**, and **glory**, and **blessing**."* This is awesome and deserved praise to our Lord Jesus Christ, but in all of this description one word is missing. It is **not said** that they **worshiped the Lamb**, as they did God the Father in Chapter 4, verse 10. This is significant. Now verse 13 tells us:

> *"Every creature which is in heaven, and on earth, and under the earth, and such as are in the sea, and all that are in them, heard I saying, Blessing, and honor, and glory, and power, **be unto him that sitteth upon the throne** (God), **and unto the Lamb** (Jesus) forever and ever."*

Again, *"**Blessing**, and **honor**, and **glory**, and **power**,"* to God the Father and to His Son Jesus. Now verse 14, *"And the four beasts said, Amen. And the four and twenty elders fell down, and **worshiped him** (God the Father) that liveth forever and ever" (see 4:8-10).*

Why does this account not say that they worshiped the Lamb? Perhaps the answer can be found in these verses:

> (Jesus speaking) *"For it is written, Thou shalt **worship the Lord thy God**, and him only shalt thy serve" (Luke 4:8).*

> (Jesus speaking) *"We know what **we** worship"* (the Father) *(John 4:22).*

> (Jesus speaking) *"The true worshipers shall **worship the Father**...for the Father seeketh such to **worship him**" (John 4:23).*

> *"Who shall not fear thee, **O Lord** (Lord God Almighty) and glorify thy name? for thou only are holy: for all nations shall come and **worship before thee**" (Rev. 15:4).*

> *"And I* (John) *fell at his feet* (the angel's) *to worship him. And he said unto me, See thou do it not: I am thy*

> *fellow servant, and of thy brethren that have the*
> *testimony of Jesus:* ***worship God"*** *(Rev. 19:10).*
> ***"Worship God"*** *(Rev. 22:9).*

NOW BACK TO HEBREWS CHAPTER TWO.

Verse 9 says: *"But we see Jesus.......crowned with glory and **honor**; that he by the grace of God should taste death for every man."* Let's look at the **honor** with which he is crowned. The **Lord God Almighty** *(not Jesus)* is the Supreme ruler, **the great King of heaven.**

> *"For **God is my King** of old, working salvation in the*
> *midst of the earth" (Ps. 74:12).*
> *"Who is the **King** of **Glory**? The **Lord of hosts**, he is the*
> *King of Glory" (Ps. 24:10).*
> *"The King answered unto Daniel, and said, of a truth it*
> *is, that your **God, is a God** of **gods**, and a **Lord of***
> ***kings"** (Dan. 2:47).* **The king of the universe is God!**
> *"Now I Nebuchadnezzar praise and extol and honor the*
> ***King of heaven"** (Dan. 4:37).* **God,** the **King** of
> heaven!

God the Father has made His son Jesus a **Prince.** *(**A prince is under a king).***

- *"The Messiah, the **Prince"** (Dan. 9:25).*
- *"The **Prince** of Peace" (Isa. 9:6).*
- *"The **Prince** of Life" (Acts 3:15).*
- *"A **Prince** and a Savior" (Acts 5:31).*
- *"And from Jesus Christ...the **Prince** of the kings of the earth" (Rev. 1:5).* **Jesus the Prince is under God the King.**

But what about Revelation 17:14 which says, *"These shall make war with the Lamb, and the Lamb shall overcome them: for he is **Lord** of **lords**, and **King** of **kings**?"* This is a very high and exalted position, above all of the rulers on earth, but **this does not mean** that the Lamb *(Jesus)* is **King of heaven**.

93

The prophet Daniel told Nebuchadnezzar, *"**Thou**, O king, art a **king of kings**: for the God of heaven hath given thee a kingdom, power, and strength, and glory" (Dan. 2:37).* This title denotes God given authority of **one king on earth** over **other earthly kings**.

Yes, our Lord Jesus is highly exalted by the Father, he is the **only begotten Son of God**.

> *"Wherefore God also hath **highly exalted him**, and given him a **name** which is **above every** name: That at the name of Jesus every knee should bow, of things in heaven, and things in earth, and things under the earth; and that every tongue should confess that Jesus Christ is Lord, **to the glory of God the Father"** (Phil. 2:9-12).*

He is *"the **Apostle** and **High Priest** of our profession, Christ Jesus"* (Heb. 3:1). *"For every high priest is ordained to offer gifts and sacrifices: wherefore it is of necessity that **this man** (Jesus) have somewhat also to offer"* (his sinless blood) *(Heb. 8:3).*

> *"And **no man taketh this honor unto himself**, but he that is called of God, as was Aaron. So also Christ **glorified not himself** to be made a high priest; but he (God) that said unto him"* (Jesus), *Thou art my Son, today have I begotten thee (Heb. 5:4-5).*

Why did God the Father give Jesus this **glory** and **honor**? *"That he (Jesus) by the grace of God should taste death for every man" (Heb. 2:9).*

God made **a great deposit of grace**, "the grace of God," in His son Jesus, of which we are partakers.

> *"For it became him (suited God), for whom are all things, and by whom are all things, **in bringing many sons unto glory**" (Heb. 2:10).*

GOD'S PLAN INCLUDED MANY SONS.

When God the Father spoke His son at the beginning of creation, to be "brought forth" in time, he was the (logos - "thought - motive"), the **motive** for all of God's further creation. But Hebrews 2:10 helps us understand that

94

God had an additional motive, *"bringing many sons unto glory."*

Why did God bring about the death of His only begotten Son? To bring **"many sons unto glory."**

> *"He* (Jesus) *came unto his own, and his own received him not. But as many as received him,* **to them gave he power to become the sons of God"** *(John 1:11-12).*
>
> *"Behold, what manner of love* **the Father** *hath bestowed upon us, that we should be called* **the sons of God**. *Beloved,* **now are we the sons of God"** *(I John 3:1-2).*
>
> **"For as many** *as are led by the Spirit of God,* **they are the sons of God**. *For ye have not received the spirit of bondage again to fear; but* **ye have received the Spirit of adoption, whereby we cry, Abba, Father. The Spirit** *itself beareth witness with* **our spirit,** *that we are the* **children of God: And if children, then heirs; heirs of God, and joint heirs with Christ;** (joint heirs with Christ - he is our brother and we are 'joint heirs with Christ.' 'Heirs of God'). *If so be that we suffer with him,* **that we may be also glorified together.** *For I reckon that* **the sufferings of this present time** *are not worthy to be compared with* **the glory which shall be revealed in us.** *For the* **earnest expectation of the creature** (creation) **waiteth for the manifestation of the sons of God"** *(Rom. 8:14-19).*/

We are the sons of God, and God desires to **use us mightily** in these end times to bring healing and deliverance to a hurting world, **as He used His son Jesus**.

> *"Verily, verily, I say unto you, He that believeth on me, the works that I do shall he do also; and* **greater works than these shall he do;** *because I go unto my Father"*

(John 14:12).

"And his (the anti-christ's) *heart shall be against the holy covenant; and he shall do exploits,...and such as do wickedly against the covenant shall he* (the anti-christ) *corrupt by flatteries: but the people **who do know their God** shall be **strong**, and **do exploits**"* (remarkable and bold deeds) *(Dan. 11:28, 32).*

*"Because the **creature** (creation) itself also **shall be delivered from the bondage of corruption into the glorious liberty of the children of God**. For we know **that the whole creation groaneth and travaileth in pain** together until now" (Rom. 8:21-22).*

The whole creation is groaning in pain. Our friends and loved ones are groaning, we ourselves are groaning, waiting **"for the manifestation of the sons of God."** "Sons of God," we who are begotten by God, in Christ.

Dear reader, God the Father wants to empower us with His Spirit and anointing *"to preach good tidings," "bind up the broken hearted,"* to *"proclaim liberty to the captives,"* and the *"opening of the prison to them that are bound,"* to *"comfort all that mourn." "That they might be called trees of righteousness, the planting of the Lord (God) that **He might be glorified**. And they shall build the old wastes, they shall raise up the former desolations, and they shall repair the waste cities, the desolations of many generations" (Isa. 61:1-4).*

POWER WITHOUT KNOWLEDGE AND UNDERSTANDING IS DANGEROUS.

When the Samaritans did not receive Jesus, the disciples without proper understanding said, *"Lord wilt thou that we command fire to come down from heaven and consume them, even as Elijah did?"* **Dangerous!**

"But he (Jesus) *turned, and rebuked them and said, Ye know not what manner of spirit ye are of. For the Son of man is not come to destroy men's lives, but to save them" (Luke 9:55-56).* The "foolish Galatians" were

96

becoming dangerous.

"O Foolish Galatians, who hath bewitched you" (Paul) *(Gal. 3:1).*

"I am afraid of you, lest I have bestowed upon you labor in vain (Paul) *(Gal. 4:11).*

"But if ye **bite and devour** *one another, take heed that ye be not consumed one of another"* (Paul) *(Gal. 5:15).*

Dangerous!

"That ye may be **blameless** *and* **harmless, the sons of God"** (Paul) *(Phil. 2:15).*

Even Jesus, the only begotten son was not empowered **until he had learned obedience.**

"Though he (Jesus) **were a Son, yet learned he obedience by the things which he suffered; and being made perfect,** *he became the author of eternal salvation unto all them that obey him"* (Heb. 5:8-9).

"I am a witness of the **sufferings of Christ"** (Peter) *(I Peter 5:1).*

"He (Jesus) *himself hath* **suffered being tempted"** *(Heb. 2:18).*

"And **Jesus increased** *in wisdom and stature* **and in favor with God** *and man" (Luke 2:52).* **Obedient sons do grow in favor.**

"And John (the Baptist) *bare record, saying* **I saw the Spirit descending from heaven like a dove, and it abode upon him"** *(John 1:32).*

"Now when all the people were baptized, it came to pass, that **Jesus** *also* **being baptized,** *and* **praying,** *the heaven was opened, and the Holy Ghost descended in a* **bodily shape like a dove** *upon him, and a voice came from heaven, which said,* **Thou art my beloved Son;** *in thee* **I am well pleased"** *(Luke 3:21-22).*

97

*"And Jesus being full of the Holy Ghost returned from Jordan, and was led by the Spirit into the wilderness, being forty days **tempted** of the devil" (Luke 4:1-2).*

If Jesus was "filled with the Holy Ghost, even from his mother's womb," as Luke very clearly says his cousin John the Baptist was *(Luke 1:15)*, the **Bible is silent** on this fact. Jesus was not the Holy Ghost, the Spirit of God, for the Holy Ghost overshadowed his mother Mary to generate him in her womb. After the Holy Ghost came in His office as the Comforter, He is called the spirit of Christ two times *(Rom. 8:9, 1 Peter 1:11)*. This is because the comforter *(Holy Ghost)* was sent through Jesus' prayers to the Father *(John 14:16)*, was sent in Jesus' name *(John 14:26)*, "proceeded from the Father," but was sent by Jesus "from the Father *(John 15:26)*," and was purchased through Jesus' death on the cross *(Acts 2:31-32)*.

"Therefore being by the right hand of God exalted, and having received of the Father the promise of the Holy Ghost, he (Jesus) **hath shed forth** (sent) **this**, *which ye now see and hear"* (the Holy Ghost with speaking in tongues) *(Acts 2:33)*.

Jesus is said to be "full of the Holy Ghost" in Luke Chapter 4, verse 1. But it is after his time of severe temptation and triumph that he is said to have *"returned in the **power of the** Spirit into Galilee: and there **went out a fame** of him through all the regions round about" (Luke 4:14).*

Brethren, we will not be empowered by the Spirit and manifested to the world as the **sons of God**, until we are **God fearing, obedient overcomers! THERE IS AT LEAST ONE OTHER REQUIREMENT TO HAVE GOD'S POWER.**

We must know for sure who our God is! Look again at Daniel 11:32, *"But **the people that do know their God** shall be strong, and do exploits."* God in His wisdom will not empower a church that does not know **who He is. God is not a trinity**, as some two billion "Christians" think. **Jesus Christ is not God Almighty** as another, smaller segment of Christianity thinks. The Most High God is **not a man**, and **a man cannot be** and **never will be the Lord**

98

God. Men die. **God cannot die!** Every man is tempted. God cannot be tempted *(James 1:13-14)*. "God is not a man" *(Num. 23:19, I Sam. 15:29)*, "neither the son of man" *(Num. 23:19)*.

In our minds we have made Jesus, God. Such thinking is dangerous! When a man, the anti-christ steps onto the world's stage with lying signs, wonders, and miracles, and a **cunningly devised formula for peace**, and declares that he is God, **those people**, even Christians, **who believe that a man can be God, do not stand a chance!**

> *"And **all the world** wondered after the beast and **they worshiped the dragon** (Satan) which gave power unto the beast: and **they worshiped the beast** saying, 'Who is like unto the beast? Who is able to make war with him?' And all that dwell upon the earth **shall worship him**, whose names are not written in the book of life of the Lamb slain from the foundation of the world" (Rev. 13:3-4, 8).*

> *"If it were possible, they shall **deceive the very elect"*** (Jesus speaking) *(Matt. 24:24).*

For over fourteen centuries a long series of popes *(meaning papa)* have declared themselves to be "the Vicar of Christ," "God," and "God Almighty" here on earth, and over a billion followers love to have it so. They call him "Holy Father" knowing, or perhaps not knowing, that Jesus said, *"And call no man your Father upon the earth: for one is your Father, which is in heaven" (Matt. 23:9).*

For some 500 years since the Reformation the second largest segment of Christianity, the Protestants, have accepted the Catholic doctrine regarding God. The "Trinity, God in three Persons, Father, Son, and Holy Ghost - the glory equal; the Majesty coeternal." *"At the time of the Reformation, the Protestant Church took over the doctrine of the Trinity without serious examination."* [2] What deserves **"serious examination," more** than who our God is ?"

A MAN CANNOT BE GOD!

The Oneness Pentecostals have embraced a doctrine equally as unbiblical and have had those who were *"in place of Christ"*. A Baptist preacher many years ago *(1940's)* began to see visions and experience apparent miracles of healings and gathered a large following. He conducted healing campaigns, attracted huge crowds, and converted to the Oneness faith. I witnessed first hand his ability to call people out of the audience and tell them things which one would not normally know. He said in that service that he explained this ability to his personal physician thus: "The subconscious of a man knows things that his conscious mind does not know." He said that some people such as himself were born with an "overlap," the conscious mind overlapping the subconscious mind, so that they are "conscious of the subconscious." *(I only know what he said.)* Perhaps the dead were raised, perhaps the sick were healed, but his message went seriously awry *(I listened to various tapes and read books of his and this is what I understood)*. He began to venture into strange doctrines such as the "serpent seed," that Eve had sexual relations with the serpent, and produced a lineage, "the Serpent Seed" *(this is gross heresy!)*. Making much of the similarities in the names Abra**ham**, Gra**ham**, and Bran**ham**, he decided that he and Billy Graham *(whom I respect)* were the two angels to the Church of Laodicea, similar to the two angels who went to destroy Sodom: Graham being the angel to the world and Branham the angel to the Church. His ministry ended tragically in 1965 when he was killed in a car wreck in Texas. Every message and doctrine bears fruit, and **error bears bitter fruit**. I am told that his followers after his death waited to bury him, expecting him to resurrect in 3 days, 10 days, 40 days , and then on Easter; of course he didn't, but this did not keep many from continuing to worship him. They are called Branhamites, and reportedly can be found all over the world. It is said the fourth largest church in Zaire is Branhamite. Some baptize in his name,write and sing praise choruses to him, and have shrines to him in their homes, cars and churches, featuring an 8x10, black and white picture of him with a "halo of light" at the back of his head. They hold "Branham" conventions, where they worship him, listen to his tapes and trade his material. This is idolatry!

100

When challenged for this blasphemy a stock answer is, "You just don't know who he is." Who is he? **A man**, whom they made "a god!" Shame on him and them and may they receive God's mercy.

GOD THE FATHER IS JEALOUS REGARDING HIS WORSHIP.

"Thou shalt not bow down thyself to them, nor serve them: for I the Lord thy God am a jealous God" (Ex. 20:5).

*"For thou shalt worship no other god: for the Lord, **whose name is Jealous**, is a jealous God" (Ex. 34:14).*

"For the Lord thy God is a consuming fire, even a jealous God" (Deut. 4:24).

"Thou shalt not bow down thyself unto them, nor serve them: for I the Lord thy God am a jealous God" (Deut. 5:9).

"(For the Lord thy God is a jealous God among you) lest the anger of the Lord thy God be kindled against thee, and destroy thee from off the face of the earth" (all a quote from Deut. 6:15).

"And Joshua said unto the people, ye cannot serve the Lord: for he is a holy God; he is a jealous God; he will not forgive your transgressions, nor your sins. If ye forsake the Lord, and serve strange gods, then he will turn and do you hurt, and consume you, after that he hath done you good" (Josh. 24:19-20).

*"**God is jealous, and the Lord revengeth**; the Lord revengeth and is furious; the Lord will take vengeance on his adversaries, and he reserveth wrath for his enemies. The Lord is slow to anger, and great in power, and will not at all acquit the wicked: the Lord hath his way in the whirlwind and in the storm, and the clouds are the dust of his feet. He rebuketh the sea, and maketh it dry, and drieth up all the rivers: Bashan*

languisheth, and Carmel, and the flower of Lebanon languisheth. **The mountains quake at him, and the hills melt,** *and the earth is burned at his presence, yea,* **the world, and all that dwell therein.** *Who can stand before his indignation? And who can abide in the fierceness of his anger? His fury is poured out like fire, and the rocks are thrown down by him.* **The Lord is good, a strong hold in the day of trouble; and he knoweth them that trust in him"** *(Nahum 1:2-7).*

"Neither their silver nor their gold shall be able to deliver them in the day of the Lord's wrath; but the whole land shall be devoured by the fire of his jealousy: *for he shall make even a speedy riddance of all them that dwell in the land. Therefore wait ye upon me, saith the Lord, until the day that I rise up to the prey: for my determination is to gather the nations, that I may assemble the kingdoms, to pour upon them mine indignation, even all my fierce anger:* **for all the earth shall be devoured with the fire of my jealousy"** *(Zeph. 1:18, 3:8).*

"For I am the Lord, I change not" (Mal. 3:6).

"These things hast thou done, and I kept silence; thou thoughtest that I was altogether such an one as thyself: *but I will reprove thee, and set them in order before thine eyes. Now consider this,* **ye that forget God,** *lest I tear you in pieces, and there be none to deliver.* **Whoso offereth praise glorifieth me:** *and to him that ordereth his conversation aright will I shew* **the salvation of God"** *(Ps. 50:21-23).*

Notice verse 21, "you thought that I was like you."

Do you know this God, who Jesus called, *"my God and your God" (John 20:17)* and *"the only true God" (John 17:3)*? Jesus said love Him

102

with thy **heart, soul and mind** *(Matt. 22:37)* **And He is loveable!** Jesus said fear Him:

> *"But I will forewarn you whom ye shall fear: Fear him,*
> *which after he hath killed hath power to cast into hell;*
> *yea I say unto you, **Fear him**"* (God) *(Luke 12:5).*

HOW DID WE LOSE OUR FEAR OF GOD?

Whatever happened to our fear of God, a healthy, reverential fear of the Lord God in our churches and society that produced God fearing men, and decent, moral behavior? For one thing a backslidden preacher by the name of Charles Darwin began to teach the theory of evolution around 1859 and planted, at least in the backs of people's minds, a doubt that God even exists.

Newsweek **Magazine in the November 28, 2005 issue**, had a cover story called "The Real Darwin," which said, "He had planned to enter the ministry *(in fact he had been studying for it)* but his discoveries over a fateful voyage 170 years ago shook his faith and changed our conception of the origin of life" *(p. 50).* He is named as one of four "revolutionary thinkers who have done the most to shape the intellectual history of the past century" *(p. 42).* "To a society accustomed to **searching for the truth in the pages of the Bible**, Darwin introduced the notion of evolution" *(p. 54).* To "a world taught to see the hand of God in every part of nature, he suggested a different creative force altogether" *(p. 55).* "His ideas carried to their logical conclusion, appeared to undercut the basis of Christianity" *(p. 56).* The British biologist Richard Dawkins, an outspoken defender of Darwin, wrote that evolution "made it possible to be an **intellectually fulfilled atheist"** *(p. 56).* Darwin ultimately described himself as an "agnostic" *(p. 56).* It appeared to many, including his own wife, that Darwin's **"destination was plainly hell."** **"Emma... was tormented** to think they would **spend eternity apart"** *(p. 54).* These demonic teachings have found their way into our minds, theologies, churches and institutions of higher learning. *Newsweek* asks, "**Where is God**?" Then adds, "For all of his nets, guns and glasses, **Darwin never found God"** *(p. 58) (What a shame for Darwin and the world).* He is buried in Westminister Abbey, a 1000 year old Church in

London, England, along with kings, queens, and other notables. As I visited his tomb this week and was assured by the attendants that this was the resting place of his body, I feared to imagine the place where his soul might be at that very moment. To **Charles Darwin** and **all of his followers**, and to **all in whose minds he has placed** doubts, God has an answer:

> *"The fool hath said in his heart,* (not just aloud) *There is no God" (Ps. 14:1).*

JESUS IS GOD THE FATHERS "WITNESS"!

If we miss God the Father in the life and teachings of Jesus, it is certainly not the fault of our precious Lord and Savior. Those who teach the Oneness doctrine have a saying, "The Lord God of the O.T. is Jesus Christ of the N.T." Not so! Jesus said in Revelation 1:5, *"From Jesus Christ, who is the faithful witness."* And again in Revelation 3:14 he says, *"These things saith the Amen, the faithful and true witness, the beginning of the creation of God."* So Jesus came as God's "witness." As John the Baptist came as a witness *(forerunner)* for Jesus, so Jesus came as a witness for God the Father. Jesus came, and is soon coming back **to reign on** *"the throne of his father David"* in Jerusalem, over all the earth for 1000 years *(Luke 1:32, Rev. 3:21, 20:4-6).* This is Jesus Christ and his redeemed saints in Rev. Chapter 20, reigning on the earth. But look at Rev. Chapter 21, **God himself is coming!**

> *"And I John saw the **holy city**, new Jerusalem, **coming down from God out of heaven**, prepared as a bride adorned for her husband. **And I heard a great voice out of heaven saying, Behold, the tabernacle of God is with men, and he will dwell with them, and they shall be his people, and God himself shall be with them, and be their God. And God** shall wipe away all tears from their eyes; and there shall be no more death, neither sorrow, nor crying, neither shall there be any more pain: for the former things are passed away. And **he that sat upon the throne said**, Behold I make all*

things new, And he said unto me, write: for **these words are true and faithful**. And he said unto me, It is done. **I am Alpha and Omega**, the beginning and the end. I will give unto him that is athirst of the fountain of the water of life freely. **He that overcometh** shall inherit all things; and **I will be his God, and he shall be my son**. But the fearful, and unbelieving, and the abominable, and murderers, and whoremongers, and sorcerers, and idolaters, and all liars, shall have their part in the lake which burneth with fire and brimstone: which is the second death" (Rev. 21:2-8).

God is coming to reign over and live with us, and He sent Jesus Christ His Prince, as His forerunner to tell and prepare us. Compare verse 5 above, *"these words are* **true** *and* **faithful**, *"*with what Jesus said in Revelation 3:14: *"These things saith the Amen, the* **faithful** *and* **true** *witness. "* Jesus is God the Father's "witness," "the Amen." All that God said in the O.T. Jesus said "Amen" *(so be it)* to in the N.T.

- God said that *"He created all"* in Genesis Chapter one and Jesus said, *"Amen" (Mark 13:19)*.
- God said *"The Lord (thy) God is one Lord" (Deut. 6:4)* - Jesus said, *"Amen" (Mark 12:29)*.
- God said, *"Thou shalt love the Lord thy God will all thine heart" (Deut. 6:5, 10:12)* - Jesus said, *"Amen" (Mark 12:30)*.
- God gave 10 commandments *(Ex. 20:1-17)* - Jesus said, *"Amen" (Mark 10:19, John 15:10)*.
- God said, *"Beside me there is no God" (Isa. 44:6)* - Jesus said, *"Amen" (Mark 10:18, John 17:3)*

  "Jesus Christ was a minister of the circumcision for the truth of God, **to confirm** *the promises made unto the fathers "(Paul speaking) (Rom. 15:8)*.

The Scripture clearly teachers that Jesus knew that God was his Father from young childhood. In fact, the seed of God that was in Jesus was his

105

awareness that God was his Father.

In the account given by Luke of Jesus' birth in Bethlehem and the events shortly thereafter he says:

> *"And when the days of her purification according to the law of Moses were accomplished, they brought him to Jerusalem* (about 5 miles) **to present him to the Lord"** **(God)** *(Luke 2:22).*

They brought him into the temple where he was circumcised and sacrifices were made. Verses 25-34:

> *"And behold, there was a man in Jerusalem, whose name was Simeon...waiting for the consolation of Israel:* (Israel's deliverance from her enemies) *and the Holy Ghost was upon him* (Simeon). *And it was revealed unto him by the Holy Ghost, that he should not see death, before he had seen the Lord's Christ"* (God's Messiah). *And he came by the Spirit into the temple: and the parents* (his mother and stepfather) *brought in the child Jesus...then took he him up in his arms, and* **blessed God and said, Lord**, *now lettest thou thy servant depart in peace, according to thy word: For mine eyes have seen thy salvation,* (God is our Savior, but He was going to use Jesus as the agent of our salvation) *which thou* **hast prepared** *before the face of all people; a* **light** *to lighten the Gentiles, and the glory of thy people Israel. And* **Joseph** *and his* **Mother** **marveled** *at those things which were spoken of him* (Jesus). *And Simeon blessed them and said unto Mary his mother, Behold, this child is set for the fall and rising again of many in Israel; and* **for a sign** *which shall be spoken against"(see Acts 28:22 and Isa. 7:14).*

Jesus on this occasion was also recognized for who he was by a Godly widow named Anna *(v. 38)*. *"And she coming in that instant gave thanks*

106

likewise unto the Lord (God)*, and spoke of him* (Jesus) *to all them that looked for redemption in Jerusalem. "* None of the people in Luke's account of Christ's birth in Chapters one and two, **Zechariah, Elizabeth, Mary, Joseph, the shepherds, Simeon, Anna** or the **Angel Gabriel** believed that the baby Jesus was "God the son," "the eternal Son," "second person in the triune God," or Almighty God; but they knew that he was the Messiah of Israel, whom the Lord God had promised through the mouths of His holy prophets.

> *"And when they had preformed all things according to the law of the Lord, they returned into Galilee, to their own city Nazareth* (about 70 miles from Jerusalem) *and the child grew, and waxed strong in spirit* (his human spirit)*, filled with wisdom; and the grace of God was upon him. Now his parents went to Jerusalem every year at the feast of the Passover. And when he was twelve years old, they went up to Jerusalem after the custom of the feast (*please note that Jesus was not doing miracles, but being what to Mary and Joseph seemed a normal boy)*. And when they fulfilled the days, as they returned; **the child Jesus tarried behind in Jerusalem;** and Joseph and his mother knew not of it. But they, supposing him to have been in the company went on a day's journey; and they sought him among their kinsfolk and acquaintance. And when they found him not, they turned back again to Jerusalem, seeking Him. And it came to pass that **after three days** they found him in the temple, sitting in the midst of the doctors* (Jewish teachers) *both **hearing them**, and **asking them questions**. And all that heard him were astonished at his understanding and answers" (Luke 2:39-47).*

This was not God, but a 12 year boy, schooled in the O.T., as were all Jewish boys, who was taught early in life the Creed of Israel *(Hear O, Israel the Lord our God is one Lord)* but with this exception: God had made Himself known unto him and he was beginning to see his mission. *(Also, Jesus' mother no doubt had told him of the awesome events concerning his birth)*

> *"And when they* (Mary and Joseph) *saw him,* **they were amazed***: and his mother said unto him, Son, why hast thou thus dealt with us (*Done this to us)*?* **Behold thy father and I have sought thee sorrowing***. And he said unto them, How is it that ye sought me? Wist ye not that I must be about my Father's business?* **And they understood not the saying which he spake unto them***. And he went down with them and came to Nazareth,* **and was subject unto them: but his mother kept all these sayings in her heart***. And Jesus increased in* **wisdom and stature,** *and in* **favour with God and man***"* *(Luke 2:48-52).*

Let us speak where the Bible speaks and be silent where the Bible is silent, but we learn much from these verses. Without the knowledge of Mary and Joseph, it seems that God had been speaking to Jesus: perhaps through the Scriptures, perhaps in his dreams, or perhaps as he did to the young boy Samuel, by an audible voice.

> *"The Lord called Samuel: and he answered, Here am I. Now Samuel did not yet know the Lord, neither was the word of the Lord yet revealed unto him. And the Lord came, and stood, and called as at other times, Samuel, Samuel. Then Samuel answered, Speak; for thy servant heareth" (I Sam. 3:4, 7, 10).*

This experience on the trip to Jerusalem seems to have increased Jesus' understanding, as reflected in Luke's statement in verse 51, *"And he went down with them, and came to Nazareth, and was subject unto them."* That Jesus' mind was a human mind **totally distinct from the Father's,** is clear in Scripture.

*"But of that day and hour **knoweth no man** no, not the angels of heaven, but my Father only" (Matt. 24:36).* Notice, Jesus put himself in the **"man"** category, which **he was**.

*"But to sit on my right hand, and on my left, **is not mine to give**, but it shall be given to them for whom it is prepared of my Father" (Matt. 20:23).* Notice, **"Not mine to give."**

*"The **Revelation of Jesus Christ**, which **God gave unto him**, to **show unto his servants**...and he sent and signified it by his angel unto his **servant John"** (Rev. 1:1).*

The book of Revelation was revealed to John as something he did not know. It was revealed to Jesus because **he did not know it!** We do not know when this was revealed by God the Father to Jesus, but he had been in heaven at God's right hand approximately 60 years when John wrote the book of Revelation.

Dear reader, you must know that I have shed many tears during the writing of this book, because I previously believed and taught that Jesus was God. Now I joyfully agree with Jesus when he said:

"My Father is greater than all."

"May Father is greater than I."

And the apostle Paul when he said:

*"Then shall the Son also himself be subject unto him (the Father), that God may **be all** in all" (I Cor. 15:28).*

All the wonderful things that we see in Jesus, his compassion, love, mercy, approachability, and salvation, are derived from God his Father and ours; who is **greater** in all of these things, they are the essence of His Divine nature.

JESUS LOVES GREATLY BUT "GOD IS LOVE" *(I JOHN 4:8).* This means that God is incapable of doing anything that **would be out of character with love. We see love even when He judges the wicked.**

When God sent the flood in the days of Noah, mankind had become so wicked and violent that the race could no longer continue. The flood was **God's act of mercy** on all succeeding generations.

When God sent fire and brimstone to destroy Sodom and Gomorrah, homosexuality and sexual immorality had spread to a shocking degree. If God had not wiped out those immoral people, the **AIDS** virus from which over 25 million people have died in the past 25 years on planet Earth, and from which 40 million people are presently dying, would probably have developed many centuries before it did.

When Jesus platted a whip of cords and drove the moneychangers from the temple of God in Jerusalem, he showed the **love of God**. They were under the judgement of God for defiling His house, so Jesus did them **a great favor!**

NOW LET'S RETURN TO HEBREWS CHAPTER TWO.

Verse 11 gives further understanding regarding **"the man Christ Jesus."**

"For both he (Jesus) *that sanctifieth and they who are sanctified* (those of us who are in Christ) *are all of one. "* The statement above means that we and Jesus are of **one substance,** Jesus is **one in humanity** with us. The word substance means, *1. "the real or essential part or element of anything; essence, reality, or basic matter"* or *2. "the physical matter of which a thing consists; material."*

The Nicene Creed of 325 A.D., to which the Catholic church and most Protestant churches hold, declares belief in, "one Lord Jesus Christ, the only begotten Son of God; Begotten of his Father before all worlds....Light of Light, Very God of very God; begotten, not made; **Being of one substance with the Father**." There is much error in that Creed, which we have dealt with, and will deal with further, but the part which we will consider at this point is the last statement, "Being of one substance with the Father." If Jesus was and is **of the same substance with the Father**, the inspired writer of Hebrews did not know it. He says in verse 11 that Jesus ("he that sanctifieth") and those sanctified by him **"are all of one."** That is **one** substance. For proof look at his next statement, *"for which cause he* (Jesus)

110

is not ashamed to **call them brethren**.*"* He is a **brother in the flesh** *(human family)* to those he saves. Then for further proof the writer of Hebrews quotes from O.T. prophecies that pertain to Jesus. From Ps. 22 which begins, *"My God, my God, why hast thou forsaken me,"* he quotes verse 22, *"I will declare thy name* (God's) *unto* **my brethren** *(***us his brothers***): in the midst of the congregation will I praise thee* (God)*."* And again, *"I will put my trust in him"* (God) *(Ps. 18:2, Isa. 12:2).* And again, *"Behold I* (Jesus) *and the children which God hath given me" (Isa. 8:18).* This is Jesus and his "brethren."

Now verse 14, *"Forasmuch then as the children are partakers of* (the children are) **flesh and blood**, *he* (Jesus) *also himself likewise took* **part of the same** *(*flesh and blood*)."* Jesus did not come in the God family *("There is one God the Father," I Cor. 8:6)*, nor the angel family *(v. 16 "Verily he took not on him the nature of angels.")*, but he came in the **human family** *(flesh and blood).* Compare this with the apostle John's statement in I John 4:3, *"And every spirit that confesseth not that Jesus Christ is come* **in the flesh** *(as a human) is not of God; and this is the spirit of anti-christ, whereof ye have heard that it should come; and even now already is it in the world."* **The Lord God needed no help in the Godhead: He is Almighty, all sufficient, self existent God of more than enough!** He did not need another angel! Hebrews 12:22 speaks of "an innumerable company of angels." John saw *"ten thousand times ten thousand, and thousands of thousands"* (100 million) *(Rev. 5:11)*; and Jesus said to Peter in Matt. 26:53, *"Thinkest thou that I cannot now pray to my Father, and he shall presently give me more than twelve legions* (72,000?) *of angels?"*

What God needed to redeem fallen man (adam) was a sinless, righteous **man.** *(v. 17) "Wherefore* **in all things it behooved** (was necessary for) *him* (Jesus) **to be made like unto his brethren**, *that he might be a* **merciful** *and* **faithful** *high priest in things pertaining to God, to make reconciliation for the sins of the people."* Study that verse for a few moments. It was necessary for ("behooved") Jesus to be made **in all things like us. "In all things! "**We are not God-men, **neither was he.** We are not eternal Sons,

neither was he. We are not of one substance with God, **neither was he.** Look at verse 16, *"For verily he took not on him the nature of angels, but he took on him the seed of Abraham."* All of the seed of Abraham are **flesh and blood human beings.** God needed a man *(an adam)* **to make reconciliation for the sins of the people.** Why? Because the first "adam," Adam, sinned in the garden and brought upon himself and all of his lineage death. *(The physical death and spiritual separation* that God had warned him of).

> *"For since by man came death, by man came also the resurrection of the dead. For as in Adam all die, even so in Christ shall all be made alive" (I Cor. 15:21-22).*
> *"By man came death, by man came resurrection."* **By man!**
> *"The first man Adam was made a living soul: the last Adam was made a quickening spirit" (I Cor. 15:45).*

LET'S LOOK AT THE FIRST ADAM.

> *"This is the book of the generations of Adam. In the day that God created man, in the likeness of God made he him; Male and female created he them; and blessed them, and called their name Adam, in the day when they were created. And Adam lived an hundred and thirty years, and begat a son in his own likeness, after his image; and called his name Seth" (Gen. 5:1-3).*

God is a spirit but he has a form, a "likeness". When the prophet saw Him on His throne in Ezekiel Chapter one, His appearance *"was the likeness as the appearance of a man" (v. 26).* This was *"the appearance of the likeness of the glory of the Lord" (v. 28).*

The first Adam was created by God, **in God's own image and likeness,** and when his son Seth, the second generation was born, it is said that Adam *"begat* (Seth) *a son in his own likeness after his image."* So Adam and all his generations thereafter were in the image and likeness of God. Look at

112

the creation of Adam:

> *"And the Lord God formed **man** of the **dust of the***
> ***ground**, and breathed into his nostrils the breath of life;*
> *and man became a living soul" (Gen. 2:7).* **This was a**
> **creative act.**

Now look at Luke's account of **Jesus' baptism**:

> *"And the Holy Ghost descended in a bodily shape like a*
> *dove upon him, and a voice came from heaven, which*
> *said, **Thou art my beloved Son**; in thee I am well*
> *pleased" (Luke 3:22).*

(Verse 23) "And Jesus himself began to be about thirty years of age, being (as was supposed) the son of Joseph, which was the son of Heli." And then begins a series of **14 verses** which trace the lineage of Jesus through King David *(which establishes his legal right to the throne of Israel)* and ends at **verse 38** which says, *"Which was the son of Enos, which was the son of Seth, which was the son of **Adam, which was the son of God.**"* Luke wants to make sure that we understand that **created Adam**, whose body came from the dust of the ground, in whom was none of God's DNA, **was also the son of God.** This is **very significant**, coming so soon after this account of Jesus' baptism, where God spoke from heaven saying, "Thou art my beloved Son; in thee I am well pleased" *(v. 22)*. Luke says, **and Adam** was also **"the son of God."**

NOW LET'S LOOK AT THE CREATION OF JESUS.

> *"These things saith the Amen* (Jesus)*, the faithful and*
> *true witness, **the beginning of the creation** of God"*
> *(Rev. 3:14).*

> *"In whom we have redemption through his blood, even*
> *the forgiveness of sins: who is the **image** of the invisible*
> *God, the **firstborn of every creature**" (Col. 1:14-15).*

> *"The image of him* (God) ***who created him**" (Col. 3:10).*

> *"Also I will make him my **firstborn*** (Jesus)*, higher than*

the kings of the earth" (Ps. 89:27).

"I will declare the decree: the Lord hath said unto me,

Thou art my Son: **this day** have I begotten thee" (Jesus)

(Ps. 2:7).

The word image in Col. 1:15 refers to Jesus' creation in Adam, not from having God's DNA in him. Jesus said, "*God is a spirit" (John 4:24).* Jesus said *"a spirit hath not flesh and bones, as ye see me have" (Luke 24:39).* Without flesh and bone **a spirit does not have seed** nor DNA. Thus, whatever the Holy Spirit did in the womb of Mary was **a creative act**. Remember, when the saints are *"changed in a moment, in the twinkling of an eye, at the last trump" (I Cor. 15:51-52),* **that will also be a creative act**, for *"this corruptible shall put on incorruption, and this mortal shall have put on immortality" (I Cor. 15:54).* Our vile bodies will then *"be fashioned like unto his* (Jesus') *glorious* (glorified) *body" (Phil. 3:21).* **These are creative acts of God the creator.** Adam was made in the image of God. The Hebrew word for **"image"** is "tselem" and means **"resemblance, a representative figure."** Adam was made in resemblance; a representative figure of God. **Seth**, Adam's son was born in **"resemblance a representative figure"** of **Adam** and **God**. The word "image" in the Greek, the language in which the N.T. was given to us, is "eikon" and means, "a likeness, representative resemblance." So the word "image" means the same in Bible usage when speaking of **Adam, Seth**, and **Jesus**. They are all three **in the image of God.**

Look at what Paul says regarding **every male descendent** of the first Adam (adam, man) in I Cor. 11:7: *"For a man indeed ought not to cover his head,* (during prayer), *forasmuch as **he is the image** and glory of God."* This speaks of our creation in Adam. Paul says again in Acts 17:28-29:

"For we are also his (God's) **offspring**. Forasmuch

then as we are the **offspring** of God."

This is not kinship, this is **relationship through creation**. Look at Jesus' statement in Rev. 22:16: *"I am the root and the **offspring** of David."*

This word **"offspring"** means **kinship**, as **Jesus was by lineage**, "the Son of David." *"Hosanna to the son of David" (Matt. 21:9).*

Jesus is the Son of God by a creative act in the womb of Mary:

> *"Then said Mary unto the angel, How shall this be, seeing I know not a man? And the angel answered and said unto her, The Holy Ghost shall come upon thee, and the power of the Highest shall overshadow thee:* ***therefore*** **(for this reason)** *also that holy thing which shall be born of thee* ***shall be called the Son of God"*** *(Luke 1:34-35).*

David's son Solomon was also called by God **"my son"**. God said to David in II Sam. 7:12-14:

> *"And when thy days be fulfilled, and thou shalt sleep with thy fathers,* ***I will set up thy seed after thee****, which shall proceed out of thy bowels, and I will establish his kingdom. He shall build an house for my name, and I will stablish the throne of his kingdom for ever.* ***I will be his father,*** *and he* ***shall be my son. If he commit iniquity****, I will chasten him with the rod of men, and with the stripes of the children of men."*

This is David's **"great"** son Solomon called the son of God **by adoption**, and the account in Luke 2 is David's **"greater son" Jesus, Messiah, called the son of God because of a creative act in the womb of Mary**.

We may never understand fully how this was accomplished by the Holy Ghost. For example, how do words spoken from the mouth of one person, enter through the ear into the mind of another person, and **cause that mind to conceive a thought**. This is seen in the Scripture where David says of the wicked in Ps 7:14, *"Behold, he* ***travaileth*** *with iniquity, and hath* ***conceived*** *mischief, and* ***brought forth*** *falsehood."* Isaiah 59:13 says, *"Speaking oppression and revolt* ***conceiving*** *and uttering from the heart words of falsehood."* Peter said in Acts 5:4, *"Why hast* ***thou conceived*** *this thing in* *thine heart?"* So the mind **conceives thoughts**, which according to scientists can and do have a physical effect on the brain, even changing its shape. We do not understand how this happens, but we accept it as something done in us by our Creator. In these days when puny man is cloning mammals in laboratories, can we not believe that God, the Holy Ghost, overshadowed a virgin and **created a seed** which produced a child, **a second Adam** in whose body **righteous, sinless blood flowed**, untainted by the sin and death of Mary's father in the flesh, **the first Adam**.

Notice John the Baptist's words to the unrepentant multitude, *"and begin not to say within yourselves, we have Abraham to our father: for I say unto you, that **God is able of these stones** to raise up children unto Abraham."* **Of stones**, cold, dead stones, no life, no blood, but *"God is able....."*. This great prophet certainly knew the **creative power** of the One who sent him.

Look at Matt. 1:18:

"Now the birth of Jesus Christ was on this wise."

The English word "birth" in this verse is **"genesis"** in the Greek, and means "to make, generate or spring forth." Matthew says this is the **beginning** of Jesus: Like the first Adam who had his beginning *(genesis)* in the **book of Genesis Chapter one,** the second Adam Jesus, had his literal beginning *("genesis")* in the womb of Mary, in **Matthew Chapter one.** He was the first creative thought *(logos)* of God, spoken before time, before all else, *"and when the fulness of time had come,"* caused by the Holy Spirit to be received and conceived in the womb of a virgin. *"And the word was made flesh, and dwelt among us, and we beheld his glory, the glory as of the **only begotten of the Father**."* God had previously **created** a son *(Adam)*, **adopted** a son *(Solomon)*, but this is the one and only time He has ever "sired" and **brought forth** a son from the womb of a woman, *"the only begotten Son."*

God spoke of him through the centuries.

In Gen. 3:15 he is *"the seed (posterity) of the woman"*.

In Gen. 15:5 he is *"the seed of Abraham" (Rom. 4:18)*.

116

In Ps. 89:4 he is *"the seed of David."*

We know that **it was sinless human seed** that God created within the womb of Mary by what it produced. Every seed **must bring forth** after his **own kind**. God **commanded this** in Genesis before he created man.

> *"And God said, Let the earth bring forth grass, the herb yeilding **seed**, and the **fruit tree yielding fruit after his kind**, whose **seed** is in itself, upon the earth: and it was so. **And the earth brought forth grass, and herb yielding seed after his kind, and the tree yielding** fruit, whose **seed** was in itself, **after his kind**: and God saw that it was good. And God said, Let the earth bring forth the **living creature after his kind**, cattle, and creeping thing, and beast of the earth **after his kind: and it was so.** And God made the beast of the earth **after his kind**, and cattle **after their kind**, and every thing that creepeth upon the earth **after his kind**: and **God say that it was good"** (Gen. 1:11-12, 24-25).*

This is an immutable law of God spoken at creation, that **never has** and **never will be broken**. Jesus said in John 10:35, "the Scripture **cannot be broken**." So the Holy Ghost created **man seed** in the womb of Mary and it produced **a man**, not a God!

LET'S REVIEW THESE SCRIPTURES REGARDING JESUS' MANHOOD.

- *"**A man** of sorrows and acquainted with grief" (Isa. 53:3).*
- *"David shall never want **a man** to sit upon the throne of the house of Israel" (Jer. 33:17).*
- *"Awake, O sword against **the man** that is my fellow" (Zech. 13:7, Matt. 26:31).*
- *"And **this man** shall be the peace" (Micah 5:5).*
- *"This is he of whom I* (John the Baptist) *said, after me cometh **a man** who is preferred before me" (John 1:30).*

117

- *"Come see **a man**" (John 4:29).*
- *"Never a man spake like **this man**" (John 7:46).*
- *"All things that John spake of **this man** were true" (John 10:41).*
- *"Jesus of Nazareth, **a man** approved of God"* (Peter at Pentecost) *(Acts 2:22).*
- *"**Every man** in his own order: Christ the firstfruits" (I Cor. 15:23).*
- *"Through **this man** is preached unto you the forgiveness of sins"* (Paul) *(Acts 13:38).*
- *"He* (God) *will judge the world...by **that man** whom he hath ordained"* (Paul) *(Acts 17:31).*
- *"The gift of grace, which is by **one man**, Jesus Christ"* (Paul) *(Rom. 5:15).*
- *"And being found in fashion as **a man**"* (Paul) *(Phil. 2:8).*
- *"Put on the **new man**"* (Christ) (Paul) *(Col. 3:10).*
- *"For **this man** was counted worthy of more glory than Moses" (Heb. 3:3).*
- *"But **this man**...hath an unchangeable priesthood" (Heb. 7:24).*
- *It is of necessity that **this man** have somewhat to offer" (Heb. 8:3).*
- *"But **this man**...sat down on the right hand of God" (Heb. 10:12).*
- *"**The man Christ Jesus**" (I Tim. 2:5).*

There is not one Scripture in the Bible that calls Jesus **"this God," "that God," "our God,"** or the **"Lord God."** So with these 20 foregoing Scriptures, and many more calling him a **"man,"** let's settle it once and for all that Jesus Christ is a virgin born, sinless, righteous **man!** Jesus is the **perfect man**, a **glorified man,** but he is a man nevertheless! Think again of how he is portrayed in the Gospels. He asks questions to obtain information; He feels and expresses surprise; He looks for fruit on the fig tree; and there is none. His miracles are done through faith in the power of God. He asks for these miracles in prayer and receives them with thankfulness *(Matt. 14:19, Mark 7:34, John 6:11, 11:40-42).* He is the **perfect revealer of God** and the **destined ruler of the world;** but his life was a life **in the flesh**, a

118

distinctly **human existence,** which moved within the normal lines of a human mind and will. [3] Look at two examples. Mark 9:16-17, 21:

> *"And he* (Jesus) *asked the scribes, What question ye with them* (the disciples)? *And one of the multitude answered and said, Master, I have brought unto thee my son, which hath a dumb spirit; And he* (Jesus) *asked his father, How long is it ago since this came unto him? And he said, of a child."* (He asked questions to get information).

Mark 11:12-13:

> *"And on the morrow, when they came from Bethany, he* (Jesus) *was hungry: And seeing a fig tree afar off having leaves, he came, if haply* (perhaps) *he might find anything thereon: And when he came to it, he found nothing but leaves; for the time of figs was not yet."* (If he was God, would he not have known? When he cursed the fig tree and it withered, he explained it to his disciples as an act of faith in God, verses 21-23).

His understanding and miracles, rather than proving omniscience and omnipotence, proved that he was anointed, appointed, empowered and sent by God his Father. He prayed at the tomb of Lazarus, *"Father, I thank thee that thou hast heard me. And I know that thou hearest me always: but because of the people which stand by I said it, **that they may believe that thou hast sent me"** (John 11:41-42).* Look at Mark 6:3-6 and see how he was **limited by the unbelief** of the people in his home town:

> *"And he **could** there **do no mighty work"** (Mark 6:5, 9:23).*

HOW JESUS SAW HIMSELF AS HE CERTAINLY KNEW THE TRUTH.

Jesus spoke of himself as a **man** on more than one occasion. To the Pharisees he said:

> *"But now ye seek to kill me, **a man** that has told you the*

119

truth, which I have heard of God" (John 8:40). **Hear Jesus!** "**A man** that has told you the truth!" "**A man!**" "**A man!**"

He spoke of his coming death in John 15:13-14 and said:

"Greater love hath no **man** *than this, that* **a man** *lay down his life for his friends. Ye are my friends... ."*

He said again in verse 24:

"If I had not done among them the works which **none other man** *did, they had not had sin."*

THE SON OF MAN.

Though Jesus is the Son of God by virtue of his being begotten from the womb of Mary, his favorite title for himself was "**Son of man.**" This is a title which means "**a human being**" and was used by God to address the prophet Ezekiel some 90 times in the book which bears his name. *"And he said unto me, Son of man, stand upon thy feet, and I will speak unto thee"* *(Ezek. 2:1).* It's also a Messianic title taken from Ps. 8:4, which refers to Jesus as seen also in Daniel 7:13. The prophet Daniel describes in this Chapter, visions which correspond to those seen by the apostle John in Revelation 4 and 5. In Daniel Chapter seven, the **one** on the throne, the Lord God, is called the "Ancient of days." "Thousand thousands ministered unto him and ten thousand times ten thousand stood before him," as they did in John's account. Then Daniel 7:13 says:

"I saw in the night visions, and behold, one like **the son of man** *came with the clouds of heaven, and came to the Ancient of days, and they brought him near before him."*

This is a picture of our Lord Jesus brought to the throne of our Lord God, an event at least 500 years in the future for Daniel, but already firmly fixed in the foreknowledge and unchangeable purpose of God. Jesus as God's Messiah *adopted this title, "son of man, "*and referred to himself thus, as is noted some **84 times** in the gospel accounts. *(Jesus is "Son of man" 32 times in Matt., 14 times in Mark, 26 times in Luke, and 12 times in John)*

The fact that he is referred to as **"Son of God"** **28 times** in the gospels, helps us understand who he is. (He was called "Son of man" exactly 3 times as many as he was called "Son of God".) He was saying I am a child of man *(adam)* **"a human being."** **How did we miss it?** Stephen told his tormenters in Acts 7:56, *"Behold, I see the heavens opened and **the Son of man** standing on the right hand of God."* In heaven he is **still the "Son of man."** Many Scriptures state that he will return as the "Son of man."

> *"And then shall they see **the Son of man** coming in the clouds with **great power and glory"** (Mark 13:26, Matt. 24:30, Luke 21:27).*

> *"Nevertheless, when **the Son of man cometh,** shall he find faith on the earth" (Luke 18:8)?*

UNDERSTANDING THE PHRASE "CAME DOWN FROM HEAVEN."

Do not misunderstand Jesus' statement in John 3:13 that, *"No man hath ascended up to heaven, but he that came down from heaven, even the Son of man which is in heaven."* Jesus was speaking to Nicodemus, a Pharisee, and had said in the previous verse *(v. 12)*, *"If I have told you earthly things, and ye believe not, how shall you believe if I tell you of heavenly things?"* The Pharisees loved to challenge Jesus' claim to being the Messiah, so he spoke parables to them, which he knew they would not understand. His words "the Son of man which is in heaven" are not to be taken to mean that Jesus was in fact in heaven while he was standing on earth. It means that Daniel 7, which refers to the "Son of man," **pictured** Jesus in heaven; therefore it was **already accomplished in God's reality**, though it was yet to happen in the life of Jesus. Likewise, Jesus could say to the Father in John 17:11, *"And now I am no more in the world, but these are in the world,"* because it was foreordained in the unchangeable plan of God.

When Jesus speaks of coming "down from heaven" this in no way implies that he preexisted in heaven as a person before his birth in Bethlehem. This would not harmonize with many other Scriptures. Look at John 6:31 where the doubters asked Jesus for a sign that he was from God.

121

"Our Fathers did eat manna in the desert; as it is written, He gave them **bread from heaven** *to eat."* They and Jesus knew that the bread *(manna),* which God had given their fathers in the desert, did not rain down on them all the way from the throne of God, but was **a gift sent from God**; therefore it was said, *"He gave them bread from heaven."* The phrase "down from heaven" means, "sent from God." James 1:17 says, *"Every good gift and every perfect gift is from above, and* **cometh down from the Father** *of lights."* Look at II Kings 1:10 where the prophet Elijah called down fire upon his enemies, *"And Elijah answered and said to the captain of fifty, If I be a man of God, then* **let fire come down from heaven...** *and* **there came down fire from heaven.** *"* In John 6:33 Jesus says, *"For the bread of God is he which cometh down from heaven* (himself).*"* Verse 35, *"I am the bread of life."* Verse 38, *"For I came down from heaven, not to do mine own will, but the will of him that sent me."* Compare these Scriptures with what the resurrected Jesus said to Mary at the tomb, *"Touch me not: for I am not yet* **ascended** *to my Father" (John 20:17).*

I found 17 Bible references where Jesus spoke of his pending ascension in this manner:

- *"I* **go** *unto him that sent me" (John 7:33).*
- *"Whither I* **go** *" (John 8:21).*
- *"I* **go** *to prepare a place for you" (John 14:2).*
- *"I* **go** *unto my Father" (John 14:12).*
- *"I* **go** *to my Father" (John 16:10).*

I found **not one** reference where Jesus said *"I* **go back** *to heaven," "***back** *to my Father,"* or *"I* **return** *to heaven,"* which is a strong indication that he had not previously been there. Jesus was born on earth, is **now in heaven** with the Father, and will soon **"return"** to *"receive for himself a kingdom "(Luke 19:12).*

GOD NOW HAS MANY SONS.

One final note before we close this Chapter. Please receive and accept this Bible truth. In a broad sense Jesus is **not now** the only begotten son of God, but is the **"first-begotten,"** our elder **brother**. The word "begot" means to "sire, or to bring into being."

> *"And again when he* (God) *bringeth the first-begotten into the world, he saith, And let all the angels of God worship him" (Heb. 1:6).*

> *"And from Jesus Christ, who is the faithful witness, and the first-begotten of the dead" (Rev. 1:5).*

> *"Blessed be the* **God** *and* **Father** *of our Lord Jesus, which according to his abundant mercy* **hath begotten us** *again unto a lively hope by the resurrection of Jesus Christ from the dead" (I Peter 1:3).*

> *"He that is* **begotten of God** *keepeth himself, and that wicked one toucheth him not" (I John 5:18).*

> *"Of his* (the Father's) *own will* **begot he us** *with the word of truth, that we should be a kind of firstfruits of his creatures" (James 1:18).*

> *"In Christ Jesus I have* **begotten you** *through the gospel" (I Cor. 4:15).*

> *"To be conformed to the image of his Son, that he* (Jesus) *might be the firstborn among many brethren" (Rom. 8:29).*

> *"And if children, then heirs;* **heirs of God,** *and* **joint heirs** *with Christ" (Rom. 8:17).* *"Heirs of God and joint heirs with Christ."* **Joint heirs with Christ!** Remember that under the **rules** that God ordained in the O.T., the first born son received the birthright, a **double portion** of the inheritance. So it is with Jesus.

> *"But ye have received the Spirit of adoption, whereby* **we cry, Abba Father"** *(Rom. 8:15).* 'Abba' is Father in Greek and is the term Jesus used in the Garden of Gethsemane.

> *"And he said,* **Abba Father,** *all things are possible unto thee; take away this cup from me" (Mark 14:36).*

Remember the term, 'Son of God' **does not denote kinship, but position**, a work of the Holy Ghost who begot Jesus, and **begot us his brethren, in him**.

*"And because **ye are sons**, God hath sent forth the **Spirit** of his Son* (the Holy Ghost) *into your hearts, crying **Abba Father**. Wherefore thou art no more a servant, **but a son**; and **if a son then an heir of God through Christ"** (Gal. 4:6-7).* We call God through the Spirit of His son, exactly what Jesus did, **Abba Father**. *(See also Rom. 8:15).*

*"To the general assembly and **church of the firstborn*** (Jesus), *which are written in heaven" (Heb. 12:23).* Jesus is building his church but he is building it according to **God's plan,** and on **God's authority**.

*"Known unto God are all his works **from the beginning of the world"** (Acts 15:18).*

"Now therefore are ye no more strangers and foreigners, but fellow citizens *with the saints, and of the **household of God**. And are built upon the foundation of the apostles and prophets, Jesus Christ himself being the chief cornerstone; **In whom all the building** fitly framed together groweth unto a **holy temple** in the Lord: In whom* (Jesus) *ye also are builded together for a **habitation of God** through the Spirit" (Eph. 2:19-22).*

Notice, **"Builded together for a habitation of God."** **Jesus is part of this building as we are**.

*"Because **as he is**, so are we in this world" (I John 4:17).*

"Ye are God's building" (I Cor. 3:9).

"He that built all things is God" (Heb. 3:4).

*"The works **were finished** from the **foundation of the***

124

world" (Heb. 4:3).

"Behold , what manner of love the Father hath bestowed upon us, that we should be called the sons of God ("therefore also that holy thing which shall be born of her shall be called the Son of God" Luke 1:35) therefore the world knoweth us not, because it knew him not. Beloved, now are we the sons of God, and it doth not yet appear what we shall be: but we know that, when he (Jesus) shall appear, we shall be like him; for we shall see him as he is" (I John 3:1-2).

"We shall be like him," not **"Gods"** but glorified men and women. (Before Jesus died and was resurrected John 7:39 says: *"Jesus was not yet glorified"*).

JESUS IS AWESOME!

- ▸ Jesus is *"the way, the truth and the life" (John 14:6).*
- ▸ Jesus is *"the door,"* the only way to the Father *(John 10:9).*
- ▸ Jesus has *"the keys of hell and of death" (Rev. 1:18).*
- ▸ Jesus' name is the only *"name under heaven given among men whereby we must be saved "(Acts 4:12).*
- ▸ Jesus is a man "appointed" of God *(Heb.3:2).*
- ▸ A man "anointed" of God *(Acts 10:38).*
- ▸ A man "ordained" of God *(Acts 17:31).*
- ▸ A man "approved" of God *(Acts 2:22).*
- ▸ A man "chosen" of God *(I Peter 2:4).*

And he is so much more, **but he is not God.** *He is, the Man Christ Jesus!*

125

(The Doctrine of the Trinity is) "an unintelligible proposition of Platonic *(Plato)* mysticisms that three are one and one is three, and yet one is not three, and the three are not one. I never had sense enough to comprehend the Trinity, and it has always appeared to me that comprehension must precede assent *(agreement)*"...*(It is a relapse from the true)* "**religion of Jesus**, founded in the unity of God, into unintelligible polytheism"...*(Trinitarian Christians)* "undertook to make of this articulation a second pre-existing being, and ascribe to him, and not to God, the creation of the universe. The world was created by the Supreme, intelligent being...The Trinitarian idea triumphed in the Church's Creeds, not by the force of reason but by the word of ...Athanasius, and grew in the blood of thousands and thousands of martyrs." *(I wish to)* "do away with the incomprehensible jargon of the Trinitarian Arithmetic, that three are one and one is three and knock down the artificial scaffolding reared to mask from view the sturcture of **Jesus' doctrine**," *(so that people may be)* "**truly and worthily His disciples**." [4]

Thomas Jefferson

3rd President of the United States and

Author of the Declaration of Independence

Chapter 5

What Is God's Name?

*"Therefore, behold, I will this once cause them to know,
I will cause them to know mine hand and my might; and
they shall know that **my name is The Lord"** (Jeremiah
16:21).*

*"Who ascended up into heaven, or descended? Who
hath gathered the wind in his fists? Who hath bound
the waters in a garment? Who hath established all the
ends of the earth? **What is his name,** and **what is his
son's name, if thou canst tell"** (Proverbs 30:4)?*

D ear reader, I begin this chapter by acknowledging to you that I do not
have all the answers pertaining to the Godhead. I am writing as one who
was raised in the Oneness *(Jesus Only)* faith. In young adulthood I was
called to preach, and for many years I evangelized and pastored as a minister
of that persuasion. I dearly love the people who hold to that doctrine, they
are my brethren; but I now see that it is one that cannot be supported by
Scripture. However, I still believe that converts should be baptized in the
name of Jesus, *"for there is **none other name under heaven** given among
men, whereby we must be saved" (Acts 4:12).* And in all Bible accounts of
water baptisms after Pentecost, they were baptized in the *"**name of Jesus
Christ"** (Acts 2:38), "**the Lord Jesus"** (Acts 8:16), "**in the name of the
Lord"** (Acts 10:48), "**the name of the Lord Jesus"** (Acts 19:5).* The
historical record says the same. *The Encyclopedia Britannica* says, "The
triune and trinity formula was not used from the beginning and up until the
third century, baptism in the name of Christ only was wide spread...."
(Baptismal formula changed by the Roman Catholic Church) "Now the

127

formula of Rome is 'I baptize thee in the name of the Father and of the Son and of the Holy Ghost'." [1] So while we are on our search for truth, **please embrace this one**. Because of what I understand from the Bible, I would not baptize a convert in water without speaking the name of Jesus over him or her.

However, the doctrine of Jesus as Lord God Almighty, the one true God, is not supported by Scripture. He is who he, and all of the N.T. writers say he is, the virgin born, sinless, Son of God. I am not pastoring a church at this time, nor do I belong to a certain denomination, so I do not have a doctrinal position to support nor a statement of faith to defend. I want only the truth as clearly stated in God's word. I started on the road to my present understanding of the Godhead one day while I was reading Acts Chapter 4. Oneness people lean heavily on the book of Acts, but a closer look at this Chapter shook me.

The Oneness brethren have a proper understanding of one thing: there are not three coequal, coeternal persons in the Godhead; **God is not a trinity**. There are absolutely too many Scriptures that do not fit that belief.

Deut. 6:4 says:

>*"Hear, O Israel: The Lord our God is **one Lord**."*

Isa. 44:6 says:

>*"Thus saith the Lord the King of Israel, and his redeemer, the Lord of hosts; I am the first, and I am the last: and **beside me there is no God**."*

Isa. 45:11-12 says:

>*"Thus saith the Lord, the **Holy One** of Israel, and his maker, I have made the earth, and created man upon it....I, even my hands, have stretched out the heavens, and all their host have I commanded."*

Jesus said in Matt. 19:17:

>*"Why callest thou me good? There is none good but **one, that is, God**."*

He says in his prayer to the Father in John 17:3:

128

*"And this is life eternal, that they might know thee **the***
only true God, and Jesus Christ, whom thou hast sent."

There are so many more, but these should suffice. There is other solid, non-biblical evidence against holding to the doctrine of the trinity. *The New International Encyclopedia* says of the trinity, "The Catholic Faith is this: We worship one in trinity, but there is one person of the Father, another of the Son and another of the Holy Ghost. **The Glory equal; the Majesty coeternal**. The doctrine is not found in its fully developed form in the Scriptures. Modern theology does not seek to find it in the O.T. At the time of the Reformation **the Protestant Church took over the doctrine of the Trinity without serious examination."** [2]

When it **was** given "serious examination" after the latter day outpouring of the Holy Spirit in the early 1900's, those brethren who rejected the "trinity doctrine," took the other extreme, non-biblical position, that Jesus is all, "Jesus only," the "Oneness" belief. This divide remains until the present in two different Pentecostal camps, the Assemblies of God being the largest Trinitarian organization and the United Pentecostal Church the largest Oneness. We minister with and among people of both beliefs, and count them as our dear friends. They are precious, and my purpose in this book is to show both sides, and all Christians that there is another way, the Bible way of viewing God and His son Jesus Christ. Now back to the beginning of my departure from the Oneness *(Jesus only)* belief. In Acts Chapter 3 a lame man was sitting at the temple gate called Beautiful, when Peter and John went there to pray, and Peter lifted him up in the name of Jesus Christ. His healing caused quite a stir in Jerusalem and 5000 new believers were added to the church. Peter preached a powerful message to the multitude about the crucifixion and resurrection of Jesus, ending it with verse 26:

*"Unto you first **God, having raised up his Son Jesus**,*
sent him to bless you, in turning away every one of you
from his iniquities."

This sermon got them arrested and put into prison overnight, and the next day they were brought before a council made up of Caiaphas the high priest and several of his relatives. Peter gave another powerful message *(Acts 4:8-12)*; and after the council conferred they sent Peter and John away with threats, warning them to preach no more in the name of Jesus. Verses 23-26 say:

> *"And being let go, they went to their own company, and reported all that the chief priests and elders had said unto them. And when they heard that, they lifted up **their voice to God** with one accord, and said, **Lord, thou are God**, which hast made heaven, and earth, and the sea and all that in them is: Who by the mouth of thy servant David hast said, Why did the heathen rage, and the people imagine vain things? The kings of the earth stood up, and the rulers were gathered together **against the Lord, and against his Christ.**"*

I saw first that these apostles who had just seen Jesus ascend into heaven, and had tarried in Jerusalem until the outpouring of the Holy Ghost on Pentecost *(Acts Chapter 2),* are now addressing this very urgent prayer in Chapter 4 to "God, the Lord God, **which hast made heaven and earth.**" And they referred in this prayer back to Psalm 2, which I knew was a prophetic Psalm of David, written some 1000 B.C., which speaks of God exalting His Son, His anointed Messiah, "his Christ." It did not seem that in their minds Jesus was **"God," or "Lord God,"** so they must not be as I was, "Jesus only." This much had me on the ropes but verses 27-30 delivered the "knock out punch."

> *"For of a truth against **thy holy child Jesus**, whom thou has anointed, both Herod, and Pontius Pilate, with the Gentiles, and the people of Israel, were gathered together, For to do whatsoever thy hand and thy counsel determined before to be done. **And now, Lord,** behold their threatenings: and grant unto thy servants, that with all boldness they may speak thy word. By stretching forth thine hand to heal; and that signs and*

wonders may be done **by the name of thy holy child Jesus**."

At this time Jesus was clearly in heaven, but they were praying to the "Lord" *(God)* regarding "**thy holy child Jesus**," and "**by the name of thy holy child Jesus**." This did not sound like anything I had preached or heard preached in all of my years in Oneness Pentecostal churches. In fact using such terminology might have gotten you thrown out of some, or at least kept you from being invited back. We were taught that Jesus *was* "Lord God." Since Jesus was God, He should be addressed by His name "Jesus," and the use of the name "God" was to be limited. God would never have been prayed to in "the name of thy holy child Jesus." There was obviously something wrong with my doctrine and understanding of **who God is**. Why hadn't I seen this before? And God's response to this prayer is recorded in verse 31:

> "And when they had prayed, the **place was shaken** where they were assembled together; and they were **all filled with the Holy Ghost**, and they spake the word of God with boldness."

God was clearly pleased with their prayer and their understanding of Him and His relationship to His son Jesus; and He showed it by shaking the house and refilling them with the Holy Ghost. For a short time after I came to this realization, I took another look at the *Trinitarian* message, but it just did not fit what I knew of God's word. It was clearly unscriptural. Therefore I did for a while what I feel that many more have done, I put the doctrine of the Godhead in my mental "I don't understand box," and went on loving and trying to work for the Lord. This is an uncomfortable place to be; for how can we worship God "in spirit and **in truth**," which is how Jesus said we **must** "worship the Father" *(John 4:23-24)*, if we don't know **the truth** as to who He is? I knew that the Apostle Paul had said in Romans 1:19-20:

> "Because that which may be **known of God** is manifest in them: for God hath **shown it unto them**. For the

*invisible things of him from the creation of the world
are **clearly seen, being understood** by the things that
are made, even his eternal power and **Godhead**; so that
they are without excuse."*

The next question was, had I in my sincere desire to exalt Jesus the Son of God, given him a place in my **heart, mind** and **worship** that should be reserved only for the Lord God, Jesus' Father and mine *(John 20:17)*? I continued praying to both God and Jesus, which I thought was proper, and ending my prayers in the name of Jesus, which I knew was right.

In 1986 I experienced a spiritual breakdown, which would have been fatal, except for the fact that the Lord sent a man to me, which He used as a prophet over a few weeks period and rescued me from my failure. The revival that ensued in our family and ministry was reported in *Charisma* Magazine in the July 1988 issue in a article titled "*A Family In Revival*." My wife LaBreeska also covered it very well in her book "*Partners In Emotion*," published by Trumpet Call Books.

When God spoke to me through this prophet, He identified Himself as "The God of Abraham, Isaac, and Jacob, the God of your father, and also your God." He called himself the "Lord God of the Mighty Hosts." He said that I should know that "Elohim had turned His vision toward my pathway." He said through this prophet, whose background also was Oneness, and who was just as amazed and awed as I was by what was spoken, "You call me Lord, and I am He, you say to me Jesus **and I hear thee**." Please note that he did not say "I am Jesus." God said to me, "When you call me Father and acknowledge me as Father, I in turn acknowledge you, and call you Son." This was clearly the God of the O.T.

I was overwhelmed with appreciation to God for intervening in my life and rescuing me, and I hung on to every word that He spoke. I also realized that God was speaking in what I considered to be O.T. terms and using names that I knew to be O.T. names. We must understand that the division in our Bibles, named Old Testament and New Testament, is an artificial division put there by the Bible translators, and may or may not be helpful in

132

understanding what God is saying to us today. Some people have a wall built up in their minds as to what is "Old Testament" and they just don't go back there. A very prominent preacher said several years ago in my hearing, "I don't know why we have the O.T. in the Bible. It's not for us today and I don't read it." Yes, there was an O.T. *(covenant)* given to Moses which contained the "blood of bulls and goats," but there is **much more to it**; and a N.T. (covenant) which Jesus called *"the new testament in my blood, which is shed for you" (Luke 22:20, I Cor. 11:25)*. Hebrews tells us that the testament of Jesus is *"a better testament" (Heb. 7:22)*, but in the Bible there certainly is an overlap, and you can't understand one without the other. We for sure will not ever understand the Godhead unless we study and love both, because it is the same God and He has not changed. As someone has rightly said, "The O.T. is the N.T. concealed, and the N.T. is the O.T. revealed." Paul said to Timothy:

> *"**All scripture** is given by inspiration of God, and **is profitable** for doctrine, for reproof, for correction, for instruction in righteousness: That the man of God may be perfect, throughly furnished unto all good works" (II Tim. 3:16-17).*

I spent much time in the ensuing days and months feeding on the words of life which God had spoken to me and also reflecting on the names by which He had identified Himself.

Since we usually address people, using the names by which they identify themselves to us, I began to study these names of God in the Scripture and use them in my prayer times, always approaching Him through the blood of Jesus and praying in the name of Jesus. In other words I invoked the righteousness of Jesus on my behalf, and claimed through Jesus what I knew he had purchased for me by his death on the cross. I found something very interesting in Exodus Chapter 3. When God appeared to Moses in a burning bush on the backside of the desert, He said:

> *"I am the God of thy father, the God of Abraham, the God of Isaac, and the God of Jacob. And Moses hid his*

133

face; for he was afraid to look upon God" (v. 6).

Verse 15 says:

> *"And God said moreover unto Moses, Thus shalt thou*
> *say unto the children of Israel, The **Lord God** of your*
> *fathers, the God of Abraham, the God of Isaac, and the*
> *God of Jacob, hath sent me unto you: **this is my name***
> ***forever, and this is my memorial unto all generations.***"

God says, "This is my name forever." That was some 4000 years ago, but if today is still a part of "forever," God's name is still, "*The Lord God of your fathers, the God of Abraham, the God of Isaac, and the God of Jacob.*" It is beautiful to read in Genesis how God called out these three men to serve Him and chose to be identified with them "forever." When Abraham was 90 years old, God appeared to him again and changed his name from Abram to Abraham *(Father of nations),* saying in Genesis 17:1, *"I am the Almighty God; walk before me and be perfect."* He made Himself known to Isaac, Abraham's son in Genesis 26:24 saying:

> *"I am the **God of Abraham thy father**: fear not, for I*
> *am with thee, and will bless thee, and multiply thy seed*
> *for my servant Abraham's sake."*

God appeared to Jacob in a dream about angels, and a ladder reaching to heaven in Gen. 28:13:

> *"And, behold, the **Lord stood above it**, and said, **I am***
> ***the Lord God of Abraham** thy father, and the **God of***
> ***Isaac**: the land whereon thou liest, to thee will I give it,*
> *and to thy seed."*

See how this progressed? God is called by this name several more times in the Scriptures, including at least three times by Jesus, as quoted by the Gospel writers. No wonder, for He said to Moses, *"This (name) is my memorial unto **all generations**."* In Deut. 7:9 God speaks of keeping His covenant and mercy with those that love Him to a thousand generations. That means at least 30,000 years, so for **at least 25,000 years past** the 1000 year Millennium, God's name will still be "The Lord God of your fathers, the

God of Abraham, the God of Isaac, and the God of Jacob."

Regarding the name by which God spoke to me in 1986, "The Lord God of the Mighty Hosts": neither I, nor the man through whom He spoke, knew how many times God is called by that name in the Bible. He is called "God of Hosts" 11 times including Amos 5:27:

> *"Therefore will I cause you to go into captivity beyond Damascus, saith the **Lord, whose name is The God of hosts.**"*

God is called "**Lord God** of hosts" several times in the O.T. I found no less than 230 times where He is called "the **Lord** of Hosts," including no less than 12 times where it specifically says His **name** is the "Lord of Hosts." To the best that I can determine, it means "the Lord God of heavens armies of angels."

> *"Who is the King of glory?* ***The Lord of hosts,*** *he is the King of Glory" (Ps. 24:10).*

As to "Elohim," it is the Hebrew name for God and He is so called 2700 times in the Bible. It is always translated into our English word "God." It is not **plural**, as some would try to say, but **singular** because our Elohim, God *"is **one Lord**" (Deut. 6:4).* When used of the one God it **always** takes a **singular verb**.

Have we thrown away the O.T. in our hearts and minds and along with it these mighty names of our God? Names by which the heroes of old:

> *"Through faith subdued kingdoms, wrought righteousness, obtained promises, stopped the mouths of lions, quenched the violence of fire, escaped the edge of the sword, out of weakness were made strong, waxed valiant in fight, turned to flight the armies of the aliens. Women received their dead raised to life again" (Heb. 11:33-35).*

The Oneness Pentecostal people believe and teach that God's N.T. name is Jesus. Let's see from God's Holy Bible if it is?

Let me pause to say that I love the name of Jesus. It is a beautiful name, a lovely name, a powerful name. It is the name through which I was saved, in which I was baptized in water at the age of 10, about which I have written songs and the name to which I humbly bow. I joyfully give honor, praise and glory to the name of Jesus Christ, my Lord and Savior. But this is not the name of the Lord God, the most High God! Look at Luke 1:30-35:

> *"And the angel said unto her, Fear not, Mary: for thou hast found **favour with God**. And, behold, thou shalt conceive in thy womb, and bring forth a son, and shalt call his name Jesus. He shall be great, and shall be called the Son of the Highest: and the **Lord God** shall give unto him the **throne of his father David**: And he shall reign over the house of Jacob for ever; and of his kingdom there shall be no end. Then said Mary unto the angel, How shall this be, seeing I know not a man? And the angel answered and said unto her, The Holy Ghost shall come upon thee, and the power of the Highest shall overshadow thee: **therefore also that holy thing which shall be born of thee shall be called the Son of God."***

The angel Gabriel spoke to the virgin Mary about **God**, the **Lord God** and of **Jesus** who shall be called the **Son of God**, but gave her no indication that they were one and the same. Look at what the angel said in verse 35, *"The Holy Ghost shall come upon thee and the power of the Highest shall overshadow thee: therefore* (**which means for this reason**) *also that holy thing which shall be born of thee shall be called the Son of God."* Notice, the "**Lord God**" of the O.T. is still "**Lord God**" in the N.T.

Mary's response is recorded in verses 46-47:

> *"And Mary said, My soul doth magnify the **Lord**, And my spirit hath rejoiced in **God my Saviour**."*

She magnifies the Lord God and rejoices in "God my Saviour." In no way was this sweet Jewish girl led to believe, **nor did she ever believe**, that God, the Holy one of Israel, had moved into her womb, nor that she would give birth to God the Son, second person of the triune Godhead, a preexistent being.

The angel of the Lord came to Joseph as recorded in Matthew1:20-21 and said:

> *"Fear not to take unto thee Mary thy wife: for that which is **conceived in her is of the Holy Ghost**. And she shall bring forth a son, and thou shalt call **his name Jesus**: for he shall save his people from their sins."*

The angel did not speak the English name "Jesus" to Joseph, but "Yeshua" which is his Hebrew name. *(There was no letter "J" in the Hebrew)*. The name "Yeshua" means "Jehovah has become our salvation," and is the **same as Joshua in the O.T.** It should be noted here that the name "Jehovah" is not recognized by Jewish scholars but came into Christian usage about 1520. It is a transliteration of the "Tetragrammaton," the four consonants of the sacred name, "YHWH," and the vowel points of "Adonai" *(the Lord)*. I have used it in this book because of its common usage by English speaking people. In our Bibles it is translated "LORD."

Look at the announcement that the angel of the Lord gave to the shepherds in the field, Luke 2:11-12:

> *"For unto you is born this day in the city of David a **Saviour**, which is Christ the Lord."*

They left immediately for Bethlehem expecting to see, and they did see, not God but a "Saviour, Messiah the Lord."

> *"And suddenly there was with the angel a multitude of the heavenly host **praising God**, and saying, **Glory to God in the Highest** and on earth peace, good will toward men" (Luke 2:13-14).*

God was still "in the highest," but there was rejoicing among the angels and rejoicing among men because the *Lord God's* only begotten son Jesus, the *Lord Messiah* had been born in Bethlehem. And at the stable as Mary held this precious baby and kissed his cheeks, she knew beyond a shadow of a doubt that she **had not** in fact **"kissed the face of God,"** as is stated in a popular Christmas song. She was a Jewish girl, taught strongly all of her life the "Shema"" of Israel, God's greatest commandment, which begins, "Hear, O Israel, the Lord thy God is one Lord." She would have been horrified to know that one day in the future millions of Catholics would pray to her and proclaim her "Mother of God." *(These things must be stated plainly because they have become so scrambled in our thinking).*

Who was this child? Let's look back at who the prophets said he would be. Psalm 2, that great Messianic Psalm holds a very important key. Verse 2 says the kings and rulers of the earth *"take council together against the Lord* (God), *and against his anointed* (Messiah), *"* Remember the disciples' prayer in Acts 4:27, which said this was *"against thy holy child Jesus, **whom thou hast anointed.**"* Now look at Psalm 2:7:

> *"I will declare the decree: the Lord hath said unto me,*
>
> ***Thou art my Son; this day have I begotten thee.***"

So **Jesus was begotten on a certain day**, and not in eternity past. **God has no beginning; He is eternal**. Jesus had a beginning! Jesus says so himself in Revelation 3:14, *"These things saith the Amen, the faithful and true witness, **the beginning of the creation of God.** "* Please receive this as he said it, "I am the beginning of the creation of God." Paul confirms it in Colossians 1:15 when he speaks of Jesus and says, *"Who is the image of the invisible God, the firstborn of every creature,"* and in Col. 3:10 when he says *"him* (God) *that created him."* God spoke His son Jesus **before time** as we know it, to be begotten and brought forth **in time**, generated by the Holy Ghost in the womb of Mary. The words "begot" or "begotten" mean to "father or sire, to bring into being." Jesus was "sired" by his Father God in the womb of the virgin Mary, when she was overshadowed "by the Holy Ghost." That's why Paul says in Gal. 4:4:

> *"But **when the fulness of the time was come**, God sent*
>
> *forth his Son, **made of a woman**, made under the law."*

Heb. 9:26 says:

> *"Now **once in the end of the world hath he** (Jesus)*
>
> ***appeared** to put away sin."*

138

Heb. 1:1-2 says:

> *"God, who at sundry times and in divers manners spake*
> *in time past unto the fathers by the prophets, Hath in*
> *these last days spoken unto us by his Son."*

Please understand why God did not speak to the "fathers" in times past by Jesus but rather by the prophets. **Jesus was not there** in our reality. He appeared "in these last days" in Bethlehem. Hebrews 1:6 says, *"When he* (God) *bringeth the first begotten into the world, he saith, and let all the angels of God worship him."* When did God decree that Jesus should be worshiped by the angels of God? Not in eternity past, **he wasn't there**, but the "first begotten" certainly was worshiped by angels and men when God brought him "into the world." Jesus was the beginning of God's creative thought, and in the mind and plan of God existed as the *logos ("word")* of John 1:1 in God's reality, **before all of creation**. But in our reality he came in "time," begotten in and born from the womb of a virgin around 2 or 3 B.C. Notice, John **did not say**, "In the beginning was the Son, and the Son was with God." In Rom. 4:17 Paul shows us the difference between God's reality and ours when he says, *"God...calleth those **things which be not as though they were.**"* When **we** speak an intention, it may or may not happen, but when God speaks an intention **it is done**. This is why Rev. 13:8 can call Jesus, *"the Lamb slain before the foundation of the world,"* since it was done back then in God's plan and purpose *(His reality)*, but it happened around 32 A.D. in our reality. *(More on this important subject in the next chapter.)*

Look at Jesus' prayer to the Father in John Chapter 17:

> *"The glory which I had with thee **before the world was**"*
> *(v. 5).*
> *"For thou lovedst me **before the foundation of the** **world**" (v. 24).*

Neither of these verses say, "from eternity past," as Jesus was not there in eternity past, but his glory was spoken and he was loved before the *"foundation of the world."*

In closing this chapter let's answer one further question. When Jesus said in John 5:43 *"I am come in my Father's name,"* did he mean as the Oneness say, that the name of God the Father is Jesus Christ *(Messiah)*? No way! Jesus said in John 10:25, *"the works that I do in my Fathers name."* Look at I Sam. 17:45 where David said to the giant, *"I come to thee in the name of the Lord,"* and ask yourself, does this mean the Lord's name was David? Of course not! It means that **David came** in the **power and authority of the Lord**, even as **Jesus came** to earth in the **power and authority of the Father**. If Jesus had wanted us to believe such an earthshaking truth as, "God the Father's name is Jesus," he would have told us plainly and in more than one verse. Jesus said in John 17:11, *"Holy Father, **keep through thine own name** those whom thou hast given me."* God the Father has his **own name**, and it is not Jesus Christ.

Look at I Chron. Chapter 16 where David brings the ark of the covenant to Jerusalem. Verse 4 says:

> *"And he appointed certain of the Levites to minister...*
> *and to thank and praise the **Lord God*** (Jehovah
> Elohim) *of **Israel**."*

Verse 29 says:

> *"Give unto the Lord the **glory due unto his name**."*

What name? **The Lord God of Israel!** Jesus is not the Lord God of Israel, but he is their Messiah *(anointed one)*, sent to them by their "Lord God." Now see verses 35 and 36:

> *"And say ye, Save us, O God of our salvation...that we*
> *may give thanks to **thy holy name**, and glory in thy*
> *praise. Blessed be the **Lord God of Israel** for ever and*
> *ever."*

Look again at Ex. 34:5-6 where God proclaimed his name to Moses:

> *"And the Lord descended in the cloud, and stood with*
> *him there and proclaimed **the name of the Lord**. And*
> *the Lord passed by before him and proclaimed, **The***
> ***Lord, The Lord God**."*

What is God's name? **"The Lord," "The Lord God."** It may be The

140

Lord God of the Mighty Hosts, The Lord God of Israel, or The Lord God of Abraham, Isaac and Jacob, but it is forever, **"The Lord God."**

David says two more times, "Give unto the Lord the **glory** due unto **his name** *(Ps. 29:2, 96:8)*. This shows the importance of it. We must quit giving to Jesus the glory that is due only to God his Father. The Lord God of the O.T. is still the Lord God of the N.T. Peter said in Acts 3:13:

> *"The God of Abraham, and of Isaac, and of Jacob, the*
> *God of our fathers, hath glorified his son Jesus."*

He says again in Acts 5:30:

> *"The God of our Fathers raised up Jesus, whom ye*
> *slew and hanged on a tree. Him hath God exalted with*
> *his right hand to be a Prince and a Savior."*

After Paul's experience on the Damascus road, he quotes Ananias as saying to him:

> *"The God of our fathers hath chosen thee, that thou*
> *shouldest know his will, and see that just one* (Jesus)
> *and shouldest hear the voice of his mouth" (Acts 22:14).*
> *"Have I not seen Jesus Christ"* (Paul) *(I Cor. 9:1)*?
> (Notice, he did not say he had seen God).

Please keep these facts in mind while you study the Godhead in Scripture. Over 1300 times in the N.T. the term "God" clearly refers to God the Father. In Paul's writings the term "theos" *(Greek for God)* occurs more than 500 times and there is not one provable instance where it applies to Jesus. Paul always distinguished between the two. This says it all!

Blessed be the Lord God of Israel!

John 5:44-45 (Jesus speaking):

*"You receive glory from one another and you do not seek the glory that is from the **one and only God...the father"*** (New American Standard Bible).

*"You don't seek the glory that comes from **the only God...the Father"*** (Holman CSB).

You...*"care nothing for the honour that comes from **him who alone is God...the Father"*** (The New English Bible).

You...*"do not seek the glory that comes from **the only God...the Father"*** (English Standard Version).

You...*"make no effort to obtain the praise that comes from **the only God...the Father"*** (New International Version).

*"You don't care about the honor that comes from **the one who alone is God...the Father"*** (New Living Translation).

You...*"do not seek the honor that comes from **the only God...the Father"*** (New King James Version).

Chapter 6

Where Is Jesus Now?

*"The Lord said unto my Lord, Sit thou **at my right hand**, until I make thine enemies thy footstool"* (King David of Israel) *(Psalm 110:1).*

*"So then after the Lord had spoken unto them, he was received up into heaven, and **sat on the right hand of God"*** (Mark, Gospel writer) *(Mark 16:19).*

It is said that there are no less than thirty-three quotations and allusions to Ps. 110 scattered throughout the N.T., making it the verse from the O.T. that is **most referred to in the New.** [1] This gives us a strong indication of its importance, if we are to have a clear understanding of who Jesus is in relationship to God his Father, whom he calls "my God" numerous times in the N.T. *(Matt. 27:46, John 20:17, Rev. 3:12).* Jesus quotes this Psalm in Matthew 22:42-45 in answer to his critics who did not believe his claim to be Christ *(Messiah)*, son of David. In verse 45 he asked them, *"If David then call him Lord, how is he his son?"* Jesus left no doubt that he was the son of David, but also David's Lord, the second Lord mentioned in Ps. 110:1. Notice again, *"**The** Lord said unto **my** Lord."* It is very important to note that sometimes when the Scriptures use the term "Lord" it can be *Adonai* used only of the Lord God and never of men, or *Adoni* "master" and is used at least 195 times in the Bible in reference to men of honor, and means master, owner, or superior. The verse properly understood from the Hebrew reads, *"The Lord* (Adonai - God Almighty) *said unto my Lord* (Adoni - Master - Messiah), *sit thou at my right hand, until I make thine enemies thy footstool."*

The next question is, did it happen? Is Jesus the Son of God seated at the right hand of God his Father, the Supreme God, today? First let us

143

determine some things regarding God the Father. He is a spirit. Jesus said, *"God is a spirit" (John 4:24)*. A spirit does not have flesh and bones *(Luke 24:39)*. But God has a form, a shape. Gen. 1:27 says, *"So God created man in his own image, in the image of God created he him."* Genesis 9:6 says, *"Whoso sheddeth man's blood, by man shall his blood be shed: For in the image of God made he man."* Genesis 5:1 says, *"In the day that God created man, in the likeness of God made he him."* To be sure that we knew what "in the image of God' and "in the likeness of God" meant, verse 3 says, *"And Adam....begat a son in **his own likeness, after his image;** and called his name Seth."* So as Seth looked like Adam, Adam looked like God. This is simple Bible truth and we should not try to make something else of these verses. No man has seen God in **His full and awesome glory**. *"No man hath seen God at any time" (John 1:18, I John 4:12)*. Jesus said to the Jews who stood looking at and listening to **him**, as further proof that **he is not** God the Father, *"and **the Father himself**, which hath sent me, hath borne witness of me. Ye have neither **heard his voice at any time, nor seen his shape."** Of course God has appeared to man using many different forms through the ages, and as God, is free to do so as He pleases. God appeared to Adam and Eve in some form in the Garden of Eden to fellowship and talk with them *(Gen. Chapters 2 & 3)*. God along with two angels visited Abraham and Sarah at their tent in Mamre, on the way to destroy Sodom, and they saw the Lord in human form *(v. 2)* and prepared a meal and visited with them, while He *(the Lord)* and the angels ate. *(This may challenge you a little bit but take the word of God for what it says)*. Stephen said in Acts 7:2 that it was the *"God of glory" (obviously veiled)*, that appeared to Abraham. God appeared to Moses in the form of a burning bush *(Ex. 3:4)*. God was seen by the children of Israel in *"a pillar of a cloud and in a pillar of fire" (Ex. 13:21)*. Numbers 11:25 says that *"the Lord came down in a cloud."* Exodus 24:6-11 gives an awesome account of God visiting with men, in some form which they could see. After the sprinkling of blood and the reading of the covenant verses 9-11 say:

> *"Then went up Moses, and Aaron, Nadab, and Abihu,*

> *and **seventy of the elders of Israel: And they saw the
> God of Israel**: and there was under his feet as it were a
> paved work of a sapphire stone, and as it were the body
> of heaven in his clearness. And upon the nobles of the
> children of Israel he laid not his hand: **also they saw
> God, and did eat and drink**."*

The prophet Isaiah saw the Lord God in some awesome form, as described in Isaiah 6:1 & 5. Notice that Isaiah did not say that he saw a vision.

> *"In the year that king Uzziah died **I saw also the Lord**
> sitting upon a throne, high and lifted up, and his train
> filled the temple. Then said I, Woe is me! For I am
> undone; because I am a man of unclean lips, and I
> dwell in the midst of a people of unclean lips: for **mine
> eyes have seen the King, the Lord of hosts**."*

There are many other examples, but these and one more should suffice. Luke 3:21-22 says:

> *"Now when all the people were baptized, it came to
> pass, that Jesus also being baptized **and praying, the
> heaven was opened**. And the Holy Ghost* (God)
> *descended in a **bodily shape like a dove** upon him, and
> a **voice came from heaven**, which said, Thou art my
> beloved Son; in thee I am well pleased."*

This was **not** the Holy Ghost in his office as baptizer, "the promise of the Father," which Jesus had told them of:

> *"But this spake he of the Spirit, which they that believe
> on him should receive: **for the Holy Ghost was not yet
> given**; because that Jesus was not yet glorified" (John
> 7:39).*

Of course the Holy Ghost and the Spirit of God are the same person, for there is "one spirit" *(I Cor. 12:4-11, II Cor. 3:17, Eph. 2:18, 4:4)*, whom the writer of Hebrews calls *"the eternal spirit" (Heb. 9:14)*. Matthew 3:16 says it was *"the Spirit of God descending like a dove"* upon Jesus. This of course does not mean that God is a dove, but only used "a **bodily shape like a dove**" to appear at this very special occasion, the water baptism of His only begotten Son.

In Spirit, God is everywhere in the universe, *Omni-present*, in all places at all times. **But God has a presence!**

- Adam and Eve *"hid themselves from the presence of the Lord" (Gen. 3:8)*.
- *"Cain went out from the presence of the Lord" (Gen. 4:16)*.
- David prayed, Lord *"Cast me not away from thy presence" (Ps. 51:11)*.
- *"Sinai itself was moved at the presence of God, the God of Israel" (Ps. 68:8)*.
- God says, *"All the men that are upon the face of the earth shall shake at my presence" (Ezek. 38:20)*.
- God's *presence* has been seen (In the temple) *(II Chron. 5:13-14)*.
- God's *presence* has been felt *(Job 4:14-17)*.
- God's *presence* has been heard *(Acts 2:2)*.
- God's *presence* brings healing. *"The power of the Lord* was *present* to heal them" *(Luke 5:17)*.
- *God's presence* brings joy. *"In thy presence* is fullness of joy" *(Ps. 16:11)*.

Yes, the most High God, the Lord God of the Mighty Hosts (heaven's army of angels) the Eternal Spirit, fills all of heaven and earth and is so awesome no words can describe Him. But let us not forget that He is a person, having personality, feelings, emotions and a sweet and divine nature. Those who disregard and do not study the O.T. cannot possibly understand His mercy, forbearance, patience and forgiveness in His tender dealings with man. For example:

- Picture God alone in the Garden of Eden, the day after He had been forced by his absolute righteousness to evict His children, Adam and Eve, because **He cannot fellowship with sin.**
- Picture God killing precious animals that He created and loved,

shedding the first blood on planet earth to get skins to cloth this naked pair of sinners *(Gen. 3:21).*

- Picture God grieving over fallen humanity in the days just before Noah's flood, because man had become "violent" and "wicked" and *"every imagination of the thoughts of his heart was only evil continually, and it repented the Lord that He had made man on the earth, and it **grieved him at His heart"** (Gen. 6:5-6).* That last line literally means, "and His heart was **filled with pain**."

- Hear God saying to Israel, with whom He dwelt, *"Thou shalt not seethe a kid in his mother's milk,"* because it would be improper and God is tenderhearted and didn't want to see it *(Ex. 23:19, 34:26, Deut. 14:21).*

- Hear God's words of caution regarding disturbing a mother bird on a nest with her babies, and feel the compassion of His heart *(Deut. 22:6-7).* Now read again the Golden Text of the entire Bible, **John 3:16**.

Only one man, other than His only begotten Son has come close to seeing Almighty God on earth **in His Glory**. Moses the great prophet of Jehovah, whom Num. 12:3 calls the meekest man "upon the face of the earth," and who was a prototype of Jesus, was having a difficult time leading the Israelites to the promised land. God reassured him in Ex. 33:14 with these words, *"My presence shall go with thee and I will give thee rest."* But Moses wanted more, and said in verse 18, *"I beseech thee **show me thy glory."*** And the Lord said:

> *"I will make **all my goodness** pass before thee, and I will proclaim the **name of the Lord** before thee; And he said, **Thou canst not see my face; for there shall no man see me, and live**. And the Lord said, Behold, there is a place by me, and thou shalt stand upon a rock: And it shall come to pass, **while my glory passeth by**, that **I will put thee in a clift of the rock, and will cover thee with my hand while I pass by**: And I will take away mine hand, and **thou shalt see my back parts**: but my face shall not be seen" (Ex. 33:19-23).*

147

We see from these verses that the God of the O.T. had a "face," a "hand," and "back parts." God instructed Moses to hew out two tablets of stone on which He would write the ten commandments, and to ascend Mt. Sinai the next morning, which he did.

> *"And the Lord descended in the cloud, and stood with him there, and proclaimed the **name of the Lord**. And the Lord passed by before him, and proclaimed, **The Lord, The Lord God**, merciful and gracious, longsuffering, and abundant in goodness and truth, Keeping mercy for thousands, forgiving iniquity and transgression and sin, and that will by no means clear the guilty; visiting the iniquity of the fathers upon the children, and upon the children's children, unto the third and to the fourth generation. And Moses made haste, and bowed his head toward the earth, and worshiped" (Ex. 34:5-8).*

When Moses came down from the mountain with the two tablets, after only this brief glimpse of God's "back parts," he did not know that the skin of his face shined so brightly that, *"the children of Israel could not steadfastly behold the face of Moses for the glory of his countenance" (II Cor. 3:7).*

Look at Ex. 34, verses 30, 31, 33 & 35:

> *"And when Aaron and all the children of Israel saw Moses, behold, the **skin of his face shone; and they were afraid** to come nigh him. And Moses called unto them; and Aaron and all the rulers of the congregation returned unto him: and Moses talked with them. And till Moses had done speaking with them, **he put a veil on his face**. And the children of Israel saw the face of Moses, that the skin of Moses' face shone: and Moses put the veil upon his face again, until he went in to speak with him* (God)."

Moses and the children of Israel had encounters with Elohim that left them with no doubt that He was the **one and only Lord God** of the universe, **and God made sure that it was so.** Consider this encounter described in Exodus Chapters 19 and 20:

> *"And it came to pass on the third day in the morning, that there were **thunders and lightnings**, and a **thick cloud** upon the mount, and the **voice of the trumpet exceeding loud**: so that all the people that was in the camp **trembled.** And Moses brought forth the people out of the camp to meet with God; and they stood at the nether part of the mount. And mount Sinai was altogether on a smoke, because **the Lord descended upon it in fire**: and the smoke thereof ascended as the smoke of a furnace, and **the whole mount quaked greatly.** And when the **voice of the trumpet sounded long**, Moses spake, and **God answered him by a voice"** (Ex. 19:16-19).*

> *"And all the people saw the **thunderings**, and the **lightnings**, and the noise of the **trumpet**, and the **mountain smoking**: and when the people saw it, they removed, and stood afar off. And they said unto Moses, Speak thou with us, and we will hear: **but let not God speak with us, lest we die.** And Moses said unto the people, Fear not: for God is come to prove you, **and that his fear may be before your faces, that ye sin not.** And the people stood afar off, and Moses drew near unto the thick darkness where God was. And the Lord said unto Moses, Thus thou shalt say unto the children of Israel, **Ye have seen that I have talked with you from heaven.** Ye shall not make with me gods of silver, neither shall ye make unto you gods of gold"* (Ex. 20:18-23).

God knew that this special people, whom He had called out to be His own and with whom He had made an everlasting covenant at Sinai, people through whom He would give to all mankind the Ten Commandments and the Messiah, had been and would be exposed to many false gods; and **He never wanted them to forget this day**! In their minds were fresh memories of the many gods of the Egyptians. Moreover, they would soon encounter idolatrous Canaanite nations whose plural gods demanded such abominable practices as temple prostitution and child sacrifice, and He wanted to teach them a lesson. **"I am one**, and there is **no God beside me**. I am Almighty. I am not an impersonal god force, I am the God who **knows all and speaks from heaven** with a **mighty voice that shakes the world!"** And it produced a healthy fear of God, so much so that all of Israel, even the man of God, Moses, did *"exceeding fear and quake" (Heb. 12:21).* What has happened to the fear of God today among Christians, even some ministers *(T.V. and radio preachers)*, who act as if God is their buddy, someone to whom they can beckon to come do this or that? Part of the answer lies in this: We have reduced God in our minds to a six-foot man, the lowly Nazarene, and what we see, we do not fear! Jesus never said fear him, but he gave us a serious warning regarding the Supreme God, who *"after he hath killed hath power to cast into hell; yea, I say unto you, **Fear him"** (Luke 12:5).*

If God rules over all, where is His throne? If we can answer this question from the Scripture, then we will answer the question at the beginning of this chapter, **Where is Jesus now?**

In God's omni-presence "The heaven is his throne and the earth is his footstool" *(Isa. 66:1).* But the Scriptures clearly teach that, in a very real sense, there is a geographical place called "Heaven" where the true temple of God is and where God Almighty sits enthroned in heaven above. When Jesus fed the multitude the Bible says:

> *"Then he took the five loaves and the two fishes, and*
> ***looking up to heaven***, *he blessed them: (Luke 9:16;*
> *Matt. 14:19).*

King David says in Ps. 11:4, *"The Lord is in his holy temple, **the Lord's throne is in heaven."*** The prophet of God, Micaiah described a scene at God's throne thus:

> *"And he said, Hear thou therefore the word of the Lord;*
> ***I saw the Lord sitting on his throne**, and all the host of heaven standing by him on his **right hand and on his left**. And the Lord said, Who shall persuade Ahab, that he may go up and fall at Ramoth-Gilead? And one said on this manner, and another said on that manner. And there came forth a spirit, and stood before the Lord, and said, I will persuade him. And the Lord said unto him, Wherewith? And he said, I will go forth, and I will be a lying spirit in the mouth of all his prophets. And he said, Thou shalt persuade him; and prevail also: go forth and do so" (I Kings 22:19-22).*

God's throne is the place where He is attended by a host of angels, receives and dispatches His messengers and where Satan comes to accuse the brethren. *(See also Matt. 5:34, 18:10, Mark 13:32, Job 1:6-7, 2:1, Rev. 12:5, 7-10).* Jesus said in Matthew 18:10 regarding small children:

> *"Take heed that ye despise not one of these little ones;*
> *for I say unto you, That **in heaven their angels do always behold the face of my Father which is in heaven."***

When the angel Gabriel was sent to Zechariah to announce the coming birth of his son John, who would be the forerunner of Jesus, he said, *"I am Gabriel, that stand in the presence of God; and am sent to speak unto thee" (Luke 1:19).* Six months later when Gabriel was sent to the virgin Mary to announce the conception of Jesus in her womb, Gabriel knew that he was **not telling Mary about the coming birth of God, whose presence** he had left in heaven and **whose face** he always beheld in heaven *(Matt. 18:10)*, but the **son** of God. *"And the angel answered her, the Holy Ghost shall come upon thee, and the power of the highest shall overshadow thee: therefore* (for that reason) *also that holy thing which shall be born of thee shall be called the Son of God."* Gabriel was announcing Jesus, the **Messiah**, who was later to enter "into **heaven itself**, now to appear in the **presence of God for us**" *(as our High Priest) (Heb. 9:24).*

God's throne is the place of unspeakable splendor where God is seated and receives worship and where Jesus says in Rev. 3:21 he is seated also.

> *"To him that overcometh will I grant to sit with **me in my throne**; even as I also overcame, and am set down with my Father in his throne."*

The Gospel writer Mark describes Jesus' departure from earth and arrival in heaven thus:

> *"So then after the Lord had spoken unto them, he was received up into heaven, and **sat on the right hand of God**" (Mark 16:19).*

This is exactly where David had prophesied some 1000 years before that he would be, in Psalm 110:1. Can this be taken literally? Those who teach the so called "Oneness of the Godhead" message claim that this phrase, "set on the right hand of God" is not meant in a literal sense but is symbolic; as if we would say of a top White House advisor, "He is the President's right hand man." I am in possession of a Oneness tract, which has been distributed widely by that movement, titled, "The Truth About God," and on page 5 it says,"the term right hand does not form a part of **another person** or Deity. It is **symbolic** of the **power and authority** of God." [2] Of course they must say this because they teach that Jesus came to earth as God and man, "The Godman," in a "dual nature" and that the Son of God is, in fact, God Almighty, the Father. To support this they claim that Jesus is actually the one seated on the throne of God above, and that "right hand" only expresses favor of the Spirit. Is this Bible doctrine? Can this be supported by Scripture? Let's see.

Hebrews 1:3 says:

> *"Who being the brightness of his **glory**, and the express image of **his person**, and upholding all things by the*

152

> *word of his power, when he had by himself purged our*
> *sins,* **sat down on the right hand of the Majesty on**
> **high."**

The first "his" in this verse, "the brightness of *his* glory "is in italics in the King James, which means it was supplied by the translators and was not in the original.

Hebrews 8:1 says:

> *"Now of the things which we have spoken this is the*
> *sum: We have such an high priest, who is* **set on the**
> **right hand of the throne of the Majesty in the**
> **heavens."**

Hebrews 10:12-13 says:

> ***"But this man,*** *after he had offered one sacrifice for*
> *sins for ever,* **sat down on the right hand of God;**
> *From henceforth* **expecting** *till his enemies be made his*
> *footstool."*

This is Jesus, God's only begotten Son, Messiah and David's Adoni *(Lord)* expecting what he was promised prophetically in Ps. 110:1. May I humbly say that God the Father is not "expecting" anything, but simply speaks and it is done. Jesus His Son, has a right to **expect** what the Father promised him.

Hebrews 12:2 says:

> *"Looking unto Jesus the author and finisher of our*
> *faith; who for the joy that was set before him endured*
> *the cross, despising the shame, and is* **set down at the**
> **right hand of the throne of God."**

Acts 2:32-36 says: (Peter speaking at Pentecost) This is so important!

> *"This Jesus hath God raised up, whereof we all are*
> *witnesses. Therefore* **being by the right hand of God**
> **exalted,** *and having* **received of the Father the promise**
> **of the Holy Ghost, he hath shed forth this, which ye**
> **now see and hear. For David is not ascended into the**

heavens; but he saith himself, The Lord said unto my
Lord, Sit thou on my right hand, Until I make thy foes
thy footstool. Therefore let all the house of Israel know
*assuredly, that **God** hath made that same **Jesus**, whom*
*ye have crucified, both **Lord** and **Christ**"* (Lord, Adoni,
Master and Messiah).

In Acts Chapter 6, the Bible tells of Stephen, one of seven deacons of the church at Jerusalem, who *"full of faith and power, did great wonders and miracles among the people" (Acts 6:8)*. There were unbelieving Jews who disputed with Stephen regarding the Christian message:

"And they were not able to resist the wisdom and the
spirit by which he spake. Then they suborned men,
which said, We have heard him speak blasphemous
words against Moses, and against God. And they
stirred up the people, and the elders, and the scribes,
and came upon him, and caught him, and brought him
to the council" (Acts 6:10-12).

When Stephen was permitted to speak, he preached one of the greatest sermons recorded in the pages of Scripture. He began with Abraham and told the story of God's dealings with Israel down to their recent crucifixion of Jesus.

"When they heard these things, they were cut to the
heart, and they gnashed on him with their teeth. But he,
*being **full of the Holy Ghost**, looked up steadfastly into*
*heaven, **and saw the glory of God, and Jesus standing***
***on the right hand of God**, And said, Behold, I see the*
*heavens opened, and the Son of man **standing on the***
***right hand of God**" (Acts 7:54-56)*.

These are the words of a man on trial for his life, a dying man. The words of dying men are admissible in a court of law today, because it is believed that if a man is ever going to tell the truth it is in his dying hour. How much more a man "full of the Holy Ghost." Stephen saw this scene and told what he saw. This is real and is certainly not as many teach, "symbolic." Notice, Stephen saw Jesus "standing," perhaps to welcome home his faithful servant who was becoming the first of many martyrs for the truth.

There is one other thing that we should notice regarding this account in order to further establish the truth. Verse 59 is used by those who teach that Jesus is Almighty God. It says,

> *"And they stoned Stephen, calling upon God, and saying, Lord Jesus, receive my spirit."*

Their claim is that when Stephen said *"Lord Jesus receive my spirit,"* he was "calling upon God," and thus they are one and the same. There are several things wrong with that argument. For one, the word "God" is in italics in the King James verison of the Bible, which means that it was supplied by the translators. This makes for a weak argument that Jesus and God are one person. He could have indeed been calling upon both, because he said he saw God and Jesus, and would it seems have been justified in calling upon the two of them at such a time as this. He was probably praying to God and commending his spirit to the Lord Jesus.

This should be sufficient to prove where Jesus is now, but there is more. Romans 8:34 says:

> *"Who is he that condemneth? It is Christ that died, yea rather, that is risen again, who is even at the **right hand** of **God**, who also maketh intercession for us."*

So the apostle Paul tells us in this verse, not only where Jesus is, but what his purpose is for being there. He is there as an **intercessor**, our **advocate**, our go between. The word intercessor speaks of three parties: the one who intercedes, the one interceded to, and the one who is interceded for. This is why Hebrews 7:25 says:

> *"Wherefore he is able also to **save them to the uttermost** that **come unto God by him**, seeing he **ever liveth to make intercession for them**."*

Isaiah 59:16 tells us some 700 years before Christ, that God "saw that there was **no man**, and wondered that there was no **intercessor**." So, thank God He birthed one from the womb of the virgin Mary, His righteous Son "the **man Christ Jesus**."

I John 2:1 says:

> *"My little children, these things write I unto you, that ye sin not. **And if any man sin, we have an advocate with the Father, Jesus Christ the righteous.**"*

The book of Hebrews goes into great detail in the first 10 Chapters to explain Jesus' ministry on our behalf. In Chapter 3 verse 1 he calls Jesus Christ, *"the apostle and High Priest of our profession."* The High Priest under Moses law went into the Holy of Holies of the Tabernacle or Temple to present to God, for himself and the people, an offering of blood for atonement for sins. This pointed to Jesus who would present to God in the true tabernacle above "once and for all," **his blood** shed on the cross **for the sins of all mankind**. Please understand this Bible fact. The ministry of Jesus on our behalf did not end when he went to heaven. Look at Hebrews 8:1-2:

> *"**We have** such a high priest who is set on the right hand of the throne of the Majesty in the heavens; a **minister** of the sanctuary, and of the true tabernacle, which the Lord* (God) *pitched, and not man"* (in heaven).

Hebrews was written about 32 years after Jesus' ascension, but to the inspired writer, Jesus was still "a minister." Verse 6 says:

> *"**But now** hath he obtained a more excellent **ministry**, by how much also **he is** the mediator of a better covenant."*

Jesus, who as a priest ministers **to** God, **cannot be God,** and his ministry as a priest will last forever.

> *"Thou art a priest **for ever"** (Heb. 5:6).*

> *"Jesus, made an high priest **for ever"** (Heb. 6:20).*
>
> *"For He* (God) *testifieth, thou* (Jesus) *art a priest for ever...Thou art a priest **for ever"** (Heb. 7:17, 21).*
>
> *"The Son, who is consecrated* (a high priest) *for evermore" (Heb. 7:28).*
>
> *"But this man* (Christ),...**hath** *an unchangeable priesthood" (Heb. 7:24).*

Paul speaks of God's power in Ephesians 1:19 and says in verse 20:

> *"Which he wrought in Christ, when he raised him from the dead, and **set him at his own right hand in the heavenly** places."*

Here again a word in italics *"places,"* is not in the original but supplied by the translators, and it may or may not add to what Paul meant. We as Christians are seated in "heavenly places" *(Eph. 2:6)* but God and Jesus are seated in a **heavenly place**. See Isa. 57:15 when God says, "I dwell in the high and holy *place*."

Colossians 3:1 says:

> *"If ye then be risen with Christ, seek those things which are **above, where Christ sitteth on the right hand of God."***

> *"Jesus Christ, Who is gone into heaven, and **is on the right hand of God"** (I Peter 3:21-22).*

> *"Hereafter shall ye see the Son of man **sitting on the right hand of power**, and coming in the clouds of heaven"* (Jesus speaking) *(Matt. 26:64).*

Why so many Scriptures on this subject? Obviously God the Father did not want us to be in doubt about the answer to this very important question, Where is Jesus now? And where has he been for almost 2000 years prior to his second coming? **Seated in heaven at the right hand of God**.

Two persons, one Almighty God and the other His virgin born, sinless Son, spoken before the foundation of the world *(the "word")*, and begotten and bought forth in *time*.

(Incarnation) refers to the Christian doctrine that the pre-existent Son of God became man in Jesus. None of these writers *(Matthew, Mark, Luke)* deals with the question of Jesus' pre-existence. Paul does not directly address the question of the incarnation...**It is only with the fathers of the church in the third and fourth centuries, that a full-fledged theory of the incarnation develops.**

The use of the word *"appointed"* in Rom. 1:4 indicates that at this stage in the history of Christian thought the **title "Son of God" denoted an office or function** in salvation history, rather than a metaphysical quality as in later dogmatics. This usage is in accord with **O.T. Jewish thinking**. *(The birth narratives of Matthew and Luke)* "do **not imply a pre-existence - incarnation** Christology or a divine son-ship in the metaphysical sense. Rather, it implies Jesus' **predestination** from the womb for a messianic role in salvation history. The functional meaning of divine son-ship is made clear in Luke 1:32-33.

It is generally acknowledged that the Church father Tertullian *(A.D. 145-220)* either coined the term *(trinity)* or was the first to use it with reference to God. The explicit **doctrine** was thus formulated in the **post-biblical period**...Attempts to trace the origins still earlier to the O.T. literature cannot be supported by historical-critical scholarship. **The formal doctrine of the Trinity as it was defined by the great Church Councils of the fourth and fifth centuries is not to be found in the N.T.**

Harper-Collins Bible Dictionary
Paul J. Achtemeier, Editor, 1996 Edition
p. 452-453, 1052-1053, 1178-1179

Chapter 7

I and My Father Are Two

*"And yet if I judge, my judgement is true: for **I am not alone, but I and the Father that sent me**. It is also written in your law, that the **testimony of two men** is true. **I am one** that bear **witness** of **myself**, and the **father** that sent me **beareth witness** of me" (John 8:16-18).*

*"All are yours; and **ye are Christ's**; and **Christ is God's"** (I Cor. 3:22-23).*

*J*will ask what for some of you will seem like a strange question, but for me it is a very sad one, **how did we lose God**? Living in a world that He made, reading His book, the Holy Bible, wherein His prophets, His apostles and most important of all His Son Jesus talked so much about Him, how did we lose the **Lord God, Holy one of Israel?** The overwhelming majority of Christian people in the world today do not have a true Biblical concept of **who He is**. The largest segment of Christianity has seperated Him into three persons, "a trinity,"The Glory equal; the majesty coeternal." Another segment, the Oneness, has taken the place in their **minds**, **hearts** and **worship** that should be reserved for the **Lord God alone**, *"the only true God" (John 17:3)*, and given it to His Son, *"Jesus Christ whom thou hast sent" (John 17:3)*.

Is God "three persons," a committee? The Bible's answer is no! Over 10,000 times in the Scripture, **singular** pronouns and verbs are used in reference to God. Over 1300 times in the N.T., the term "God" clearly refers to God the Father. In Paul's writings he refers to "God" (the Greek is theos) 500 times and not one time can it be proven that he is speaking of Jesus.

God is **one person**! Is Jesus that **one** person? Again the Bible's answer is **no**. The writer of Hebrews says that the *"Son* (Jesus) *is the express image of His* (God's) *person" (Heb. 1:2-3).* So God in the Bible is stated to be "His person." That makes one person, God. Pilate said in Matthew 27:24, *"I am innocent of the blood of this just person."* So Jesus also is a "person." That makes **two persons, one** Lord God, "the only true God," and **one** Lord Messiah, *"Jesus Christ whom thou hast sent" (John 17:3).*

When God is spoken of in the Bible as to "His person", He is not to be thought of as in any way "human." It does mean that He is not just a force, "the God-force" but He is an entity, The Divine Being, having existence, with a mind, personality, emotions and will. Does God, as pictured in the Bible, possess these qualities that cause Him to be thought of in a very special way as a "person?" Go back to Genesis Chapter one and see what we can learn about God. Verse 1 teaches us that He creates, He is **the** Creator, and that he is **one "God,"** singular. Verse 2 teaches us that **He moves,** *"The Spirit of God moved."* Verse 3 teaches us that **God speaks,** *"And God said."* Verse 4 teaches us that **God has feelings,** *"And God saw the light that it was good."* God felt good about the light that He had created in verse 3. Verse 26 teaches us that **God has a form,** *"in our image, after our likeness."* Don't let the "us and "our" of this verse throw you off, and make you forget what we learned in verse one, **that God is one**. Who was God talking to, if not to another god or another member of the Godhead? In Job 38:4-7, God tells Job that when He laid the *"foundations of the earth", the angels,* (Sons of God) *were there, and "shouted for joy."* So the angels were there and **we** were created in **their image** as well as **God's**. That's why most angels who appear in Scripture look like men. Those who came to Abraham's tent and visited in Genesis 18 looked like men. The two who went to Sodom in Chapter 19 looked so much like men that those perverted people tried to molest them. Angels look so much like men that Heb. 13:2 says that some people, *"have entertained angels unaware."*

Verse 27 teaches us that **we** also **look like God,** *"So God created man in His own image"* (See also 1 Cor. 11:7). Genesis 5:1 says, *"In the likeness* *of God."* Verse 28 teaches us that God **blesses**, *"And God blessed them."* **He gives commands,** *"Be fruitful and multiply."* **He** also **delegates authority,** *"And have dominion over the fish of the sea, and over the fowl of the air and over every living thing that moveth upon the earth."*

Chapter 2, verse 17 teaches us that **God has rules**, *"But of the tree of the knowledge of good and evil thou shalt not eat."* And also that **breaking His rules has consequences,** *"Thou shalt surely die."* So **God can take away** the **life** that He has given. Verse 23 teaches us that **God is not the only one who speaks**, *"And Adam said."* Chapter 3 verse 2, *"And the woman said."* Verse 4, *"And the serpent said,"* and he contradicts God, *"ye shall not surely die."* They heeded the wrong voice, sinned against God, were cast out and died spiritually that day, and physically that 1000 year day. *"A thousand years are as one day with the Lord" (II Peter 3:8).* *"By one man sin entered into the world, and **death by sin**; and so death passed upon all men, for that all have sinned. Nevertheless, **death reigned from Adam.....**" (Rom. 5:12, 14).*

But God had a plan! Though Jesus wasn't there in Genesis one, two and three in reality, *(as we know reality)*, we understand from Scripture that God had already, before He created anything else, spoken His intention to have a Son. He spoke His Son before all! Spoken **before time**, to be begotten and brought forth **in time**, from a virgin. **Jesus,** *"the beginning of the creation of God" (Rev. 3:14).* **Jesus,** *"the firstborn of every creature" (Col. 1:15).* He was not at the creation in our reality; **God did not need help.**

> *"Thus saith the Lord, thy redeemer, and he that **formed thee** from the womb, that **stretcheth forth the heavens alone**; that spreadeth abroad the earth **by myself"** (Isa. 44:24).*
>
> *"Thus saith the Lord, the Holy **one** of Israel, and his maker. **I** have made the earth and created man upon it: **I** even **my** hands have stretched out the heavens, and all their host have **I** commanded" (Isa. 45:11-12).*

161

*"By the word of the Lord were the heavens made; and all the host of them by the **breath of his mouth"** (Ps. 33:6).*

*"Have we not all **one father**? Hath not **one God** created us" (Mal. 2:10)?*

Who created all? God the Father alone!

*"O the depth of the riches both of the wisdom and knowledge of **God**! For **of him** and **through him** and **to him** are all things: to whom be glory forever, Amen" (Rom. 11:33, 36).*

What was the driving force behind all of God the Father's creative works, after he spoke His Son? The answer is found in Rom. 8:38-39:

*"For I am persuaded, that neither death, nor life, nor angels, nor principalities, nor powers, nor things present, nor things to come, nor height, nor depth, nor any other creature, shall be able to separate us from **the love of God, which is in Christ Jesus our Lord**."*

He spoke him **before time** and brought him forth **in time**.

*"But when the **fulness of the time** was come, God sent forth his Son, made of a woman" (Gal. 4:4).*

*"Be thou partaker of the afflictions of the gospel according to the power of **God: Who hath saved us**, and called us with an holy calling, not according to our works, but **according to his own purpose and grace,** which was **given us in Christ Jesus before the world began. But is now made manifest** by the appearing of our Saviour Jesus Christ"(II Tim. 1:8-10).*

Yes, God promised Himself a son. Just as hundreds of years later, He promised his friend Abram a son, when Abram was 75 years old and his wife Sarah was barren. Abram was very rich in cattle, in silver and in gold, and his nephew Lot lived with him, but all of that meant little without a son. And occasionally through the years God appeared to him and reminded him of his son *(seed)*, and named him Isaac. But Abram and his wife Sarah became impatient and tried things on their own. Things like adopting their favorite servant boy as their son, or Abram having a son Ishmael, by their slave girl Hagar. *(The descendants of Ishmael are causing much pain in the world today.)* All the while Abram's brother Nahor was having **12 sons**, 8 by his wife and 4 by his concubine, which must have added to Abram's pain. And then God appeared to Abram in Gen. 17:5 and said:

> *"Neither shall thy name any more be called Abram, but thy name shall be Abraham; for a father of many nations have I made thee."*

Why did God change his name to Abraham *(father of nations)* and say **"a father of many nations have I made thee,"** when the promised son still had not been born? Because God *"calleth those things which be not as though they were" (Rom. 4:17).* In God's mind it was **done**! In Abraham's mind it was still in the **doing**.

> *"And the Lord visited Sarah as he had said, and the Lord did unto Sarah as he had spoken. For Sarah conceived, and bare Abraham a son in his old age, at the set time of which God had spoken to him. And Abraham called the name of his son that was born unto him, whom Sarah bare to him, Isaac. And Abraham was an hundred years old, when his son Isaac was born unto him. And Sarah said, God hath made me to laugh, so that all that hear will laugh with me" (Gen. 21:1-3, 5-6).*

How Abraham and Sarah loved this boy!

> *"And the child grew, and was weaned: and Abraham made a great feast the same day that Isaac was weaned" (Gen. 21:8).*

However, through this beloved son, this son of promise, of whom he had talked, dreamed and planned for long before his birth, Abraham was put to a severe test. When the lad was about 17 years old, God spoke to his father and said:

*"Abraham: and he said, Behold, here I am. And he said, Take now thy son, **thine only son Isaac**, whom thou lovest, and get thee into the land of Moriah; and **offer him** there for a burnt offering upon one of the mountains which I will tell thee of. And Abraham rose up early in the morning, and saddled his ass, and took two of his young men with him, and **Isaac his son**, and clave the wood for the burnt offering, and rose up, and went unto the place of which God had told him And Isaac spake unto Abraham his father, and said, My father: and he said, Here am I, my son. And he said, Behold the fire and the wood: but where is the lamb for a burnt offering? And Abraham said, My son, **God will provide himself a lamb** for a burnt offering; so they went both of them together. And they **came to the place which God** had told him of; and Abraham built an altar there, and laid the wood in order, and bound Isaac his son, and laid him on the altar upon the wood. And Abraham **stretched forth his hand, and took the knife to slay his son**. And the angel of the Lord called unto him out of heaven, and said, Abraham, Abraham; and he said, Here am I. And he said, Lay not thine hand upon the lad, neither do thou any thing unto him: for now I know that thou fearest God, **seeing thou hast not withheld thy son, thine only son from me**. And Abraham lifted up his eyes, and looked, and behold behind him a ram caught in a thicket by his horns: and Abraham went and took the ram, and offered him up for a burnt offering in the stead of his son. **And Abraham called the name of that place Jehovah Jireh;** as it is said to this day, **in the mount of the Lord it shall be***

seen" *(Gen. 22:2-3, 7-14).*

Jehovah-Jireh, "The Lord will provide." Abraham spoke a prophecy in the moment when God spared his son Isaac, "In the mount of the Lord it shall be seen." But Abraham did not know what God knew, that some 1900 hundred years later God's son of promise, for whom He had waited patiently, of whom He *(God)* had spoken often *(to Moses, David, Isaiah, and in veiled words to Abraham himself)*, would be born of a mother *(Mary)*, who would also rejoice. And God his Father would send heaven's angels to herald **his birth** and would even hang out a bright star to say, **It's a boy!** And then at the age of 33 God's only begotten son would walk up this same Mt. Moriah, as Abraham's only son had done so long before, to a place called Calvary, **to die**. But this time there would be no lamb in the bushes. **He was the Lamb, he was slain**! *"And God so loved the world that He gave His only begotten Son that whosoever believeth in him should not perish but have everlasting life" (John 3:16)*. No, he did not preexist, but he certainly was preordained! So much so that Peter, and John the Revelator could call Jesus *"the Lamb slain from the foundation of the world." "In the book of life of the Lamb slain from the foundation of the world" (Rev. 13:8)*.

> *"Forasmuch as ye know that ye were not redeemed with corruptible things, as silver and gold, from your vain conversation received by tradition from your fathers; But with the precious blood of **Christ, as of a Lamb** without blemish and without spot: Who verily was **foreordained before the foundation of the world**, but was **manifest in these last times** for you" (I Peter 1:18-20).*

In our reality it did not happen back then, but in God's reality it did! Even when Jesus taught by parables, Matthew said he fulfilled words spoken by the prophet long ago, who said *"I will open my mouth in parables: I will utter things which have been **kept secret** from the **foundation of the world**" (Matt. 13:35)*. Do not confuse the terms **"foreordained"** with **"preexisted."** Jesus surely saw himself as a separate "being" or "person" from the

165

Father. My Oneness brethren make much of what Jesus said in John 10:30, *"I and my father are one."* Is Jesus telling us in this one verse what would have been such an earthshaking revelation as, "I and my father are one person, entity, **God**," or rather that they are one in spirit, unity, love, fellowship, etc. The key to the way in which they are **one** is found in this same book of John *(17:11)*, when Jesus prays, *"Holy Father, keep through* ***thine own name,*** *those whom thou hast given me,* ***that they may be one, as*** ***we are."*** Not **one person!** He says again in verse 22:

> *"That they may be one,* ***even as we are one."***

JESUS SAID THAT HE AND THE FATHER MADE TWO WITNESSES. *(John 8:18).*

On this occasion his detractors, the scribes and Pharisees, were testing him and looking for something to accuse him of. The Pharisees said in verse 13, *"Thou bearest record of thyself, thy record is not true."* His response was, *"I am not alone, but I and the Father who sent me" (v. 16).* Then he reminds them that in their law *(Moses' law)* "at the mouth of two witnesses, or at the mouth of three witnesses shall the matter be established" (see Deut.19:15). If Jesus and his Father are **one** person then he in his wisdom would not have made this argument. Verse 18: *"**I am one** that **bear witness** of myself. And* ***the Father*** *that sent me* ***beareth witness of me."*** Jesus is clearly saying, "I and my Father are two, two witnesses."

The writer of Hebrews shows clearly the distinction between God and Jesus in the list of things that he says believers have come to:

> *"But ye are come unto Mount Zion, and unto the city of the living God, the heavenly Jerusalem, and to an innumerable company of angels" (Heb. 12:22).*
>
> *"**And to God** the judge of all..." (v. 23).*
>
> *"**And to Jesus** the mediator of the new covenant" (v.24).*

To him they are not the same.

When Jesus says in John 14:9, *"Philip, he that hath seen me hath seen the Father,"* is he telling Philip and us that he and God the Father are the same person? Not so, for the writer of this Gospel, John the beloved disciple

166

says twice in his writings, *"No man hath seen God at any time" (John 1:18, I John 4:12)*. Jesus had said previously in John 5:37, *"The Father himself, which hath sent me, hath borne witness of me. Ye have **neither heard his voice** at any time, nor seen his shape."* They were looking at and listening to Jesus, but they had **never heard nor seen** the Father. The Bible does not contradict itself, but it must be *"rightly divided" (II Tim. 2:15)*.

Jesus and God the Father are two "Lords." I know this will not fit the doctrine of many whose minds will go immediately to Eph. 4:5 which says, *"One Lord, one faith, one baptism,"* but in our minds we have put a period after the word "baptism," when in God's Holy Bible there is a comma. *(Remember we are on a search for truth.)* That is what's wrong with much of our theology and what causes such division among Christians. We have taken fragments of Scriptures, incomplete verses, and built huge doctrines that are without foundation. There is no **period** after the word "baptism," which would mean that the thought was completed, but there is a **comma**, which means that the statement includes this thought, that, in **addition** to *"**One Lord, one Faith, one baptism,**"* there is *"**one God and Father** of all."* This agrees with Jesus' statement that, *"My father is greater than all" (John 10:29)* and *"My father is **greater than I**."* One question, if Jesus truly is God the Father, how can he be greater than himself? Do not fall in the trap into which many "Oneness" people have fallen, that is, when they read "God," or "Father" in the Bible, their minds automatically register "Spirit,"and when they read Jesus they register "body." God is a Spirit, the Holy Spirit, but he is a "person," and Jesus was not just a "body", **he is a person**, *"the man Christ Jesus" (I Tim. 2:5)*. Now we see what Paul meant when he said in I Cor. 8:6, *"But to us there is but **one** God, the Father* (the **Lord God** of the Old and New Testaments) ***of whom** are all things, and we in him; and one **Lord** Jesus Christ, **by whom** are all things, and we **by** him."* The apostle Paul was not "Jesus only," for he proclaimed one **Lord God** the Father and one **Lord Jesus Christ**. Please note that the apostle Paul speaks of God *(Gk. theos)* 500 times in his writings and not one time can it be proven that he was speaking of the Lord Jesus. **There are clearly in**

167

Scripture two Lords, the **Lord God** and his son, the **Lord Jesus**. For further proof that the Bible teaches there are two Lords, turn to Ps. 110:1. David was speaking prophetically when he said, *"The Lord said unto my Lord, sit thou at my right hand, until I make thine enemies thy footstool."* David makes it clear in verse 4 who the first Lord is, *"The **Lord** hath sworn, and will not repent, Thou are **a priest forever after the order of** Melchizedek."* This was the Lord God speaking to his son our High Priest. Look at Heb. 5:8 & 10 where it is said, *"Though he* (Jesus) *were a son..called of God an high priest after the order of Melchizedek."* In Matt. 22:42-44 Jesus confirms that he is David's son, the second Lord spoken of in Ps. 110:1. So David's Lord God said to his (David's) son the Lord Jesus, *"Sit thou on my right hand, till I make thine enemies thy footstool."* Now, look with me at Mal. 3:1 and see two Lords.

> *"Behold, I will send **my messenger**, and he shall prepare the way before me: and the **Lord, whom ye seek**, shall suddenly come to his temple, even **the messenger of the covenant**, whom ye delight in: behold, he shall come, saith the **Lord of hosts**."*

This is a promise of John the Baptist *("my messenger")* and Jesus Messiah, *"the messenger of the covenant." "The Lord whom ye seek"* is the Lord Jesus and *"the Lord of hosts"* is the Lord God who **sent them**. In Matt. 11:10 Jesus, speaking of John says:

> *"For this is he, of whom it is written, Behold, I send **my messenger** before **thy face**, which shall prepare **thy way** before thee."*

Thus **the Lord God** sent John to prepare the way for **the Lord Jesus**. And Peter said the **Lord God** will send the Lord Jesus again.

> *"Repent...that your sins may be blotted out, when the times of refreshing shall come from the presence of **the Lord**; And **he** shall send Jesus Christ...whom the heaven must receive until the times of restitution of all things" (Acts 3:19-21).*

Please agree with me that the Bible clearly speaks of two Lords, **one** Lord

168

God Almighty and **one** Lord Jesus Christ, His son. From now on when you see "Lord" in O.T. prophecy, and especially in the N.T., ask yourself is it speaking of the Lord God or the Lord Jesus. For example in Luke 1:43, John the Baptist leaped in his mother Elizabeth's womb, and she said to Mary, *"And whence is this to me, that the mother of my Lord* (**not her Lord God but her Lord Messiah**) *should come to me."* Mary was not the mother of Elizabeth's Lord God! She says in verse 45, *"And blessed is she that believed* (Mary)*: for there shall be a performance of those things which were told her from the Lord* (God)*."* After John's birth, *"his father Zechariah was filled with the Holy Ghost, and prophesied saying, Blessed be the **Lord God of Israel**; for he hath visited and redeemed his people (Luke 1:67-68)."* He is speaking of the "Lord God of Israel." In Luke 2:11 the angel said to the shepherds, *"For unto you is born this day in the city of David a Savior which is Christ the Lord"* (**the Lord Jesus**).

This verse in Luke brings us to our next point, that in Scripture there are plainly two Saviors. The angel spoke of a "a **Savior** which is **Christ** the Lord." In Luke 1:46-47 the virgin Mary says, *"My soul doth magnify the Lord, and my spirit hath rejoiced in **God my Savior**."* This is "God my Savior." In Isaiah 43:3 God says *"I am the Lord thy God, the Holy one of Israel, **thy Savior**."* In verse 11 He says, *"I, even I, am the Lord, and **beside me there is no Savior**."* This does not contradict II Kings 13:4-5 which says *"and Jehoahaz besought the Lord, and the Lord hearkened unto him: for he saw the oppression of Israel, because the king of Syria oppressed them. And the Lord gave Israel a **savior**, so that they went out from under the Syrians."* This means that God, **Israel's only true Savior**, sent a man to save them from the Syrians, "**a savior**." Nehemiah 9:27 tells us that God had sent Israel many "**saviors**," *"who saved them out of the hand of their enemies."* **God saved them** but he used a man, "**a savior**." *("And saviours shall come up on mount Zion"* Obadiah 1:21). Thus we understand why Jesus is called **our Savior**. God Almighty, our true Savior, sent his Son Jesus, whose name, Yeshua in Hebrew means, "God has become my salvation," **to save us**, and God's angel Gabriel said, *"Call his name Jesus* (Savior)*, for he*

169

*shall **save** his people from their sins" (Matt. 1:21).* Thus God our Savior sent his son Jesus into the world to act as His **exclusive agent** in salvation. II Peter 1:1 speaks of both when he says, *"God and our Savior Jesus Christ."* That is why throughout the N.T. God and His son Jesus, are both called "Savior." *(See Titus 1:4, 2:10, II Peter 2:20, Jude 25)*

This should not be hard. Just look in the context to see which one it is speaking of, and the Holy Spirit will help you. Keep one thing in mind, God is the "I am that I am." He is **"underived."** He is the **self existent one.** All that our Lord and Savior Jesus Christ has given or ever will give us, is "derived" from God his Father and ours.

WHAT GOD GAVE JESUS.

➢ Works to finish. *"The works which the Father hath given me to finish" (John 5:36).*

➢ Power to forgive sins (Matt. 9:1-8). *"They marveled, and **glorified God**, which had given such power unto men (v. 8).*

➢ Power to raise the dead (John 5:19-28). *"And this is the will of **him that sent me**...and I will raise him up at the last day"* (believers) *(John 6:40).*

➢ A throne. *"The Lord God shall give unto him the throne of his father David" (Luke 1:32).*

➢ Power to execute judgement. The Father *"hath given him* (Jesus) *authority to execute judgement also" (John 5:27).*

Think of the Sun and the Moon. Paul says in I Cor. 15:41, *"There is one glory of the sun, and another glory of the moon, and another glory of the stars."* When you see the Moon on a beautiful night, its glory is really a reflection of the Sun's glory, its light a reflection of the Sun's light. God the Father is the light. This is the light of which I John 1:7 speaks, *"But if we walk in the light, as he* (God) *is in the light, we have fellowship one with another, and the blood of **Jesus Christ his son** cleanseth us from all sin."* To God be the Glory!

Chapter 8

Does Jesus Have A God?

"My God, my God, why hast thou forsaken me" (Jesus
speaking) *(Matthew 27:46).*

*"But thou Bethlehem Ephrathah, though thou be little
among the thousands of Judah, yet out of thee shall he
come forth unto me that is to be ruler in Israel. And he
shall stand and feed in the strength of the Lord, in the
majesty of the name of **the Lord his God"** (Micah
5:2,4).*

lease understand two things about the verse just above. God says
through the prophet Micah to the little town of Bethlehem, *"out of thee shall
he come forth unto me."* Notice how many times the phrase "brought forth"
is used regarding the birth of Jesus. Matthew 1:25 says, *"And he* (Joseph)
*knew her not till she had **brought forth** her firstborn son."* The angel of
God had said to Joseph in a dream, *"And she shall **bring forth** a son and
thou shalt call his name Jesus."* So when Jesus came in Bethlehem he was
not just born, he was **brought forth** unto God his Father. He had been
spoken before time by God as His first creative thought *(the logos),* but now
as the prophet had said, *"Shall he come forth **unto me.**"* He had not been
with God in heaven as a separate person but is "brought forth" to God in
time, generated in the womb of a virgin, by the Holy Ghost. *"But when the
fullness of time was come, **God sent forth his Son**, made of a woman, made
under the law" (Gal. 4:4).* Jesus' "sending forth" and his "bringing forth" are
the same. *"And again when **he bringeth in** the first - begotten into the
world, he saith, and let all the angels of God worship him" (Heb. 1:6).* To
make sure we understand what the Bible means when it says God sent Jesus

171

into the world, look at John 17.

> *"They have known surely that I came out from thee, and*
> *they have believed that thou didst send me" (v. 8).*
> *"As thou hast **sent me into the world**, even so have I*
> *also **sent them into the world**" (v. 18).*

Jesus sent his disciples into the world, just like God sent Jesus into the world, chosen, anointed and empowered.

> *"There was a man sent from God, whose name was*
> *John"* (the Baptist) *(John 1:6).*

The day Jesus was born was one of the greatest days in the history of the world, a day for which the God of eternity had patiently waited, the birth of His Son, "His only begotten." No wonder He commanded angels to worship and hung out a star to say, **"It's a boy!"** *"But now **once in the end of the world hath he appeared** (brought forth) to put away sin by the sacrifice of himself" (Heb. 9:26).* Regarding the word "begotten," please understand that it is the act of "fathering" and it means "to sire." If you have ever wondered why all of the "begot's" and "begat's" are in the Bible, God put them there so we could understand for all of time and eternity that when He "brought forth" Jesus, and called him his "only begotten son," He meant that he was the only child **"sired"** by Him in the womb of a mother, the virgin Mary. This gives added meaning to the crucifixion, for though God had many **created Sons**, He sent His only "sired" son to the cross to die for our sins.

The second thing we should see from Micah 5:4 is the phrase, *"In the majesty of the name **of the Lord his God.**"* **Does Jesus have a God**?

The Bible's answer to this question should do much to clear up the confusion among believers as to the relationship between the Eternal God and His son Jesus. Hear again Jesus' cry from the cross as recorded in Matthew 27:46 and Mark 15:34:

> *"And about the ninth hour Jesus cried with a loud*
> *voice, Eli, Eli, lama sabachthani? that is to say, **My***
> ***God, my God,** why hast thou forsaken me?"*

The resurrected Jesus said to Mary near the garden tomb in John 20:17:

> *"Go to my brethren, and say unto them, I ascend unto* ***my Father,*** *and* ***your Father;*** *and* ***to my God,*** *and* ***your God.***"

Paul says in Ephesians 1:3 *"Blessed be the* ***God and Father*** *of our Lord Jesus Christ"* and again in verse 17:

> *"That the* ***God of our Lord Jesus Christ,*** *the* ***Father of glory,*** *may give unto you the spirit of wisdom and revelation in the* ***knowledge of him.***"

The writer of Hebrews says of the Son in Hebrews 1:9:

> *"Thou hast loved righteousness, and hated iniquity; therefore God,* ***even thy God,*** *hath anointed thee with the oil of gladness above thy fellows."* This is a quote from a Messianic psalm of David *(Ps. 45:7).*

Peter begins his first epistle by saying:

> *"Blessed be* ***the God and Father*** *of our Lord Jesus Christ" (I Peter 1:3).* Peter and Paul believed alike! Notice, **Jesus was** ascended and **in heaven** with the Father when Paul, Peter, and the author of Hebrews wrote, but to them **Jesus still had a God!**

The ascended Jesus says in Revelation 3:12:

> *"Him that overcometh will I make a pillar in the* ***temple of my God,*** *and he shall go no more out: and I will write upon him the* ***name of my God,*** *and the name of the* ***city of my God,*** *which is new Jerusalem, which cometh* ***down out of heaven from my God.***" (One cannot be the Supreme God and **have a God** at the same time).

So the Bible's answer to the question, Does **Jesus have a God**, is one resounding **"yes"**. To acknowledge the most High, Creator as your "God" is to say that He is your "higher power," whom you worship, fear, obey, love and to whom you submit.

Did Jesus worship God? Yes, see John 4:21-23 where Jesus says to the woman at the well:

> *"Woman, believe me, the hour cometh, when ye shall neither in this mountain, nor yet at Jerusalem, **worship the Father**. Ye worship ye know not what: **we know what we worship**: for salvation is of the Jews. But the hour cometh, and now is, when the **true worshipers** shall **worship the Father** in spirit and in truth: for the **Father** seeketh such **to worship him**."* Please notice that Jesus did not say the Father seeketh worshipers to worship the Son but *"true worshipers"* to *"worship the Father"* (God).

So, Jesus says *"**we** worship the Father"* (his God and our God). The final thing that Jesus did with his disciples at the "last supper," before going to the garden of Gethsemane, is recorded in Matthew 26:30 and Mark 14:26:

> *"And when they had **sung an hymn**, they went out into the mount of Olives."*

A hymn is a song of **worship** and praise to God. John the Revelator saw the overcoming saints standing on "a sea of glass mingled with fire," holding harps and singing to God the song of Moses and **the Lamb** *(Jesus)*, and what did the Lamb's song of worship to his Father say?

> *"Great and marvelous are thy works, **Lord God Almighty**; just and true are thy ways, thou **King of saints**. Who shall not fear thee, O Lord, and glorify thy name? for thou only are holy: for all nations shall come and **worship before thee**; for thy judgements are made manifest"* (Rev. 15:3-4).

In Romans 15:9 Paul quotes from Psalm 18:49, a great messianic psalm, and portrays Jesus as saying to God his Father, *"For this cause I will confess to thee among the Gentiles, **and sing unto thy name**."*

The writer of Hebrews in Chapter 2, verse 12 quotes from Psalms 22, and has Jesus saying to God, *"**In the midst of the church will I sing praise unto thee**."* Jesus joins us in singing praises unto God.

174

Did Jesus fear his God? Yes. Isaiah, under the inspiration of the Holy Spirit, penned one of the Old Testament's greatest prophecies pertaining to the coming Messiah of Israel *(Jesus)*, in Isaiah 11:1-5:

> *"And there shall come forth **a rod out of the stem of Jesse**, and a Branch shall grow out of his roots: And the spirit of the Lord shall rest upon him, the spirit of wisdom and understanding, the spirit of counsel and might, the spirit of knowledge and of the **fear of the Lord** (God); And shall make him of quick understanding in the **fear of the Lord**: And **righteousness** shall be the girdle of his loins, and **faithfulness** the girdle of his reins."*

Look at Hebrews 5:7 and see how Jesus prayed:

> *"Who in the days of his flesh, when he had offered up prayers and supplications with strong crying and tears unto him that was able to save him from death, and **was heard in that he feared.**"*

Compare this with Mark 1:12-13 and you will understand the fear that Jesus had for his heavenly Father:

> *"And immediately **the Spirit driveth him into the wilderness**. And he was there in the wilderness forty days, tempted of Satan; and was with the wild beasts."*

Jesus' fear of God, "the Lord" *(Isa. 11:2-3)* was not a cowering fear, but a respectful, reverential fear, which King David compared to the fear of an obedient child toward a kind father *(Ps. 103:13)*. This is the fear that **we should have** for God as well, a fear that produces obedience. It is altogether fitting that Jesus should walk "in the fear of the Lord" as it was prophesied of him, for *"the fear of the Lord is wisdom" (Job 28:28)* and *"the fear of the Lord is the beginning of knowledge" (Prov. 1:7)*. When in the presence of Almighty God, Moses, a prototype of Jesus *(Deut. 18:18, Acts 3:22)* said, *"I exceeding fear and quake" (Heb. 12:21)*.

Now back to Hebrews where its author, likely Paul, makes this awesome

175

statement regarding Jesus:

> *"Though he were a Son, **yet learned he obedience by***
> ***the things which he suffered; And being made perfect,***
> *he became the author of eternal salvation unto all them*
> *that obey him" (Heb. 5:8-9).*

God does not need to learn anything, much less obedience, but Jesus "learned obedience."

Hebrews 2:18 says:

> *"For in that he himself hath **suffered being tempted,** he*
> *is able to succour* ("help and relieve when in difficulty
> or distress") *them that are tempted."*

Hebrews obviously is not speaking in regard to Jesus' suffering on the cross, by which he "learned obedience," for it was this **"learned"** obedience which **took him to the cross**. For Paul says in Phil. 2:8-9:

> *"And being found in fashion as a man, he humbled*
> *himself, and became **obedient unto death, even the***
> ***death on the cross. Wherefore** God also hath highly*
> *exalted him, and given him a name which is above*
> *every name."*

Therefore, the suffering of which Heb. 5:8 speaks must have been the life experiences which the Father led him through that brought him to this final point of obedient sacrifice and victory. I know this is not the message that many teach, but this is the message of the Bible!

Did Jesus love his God and Father? Yes. In John 14:15, Jesus tells his followers to prove their love for him by keeping his commandments. He says this regarding the love he has for his Father:

> *"But that the world may know that **I love the Father;***
> *and as the Father gave me commandment **even so I do"***
> *(v. 31).*

Lastly, Did Jesus submit to the will of "his God"? Yes. Here are a few powerful Scriptures to prove it. In Isaiah 52:13, 53:11 and Zechariah 3:8 the Lord God calls the coming Messiah *(Jesus)* **"my servant"** and

176

Matthew 12:18 says:

> *"Behold **my servant**, whom I have chosen; my beloved,*
> *in whom my soul is well pleased: **I will put my Spirit***
> ***upon him**, and he shall shew judgement to the*
> *Gentiles."*

Likewise, Abraham, Moses, Paul, James and John are called "servants" of God. Jesus cannot be the Most High God and also be the **servant** of the Most High God! John 5:19, 30 says:

> *"Then answered Jesus and said unto them Verily, verily,*
> *I say unto you, The Son can do nothing of himself, but*
> *what he seeth the Father do: **I can of mine own self do***
> ***nothing**: as I hear, I judge: and my judgement is just;*
> *because **I seek not mine own will, but the will of the***
> ***Father** which hath sent me."*

In Hebrews 10:7 Christ is quoted from an O.T. prophecy of him as saying:

> *"Then said I, Lo, I come (in the volume of the book it is*
> *written of me,) **to do thy will, O God**."*

Jesus, as a person did have a will of his own, but he always submitted it to the will of his Father. The greatest struggle Jesus experienced with his will while on earth, as divergent from God's, is found in Matt. Chapter 26, Mark Chapter 14, and Luke Chapter 22. Matthew says in verses 39, 42-44:

> *"And he went a little farther, and fell on his face, and*
> *prayed, saying, **O my Father**, if it be possible, let this*
> *cup pass from me: nevertheless **not as I will**, but as*
> ***thou wilt**. He went away again the **second time**, and*
> *prayed, saying, **O my father**, if this cup may not pass*
> *away from me, except I drink it, **thy will be done**. And*
> *he came and found them, asleep again: for their eyes*
> *were heavy. And he left them, and went away again,*
> ***and prayed the third time**, saying the **same words**."*

Mark 14:36 sheds light as well:

177

"And he said, Abba, Father, all things are possible unto thee; **take away this cup from me***; nevertheless* **not what I will***, but what* **thou wilt***."* (Their wills were definitely not the same at this point in time).

Jesus had known for much of his life, and for all of his ministry, that it was his Father's will for him to die on the cross for the sins of mankind. As the time approached, the struggle within Jesus began to intensify to the point that, a few days before his death when Peter spoke words of discouragement and rebuked Jesus for saying he was going to die, Jesus saw it as Satan, who was using Peter. *(Note that if Satan cannot get to you, he will try to use someone close to you.)* Jesus said to Peter, *"Get thee behind me, Satan: thou art an offense to me: for thou savourest* (understandest) *not the things that be of God, but those that be of men" (Matt. 16:23).*

About 24 hours before his arrest Jesus' inner pain is evident in a prayer to his Father *(John 12:27):*

> *"Now is my soul troubled; and what shall I say?*
> **Father, save me from this hour***: but for this cause came I unto this hour."*

But even more in the final moments, he drew back from the pain, the shame, and the separation from his Father. This produced a struggle within Jesus that is expressed three times in prayer, when he prayed: *"take away this cup from me,"* and *"nevertheless* **not as I will***, but* **as thou wilt***."* The struggle of two wills......and submission, a struggle so intense that it caused the tiny blood vessels that carried his precious, sinless blood to burst, mixing with the sweat from his sweat glands.

> *"And* **being in agony he prayed more earnestly***; and his sweat was as it were great drops of blood falling down to the ground" (Luke 22:44).*

These verses are very painful to read, but thus we see how Jesus Christ our Lord, *"slain from the foundation of the world" (Rev. 13:8),* in God's reality, but actually slain about 32 A.D. in our reality, **purchased our eternal salvation**. Not as God but as the **perfect man**, the spotless "Lamb

178

of God." The prophet Isaiah had written some 700 years before this time *(Isa. 53:11)*, *"He* (God the Father) *shall see of the travail of his* (Jesus') *soul, and shall be satisfied: by his knowledge shall **my righteous servant** (Jesus) justify many, for he shall bear their iniquities."*

Thank God, our sin debt is paid!

Let's look again at Jesus' words in John 20:17:

> *"I ascend unto my Father, and your Father; and **to my***
> ***God and your God."***

Does Jesus have a God? **Yes!** Now, may I ask, Is **Jesus** your God, or is Jesus' **God** your God? **God is waiting for your answer!**

The doctrine of the Trinity is a **postscriptural attempt** to bring to coherent expression diverse affirmations about God...For Christians the one God appeared in what they called a threefold "economy," in, so to speak, three forms or modes. Difficulties soon emerged in formulating and understanding the threefold "economy." Catholic and Protestant theology has sought in various ways to **make the doctrine stated at Nicaea comprehensible**. In the religious thought of the Enlightenment (17th and 18th centuries) there was a strong reaction against Trinitarianism as an "orthodox" mystery without basis in either experience or reason.

Academic International Encyclopedia;
Lexicon Publications 1992 Edition
p. 300-301

Chapter 9

When Jesus Received Worship

"Then came to him the mother of Zebedee's children with her sons, worshiping him, and desiring a certain thing of him" (Matt. 20:20).

The mother of James and John brought her sons to Jesus and worshiped him, then told him her request:

"Grant that these, my two sons may sit, the one on thy right hand, and the other on thy left, in thy kingdom" (v. 21).

As a Hebrew, this mother knew what all Hebrews knew, that no man could be God, but in her heart she believed that the one whom she worshiped and made her request to was God's promised Messiah. As such he would soon have a kingdom, and she wanted a special place for her sons.

Jesus' answer is very enlightening:

*"To sit on my right hand, and on my left, is **not mine to give**, but it shall be given to them **for whom it is prepared of my Father**" (v. 23).*

His response to her teaches us several things about Jesus. One, there is someone over him, with greater authority than he, who has not told him all of His plan *(Mark 13:32, Rev. 1:1).* Number two, God had not given everything into his hands. Look at his words again, *"**It is not mine to give**, but it shall be given to them for whom **it is prepared** of my Father."*

This agrees with what Jesus said in Acts 1:7 in response to his disciples question, *"Wilt thou at this time restore again the kingdom of Israel?" And he said unto them, "It is not for you to know the times or the seasons, which the Father hath put **in his own power**."*

Yet he received this mother's worship. The statement is made that since

181

Jesus receives worship he must in fact be God. This chapter will prove from Scripture that that statement is not true.

While Jesus was on earth in God's stead, he received worship, and rightly so. Matthew 2:11 says of the wise men who came from the east, following a star:

> *"And when they were come into the house, they saw the young child with Mary his mother, and fell down, and worshiped him: and when they had opened their treasures, they presented unto him gifts; gold, and frankincense, and myrrh."*

Many other such events are recorded in the Bible.

▸ A leper needing healing came and worshiped him and he was healed. *(Matt. 8:2)*

▸ A certain ruler needing resurrection for his daughter, came and worshiped him and she was raised. *(Matt. 9:18)*

▸ After Jesus walked on the sea and calmed the storm, those who were in the ship worshiped him. *(Matt. 14:33)*

▸ Mary Magdalene and the other Mary, when they saw the risen Lord, came and held him by the feet and worshiped him. *(Matt. 28:9)*

▸ The man possessed with a legion of demons in Gadara, when he saw Jesus afar off, ran and worshiped him. *(Mark 5:6)*

▸ The blind man who was healed when he washed mud from his eyes in the pool of Siloam, found Jesus and worshiped him. *(John 9:38)*

But, you may ask, if Jesus is not Almighty God or "God the Son," second person of the triune God, why did he receive worship? That is a very good question and the answer is found in Hebrews 1:6:

> *"And again, when he* (God) *bringeth in the first begotten* (Jesus) *into the world, He saith, and let all the angels of God worship him."*

God had decreed worship for Jesus, His son, even from the angels. Jesus came as a man *(Matt. 8:20, Luke 9:58, I Tim. 2:5)* and as such **was made**, as are all men, lower than the angels *(Ps. 8:5, Heb. 2:7)*. Hebrews

2:9 says:

> *"But we see Jesus, **who was made** a little lower than the angels for the suffering of death, crowned with glory and honor; that he by the grace of God should taste death for every man."*

But by birth he is the Son of God *(Luke 1:35)* and has been exalted by his Father above the angels. Look at Hebrews 1:4-5:

> *"Being made so much better than the angels, as **he hath by inheritance** obtained a more excellent name than they. For unto which of the angels said he at any time, Thou art my Son, this day have I begotten thee? And again, I will be to him a Father, and he shall be to me a son?"*

Yes they worshiped him. God commanded it saying, *"Let all the angels of God worship him"*, (the Son). Not as God Almighty, **whose angels they are**, but as God's virgin born, sinless Son, under whom He *(God)* has *"put in subjection the world to come" (Heb. 2:5)*.

To comprehend this awesome truth we must understand that in the Scriptures, others beside the Most High were worshiped with His favor. When King David, the sweet psalmist of Israel began to grow old, he sat in his palace of cedar one day and realized that the Ark of the Great God of Israel rested not far away in a tent *(I Chron. 17:1, II Sam. 7:1-3)*. He called in Nathan the prophet of God and told him of his intention to build a beautiful house, a temple, to house the ark of God. Nathan's initial reaction was, *"Go, do all that is in thine heart, for the Lord is with thee."* However, that night God spoke to Nathan in a vision with a message for David that said in essence, "Not so fast! Yes, I am honored that you desire to build me a house and your son after you will indeed do that. But I know something that you don't know: I'm going to build you a house" (i.e. a dynasty) *(II Sam. 7:4-11, I Chron. 17:11-15)*. And there is more!

> *And it shall come to pass, when thy days be expired that thou must go to be with thy fathers, that **I will raise up***

**thy seed after thee, which shall be of thy sons; and I
will establish his kingdom.** *He shall build me a house,
and* **I will stablish his throne for ever.** *I will be his
father, and* **he shall be my son:** *and I will not take my
mercy away from him, as I took it from him that was
before thee: But I will settle him in mine house and in
my kingdom for ever: and* **his throne shall be
established for evermore.** *According to all this vision,
so did Nathan speak unto David" (I Chron. 17:11-15).*

Thus, God established his covenant with his servant King David, **"for
evermore."**

> *"And thine house and thy kingdom shall be established
> for ever before thee: thy throne shall be established for
> ever" (II Sam. 7:16).*

Look at the four things the eternal God promised David in this covenant
that is called "the Davidic Covenant." God promised David **a house**, a
dynasty, a "lineage", **forever.** Therefore the "House of David" is spoken of
throughout the remainder of the O.T., for hundreds of years after David is
dead and gone. We must remember that the "House of David" in Scripture
is only one part of the tribe of Judah, and is therefore different and distinct
from the "House of Israel" *(Jacob),* which is all twelve tribes. This is what
Luke 2:4 is referring to when it says that Joseph with his espoused wife
Mary went to Bethlehem, *"the City of David"* to be taxed, *"because he was
of the house and lineage of David."* This dynasty, house, tabernacle is what
Amos and the apostle James were referring to that God will raise up in the
last days *(Amos 9:11, Acts 15:16).*

Next, God promised David **a kingdom** and a *"throne for ever"* (I Chron.
17:11-12, 14).* Notice in verse 14 God calls this throne *"my throne."* That's
why I Chronicles 29:23 says, *"Then Solomon sat on **the throne of the Lord,** "*
at Jerusalem. This is the throne of which the angel Gabriel spoke to Mary:

> *"And the Lord God shall give unto him **the throne of
> his father David:** And he shall reign over the house of*

184

> *Jacob for ever; and of his kingdom there shall be no*
> *end" (Luke 1:32-33).*

Notice Jesus was not promised **God's throne in heaven**, but "the throne of his father David" in Jerusalem. **This is important!**

The third thing that God promised David was **mercy** laid up for his descendants.

> *"And I will not take my mercy away from him, as I took*
> *it from him that was before thee" (I Chron. 17:13).*

This is the mercy that God showed in not destroying Solomon, even after he went into idolatry. This is the mercy that was seen some 106 years after David's death during the violent and wicked reign of king Jehoram.

> *"Howbeit the Lord would not destroy the house of*
> *David, because of the covenant that he had made with*
> *David" (II Chron. 21:7).*

And about 305 years after David's death in the days of Hezekiah, God vowed to defend Jerusalem from the approaching Assyrian army with these words:

> *"For I will defend this city to save it for mine own sake,*
> *and for my servant David's sake" (Isa. 37:35).*

And finally, God promised David **"seed"** or sons.

> *"I will raise up thy seed after thee, which shall be of thy*
> *sons; and I will establish his kingdom" (I Chron.*
> *17:11).*

These sons of David, the Davidic line of kings, were also to be called "sons of God."

> *"I will be his father; and he shall be my son" (v. 13).*

To see that this did not **only** apply to Jesus, look at the account of this in II Samuel 7:14:

> *"If he commit iniquity, I will chasten him with the rod of*
> *men."*

These words "his father - my son" express the special relationship God promises to maintain with the descendants of David whom he will establish on David's throne. It marks them as the ones God has chosen to rule in His name, as the official representatives of God's rule. In Jesus *(Messiah)* this promise comes to ultimate fulfillment.

> *"The book of the generation of Jesus Christ the Son of David, the son of Abraham" (Matt. 1:1).*
>
> *"And there came a voice from heaven, saying, Thou art my beloved Son, in whom I am well pleased" (Mark 1:11).*

Now let's look at the coronation of King Solomon, David's son, God's "son," to sit "on the throne of the Lord," at Jerusalem.

> *"And David said to all the congregation, Now bless the Lord your God. And all the congregation blessed the Lord God of their fathers, and bowed down their heads, and **worshipped the Lord, and the king**" (I Chron. 29:20).*

Yes, that is what it says, they "worshiped the Lord, **and the king**." They worshiped the Lord as God *("thou art God alone" Ps. 86:10)* and they worshiped the king as God's appointed, anointed regent, God's son, and they did this with God's favor and approval.

> *"And did eat and drink **before the Lord** on that day with **great gladness**. And they made Solomon the son of David king the second time, **and anointed him unto the Lord**, to be the chief governor, Then **Solomon sat on the throne of the Lord** as king instead of David his father, and prospered; and all Israel obeyed him. And all the princes, and the mighty men, and all the sons likewise of king David, **submitted themselves unto Solomon the king**. And **the Lord magnified Solomon exceedingly** in the sight of all Israel, and bestowed upon him such **royal majesty** as had not been on any king before him in Israel. Thus David the son of Jesse reigned over all Israel" (I. Chron. 29:22-26).*

Now suppose that Solomon or Israel, after he was **magnified exceedingly** with such **royal majesty and power**, had decided that he was in fact God, or part of the Godhead. Do you think God's favor would have remained? No way! Look at King Herod who took God's glory to himself.

> *"And upon a set day Herod, arrayed in royal apparel, sat upon his throne, and made an oration unto them, And the people gave a shout, saying, **It is the voice of a god**, and not of a man. And immediately the angel of the Lord smote him, **because he gave not God the glory**; and he was eaten of worms, and gave up the ghost" (Acts 12:21-23).*

Unlike Herod, Solomon gave God the glory and was worshiped as God's anointed king, His "son," **with God's approval**.

We must be careful with "worship" because God is jealous of His glory *(honor - esteem)* and will not give it to another, but on rare occasions **He has ordained worship for others**. Look at what the Lord says to **overcoming saints** in Revelation 3:9:

> *"Behold, I will make them of the synagogue of Satan, which say they are Jews and do lie; behold, **I will make them to come and worship before thy feet**, and to know that I have loved thee. "*

Will these saints be worshiped? Yes! Will they be worshiped as God? **No way!** As deity? **No way!** But they will be worshiped as overcoming saints, **for God has ordained it**. With this understanding, lets see how Jesus Messiah was worshiped. Did the angels of God who worshiped him at his birth *(not before his birth)* think they were worshiping God? No! They saw God's face continually in heaven and knew that this baby was not God, but Messiah, son of David, Son of God *(Matt. 18:10; Rev. 5:11-13).*

> *"When he* (God) *bringeth in the first-begotten* (Jesus) ***into the world*** (not before)*, he* (God) *saith, and let all of the angels of God* (these are God's angels) *worship him* (Jesus) *" (Heb. 1:6).*

Did the wise men who found the babe in Bethlehem *"and fell down and worshiped him"* think they were looking at God? No, they had come to Jerusalem asking, *"Where is he that is born **King of the Jews** " (Matt. 2:2).* When Herod had his scribes search the Scriptures to see where Christ would be born they said:

> *"In Bethlehem of Judah: for thus it is written by the prophet, And thou Bethlehem, in the land of Judah, art not the least among the princes of Judah: for out of thee **shall come a Governor**, that shall **rule my people Israel"** (Matt. 2:5-6).*

They were not searching for God, but "a Governor" sent by God. And how did they know he would be "King of the Jews." They had "seen his star," but there is no way they could have read all this in the stars. They had no doubt read it in the chronicles of Babylon, for centuries before, Daniel, a wise man and prophet in Babylon, had seen visions and foretold the coming of Israel's Prince Messiah.

> *"Know therefore and understand, that from the going forth of the commandment to restore and to build Jerusalem unto the Messiah the Prince shall be seven weeks, and threescore and two weeks"* (69 weeks - 483 years) *(Dan. 9:25).* **And he was right on time!**

Did the disciples who worshiped Jesus in the boat, after he calmed the sea in Matthew 14:32-33, think they were worshiping him as God? Let's see. In Chapter 13:37-41, he had taught great lessons in which he twice called himself "the Son of man," a human being. He closes out the teaching by referring to himself as "a prophet" *(Matt. 13:57).* In Chapter 14 Jesus comes to the disciples walking on the sea and calms it.

> *"Then they that were in the ship came and worshipped him, saying, Of a truth thou art the Son of God" (Matt. 14:33).*

Did they think they were worshiping one in the boat with them who was in fact "God" or "God the Son?" No! They ate with him, slept with him,

188

saw that he grew weary, tired and hungry and had bodily functions as they did, and knew he was **a man**. They had asked among themselves on a previous and similar occasion *"What **manner of man** is this, that even the winds and the sea obey him" (Matt. 8:27)!* **He is the perfect man** but "man" nevertheless. This incident helped their understanding that this man is indeed Messiah, Son of God, proven by his resurrection as well *(Rom. 1:4)*. Listen to their words again; *"Of a truth thou art the Son of God."* No one in the scriptural accounts worshiped Jesus as the Lord God, and **we must not!** There are several Greek words in the N.T. that are translated "worship," and are pictured as being offered to God, Jesus, the saints of Revelation, and **improperly** to angels and idols. But there is one word "latreuo" *(#3000 Strongs)* which means "to minister to God - render religious homage" and is **not** in Scripture **given to Jesus** or anyone else **but God** *(Acts 24:14; Phil. 3:3; Heb. 10:2)*. To give Jesus the Son, God the Father's place in our hearts and in our worship is to flirt with idolatry. *"Thou shalt have no other gods* (plural) *before me* (singular)*" (Ex. 20:3)*. Jesus called his Father *"the only true God"* in John 17:3, and **He alone should be worshiped as God**. It is important to note that no place can be found in N.T. Scripture where anyone "worshiped" Jesus after his ascension to heaven, nor where any N.T. writer told us to "worship" him. He is now in the presence of God, seated at the right hand of God the Father, and our "worship" is to be directed to God.

"Now to appear in the presence of God for us" (Heb. 9:24).

Twice in the Revelation a scene is described where God and the Lamb are present and both receive praise, but only God is "worshiped" *(Rev. 5:12-14; 7:9-11)*.

Jesus never said he was God. In fact he denied that he is *(Matt. 19:17, John 5:19, 30-31)*. If he was God he would have told us; he would not have left us wondering about such a serious matter as this.

David's "great son" and God's "son" Solomon received worship with God's approval. David's "greater son" Jesus Christ *("Behold a greater than*

189

Solomon is here" Matt 12:42) received worship as ordained by God his Father. Jesus was worshiped as Savior, Redeemer, Messiah, Son of God.

> *"Saying with a loud voice, **Worthy is the Lamb** that was slain to receive power, and riches, and wisdom, and strength, and honor, and glory, and blessing" (Rev. 5:12).* Please note that the word **"worship" is not included.**

But Jesus joins us in **worshiping** the "only true God," **his God** and **our God**.

> *"We know what* (whom) *we worship"* (Jesus speaking) *(John 4:22).*
>
> *"Thou shalt worship the Lord thy God, and him only shalt thou serve"* (Jesus speaking) *(Luke 4:8).*
>
> *"But the hour cometh, and now is, when the **true** worshipers shall **worship the Father** in spirit and in truth: for the **Father seeketh such to worship him.** God is a Spirit; and they that **worship him** must **worship him** in spirit and in truth"* (Jesus speaking) *(John 4:23-24).* Notice, **Jesus says that** *"true worshipers"...""worship the Father"* who is *"a Spirit".* Jesus is not a spirit nor is he God the Father, he is a man *(Luke 24:39; John 8:40).*
>
> *"A certain woman named Lydia...which **worshiped God"** (Acts 16:14).*
>
> *"And entered into a certain man's house, named Justus, one that **worshiped God"** (Acts 18:7).*
>
> *"This fellow* (Paul) *persuadeth men to **worship God"** (Acts 18:13).*
>
> *"So **worship** I the **God** of my fathers...and have hope toward God"* (Paul speaking) *(Acts 24:14-15).*
>
> *"And there come in one that believeth not...and so falling down on his face he will **worship God"** (I. Cor.*

14:24-25).

"For we are the circumcision, which **worship God** *in the spirit, and rejoice in Christ Jesus" (Phil. 3:3).* What is that again Paul? **"We worship God and rejoice in Christ Jesus."**

"Stand up and bless **the Lord your God** *for ever and ever: Thou, even* **thou, art Lord alone; thou hast made heaven, the heaven of heavens, with all their host, the earth, and all things that are therein, the seas, and all that is therein,** *and thou preservest them all; and* **the host of heaven worshipeth thee.** *Thou camest down also upon mount Sinai, and* **spakest with them from heaven,** *and gavest them right judgements...and according to thy manifold mercies thou gavest them* **saviours,** *who saved them out of the hand of their enemies" (Nehemiah 9:5-6, 13, 27).*

(An angel) *"Saying with a loud voice,* **Fear God,** *and* **give glory to him;** *for the hour of his judgement is come: and* **worship him** *that made heaven, and earth, and the sea, and the fountains of waters" (Revelation 14:7).*

"Worship God" *(Rev. 21:10).*
"Worship God" *(Rev. 22:9).*

191

(The solar system could only have proceeded) "from the counsel and dominion of an intelligent and powerful being," (and the universe of stars) "must be all subject to the dominion of One...This Being governs all things, not as the soul of the world but as Lord over all: And on account of his dominion he is wont to be called Lord God...The father is the ancient of days and hath life in himself originally essentially and independently from all eternity, and hath given the son to have life in himself John 5.26. The father hath knowledge and prescience *(foreknowledge)* in himself and communicates knowledge and prescience to the son...We may give the names of Gods to other Beings as is frequently done in scripture. Angels and Princes who have power and dominion over us we may call Gods but **we are to have no other gods in our worship but him who in the fourth commandment is said to have made the heavens and earth; which is the character of God the father**...The reason why the *Son* in the New Testament is sometimes stiled *God* is not so much upon Account of his *metaphysical Substance*, how Divine soever; as his *relative Attributes* and divine *Authority* over us." [1]

Sir Isaac Newton (1642 – 1727)

Chapter 10

How Paul Prayed

"Now I beseech you, brethren, for the Lord Jesus
Christ's sake, and for the love of the Spirit, that ye strive
*together with me **in your prayers to God** for me" (Rom.*
15:30).

*"For this cause I bow my knees unto the **Father of our***
***Lord Jesus Christ**" (Eph. 3:14).*

In our effort to understand God the Father and His relationship to our
Lord Jesus Christ and to know to whom our prayers should be directed, it
would be helpful to study the prayers of the great apostle Paul. He was a
man mightily used of God, *"an apostle of Jesus" (II Cor. 1:1), "the apostle*
of the Gentiles" (Rom. 11:13), "not a whit behind the very chiefest apostles"
(II Cor. 11:5), and *"was caught up into paradise, and heard unspeakable*
words, which it is not lawful for a man to utter" (II Cor. 12:4). He is a man
certainly qualified to write on the subject of prayer, and one whose example
we can follow.

HOW PAUL SAID HE PRAYED.

First, let's look at Paul's writings and see to whom he said he prayed.

*"For this cause I bow my knees unto the **Father of our***
***Lord Jesus Christ**" (Eph. 3:14).*

*"I thank **my God** upon every remembrance of you,*
*Always in **every prayer of mine** for you all **making***
***request** with joy" (Phil. 1:3-4).*

*"We give **thanks to God** and the **Father** of our Lord*
Jesus Christ, praying always for you" (Col. 1:3).

*"For what thanks can we render **to God** again for you,*
*for all the joy wherewith we joy for your sakes **before***
***our God**" (I Thess. 3:9).*

> *"Being enriched in every thing to all bountifulness,*
> *which causeth through us thanksgiving **to God** "(II Cor.*
> *9:11).*
>
> *"I thank **my God**, making mention of thee always **in my***
> ***prayers** "(Phm. 1:4).*

So Paul said in the six foregoing verses that he prayed to **God the Father**. We know for sure that is what he said, so that is what he practiced. I found 34 instances of Paul in prayer in Acts and in his epistles, and we will look at them in order to learn by his example.

In Acts Chapter 9, Paul *(Saul)* was on his way to Damascus to persecute the Church and had an encounter with Jesus, which left him blinded. He was led by his friends on to Damascus and continued without sight, neither eating nor drinking for three days. The Lord Jesus spoke to a disciple of that city by the name of Ananias, telling him where to find Saul, and to pray for him to receive sight. The Lord said to Ananias, *"for behold he prayeth."* There is no indication in this account as to whom he was directing his prayers, but in his recounting of his conversion in Acts 22, he gives this quote from Ananias to him.

> ***"The God of our fathers** hath chosen thee, that thou*
> *shouldest know **his will**, and see that Just One* (Jesus),
> *and shouldest hear the voice of his mouth "(Acts 22:14).*

"The God of our fathers" is the Hebrew God of the O.T. to whom he probably was praying, but since it doesn't say specifically who Saul was praying to, we will put a question mark by the prayers at the time of his conversion, until we see more clearly to whom he prayed thereafter.

We do know what Paul's **first sermon** was after his conversion, for Acts 9:20 says that *"straightway he preached Christ in the synagogues, **that he is the Son of God.**"* Notice, **not that he is God**, or the second person of the triune God, but "the Son of God." This is the message that he continued to preach throughout his ministry.

Now, for the second Bible account of Paul in prayer, look at Acts 16 where Paul and Silas had been beaten and shackled in Philippi, and thrown into jail.

> *"And at midnight **Paul and Silas prayed, and sang***
> ***praises unto God**: and the prisoners heard them. (Acts*
> *16:25).* So they sang and prayed **to God**.

Later in Acts Chapter 27, Paul was on a ship bound for Rome as a prisoner, when they encountered a severe storm and no one on board ate food for 14 days. Paul had a visit from an angel of the Lord and was told that there would be no loss of life. Paul spoke words of encouragement to all of his shipmates and verse 35 says:

> *"And when he had thus spoken, he took bread, **and gave***
> ***thanks to God** in presence of them all; and when he*
> *had broken it, he began to eat" (Acts 27:35).* Again,
> **"to God."**

When Paul and his companions were safely back on land they continued on their journey to Rome. Acts 28:15 says:

> *"And from thence, when the brethren heard of us, they*
> *came to meet us as far as Appi forum, and the three*
> *taverns: whom when Paul saw, **he thanked God, and***
> ***took courage"**(Acts 28:15).*

Now we will look at the accounts of Paul praying, as recorded in his epistles, Romans through Philemon. *(Since the authorship of Hebrews is questioned by some we will discuss it in another chapter).* Because they are 30 in number we will only list the location of each prayer and a quote from the Scripture as to whom it was addressed. [1]

Location of Prayer in Scripture	To Whom it was Addressed
Romans 1:9-10	"God"
Romans 10:1	"God"
Romans 15:5-6	"God"
Romans 15:13	"God"
Romans 15:30	"God"
Romans 16:25-27	"God"
I Corinthians 1:4-9	"God"

195

II Corinthians 1:3-5	"God even the Father"
II Corinthians 2:14	"God"
II Corinthians 9:12-15	"God"
II Corinthians 13:7-9	"God"
Ephesians 1:15-23	"God"
Ephesians 3:14-21	"the Father of our Lord Jesus Christ"
Philippians 1:9-11	"God"
Philippians 4:20	"God our Father"
Colossians 1:9-12	"the Father" (God)
I Thessalonians 1:2-4	"God"
I Thessalonians 2:13	"God"
I Thessalonians 3:11-13	"God"
I Thessalonians 5:23-24	"God"
II Thessalonians 1:11-12	"God"
II Thessalonians 2:13-17	"God"
II Thessalonians 3:5	"the Lord...God"
II Thessalonians 3:16	"the Lord of peace"
I Timothy 1:17	"God"
I Timothy 6:13-17	"God" "whom no man hath seen"
II Timothy 1:3	"God"
II Timothy 1:16-18	"The Lord" (God)
II Timothy 4:14-18	"God"
Philemon 4-6	"God"

It is very enlightening to look at these 30 prayers and see that each one was prayed **to God the Father**. I cannot find where Paul clearly prayed one prayer to the Lord Jesus; it was always to God. Neither have I found where any other apostle prayed to Jesus after his ascension, nor where any N.T. writer told us to address our prayers to Jesus. The closest thing I have found from Paul's writings, in regard to a prayer to Jesus is in I Tim. 1:11-12:

> *"According to the glorious gospel of the blessed God, which was committed to my trust. **And I thank Christ Jesus our Lord**, who hath enabled me, for that he*

*counted me faithful, **putting** me into the ministry."*

Is this a prayer or is it an attitude of the heart? You be the judge. Look at verse 17 **of this same Chapter:**

> *"Now unto the **King eternal, immortal, invisible, the only wise God,** be honor and glory for ever and ever. Amen."*

The **"king eternal, immortal, invisible"** is none other than the Lord God, the Father, whom Paul called **"the only wise God."**

Now let's look at how Paul spoke in regard to the prayers of us, the Lord's saints:

> *"Be careful for nothing; but in every thing by prayer and supplication with thanksgiving **let your requests be made known unto God.** And the peace of God, which passeth all understanding, shall keep your hearts and minds through Christ Jesus"(Phil. 4:6-7).*

> *"I exhort therefore, that, first of all, **supplications, prayers, intercessions,** and **giving of thanks,** be made for all men; For kings, and for all that are in authority; that we may lead a quiet and peaceable life in all godliness and honesty. For this is good and acceptable **in the sight of God our Savior; For there is one God,** and **one mediator between God and men, the man Christ Jesus"** (I Tim. 2:1-3, 5).*

> *"Testifying both to the Jews, and also to the Greeks, **repentance toward God,** and faith toward our Lord Jesus Christ" (Acts 20:21).*

Please note, our faith is toward our Lord Jesus Christ *(in the work he did on the cross)*, but our **repentance** is **toward God.**

> *"Judge in yourselves: is it comely that a woman **pray unto God** uncovered"*(without hair) *(I Cor. 11:13)?*

> *"Withal **praying also** for us, **that God** would open us a door of utterance, to speak the mystery of Christ, for*

197

which I am also in bonds" (Col. 4:3).

"Now I beseech you, brethren, for the Lord Jesus Christ's sake,...that ye strive together with me in your prayers to God for me" (Rom. 15:30).

"He that eateth, eateth to the Lord, for he giveth God thanks: and he that eateth not, to the Lord he eateth not, and giveth God thanks" (Rom. 14:6).

"For it is written, As I live, saith the Lord, every knee shall bow to me, and every tongue shall confess to God. So then every one of us shall give account of himself to God" (Rom. 14:11-12).

The Lord to whom "every knee shall bow" in verse 11 above is the **Lord God**. Paul is quoting from Isa. 45:23 but look at verses 22 and 23 to see who was speaking:

"Look unto me, and be ye saved, all the ends of the earth: for I am God, and there is none else. I have sworn by myself, the word is gone out of my mouth in righteousness, and shall not return, That unto me every knee shall bow, every tongue shall swear."

And yes, one day every knee will bow to God's son, Jesus.

"Wherefore, God also hath highly exalted him, and given him a name which is above every name: That at the name of Jesus every knee should bow, of things in heaven, and things in earth, and things under the earth; And that every tongue should confess that Jesus Christ is Lord, to the glory of God the Father" (Phil. 2:9-11).

"To the glory of God the Father," for He is the one who decreed this honor for His Son.

Look at I Cor. 14 and see that speaking in tongues is prayer or praise to God.

"For he that speaketh in an unknown tongue, speaketh not unto men, but unto God: for no man understandeth

198

> *him; howbeit in the spirit he speaketh mysteries "(v. 2).*
>
> *"For if I **pray in an unknown tongue**, my spirit prayeth, but my understanding is unfruitful" (v. 14).*
>
> *"What is it then? **I will pray** with the spirit, and **I will pray** with the understanding also "(v. 15).*
>
> *"For thou verily **givest thanks** well, but the other is not edified" (v. 17).*
>
> *"But if there be no interpreter, let him keep silence in the church; and let him speak to himself, **and to God"** (v. 28).*

Luke the author of Acts agrees:

> *"For they heard them speak with tongues, and **magnify God"** (Acts 10:46).*

I must confess that I have only seen these truths regarding to whom we should pray, in the past few weeks. A few months ago I was still praying to God the Father, and to Jesus. Up until the last few years I had prayed to Jesus, believing that he was in fact God the Father. My belief was called "Oneness" or "Jesus Only." In another Chapter I mentioned how I found the apostles' prayer in Acts Chapter 4 to **God the Father**, in *"the name of thy holy child Jesus: (v. 27, 30).* That was the beginning of my awakening.

I must say however that my family and I have had many prayers answered through the years by praying to Jesus. We did it in sincerity and God was gracious. In our ministry since 1959, through prayer we have seen healing for cancer, asthma, Crohn's disease, shingles and various other afflictions and diseases miraculously through prayer. In our family we have seen the dead raised to life again by calling on the name of Jesus. We have seen marriages healed and lives restored while praying to Jesus. But perhaps we could have been much more effective if we had approached God in the manner that He has prescribed in His word. In the past few weeks, as I have begun to see how Paul and the other apostles prayed, I became more aware of the public prayers of my fellow ministers. In one service the minister who opened with prayer prayed his entire prayer to Jesus. Three nights later another minister addressed the opening of his prayer to God and closed in the name of Jesus. In a wonderful service in another church this week a fine brother started off praying to "our Lord God"; later in the prayer he called him Jesus and thanked him for dying on the cross. He ended in Jesus name. Of course our "Lord God" did not die on the cross, but our Lord Jesus Messiah surely did.

But we are learning. And as we do, I believe that God the Father will require us to approach Him properly, in order to see our prayers answered. There is a protocol to approaching God. He is the **Great King**. We **enter His gates with thanksgiving and His courts with praise;** then we approach boldly **to His throne of grace**, in the **name of His son Jesus**. *(In Jesus' righteous worthiness, claiming what he purchased for us on Calvary, Isa. 53:5).*

If you have ever had a prayer answered, **God answered it!**

> *"But my **God** shall supply all your need according to **his riches** in glory by Christ Jesus "*(Paul) *(Phil. 4:19)*
> *"Every good gift and every perfect gift is from above, and cometh down from the **Father** of lights, with whom is no variableness, neither shadow of turning" (James 1:17).*

Jesus prayed to God the Father always, and this was not just a formality or to set a good example.

> *"And in the morning, rising up a great while before day, he went out, and departed into a solitary place, **and there prayed" (Mark 1:35).***
> *"And he withdrew himself into the wilderness, **and prayed" (Luke 5:16).***
> *"And it came to pass in those days, that he went out into **a mountain to pray**, and continued **all night in prayer to God" (Luke 6:12).*** (Jesus prayed **"to God"**).
> *"He took Peter and John and James, and went up into a mountain **to pray. And as he prayed**, the fashion of his*

> *countenance was altered, and his raiment was white and glistering (glistening)" (Luke 9:28-29).*
>
> *"And when he had sent the multitudes away, he went up into a mountain apart **to pray**" (Matt. 14:23).*
>
> *"Then were there brought unto him little children, that he should **put his hands on them, and pray**" (Matt. 19:13).*
>
> *"Then cometh Jesus with them unto a place called Gethsemane, and saith unto the disciples, Sit ye here, **while I go and pray** yonder" (Matt. 26:36).*
>
> *"And **being in an agony he prayed more earnestly**: and his sweat was as it were great drops of blood falling down to the ground" (Luke 22:44).*
>
> *"Who in the days of his flesh, when he had offered up **prayers and supplications** with **strong crying and tears** unto him (God) that was able to save him from death, and was heard in that he feared" (Heb. 5:7).*

Jesus was a praying man and he prayed to the one whom he called in John 20:17, *"my Father and your Father; and to my God, and your God."* Prayer is a declaration of dependence upon God, and Jesus always prayed.

Look at what he taught his disciples regarding prayer in the closing days of his earthly ministry;

> *"Again I say unto you, that if two of you shall agree on earth as touching any thing that they shall ask, it shall be done for them **of my Father** which is in heaven" (Matt. 18:19).*
>
> *"If ye then, being evil, know how to give good gifts unto your children: how much more **shall your heavenly Father give the Holy Spirit to them that ask him**" (Luke 11:13)?* Notice, *"That ask **him**....your heavenly Father."*
>
> *"**And whatsoever ye shall ask in my name**, that will I*

*do, that the **Father may be glorified** in the Son. **If ye
shall ask any thing in my name**, I will do it. If ye love
me, keep my commandments. **And I will pray the
Father**, and he shall give you another Comforter, that
he may abide with you for ever" (John 14:13-16).*

Notice, Jesus did not say "**ask me**", he said, "**Ask in my name**." "That
will **I do**," means he, Jesus, acts as the Father's agent in answering prayer. In
Matthew Chapter 9 Jesus saw the multitudes as sheep without a shepherd
and he was moved with compassion. He said to his disciples:

*"Pray ye therefore the Lord of the harvest (not himself),
that **he** will send forth labourers into **his** harvest"
(Matt. 9:38).*

He is saying in essence:

*"Pray to God about this problem." ("My father is the
husbandman," John 15:1).*

*"**And in that day ye shall ask me nothing.** Verily,
Verily, I say unto you, **Whatsoever ye shall ask the
Father in my name, he will give it you**" (John 16:23)*

*"**Hitherto have ye asked nothing in my name: Ask,
and ye shall receive**, that your joy may be full" (John
16:24).* Jesus had not included his name in the prayer
he had taught them earlier called "The Lord's Prayer"
(Matt. 6:9-13).

*"These things have I spoken unto you in proverbs:...but
I shall show you plainly **of the Father**" (John 16:25).*
Jesus is teaching them something new.

*"**At that day ye shall ask in my name**: and I say not
unto you, that **I will pray the Father** for you" (John
16:26).*

Notice Jesus words "at that day" and realize **that this was to be after
Jesus went to the Father**. Jesus prays *("to request, entreat, beseech")* for us
in heaven. *"I will pray for you."* Look at Hebrews 7:25:

202

"Seeing he ever liveth to **make intercession** ("entreat in favor of") *for them. "*

"Who is even at the right hand of God, who also **maketh intercession** *for us" (Rom. 8:34).*

Jesus' closest friends knew that while he was on earth he prayed to God for their needs. Look at what Martha said at the tomb of her dead brother Lazarus:

"Then said Martha unto Jesus, Lord, if thou hadst been here, my brother had not died. But I know that **even now, whatsoever thou wilt ask God, God will give it thee"** *(John 11:21-22).*

Brethren we must learn the lesson that Jesus taught in John 16. God desires to answer our prayers, but **we must pray to God the Father, in Jesus name**. Again, "in that day **ye shall ask me nothing**." This is **asking in prayer**. We all have lost loved ones, sick friends, we live in a dying world, and Israel is still blinded to whom her Messiah is. **We need prayers answered**!

"If any man be a **worshiper of God...him he heareth** *"* (in prayer) *(John 9:31).* We must get our worship right!

"The **Father** *seeketh such to* **worship him** *" (John 4:23).*

"If any of you lack wisdom, let him **ask of God**, *that giveth to all men liberally...and it shall be given him" (James 1:5).*

James says again *(regarding the use of the tongue):*

"Therewith **bless we God**, *even the Father" (James 3:9).*

"And if ye **call on the Father**... *" (I Peter 1:17).*

"Ye also...offer up spiritual sacrifices, acceptable **to God** *by* **Jesus Christ** *" (I Peter 2:5).*

"Giving thanks always for all things **unto God and the Father** *in the* **name of our Lord Jesus Christ** *"* (Paul) *(Eph. 5:20).*

WHAT ABOUT OUR PRACTICE OF ASKING JESUS TO COME

INTO OUR HEARTS?

Let's see what Paul says:

> **"God hath sent forth** *the Spirit of his Son* **into your hearts**, *crying Abba, Father" (Gal. 4:6).*
>
> *"For this cause* **I bow my knees unto the Father** *of our Lord Jesus Christ...that Christ may dwell* **in your hearts** *by faith" (Eph. 3:14, 17).*
>
> *"Now he which stablisheth us with you in Christ, and hath anointed us,* **is God**; *Who hath also sealed us, and given the earnest of the Spirit* **in our hearts**" *(II Cor. 1:21-22).*

As we end this chapter, let's look again at what Paul says in Philippians 4:19:

> *"But* **my God** *shall supply all your need according to* **his riches** *in glory* **by** *Christ Jesus. "*

WHO WAS PAUL'S <u>GOD</u> WHO SUPPLIES ALL OF OUR NEED <u>BY</u> CHRIST JESUS?

Verse 20 says:

> *"Now unto* **God** *and our* **Father** *be glory forever and ever. Amen" (***"One** *is your* **Father**, *which is in heaven" - "Not any man hath seen the Father" - "I ascend unto* **my Father**, *and* **your Father**; *and to* **my God** *and* **your God")** (Jesus speaking) *(Matt. 23:9; John 6:46; 20:17).*

> *"And whatsoever ye do in word or deed, do all in the name of the Lord Jesus, giving thanks* **to God** *and the Father* **by him**" *(Col. 3:17).*

Let's pray to **God the Father,** in Jesus name. Paul did!

Chapter 11

Another Jesus

*"**But I fear**, lest by any means, as the serpent beguiled*
Eve through his subtilty, so your minds should be
corrupted from the simplicity that is in Christ. For if he
*that cometh preacheth **another Jesus, whom we have***
***not preached**, or if ye receive another spirit, which ye*
have not received, or another gospel, which ye have not
accepted, ye might well bear with him" (II Cor. 11:3-4).

et us receive, believe, and understand clearly what the Bible says about Jesus. He is **a man**. To Peter in Acts 2:22, he is *"Jesus of Nazareth, **a man*** ***approved of God.** "* To John the Baptist he is *"the Lamb of God...**a man*** *which is preferred before me. "* To Jesus himself he is *"**a man** that hath told you the truth. "* His favorite title for himself was "Son of man," *(a human being)* taken from Psalm 8:4 and ascribed to Jesus in Hebrews 2:6-9. Paul says in I Tim. 2:3-6:

> *"For this is good and acceptable in the sight of **God our***
> ***Savior**; Who will have all men to be saved and come*
> *unto the knowledge of the truth.* (What truth?) *For*
> *there is **one God**, and **one mediator** between God and*
> *men, **the man Christ Jesus**; Who gave himself a*
> *ransom for all, to be testified in due time. "*

And Jesus will always be **a glorified man**.

> *"Jesus Christ the same yesterday, and today, and*
> *forever. " (Heb. 13:8).*

Please accept and understand this truth: The eternal salvation that Jesus the Messiah purchased for us through his death on the cross, he purchased as a sinless **man**, not a "God-man" who could escape into Godhood when he was tempted and the going got rough. *God cannot be tempted (James 1:13)!* Jesus was *"tempted of the devil" (Matt. 4:1), "hath suffered being tempted" (Heb. 2:18), "and was in all points tempted like as we are, yet without sin" (Heb. 4:15).* **God cannot die!** He is *"the King eternal,* **immortal,** *invisible, the only wise God" (I Tim 1:17).* He *"who* **only hath immortality,** *dwelling in the light which no man can approach unto; whom no man* **hath seen nor can see** *(I Tim 6:16).* Jesus was **mortal; he died!** But that is the good news, **the Gospel**, that Jesus **a man**, the perfect **man**, the mirror image of God *(II Cor. 3:18, 4:4)*, the "express image" of God's person, was crucified but arose from the grave three days later, victorious over death, hell, and the grave. He did it as **a man**, empowered by God. He said in John 10:17-18:

> *"Therefore doth my Father love me, because I lay down my life, that I might take it again. I have power to lay it down, and I have power to take it again. This commandment have I received of my Father."*

"He tasted death for **every man** *" (Heb. 2:9).* He *"abolished death and brought life and immortality to light through the gospel" (II Tim. 1:10).* Because he forever lives, we shall live forever! He came back from the grave *"with the keys of hell and of death" (Rev. 1:18).* He did it as a man (human) "in his flesh" *(Eph. 2:15).* Paul said he did in I Cor. 15:20-23:

> *"But now is Christ risen from the dead, and become the* **firstfruits** *of them that* **slept.** *For since* **by man came death, by man came also the resurrection of the dead.** *For as* **in Adam all die,** *even so* **in Christ shall all be made alive.** *But* **every man** *in his own order:* **Christ the firstfruits; afterward they that are Christ's** *at his coming."*

Herein lies the danger in our modern religious thinking, which is not based on the O.T. concept of God but is tainted by post-biblical Greek philosophy. We have robbed **God of His Godhood**, *("God is not a man..."*

206

Num. 23:19, I Sam. 15:29), and robbed **Jesus of his manhood** *(one billion "Catholics" call Mary, "mother of God")*. The Greeks believed that men became gods and gods became men. **A man cannot be God.** H. L. Goudge made this enlightening statement in his work, *"The Calling of the Jews"*: "When the Greek mind and the Roman mind, instead of the Hebrew mind came to dominate the church, there occurred **a disaster** from which the Church has never recovered, either in doctrine or practice." [1] This is the thinking that will soon lead our world to delusion and destruction as they worship a **man who claims to be God**.

> *"Let no man deceive you by any means: for that day shall not come, except there come a falling away first, and that **man of sin** be revealed, **the son of perdition; Who opposeth** and **exalteth himself above all that is called God**, or that is worshipped; so that **he as God** sitteth in the temple of God, **shewing himself that he is God**. Remember ye not, that, when I was yet with you, I told you these things? And now ye know what withholdeth that he might be **revealed in his time. For the mystery of iniquity doth already work**: only he who now letteth will let, (hindereth will hinder) until he be taken out of the way. And then shall that Wicked be revealed, whom the Lord shall consume with the spirit of his mouth, and shall destroy with the brightness of his coming: Even him (anti-christ), whose coming is after the working of Satan with all power and signs and lying wonders, And with all deceivableness of unrighteousness in them that perish; because **they received not the love of the truth**, that they might be saved. And **for this cause shall God send them strong delusion, that they should believe a lie**: That they all might be damned who **believed not the truth**, but had pleasure in unrighteousness" (II Thess. 2:3-12).*

Error is unrighteousness! And Paul ends his discussion of this subject with verses 15 & 16:

> *"Therefore, brethren, stand fast, and hold the traditions which ye have been taught, whether **by word, or our epistle** (not of men). Now **our Lord Jesus Christ** himself, and **God, even our Father**, which hath loved us, and hath given us everlasting consolation and good hope through grace, **Comfort your hearts**, and **stablish you** in every good word and work."*

Brethren, we must get this right! John the beloved apostle says in II John 6-7:

> *"And this is love, that we walk after his commandments. **This is the commandment, That, as ye have heard from the beginning, ye should walk in it.** For many deceivers are entered into the world, who confess not that Jesus Christ **is come in the flesh.** This is a deceiver and an antichrist."*

Perhaps John had heard that some had taken his writings regarding the "Word," "the logos," in the preface of The Gospel of John and had begun to teach that Jesus was preexistent deity, God incarnate in the womb of Mary. It is very much on his mind in his epistles that *"Jesus Christ is come in the flesh,"* **a man, human.** (He mentions it 3 times) He says in I John 4:2-3:

> **Hereby know ye the Spirit of God: Every spirit that confesseth that Jesus Christ is come in the flesh is of God: And every spirit that confesseth not that Jesus Christ is come in the flesh is not of God: and this is that spirit of antichrist,** *whereof ye have heard that it should come; and even now already is it in the world."*

These false teachers were **not denying that Jesus Christ had come**, but that **"Jesus Christ had come in the flesh"** *(a human).* John called that the spirit of anti-christ and said that it was "already in the world," at work in his day. If we look we can see its influence around us today, even in the way

208

bibles are translated. God is the custodian of His Word and has given us all we need in the Holy Bible. I believe the King James Version of 1611 is the best, but we must read it also with understanding. Its translators were Trinitarian in belief, and that influence can be seen in the words they supplied in italics. These words in italics were not in the original and may or may not add to the true meaning of the text. Take I John 3:16, *"Hereby perceive we the love of God,* because he laid down his life for us*"*. The word *"God"* is in italics, and it was not *"God"* who died for us. God cannot die! The translators were mistaken. John was there and saw the crucifixion and heard Jesus cry, "My God, my God, why hast thou forsaken me," and he knew that it was not "God" who died, but the virgin-born, sinless Son of God, **"a man"** who died! John said in I John 2:22:

> *"Who is a liar but he that denieth that Jesus is the*
> *Christ?* ***He is antichrist, that denieth the Father and***
> ***the Son. "***

Do you see what John is saying? "He is antichrist that denieth the Father and the Son." The word "and" is a conjunction and means "in addition to," so John says that he is antichrist that denieth the Father **in addition to** the Son. *(This is God's word, not mine).* The Son is not God the Father of whom Jesus spoke so much (*"...their angels do always behold the face of my Father which is in heaven"* *Matt. 18:10),* nor **is** God the Father, Jesus, though **He was in him** through the fullness of His Spirit.

Look at I John 2:23:

> "Whosoever denieth the Son, the same hath not the
> Father*: [but] he that acknowledgeth the Son hath the*
> *Father also. "*

The first part of that verse is true, the Word of God, but the last part is in italics, *"***[but]** *he that acknowledgeth the Son hath the Father also, "*was not written by John and may or may not be true. Many are acknowledging the Son today, all the while **denying** "the Father." The Bible teaches that we have one Father, **God**. *"Have we not all* **one Father***? hath not* **one God** *created us"(Mal. 2:10)?* Jesus said in Matthew 23:9, *"And call no man your* *father upon the earth: for* **one is your Father, which is in heaven** *"*(While Jesus was on earth, God was in heaven.) *(Matt. 5:45, 22:30, Mark 11:26, Luke 11:2).*

Why such a concerted effort by so many over such a long period of time to elevate Jesus to the place of God? First, John says it is driven by a "spirit," the spirit of Lucifer, the one who was the first to try to assume God's place, him that Paul called *"the mystery of iniquity" (II Thess. 2:7).*

This is the spirit of Lucifer that God told us of by the prophet Isaiah:

> *How art thou fallen from heaven,* **O Lucifer,** *son of the morning! How art thou cut down to the ground, which didst weaken the nations! For thou hast said in thine heart,* **I will ascend** *into heaven,* **I will exalt my throne above the stars of God**: *I will sit also upon the mount of the congregation, in the sides of the north:* **I will ascend** *above the heights of the clouds;* **I will be like the most High**. *Yet thou shalt be brought down to hell, to the sides of the pit" (Isa. 14:12-15).*

If my understanding of the Bible is correct, Lucifer was created as an angel *(the "anointed cherub" of Ezek. 28:14)*, along with all other angels, called sons of God, and they were present while God completed His creative work. God told Job that these created *"sons of God shouted for joy "* while He created *(Job 38:7).* But **God did not create sin**. These sons of God were given a certain amount of "free will," and sin arose through pride and rebellion in the heart of Lucifer. Please note, God created **the possibility of sin,** free will. When another being has a will, there is the possibility that **that will** may diverge from God's. This is not God's doing, and He cannot be blamed for the result. God is all righteous, **and He did not create sin!** When God says in Isaiah 45:7, *"I form the light and create darkness: I make peace and create evil, "*He is not speaking of "sin." God is saying He creates light...and the opposite "darkness," He creates peace...and the opposite "trouble." In scripture, "evil" often means "trouble." In Ecclesiastes 12:1, Solomon calls the days of old age "evil days," not days of sin but days of trouble. Some people teach in error that Satan and sin are only the dark side of God. **God has no dark side!** *"God is light, and in Him is no darkness at all" (I John 1:5).* God spoke to the prophet Ezekiel regarding the prince *(king)* of Tyre in Ezekiel 28:2, 5-6, 9, who must have been a very proud man.

> *"Son of man, say unto the prince of Tyre, Thus saith the Lord GOD; Because thine heart is lifted up, and **thou hast said, I am a God, I sit in the seat of God**, in the midst of the seas; yet **thou art a man, and not God, though thou set thine heart as the heart of God**: By thy great wisdom and by thy traffic hast thou increased thy riches, **and thine heart is lifted** up because of thy riches: **Therefore thus saith the Lord GOD;** Because thou hast **set thine heart as the heart of God; Wilt thou yet say before him that slayeth thee, I am God? But thou shalt be a man, and no God**, in the hand of him that slayeth thee."*

God speaks again to the king of Tyre in verses 12-17, but obviously is speaking past the king to the Prince of evil, Lucifer, who had motivated him to such heights of haughtiness and pride:

> *"Thus saith the Lord GOD; Thou sealest up the sum, full of wisdom, and perfect in beauty. **Thou hast been in Eden the garden of God;** every precious stone was thy covering, the sardius, topaz, and the diamond, the beryl, the onyx, and the jasper, the sapphire, the emerald, and the carbuncle, and gold: the workmanship of thy tabrets and of thy pipes was prepared in thee in the day that thou was created. **Thou art the anointed cherub** that covereth; **and I have set thee so: thou wast upon the holy mountain of God;** thou hast walked up and down in the midst of the stones of fire. **Thou wast perfect in thy ways from the day that thou wast***

*created, till iniquity was found in thee. By the multitude of thy merchandise they have filled the midst of thee with violence, and thou hast sinned: therefore **I will cast thee as profane out of the mountain of God:** and **I will destroy thee, O covering cherub,** from the midst of the stones of fire. **Thine heart was lifted up because of thy beauty,** thou hast corrupted thy wisdom by reason of thy brightness: **I will cast thee to the ground,** I will lay thee before kings, that they may behold thee. "*

We learn much from these verses regarding the one that Jesus called *"the devil" (John 8:44),* *"Satan " (Luke 22:31),* *"a murderer " and "the father of lies " (John 8:44),* and whom other Scriptures identify as *"destroyer " (Rev. 9:11),* *"angel of the bottomless pit " (Rev. 9:11),* *"prince of this world " (John 12:31),* *prince of "darkness " (Eph. 6:12),* *"adversary " and "a roaring lion " (I Peter 5:8),* *"Beelzebub" (Matt. 12:24),* *"accuser of our brethren " (Rev. 12:10),* *"dragon" (Rev. 12:7),* *"serpent" (Rev. 20:2),* and *"the god of this world" (II Cor. 4:4).*

This being had been in the Garden of Eden *(v. 13),* was created by God *(v. 13),* had been on the holy mountain of God *(v. 14),* was beautiful *(v. 17),* had been perfect in his ways for a time after his creation *(v. 15),* his heart had been lifted up in pride *(v. 17),* iniquity was found in him *(v. 15),* he corrupted his wisdom *(v. 17),* **and God has spoken his destruction** *(v. 17).*

What I do not find in these Scriptures is that Lucifer was once the worship leader in heaven, as some so boldly proclaim. I can only say for sure what the Bible says, and I would say nothing that might create "sympathy for the devil." When he fell, he led other "fallen angels" to rebel against God, perhaps one-third of heaven's total, and since that time has caused every murder, rape, child molestation, crime, heartache, tear, and death that has occurred on planet Earth. He is to be despised and opposed by all of those who love God.

The serpent, "the father of lies," was about his evil work in the Garden of

Eden in Genesis 3:4-5:

> *"And the serpent said unto the woman, Ye shall not surely die: For God doth know that in the day ye eat thereof, then your eyes shall be opened, and ye shall be as gods, knowing good and evil. "*

This is one of his favorite tricks, appealing to pride and ego and **making people think they can be "gods."** Sometimes it works as it did with Eve. It worked with Nebuchadnezzar *(Dan. 4:30)*, the Pharaohs, Caesars, Alexander *(who named himself "The Great")*, Herod, and a host of kings and rulers down through the ages. In the case of Herod it brought immediate destruction:

> *"And upon a set day **Herod, arrayed in royal apparel, sat upon his throne**, and made an oration unto them. **And the people gave a shout, saying, It is the voice of a god, and not of a man. And immediately the angel of the Lord smote him, because he gave not God the glory:** and **he was eaten of worms,** and **gave up the ghost.** But the word of God grew and multiplied" (Acts 12:21-24).*

It has worked with a long line of popes, some of them very wicked and godless men *(and women),* going back for some 1600 years, who dare to call themselves not only "Jesus Christ on earth," but "God himself on earth." [2] Pope Leo XIII, in his encyclical, The Reunion of Christendom (1885) said, "The Pope holds upon this earth the place of God Almighty." [3]

It will work one more time with the **anti-christ** *(a term which means against Christ but also **in place of Christ**).* This will bring death, destruction, and havoc to planet earth on an unprecedented scale *(Matt. 24:21-22).* He is not a false Buddha or a false Mohammed, but a **false Christ**.

> *"And shall show great signs and wonders; insomuch that, if it were possible, they shall deceive the very elect"* (Jesus speaking) *(Matt. 24:24).*

213

"And the dragon (Satan) *gave him his power, and his seat, and great authority"(Rev. 13:2).*

"Even him, whose coming is after the working of Satan with all power and signs and lying wonders, and with all deceivableness of unrighteousness" (II Thess. 2:9-10).

"So that he as God sitteth in the temple of God, showing himself that he is God" (II Thess. 2:4).

"And his power shall be mighty, but not by his own power: and he shall destroy wonderfully, and shall prosper, and practice and shall destroy the mighty and the holy people...and he shall magnify himself in his heart, and by peace shall destroy many: and **I Daniel fainted, and was sick certain days...**and I was astonished at the vision" (Dan. 8:24-27).*

"And then shall that Wicked be revealed, whom the Lord shall consume with the spirit of his mouth, and shall destroy with the brightness of his coming" (II Thess. 2:8).

Revelation 14:10-12:

"The same shall drink of the wine of the **wrath of God,** *which is poured out without mixture into the cup of his indignation; and he shall be tormented with fire and brimstone in the presence of the holy angels,* **and in the presence of the Lamb:** *And the smoke of their torment ascendeth up for ever and ever: and they have no rest day nor night, who worship the beast and his image, and whosoever receiveth the mark of his name.* **Here is the patience of the saints:** *here are they that keep the* **commandments of God,** *and the* **faith of Jesus.** *"*

Revelation 20:10:

"And the devil that deceived them was cast into the

lake of fire and brimstone, where the beast and the
false prophet *are, and shall be tormented day and night*
for **ever and ever.** *"*

But Satan's "big lie" never did and never will work with Jesus, the only begotten Son of God, *"who, being in the form* (Gk. morphi – "the external appearance by which a person or thing strikes the vision") *of God, thought it not robbery to be equal with God" (Phil. 2:6)*, the mirror image of God *(II Cor. 3:18)*, because the seed was created by God in the womb of Mary *(Matt. 1:20, Luke 1:35)*, and because of this God's blood was in his veins *(Acts 20:28)*, *"but made himself of no reputation...he humbled himself and became obedient unto death, even the death of the cross" (Phil. 2:7-8)*. When he was accused by his enemies of claiming to be God, he denied it saying, *"I said I am the Son of God" (John 10:36)*. He said, *"My Father is greater than I" (John 14:28)*, He knows things that I do not know *(Mark 13:32)*, without the Father *"my witness is not true" (John 5:31)*. *"I can of mine own self do nothing...I seek not mine own will" (John 5:30)*, and *"I ... and the Father"* are two (witnesses) *(John 8:17-18)*. He said, not *"Any man hath seen the Father" (John 6:46)* *"ye have neither heard his voice at any time, nor seen his shape" (John 5:37)*, but *"blessed are the pure in heart: for they shall see God" (Matt. 5:8)*. He said in prayer to the Father, *"And this is life eternal, that they might know thee* **the only true God**, *and Jesus Christ, whom thou hast sent" (John 17:3)*, and told his followers before he left this earth, *"I ascend unto* **my Father** *and* **your Father;** *and to* **my God** *and* **your God" (John 20:17)**. The ascended Jesus spoke to his apostle John and said *"These things saith the Amen, the faithful and true witness, the* **beginning of the creation of God" (Rev. 3:14).**

Jesus never one time has reached or will reach for God's glory but is happy with his own, given to him by the Father, as His only begotten Son *(John 17:22, John 1:14, Matt. 24:30)*.

Look again at Paul's strong warning in II Corinthians 11:3-4:

"But I fear, lest by any means, as the serpent beguiled
Eve through his subtilty, so your minds should be

215

corrupted from the simplicity that is in Christ. For if
he that cometh preacheth another Jesus, whom we
have not preached... ye might well bear with **(receive**
or accept) him. "

Notice, Paul said *"Another Jesus, whom we have not preached."* The Jesus that Paul preached was a man. *"Through* **this man** *is preached unto you the forgiveness of sins" (Acts 13:38),* and God will *"judge the world...by* **that man** *whom he hath ordained"* (appointed or specified) *(Acts 17:31).* He said Jesus is in the "creature" class, *"the firstborn of every* **creature"** *(Col. 1:15),* and was *"created"* by God *(Col. 3:10).* To Paul, Jesus was subject to God, *"the head of Christ is God" (I Cor. 11:3),* and belongs to God, *"Christ is God's" (I Cor. 3:23).* Paul would not have recognized the Jesus of the creeds, taught by most Christians in error for 1700 years, "true God from true God, begotten **not made,** of one substance with the Father." Yes, Jesus was begotten *(brought into being)* in the womb of a virgin but to Paul he was also **"made"** *(created)* by God.

"Concerning his Son Jesus Christ our Lord, which **was**
made *of the seed of David" (Rom. 1:3).*
"The last Adam (Christ) **was made** *a quickening spirit"*
(I Cor. 15:45).
"God sent forth his Son, **made** *of a woman,* **made** *under*
the law" (Gal. 4:4).
Christ Jesus *"was made in the likeness of men" (Phil.*
2:7).

These scriptures prove again just how wrong the Nicene Council was in its conclusions, and how wrong the Christian church has been to follow.

Paul says, with Psalm 110:1 in mind, that at the end, after Jesus' 1000 year reign on earth, he *(Jesus)* will **forever** be subject to the Father:

"Then cometh the end, when he (Jesus) *shall have*
delivered up the kingdom to God, even the Father;
when he shall have put down all rule and all authority
and power. For he (Jesus) *must reign, till he* (God)

216

hath put all enemies under his (Jesus') *feet...For he* (God) *hath put all things under his* (Jesus') *feet. But when he saith* (David in Psalm 8:6) *all things are put under him* (Jesus), *it is manifest that he* (God) *is excepted, which did put all things under him* (Jesus). *And when all things shall be subdued unto him* (Jesus), *then shall the Son also himself be subject unto him* (God) *that put all things under him,* **that God may be all in all"** *(I Cor. 15:24-25, 27-28).*

Paul says in I Cor. 8:6 *"To us there is but* **one God** *the Father...and one Lord Jesus Christ"* who is not God. **This is the Jesus of the Bible.**

217

"When the Greek mind and the Roman mind, instead of the Hebrew mind came to dominate the church, there occurred a disaster from which the Church has never recovered, either in doctrine or practice."

H. L. Goudge – Historian[1]

Chapter 12

God and Jesus In The Book of Revelation

It is important for us to take a walk through the Book of Revelation and see the relationship between Almighty God and His son Jesus Christ. I believe that somewhere in the foggy areas of our minds we think that Jesus the son, morphs into the Lord God in the little understood Chapters of the Apocalypse. I have studied this book extensively and I can assure you **it does not happen**.

The word apocalypse means to "disclose" or "unveil"; thus the Book of Revelation takes its name from **Chapter one, verse one:**

>*"The Revelation of Jesus Christ, **which God gave unto him**, to shew unto his servants things, which must shortly come to pass; and **he sent and signified it by his angel unto his servant John."***

Please comprehend what John the apostle is saying in the verse above as it is very important in understanding this book. **God gave this revelation to Jesus Christ**. Something is revealed or disclosed to someone because they do not know it previously. John did not know the events described in this book until Jesus sent his angel and revealed them to him: the seven churches of Asia did not know this until John wrote the book and sent it unto them *(v. 11)*: and Jesus did not know the events of Revelation until God the Father disclosed them to him. In fact Jesus likely left this earth to go to his Father in heaven, knowing that he would one day return to reign, **but not knowing when** *(Mark. 13:32)*. There are definitely **two different minds** here. One that **knows all**.

>*"Known unto God are **all his works** from the beginning of the world" (Acts 15:18).*
>
>*"It is not for you to know the times or the seasons, which the Father hath put in **his own power"** (Jesus

219

speaking) *(Acts 1:7).*

And **one that knows only** what God his Father discloses or reveals to him:

> *"As my Father hath taught me, I speak these things"*
> *(John 8:28).*
>
> *"I speak that which I have seen with my Father" (John*
> *8:38).*
>
> *"I can of mine own self do nothing: **as I hear, I judge:** I*
> *seek not mine own will, If I bear witness of myself, my*
> *witness is not true" (John 5:30-31).*

Jesus was crucified, arose from the grave and ascended around 32 or 33 A.D.. According to James Ussher, 17th century authority on Bible chronology, Revelation was written in 96 A.D. It is possible that Jesus had been in heaven at the right hand of God for over 60 years when his Father revealed the events of this book to him. Please keep this thought in mind as we go forward.

Verse 5:

> *"And from Jesus Christ...the **prince of the kings of the***
> ***earth.** "*

Not the King of heaven. That is the Lord God, Jesus' Father *(Dan. 4:37).*

Verse 8:

> *"I am Alpha and Omega, the beginning and the ending,*
> *saith the Lord, which is, and which was, and which is to*
> *come, **the Almighty"***

Alpha and Omega are the beginning and the ending of the Greek alphabet and this is "the Almighty" speaking. The phrase, "Alpha and Omega" is found four times in the book of Revelation, and each time it is God Almighty speaking. This does not change! "Almighty" is El Shaddai in Hebrew and is spoken of the Lord God 56 times in the Bible, including 8 times in Revelation. **Jesus is never one time called "Almighty" in scripture**. He is "mighty" but only God his Father is "Almighty" *(see Isa.*

*9:6). "**Which is to come.**"* Look at Rev. 4:8 and see that this is the *"Lord God Almighty, which was, and is, and is to come."*

Verse 9:

> *"I John...was in the isle that is called Patmos, for the word of God, and for the testimony of Jesus Christ."*

Notice that John separates God from Jesus Christ, something he never fails to do throughout this book.

Verses 10-11:

> *"I.....heard behind me a **great voice**, as of a trumpet saying, I am Alpha and Omega, the first and the last."*

Do not be confused if you have a red letter edition of the Bible that has these words in red. The editors who decided what words to put in red are very likely Trinitarians, as are some two billion people on earth who are called "Christians." The Trinity is not a Bible doctrine and God has given you enough intelligence to look at the context and see who is speaking. If it says Lord God or God Almighty it is not Jesus speaking. He is neither of these, but **he is** Messiah, Savior, Redeemer, the **"man Christ Jesus."** John heard "a great voice, as of a trumpet." Let's identify the trumpet voice. In Revelation 4:1 the **trumpet voice** says, *"Come up hither,"* to heaven. When John was caught up he saw one throne, and *"one sat on the throne"* and it was the *"Lord God Almighty" (v. 8).* When God spoke to the children of Israel from heaven in Exodus 19:16 the Bible says, *"The voice of the trumpet exceeding loud; so that all the people that was in the camp trembled." (See Heb. 12:19)* So the trumpet voice is the **voice of God.**

Verse 13:

> *"One like unto the Son of Man."*

"Son of man" means a human being. God called the prophet Ezekiel "son of man" 90 times in Ezekiel and Jesus is "Son of man" 84 times in the four gospels, **a human being**. Whatever Ezekiel was in regard to manhood, Jesus was.

Verse 14:

> *"His head and his hairs were white like wool, as white*

221

*as snow; and **his eyes were as a flame of fire;** and his*
***feet like unto fine brass**...and his voice as the sound of*
many waters. And his countenance was as the sun
shineth in his strength. "

John sees the Lord Jesus in "*his own glory*" *(Luke 9:26, 32)*, his "*great glory*" *(Matt. 24:30, Mark 13:26)*, and the glory given to him by God his Father *(John 17:22)*.

*"We beheld **his glory**, the glory as of the only begotten*
of the Father"(John 1:14).

To know for sure that these verses speak not of God, but of His son, look at Chapter 2, verse 18:

*"These things saith the **Son of God**, who hath his **eyes***
***like** unto a flame of **fire**, and his **feet** are **like** fine **brass**"*
(Rev. 2:18).

Notice that his voice is not the "*great voice as of a trumpet*" but a different voice, "*as the sound of many waters.*" See 14:1-2 where the voice as of "*many waters*" is again associated with the Lamb.

Verse 18:

"I am he that liveth, and was dead; and, behold, I am
alive for evermore, Amen; and have the keys of hell and
of death."

This is Jesus, "who was dead." This cannot be "the Almighty." If God Almighty can die, the universe and man are in much more trouble than we ever knew. God is **immortal** which means "**deathless.**" "Mortal" means "appointed to death." Jesus was mortal. Hebrews 9:27-28 **was speaking of Jesus** when it says, "*And as it is appointed unto **men once to die**...So Christ was **once offered**.*" Jesus was **a man**, therefore **mortal, "appointed unto death**."

*"Now unto the King eternal, **immortal**, invisible, the*
***only wise God**, be honor and **glory** for ever and ever.*
Amen" (I Tim. 1:17).

The eternal God who is **invisible to men** is "*the only wise God*" and He

222

"*only hath immortality*" *(I Tim. 6:16).* But "*our Savior Jesus Christ*" hath "*abolished death, and brought life and **immortality** to light through the gospel*" *(II Tim. 1:10).*

Chapter 2, verse 7:

> "*The tree of life, which is in the midst of the paradise of God.*"

This is Jesus speaking and he calls heaven "the paradise **of God**."

Verses 26-27:

> "*And he that overcometh...to him will I give power over the nations, and he shall rule them with a rod of iron, even as I received of my Father.*"

Jesus has received from his Father power to rule the nations, and **as his brethren** we will have power to rule the nations with him, ("*he that overcometh*").

Chapter 3, verse 5:

> "*He that overcometh...I will confess his name before my Father.*"

Jesus is still the Son, and he still calls God, "my Father."

Verse 12:

> "*Him that overcometh will I make a pillar in the temple of **my God**, and he shall go no more out: and I will write upon him the name of **my God**, and the name of the city of **my God**, which is new Jerusalem which cometh down out of heaven from **my God**: and I will write upon him **my new name**.*"

Jesus was in heaven, seated at the right hand of God when this was written, and he still calls God, "my God." Jesus has a God, someone who is superior to him, whom he fears, worships and obeys.

> "*My God, my God, why hast thou forsaken me?*" *(Ps. 22:1, Matt. 27:46).*
>
> "**The God** *and Father **of our Lord Jesus Christ***" *(II Cor. 11:31, Eph. 1:3, I Peter 1:3).*

Let me ask you a good question. Is Jesus your God, or is Jesus' God your God? Some of us have made **a man** our God, and this is serious error. Jesus knew who his God was, do you?

> *"Ye worship ye know not what: we know what we worship"* (Jesus speaking) *(John 4:22).*

Verse 14:

> *"These things saith the Amen, the faithful and true witness, **the beginning of the creation of God**."*

Do you hear what Jesus is saying, I am not God, I am "the beginning of the creation of God?" The word "beginning" here is Gk. "arche" (*Strong's #746)* and means "to commence (in order of time)." He is saying, I am a created being, I was created **by God** first in order of time. If you will not believe Jesus, it is unlikely that you will believe anyone else in regard to this truth, but let's let Paul reinforce it.

> *"**Who is the image** ("a representative likeness") of the invisible God, **the firstborn of every creature"** (Col. 1:15).*

> *"And put on the new man* (Christ), *which is renewed in knowledge **after the image** of him* (God) *that created him" (Col. 3:10).*

Listen to Peter:

> *"But with the precious blood of Christ, **as of a lamb** without blemish and without spot: Who verily was **foreordained before the foundation of the world**, but **was manifest in these last times** for you" (I Peter 1:19-20).*

This is not a preexistent "God the Son" or "eternal Son"; this is Jesus the Messiah **"foreordained"** before the foundation of the world."

> *"In the beginning* (**God has no beginning,** this is the beginning of creation - **Jesus**) *was the Word* (**logos** - "thought," "something said" "intention," "motive") *and the Word* (something said) *was made flesh, and dwelt*

among us" (John 1:1, 14).

Jesus was **spoken** by God **before time**, but generated in the womb of a virgin, **in time** *(Matt. 1:18)*. After he was spoken, he was the **motive** for God's further creative acts.

Verse 21:

>*"To him that overcometh will I grant to sit with me in my throne, even as I also overcame, and am set down with my Father in his throne."*

When we reign with Christ for 1000 years on Planet Earth, will we ever take over his throne? No! Neither will Jesus ever take over his Father's throne in heaven. He said, I *"am set down with my Father in His throne,"* the way *"him that overcometh"* will *"sit with me in my throne."* Jesus was never promised God his Father's throne, but *"the Lord God shall give unto him the throne of his father David,"* in Jerusalem (Gabriel to Mary) *(Luke 1:32)*. **Jesus has no throne of his own in heaven.**

Chapter 4, verses 2-3:

>*"And immediately I was in the Spirit: and behold, a throne was set in heaven, and one sat on the throne. And he that sat was to look upon like a jasper and a sardine stone." (Almighty God on His throne)*

Verses 8-11:

>*"And the four beasts had each of them six wings about him; and they were full of eyes within: and they rest not day and night, saying, Holy, holy, holy, Lord God Almighty, which was, and is, and is to come. And when those beasts give glory and honour and thanks to him that sat on the throne, who liveth for ever and ever. The four and twenty elders fall down before him that sat on the throne and worship him that liveth for ever and ever, and cast their crowns before the throne, saying, Thou art worthy, O Lord, to receive glory and honour and power: for thou hast created all things,*

225

and for thy pleasure they are and were created."

John saw one throne, and **"one sat on the throne,"** and it was the Creator, "Lord God Almighty." Others had seen the Lord God on His throne before John.

> *"I saw the Lord sitting on his throne, and all the host of heaven standing by him on his right hand and on his left"* (Micaiah the prophet) *(I Kings 22:19).* Notice, God had a right and left hand.

> *"I saw also the Lord sitting upon a throne; high and lifted up, and his train filled the temple. Mine eyes have seen the King, the Lord of host"* (Isaiah the prophet) *(Isa. 6:1, 5).*

> *"The heavens were opened and I saw visions of God. And above the firmament that was over their heads* (the creatures) *was the likeness of a throne, and upon the likeness of the throne was the likeness as the appearance of a man above upon it. This was the appearance of the likeness of the glory of the Lord. And he said unto me, Son of Man, stand upon thy feet, and I will speak unto thee. Thus saith the Lord God"* (Ezekiel the prophet) *(Ezekiel 1:1, 26, 28, 2:1, 4).*

Ezekiel saw God on His throne, and He had **"*the likeness* as the appearance of a man**." Should we be surprised that God looked like a man, when man was made in **His image** and in **His likeness** *(Gen. 1:27, 5:1, 9:6, I Cor. 11:7)?* God for sure wants us to know this. Look at Hebrews 1:3:

> *"Who being the brightness of his glory, and the express image of his person."*

This is Jesus, "*the express image*" of God's "person". This word "person" is the Greek word "hupostasis" and means "essence" or "substance." God is not just a "force," a mystical spirit as some would have us believe, but He has essence, substance and form. God's glory fills the universe and He is invisible to man, *("Thou canst not see my face: for there*

226

shall no man see me **and live"** *Ex. 33:20)* but **"thou shalt see my back parts"** *(Ex. 33:23).* God said of His servant Moses in Numbers 12:8 *"The similitude* ("form or likeness") *of the Lord shall he behold"* and Hebrews 11:27 says, *"He* (Moses) *endured, as seeing him who is invisible."* Those who say that the Eternal God has no "form or likeness" are deficient in their understanding of Scripture. Those in heaven and the angels see His face.

> *"Take heed that ye despise not one of these little ones; for I say unto you, That in heaven* **their angels do always behold the face of my Father which is in heaven"** (Jesus speaking) *(Matt. 18:10).*

Now to Revelation Chapter 5, verses 1-3:

> **"And I saw in the right hand of him that sat on the throne a book** *written within and on the backside, sealed with seven seals. And I saw a strong angel proclaiming with a loud voice, Who is worthy to open the book, and to loose the seals thereof? And* **no man** *in heaven, nor in earth, neither under the earth, was able to open the book, neither to look thereon."*

God Almighty who sat upon the throne had a book in his hand, which **"no man"** in creation was worthy to open. Notice, search was made for a **"man"** to open the book and Jesus is that **"man."** It had to be a sinless man!

Verses 4-13:

> *"And I wept much, because* **no man** *was found worthy to open and to read the book, neither to look thereon. And one of the elders saith unto me, Weep not: behold, the Lion of the tribe of Judah, the Root of David, hath prevailed to open the book, and to loose the seven seals thereof.* **And I beheld, and lo, in the midst of the throne and of the four beasts, and in the midst of the elders, stood a Lamb** *as it had been slain, having seven horns and seven eyes, which are the seven Spirits of God sent forth into all the earth.* **And he came and**

227

took the book out of the right hand of him that sat upon the throne. *And when he had taken the book, the four beasts and four and twenty elders fell down before the Lamb, having every one of them harps, and golden vials full of odours, which are the prayers of saints. And they sung a new song, saying, Thou art worthy to take the book, and to open the seals thereof:* **for thou wast slain, and hast redeemed us to God by thy blood** *out of every kindred, and tongue, and people, and nation;* **And hast made us unto our God, kings and priests: and we shall reign on the earth.** *And I beheld, and I heard the voice of many angels round about the throne and the beasts and the elders: and the number of them was ten thousand times ten thousand, and thousands of thousands; Saying with a loud voice,* **Worthy is the Lamb that was slain to receive power, and riches**, *and wisdom, and strength, and honor, and glory, and blessing. And every creature which is in heaven, and on the earth, and under the earth, and such as are in the sea, and all that are in them, heard I saying,* **Blessing, and honour, and glory, and power, be unto him that sitteth upon the throne, and unto the Lamb**, *for ever and ever."*

Jesus Christ the Lamb *(a man)* "*stood*" and took the book "*out of the right hand of him that **sat** upon the throne*"; and heaven rang with well deserved praises,"*for thou wast slain, and **hast redeemed us unto God** by thy blood."*

"The next day John seeth Jesus coming unto him, and saith, **Behold the Lamb of God**, *which taketh away the sin of the world"* (John the Baptist) *(John 1:29)*. **The Lamb is Jesus**.

"These shall make war with the Lamb, and the Lamb

> *shall overcome them: for he is Lord of lords, and King*
> *of kings" (Rev. 17:14).*

Verse 14:

> *"And the four beast said, Amen. And the four and*
> *twenty elders, **fell down and worshiped him that liveth***
> ***for ever and ever"***

Notice, John did not say that the hosts of heaven "worshiped" the Lamb *(who was present)*, **but they did worship** the **one** who sat on the throne, **Lord God Almighty** *(Rev. 4:10-11).*

The prophet Daniel saw a vision very similar to this one that John saw, in Daniel Chapter 7.

> *"The Ancient of days did sit, whose garment was white*
> *as snow, and the hair of his head like the pure wool; his*
> *throne was like the fiery flame. A fiery stream issued*
> *and came forth from before him: thousand thousands*
> *ministered unto him, and ten thousand times ten*
> *thousand stood before him: the judgement was set, and*
> *the books were opened" (Dan. 7:9-10).*

This is the Lord God most High seated on His throne, and *"thousand thousands ministered unto him, and ten thousand times ten thousand stood before him" (see vs. 22, 25, 27)*. This is exactly the number that was round about the throne of the "Lord God Almighty" in Revelation 5:11.

> *"I saw in the night visions, and, behold, **one like the***
> ***Son of man** came with the clouds of heaven, and **came***
> ***to the Ancient of days, and they brought him near***
> ***before him. And there was given him dominion, and***
> ***glory, and a kingdom,** that all people, nations, and*
> *languages, should serve him: his dominion is an*
> *everlasting dominion, which shall not pass away, and*
> *his kingdom that which shall not be destroyed" (Dan.*
> *7:13-14).*

So in Daniel's vision also *"one like the Son of man,"* Jesus Christ our

Lord, is brought before God his Father and **given** dominion, glory, and a kingdom to reign on earth.

Now back to Revelation Chapter 6, verse 1:

"And I saw when the Lamb opened one of the seals."

Jesus the Lamb opens the seals of the seven sealed book that he had taken from the hand of his God. Now begins 10 Chapters of the wrath of God on a wicked, Christ rejecting world.

Verse 16:

"And said to the mountains and rocks, Fall on us, and hide us from the face of him that sitteth on the throne (God), and from the wrath of the Lamb."

Chapter 7, verses 10-12:

*"And cried with a loud voice, saying, **Salvation to our God which sitteth upon the throne, and unto the Lamb.** And all the angels stood round about the throne, and about the elders and the four beasts, and fell before the throne on their faces, **and worshiped God.** Saying, Amen: Blessing, and glory and wisdom, and thanksgiving, and honour, and power, and might, be **unto our God for ever and ever.** Amen"*

God and the Lamb are both present and are praised in verse 10, **but God alone is "worshiped"** in verse 11.

Verses 14-15:

*"These are they which came out of great tribulation, and have washed their robes, and made them white in the blood of the Lamb. **Therefore are they before the throne of God**, and serve him day and night in his temple: **and he that sitteth on the throne shall dwell among them.**"*

These saints were washed in the blood of the Lamb (Jesus) "*and he that sitteth on the throne* (Lord God Almighty) *shall dwell among them.*" This will be seen very clearly in Chapter 21; and this is a fulfillment of Jesus'

230

promise to us in Matthew 5:8 *"Blessed are the pure in heart: for they shall see God."* The multitude to whom Jesus said this had already seen him.

Verse 17:

> *"For the Lamb which is in the midst of the throne shall feed them, and shall lead them unto living fountains of waters:* **and God shall wipe away all tears from their eyes.***"*

Chapter 8, verse 4:

> *"And the smoke of the incense, which came with the prayers of the saints, ascended up before God out of the angel's hand."*

It cannot be found in scripture that prayers were made to Jesus *(the Lamb)* after his ascension to heaven. Prayers were always made to God in Jesus name; thus the smoke of the incense which came with the prayers, ascended up "**before God**".

Chapter 9 verses 4 & 13:

> *"And it was commanded them that they should not hurt the grass of the earth, neither any green thing, neither any tree;* **but only those men which have not the seal of God in their foreheads.***"*
>
> *"The golden altar which is before God (v. 13)."*

It is the Lord God that is in focus in these two verses.

Chapter 10, verse 7:

> *"The mystery of God should be finished."*

God is in focus.

Chapter 11, verse 1:

> *"Rise, and measure the temple of God."*

Verse 4:

> *"The two candlesticks standing before the God of the earth."*

Verse 11:

> *"And after three days and an half the Spirit of life from*

231

God entered into them. "

Verse 13:

"The remnant were affrighted and gave glory to the God of heaven. "

Verse 15:

"The kingdoms of this world are become the kingdoms of our Lord (God)*, and of **his Christ*** (Jesus)*. " "Christ is God's" (I Cor. 3:23).*

Verses 16-17:

*"And the four and twenty elders, which sat **before God** on their seats, **fell upon their faces, and worshiped God,** Saying, We give thee thanks, **O Lord God Almighty**, which art, and wast, and art to come. "*

Verse 19:

"And the temple of God was opened in heaven. "

Chapter 12, verse 5:

"And her child (the man child) *was caught up unto God, and to his throne. "*

Verses 10-11:

*"And I heard a loud voice saying in heaven, Now is come salvation, and strength, and the kingdom of **our God**, and the power of **his Christ**: for the accuser of our brethren is cast down, which accused them before our God day and night. And they overcame him by the blood of the Lamb, and by the word of their testimony. "*

Verse 17:

*"And the dragon was wroth with the woman, and went to make war with the remnant of her seed, which keep **the commandments of God**, and have **the testimony of Jesus Christ.** "*

Notice how John always throughout this book, separated God from Jesus

Christ the Lamb.

Chapter 13, verse 6:

> *"And he opened his mouth in* **blasphemy against God**, *to blaspheme his name, and his tabernacle, and them that dwell in heaven."*

The anti-christ will blaspheme God, and also Christ.

Verse 8:

> *"And all that dwell upon the earth shall worship him, whose names are not* **written in the book of life of the Lamb slain from the** *foundation of the world."*

As Jesus the Lamb was **ordained of God** from the foundation of the world, so **he was slain back then**, in the **foreknowledge** of God *(see Acts 2:23)*.

Chapter 14, verse 1:

> *"And I looked, and, lo, a Lamb stood on the mount Zion, and with him an hundred forty and four thousand, having* **his Father's name** *written in their foreheads."*

Verses 4-5:

> *"These are they which follow the Lamb withersoever he goeth. These were redeemed from among men, being the firstfruits unto God and to the Lamb. And in their mouth was found no guile: for they are without fault before the throne of God."*

Verses 6-7:

> *"And I saw another angel fly in the midst of heaven,* **having the everlasting gospel to preach unto them that dwell on the earth,** *and to every nation, and kindred, and tongue, and people,* **Saying with a loud voice, Fear God, and give glory to him**; *for the hour of his judgement is come: and* **worship him** *that made heaven, and earth, and the sea, and the fountains of waters."*

The angel had the everlasting gospel to preach unto them that dwell on

233

the earth*("every nation")*. And what did he say *"with a loud voice"*? ***"Fear God, and give glory to him."*** In the mouth of the angel **it was a command**, but in this book I have written it is **a strong recommendation** from your brother and fellow laborer. **Give glory to God!** Quit giving His glory (honor - admiration - esteem - worshipful adoration) to others, even His highly exalted Son. (*"God also hath highly exalted him* (Jesus)" *(Phil. 2:9)*.

When we take the honor that is due to **God alone** and give it to another, we are thieves and robbers and God will require it of us. We have done this in the past and God was patient and forgiving, but if we persist after we come to the knowledge of the truth, it will be accounted to us for idolatry. *"And they repented not **to give him** (**God**) **the glory"** (Rev. 16:9)*.

We must understand what the prophet Isaiah said about **God's** glory.

> *"I am the Lord: that is my name: and **my glory will I not give to another"** (Isa. 42:8)*. This is in the context of God's promise of the Messiah, Jesus, whom He would "give."

> *"Behold, **my servant**, whom I uphold; mine elect, in whom my soul delighteth; I have put my spirit upon him; he shall bring forth judgement to the Gentiles. I the Lord have called thee in righteousness, and will hold thine hand, and will keep thee, **and give thee** for a covenant of the people, for a light of the Gentiles" (Isa. 42:1, 6)*.

Who is this who says, *"**my glory will I not give to another**?"*

> *"Ye are my witnesses, saith the Lord, and my servant whom I have chosen: that ye may **know** and **believe** me, and **understand** that I am he: **before me there was no God formed, neither shall there be after me"** (Isa. 43:10)*.

Is God more than one? No!

> *"Thus saith the Lord, your redeemer, the **Holy One of Israel**; ...I am the Lord, your **Holy One**, the creator of*

> *Israel, your King" (Isa. 43:14).*

And He says again, *"I will not give my glory to another" (Isa. 48:11).*

Verse 10:

> *"The same shall drink of the wine of the wrath of God...in the presence of the Lamb."*

Verse 12:

> *"Here are they that keep the commandments of **God**, and the faith of **Jesus**."*

Verse19:

> *"The great winepress of the wrath of God."*

John continues to separate Jesus Christ the Lamb, from God "his Father." **They do not merge in this book!**

Chapter 15, verses 1-2:

> *"The wrath of God...the harps of God."*

Verses 3-4:

> *"And they sing the song of Moses the servant of God, and **the song of the Lamb**, saying, Great and marvelous are thy works, **Lord God Almighty**; just and true are thy ways, thou King of saints. Who shall not fear thee, O Lord, and glorify thy name? For thou only art holy: for **all nations shall come and worship before thee**: for thy judgements are made manifest."*

The song of Moses, a prototype of Jesus, and the song of the Lamb *(Jesus)*, is a song of praise to the "Lord God Almighty." Hebrews 2:12 quotes Psalm 22, a Messianic Psalm of Jesus, which begins, *"My God, my God, why hast thou forsaken me?" Also* verse 22 has **Jesus saying to God**, *"in the midst of the congregation will I sing praise unto thee."* **Jesus joins all nations in worshiping his God.**

Verse 8:

> *"And the temple was filled with smoke from **the glory of God**."*

Chapter 17, verse 6:

"And I saw the woman drunken...with the blood of the martyrs of Jesus. "

Verse 14:

"These shall make war with the Lamb, and the Lamb *shall overcome them: for **he is Lord of lords, and King** **of kings:** and they that are with him are called, and chosen, and faithful. "*

The ten kings of this Chapter will not make war with God, for He is in heaven; but they will make war with the Lamb, on earth. He will overcome these kings for he is King of kings. The prophet Daniel said to Nebuchadnezzar, *"Thou, O king art a king of kings, "* which means **a king over other kings on earth**, not the **King of heaven** *(Dan. 2:37)*. Daniel 4:37 says the most High God is *"the King of heaven. "*

Verse 17:

"For God hath put in their hearts to fulfil his will. "

Chapter 18, verses 5 & 8:

"God hath remembered her (Babylon's) *iniquities...for* **strong is the Lord God** *who judgeth her. "*

Not one time in the entire Bible is Jesus called "the Lord God" *(Jehovah Elohim)*!

Chapter 19, verse 1:

*"And after these things I heard a great voice of much people in heaven, saying, **Alleluia; Salvation, and glory, and honour, and power, unto the Lord our God. "***

Alleluia means "praise ye Jah" *(an O.T. name for God)* and is always used in praise to the Lord God, **never to Jesus Messiah**. It means "God be praised."

Verses 4-6:

*"And the four and twenty elders and the four beasts **fell***

236

> **down and worshiped God that sat on the throne,**
> *saying,* **Amen; Alleluia.** *And a voice came out of the*
> *throne, saying, Praise our God, all ye his servants, and*
> *ye that fear him, both small and great. And I heard as*
> *it were the voice of a great multitude, and as the voice*
> *of many waters, and as the voice of mighty thunderings,*
> *saying,* **Alleluia: for the Lord God omnipotent**
> **reigneth.** *"*

Omnipotent means all powerful and is another way of saying Almighty.

Verse 7:

> *"Let us be glad and rejoice, and give honour to him*
> (God)*:* **for the marriage of the Lamb is come**, *and his*
> *wife hath made herself ready. "*

In this Chapter the Lamb, Jesus Christ, comes to reign on earth with his saints for 1000 years.

> *"He shall be great, and shall be called* **the Son of the**
> **Highest:** *and the* **Lord God shall give unto him** *the*
> *throne of his father David"* (in Jerusalem) *(Luke 1:32).*
> *"For he* (Jesus) *must reign, till he* (God) *hath put all*
> *enemies under his feet"* (I Cor. 15:25).
> *"***The Lord said unto my Lord, Sit thou at my right**
> **hand, until I make thine enemies thy footstool"** *(Ps.*
> *110:1).*
> *"***But this man***, after he had offered one sacrifice for*
> *sins for ever,* **sat down on the right hand of God:**
> *From henceforth* **expecting** *till his enemies be made his*
> *footstool"* (Heb. 10:12-13).

May I humbly say that God is not "expecting" anything, but Jesus Christ His Son has a right to **expect** God to do for him what He said he would do.

Chapter 19, verses 9-16:

> *"And he saith unto me, Write, Blessed are they which*

237

*are called unto the marriage supper of the Lamb. And he saith unto me, **These are the true sayings of God.** And I fell at his feet to worship him. And he said unto me, See thou do it not: I am thy fellow-servant, and of thy brethren that have the **testimony of Jesus: worship God**: for the testimony of Jesus is the spirit of prophecy. And I saw heaven opened, and behold **a white horse; and he that sat upon him was called Faithful and True**, and in righteousness he doth judge and make war. His eyes were as a flame of fire, and on his head were many crowns; and **he had a name written, that no man knew, but he himself.** And he was clothed with a vesture dipped in blood: and his name is called The Word of God. And the armies which were in heaven followed him upon white horses, clothed in fine linen, white and clean. And out of his mouth goeth a sharp sword, that with it he should smite the nations: and he shall rule them with a rod of iron: and he treadeth the winepress of the fierceness and wrath of Almighty God. **And he hath on his vesture and on his thigh a name written, KING OF KINGS AND LORD OF LORDS.** "*

This is Jesus, coming with **power** and **great glory**, called "**Faithful and True**." Look back at Chapter 3, verse 14 where Jesus says, *"These things saith the Amen, **the faithful and true witness**, the beginning of the creation of God.* " This is **not God** on the white horse, but it surely is His "faithful and true witness."

Look at verse 12 above. *"He had a name written, that no man knew, but he himself."* Jesus will have a name change as did Abraham, Jacob, and Saul of Tarsus. Look at Revelation 3:12 where Jesus says to him that overcometh, *"I will write upon him **my new name**."* This is a mystery, but a "new name" will not change who he is, our precious Lord and Savior, **the**

only way to God the Father. Contrast this with what the God of Israel told Moses at the burning bush in Exodus 3:15:

> *"Thus shalt thou say unto the children of Israel,* **The Lord God***, of your fathers, the God of Abraham, the God of Isaac, and the God of Jacob, hath sent me unto you:* **this is my name for ever, and this is my memorial unto all generations"** *(Ex. 3:15).*

Look at Deut. 7:9 and understand that *"unto all generations"* means for at least 30,000 years. **God's name will never change!**

Chapter 20, verses 1-6:

> *"And I saw an angel come down from heaven, having the key of the bottomless pit and a great chain in his hand.* **And he laid hold on the dragon, that old serpent, which is the Devil, and Satan, and bound him for a thousand years.** *And cast him into the bottomless pit, and shut him up, and set a seal upon him, that he should deceive the nations no more,* **till the thousand years should be fulfilled: and after that he must be loosed a little season. And I saw thrones, and they sat upon them, and judgement was given unto them:** *and I saw the souls of them that were beheaded* **for the witness of Jesus,** *and* **for the word of God,** *and which had not worshiped the beast, neither his image, neither had received his mark upon their foreheads, or in their hands; and* **they lived and reigned with Christ for a thousand years.** *But the rest of the dead lived not again until the thousand years were finished.* **This is the first resurrection.** *Blessed and holy is he that hath part in the first resurrection: on such the second death hath no power,* **but they shall be priests of God and of Christ, and shall reign with him a thousand years. "**

Daniel the prophet saw this time of Christ reigning on earth with his

239

saints in Daniel 7:27:

> *"And the kingdom and dominion, and **the greatness of the kingdom under the whole heaven**, shall be given to the people of the saints of the most High, whose kingdom is an everlasting kingdom, and all dominions shall serve and obey him."*

"They lived and reigned with Christ (Messiah) *a thousand years."* The prophet Isaiah foresaw this glorious time of peace and rest when Jesus Christ, the son of David, the son of Jesse shall reign as king over the earth.

> *"And there shall come forth a rod out of the stem of Jesse, and a Branch shall grow out of his roots: **And the spirit of the Lord shall rest upon him**, the spirit of wisdom and understanding, the spirit of counsel and might, the spirit of knowledge **and of the fear of the Lord**. And shall make him of quick understanding **in the fear of the Lord**: and he shall not judge after the sight of his eyes, neither reprove after the hearing of his ears: But with righteousness shall he judge the poor, and reprove with equity for the meek of the earth: and he shall smite the earth with the rod of his mouth, and with the breath of his lips shall he slay the wicked. And **righteousness** shall be the girdle of his loins, and **faithfulness** the girdle of his reins. The wolf also shall dwell with the lamb, and the leopard shall lie down with the kid; and the calf and the young lion and the fatling together; and a little child shall lead them. And the cow and the bear shall feed; their young ones shall lie down together: and the lion shall eat straw like the ox. And the sucking child shall play on the hole of the asp, and the weaned child shall put his hand on the cockatrice' den. They shall not hurt nor destroy in all my holy mountain: for the earth shall be full of the knowledge*

240

> *of the Lord, as the waters cover the sea. And in that day there shall be **a root of Jesse**, which shall stand for an ensign of the people; to it shall the Gentiles seek: and **his rest shall be glorious**" (Isa. 11:1-10).*

Now look at Jesus' words:

> *"When **the Son of man** shall come in **his glory**, and all the holy angels with him, then shall he sit upon the throne of **his glory**: And before him shall be gathered all nations: and he shall separate them one from another, as a shepherd divideth his sheep from the goats: And he shall set the sheep on his right hand, but the goats on the left. Then shall the King say unto them on his right hand, **Come ye blessed of my Father**, inherit the kingdom prepared for you from the foundation of the world "*(in the unchangeable plan and foreknowledge of God) *(Matt. 25:31-34).*

> *"And he said unto him, Well, thou good servant: because thou hast been faithful in a very little, **have thou authority over ten cities**. And the second came, saying, Lord, thy pound hath gained five pounds. And he said likewise to him, **Be thou also over five cities**"* (Luke 19:17-19).

> *"And if children, then heirs; **heirs of God**, and **joint-heirs with Christ**; if so be that we suffer with him, that we may be also **glorified together**. For I reckon that the sufferings of this present time are not worthy to be compared with **the glory which shall be revealed in us**"* (Paul speaking) *(Rom. 8:17-18).*

> *"If we suffer, we shall also reign with him"* (Paul speaking) *(II Tim. 2:12).*

But **trouble comes** briefly at the end of the thousand years!
Chapter 20, verses 7-9:

> *"And when the thousand years are expired, Satan shall be loosed out of his prison. And shall go out to deceive the nations which are in the four quarters of the earth, Gog and Magog, to gather them together to battle: the number of whom is as the sand of the sea. And they went up on the breadth of the earth, and compassed the camp of the saints about, and the beloved city"* (Jerusalem).

Please see this picture. Jesus Christ comes back to earth, subdues the nations and rules with his saints in peace for 1000 years. At the end of this millennium, Satan, who has been bound in a spirit prison below for this period of time, will be loosed. According to the book of Revelation, one half of the world's six billion population will be killed by the plagues and cataclysmic events at the time when God's wrath is poured out *(Rev. 6:8, 9:15, 18)*. The balance, perhaps 3 billion, even those who are unsaved, will be ruled over by **Christ and his own** with a rod of iron *(Rev. 2:27, 19:15)*. When Satan is loosed out of his prison, he leads some of these people in rebellion and surrounds the "camp of the saints" and the city of Jerusalem. **But there is miraculous intervention and deliverance!**

<u>**Verses 9-10:**</u>

> *"And fire came down from God out of heaven, and devoured them. And the devil that deceived them was cast into the lake of fire and brimstone, where the beast and the false prophet are, and shall be tormented day and night for ever and ever."*

Jesus is reigning over earth from Jerusalem and God is still in heaven. **And it is God the Father to the rescue.** *"Fire came down from God out of heaven and devoured them."* The beast and false prophet had been *"cast alive into a lake of fire burning with brimstone "* at the beginning of the 1000 years, and now Satan *(the devil)* joins them *"for ever and ever."* Paul says in I Corinthians 15:26, *"The last enemy that shall be destroyed is death."* Thus **God** finishes the work of putting all enemies under Messiah's feet as He said

He would and as Jesus is "expecting" Him to *(Ps. 110:1; Heb. 10:13).*

Now, God Himself Is Coming!

Verses 11-15:

> *"And I saw a great white throne, and him that sat on it, from whose face the earth and the heaven fled away;* and there was found no place for them. And I saw the dead, small and great, **stand before God**; and the books were opened: and another book was opened, which is the book of life: and the dead were judged out of those things which were written in the books, according to their works. And the sea gave up the dead which were in it; and death and hell delivered up the dead which were in them: And they were judged every man according to their works. And death and hell were cast into the lake of fire. This is the second death. And whosoever was not found written in the book of life was cast into the lake of fire. "*

This is the "great white throne" judgement and **the one on the throne is God**. God told us in Revelation 1:8 and 4:8 that **He is coming!**

> *"I am Alpha and Omega, the beginning and the ending, saith the Lord, which is, and which was, **and which is to come**, the **Almighty**" (Rev. 1:8).*

Paul said in Acts 17:31 that **God will judge the world.**

> *"Because he* (God) *hath appointed a day, in the which **he will judge the world** in righteousness by **that man** whom he hath ordained."*

Christ *("that man")* will be the standard by which all men will be judged. To pass that judgement one must be as righteous as Jesus *(which is impossible)*, or be a partaker of his righteousness.

Listen to what Paul says in I Corinthians 15:21-24:

> *"For since by man came death, by man came also the resurrection of the dead.* For as in **Adam** all die, even

243

> *so in **Christ** shall all be made alive. **But every man in***
> ***his own order: Christ the firstfruits***: *afterward they*
> *that are Christ's at his coming. **Then cometh the end,***
> ***when he shall have delivered up the kingdom to God,***
> ***even the Father***; *when he shall have put down all rule*
> *and all authority and power. "*

Jesus the Messiah has been appointed, anointed, and empowered to build a kingdom. But what will he do with this kingdom? **He will deliver it up** *"to God even the Father."* Verse 25 *(I Cor. 15)* says *"For he* (Christ) *must reign, till he* (God) *hath put all enemies under his* (Christ's) *feet. " (Remember Ps. 110:1, "The Lord said unto my Lord, sit thou at my right hand, until I make thine enemies thy footstool, "* and Hebrews 1:13, *"But to which of the angels said he at any time, Sit on my right hand, until I make thine enemies thy footstool? ")*

> *"The last enemy that shall be destroyed is death" (I Cor.*
> *15:26).*

That is at the end of the Millennium when *"death and hell (are) cast into the lake of fire. "*

> *"For he* (God) *hath put all things under his* (Jesus') *feet.*
> *But when he* (David) *saith all things are put under him*
> (Jesus-Messiah), *it is manifest* (evident) *that he* (God) *is*
> *excepted, which did put all things under him* (Jesus)"
> (Paul speaking) *(I Cor. 15:27).*

Do not let this confuse you. Paul is saying, When David said in Psalm 8:6 that all things are put under Christ, **there is one exception**, God who put all things under Christ, is not under him. **God is not under Christ, Christ is under God**.

> *"The head of Christ is God" (I Cor. 11:3).*
> *"And when all things shall be subdued unto him, **then***
> ***shall the Son also himself be subject unto him that put***
> ***all things under him, that God may be all in all"** (I*
> *Cor. 15:28).*

Many of us have made Jesus all, but the apostle Paul says, **God is all!**

Back to Revelation Chapter 21, verses 2-7:

> *"And I John saw the holy city, new Jerusalem, **coming
> down from God out of heaven**, prepared as a bride
> adorned for her husband. And I heard a great voice out
> of heaven saying, Behold, the tabernacle* (habitation) *of
> God is with men, and **he will dwell with them**, and they
> shall be his people, and **God himself shall be with
> them,** and be their God. And **God shall wipe away all
> tears from their eyes**. And he that sat upon the throne
> said, Behold I make all things new. And he said unto
> me, **It is done**. I am Alpha and Omega, the beginning
> and the end.. He that overcometh shall inherit all
> things; and **I will be his God**, and **he shall be my son**."*
>
> (Notice, *"I will be his God"*).

We will live and reign with Jesus the Lamb for 1000 years on earth, and that will be glorious, the day for which we have longed. **But this will be the ultimate! God will** *"dwell"* **with us,** *"God himself"* shall be with us and *"**God will wipe away all tears**"* from our eyes. Notice verses 5 and 6, *"And he that sat upon the throne* (God) *said, **Behold I make all things new**. And he said unto me, **It is done**."* The day God said this to John over 1900 years ago, **it was "done."** All things were made new in the unchangeable plan and purpose of God. In our reality it is **not yet done**, but in the "foreknowledge of God" **it is done!** God *"calleth those things which be not as though they were" (Rom. 4:17)*. Thus it was with the birth of Jesus. When God spoke it **before** time **it was done**, but he came forth **in time**, from the womb of a virgin.

Verses 10-11:

> *"And he carried me away in the spirit to a great and
> high mountain, and showed me that great city, the holy
> Jerusalem, descending out of heaven from God, Having
> the glory of God."*

Remember, Jesus called this city in Rev. 3:12, *"The city of my God which is new Jerusalem, which cometh down out of heaven from my God."*

No wonder Jesus said in Matthew 5:35:

> *"Neither* (swear) *by Jerusalem; for it is the city of the great King" (Matt. 5:35).*
>
> *"I am a **great King**, saith the Lord of hosts" (Mal. 1:14).*
>
> *"For **the Lord most high** is terrible; he is a **great King** over all the earth" (Ps. 47:2).*
>
> *"For the Lord is a great God, and a **great King** above all gods" (Ps. 95:3).*

Verses 22-23:

> *"And I saw no temple therein: for the **Lord God Almighty and the Lamb are the temple of it.** And the city had no need of the sun, neither of the moon, to shine in it: **for the glory of God did lighten it, and the Lamb is the light thereof."***

The Lord God Almighty and the Lamb are still spoken of by John as two distinct persons. This is seen in the words used to describe the light that shines from them. The word **"lighten"** in the phrase *"the glory of God did lighten it"* is the Greek **"photizo"** *(#5461 in Strong's Concordance)* and it means to **"shed rays, to brighten up."** These are the rays of God's glory that we could not look upon except in our new glorified bodies. The word **"light"** in the phrase, *"the Lamb is the light thereof,"* is the Greek word **"luchnos"***(#3088 in Strong's)* and means "a portable lamp or a candle." This is not my truth; this is the Word of God, but there is a vast difference in "rays of glory" and "a portable lamp."

Chapter 22, verses 1 & 3-6:

> *"And he shewed me a pure river of water of life, clear as crystal, proceeding out of the **throne of God and of the Lamb**. And there shall be no more curse: but **the throne of God and of the Lamb shall be** in it; and his servants shall serve him: **And they shall see his face***

> **(God's)***: and his name shall be in their foreheads. And there shall be no night there; and they need no candle, neither light of the sun; for **the Lord God giveth them light*** ("photizo" - rays of glory)*: and they shall reign for ever and ever. And he said unto me, These sayings are faithful and true: and **the Lord God of the holy prophets** sent his angel to shew unto his servants the things which must shortly be done. "*

"The throne of God and of the Lamb." Remember Jesus' words in Rev. 3:21, *"Even as I also overcame, and am **set down with my Father in his throne**. "*

Verse 9:

> *"Worship God. "*

Please consider this fact. Not one time in the book of Revelation is the word "worship" used in regard to Jesus Christ, the Lamb. I am not saying that Jesus should not receive worship as the Son of God, but I am saying that it is absent from this book. *"They shall see his face. "* **The Lord God has a face** and we shall see it. "The Lord God giveth them light" *(again photizo - rays of God's glory).*

Verses 16-21:

> *"I Jesus have sent mine angel to testify unto you these things in the churches. **I am the root and offspring of David**, and the bright and morning star. And the Spirit and the bride say, Come. And let him that heareth say, Come. And let him that is athirst come. And whosoever will, let him take the water of life freely. For I testify unto every man that heareth the words of the prophecy of this book, If any man shall add unto these things, God shall add unto him the plagues that are written in this book: And if any shall take away from the words of the book of this prophecy, God shall take away his part out of the book of life, and out of the holy city, and from*

the things which are written in this book. He which
testifieth these things saith, Surely I come quickly.
Amen. Even so, come, Lord Jesus. The grace of our
Lord Jesus Christ be with you all. Amen. "

One final note. The book of Revelation is primarily about God. "God" is mentioned 99 times. Jesus is mentioned 14 times and the Lamb *(Jesus)* is mentioned 29 times. ***To God be the Glory!***

---

*"Our opponents sometime claim that no belief should be held dogmatically which is not explicitly stated in Scripture...but the **Protestant churches** have themselves accepted such dogmas as **the Trinity**, for which there is **no such precise authority** in the Gospels."*

Noted Catholic scholar Graham Greene
Defending the dogma of the Assumption of Mary.
(Chapter 13 ~ Note 19)

Chapter 13

Fables - Catholicism

"And Jesus answered and said unto them, Take heed
*that no man **deceive** you. For many shall come in my*
*name, saying, I am Christ; and shall **deceive** many.*
*And many false prophets shall rise, and shall **deceive***
many. For there shall arise false Christs, and false
prophets, and shall show great signs and wonders;
*insomuch that, if it were possible they shall **deceive** the*
very elect" (Jesus) *(Matt. 24:4-5, 11, 24).*
*"Neither give heed to **fables"** (Paul) (I Tim. 1:4).*
"For the time will come when they will not endure
sound doctrine...and they shall turn away their ears
*from the truth, **and shall be turned unto fables"** (Paul)*
(II Tim. 4:3-4).

$\mathcal{S}$ince this book is about the glory of God, the Holy One of Israel, and since we are on a search for His truth, and ready to explore any error that takes glory from Him, we need to address some fables that are deceiving the hearts and minds of modern man, and leading millions to destruction. Notice that Jesus used the word **"deceive"** four times in Matthew chapter 24, which contains our Lord's greatest recorded teaching on end time events. The disciples had come to Jesus privately as he sat upon the mount of Olives overlooking Jerusalem, and asked him a question, *"What shall be the sign of thy coming, and of the end of the world" (v.3)?* Jesus began his answer to their question with this warning, *"Take heed that no man **deceive** you" (v.4).* From his repeated use of the word "deceive" we understand that deception will be the hallmark of the age before he returns. Deception is insidious and

249

creeps in where we least expect it. **Good people become deceived. Good intentioned people become deceived.** In fact, Jesus said that at the end time deception would be so cunning, *"that if it were possible, they would deceive the very elect."*

The apostles of our Lord were troubled by deception that crept in, in their time. John saw the spirit of anti-christ already at work in his day and wrote, *"even now are there many anti-christs; whereby we know that it is the last time" (I John 2:18).* Please keep in mind that the term "anti-christ" means not only **"against"** Christ but also **"in place of"** Christ.

Paul devoted much of his epistles to dealing with deceptions. One notable example is found in Paul's letters to Timothy. In I Tim. 1:19-20 he writes, *"**Holding faith**, and a good conscience; which some having **put away** concerning faith have **made shipwreck**: Of whom is Hymenaeus and Alexander; whom I have delivered unto Satan, that they may learn not to blaspheme."* These men were Christian brothers and they had **blasphemed**, but how? Had they cursed God? Had they taken His name in vain? No, they had preached and taught **false doctrine**. Paul sheds more light on this situation in II Tim. 2:15-18 where he says:

> *"Study to show thyself approved **unto God**, a workman that **needeth not to be ashamed, rightly dividing** the word of truth. But **shun profane** and **vain babblings**: for they will increase unto more ungodliness. And their **word will eat** as doth a canker* (gangrene)*: of whom is Hymenaeus and Philetus; Who concerning the **truth** have erred, **saying that the resurrection is past already;** and overthrow the faith of some."*

These Scriptures help us understand how "the God of truth" views false teaching. Those of us who take up the Bible to teach and preach it have a grave responsibility before God to seek Him for guidance of the Holy Spirit, "the spirit of truth" so we can "rightly divide the word of truth." What these men taught, "that the resurrection is past already," seems mild compared to some of the things that are taught today under the banner of "Christian doctrine."

The great apostle Paul, inspired by the Holy Spirit, looked down through the telescope of time and wrote of the day in which we are living:

> *"For the time will come when they will not endure sound doctrine; but after their own lusts shall they heap* ***to themselves teachers****, having itching ears, and shall* ***turn away their ears from the truth****, and shall be* ***turned unto fables"*** *(II Tim. 4:3-4).*

God's man, the apostle Peter, also speaks of **fables** in II Peter 1:16 saying:

> *"We have not followed **cunningly devised fables."***

What is a fable? Webster's dictionary gives these definitions, #1 - "a **fictitious story** meant to **teach a moral lesson**: the characters are usually **talking animals**." #2 - "*a **myth** or **legend**. #3 - "*a **story that is not true; falsehood."*** With these definitions firmly in mind, let us look at some of the major deceptions in our world today to understand how Satan, the master deceiver, has used "cunningly devised fables" to lead multiplied millions of people, many of them well intentioned, along the road to hell.

A FABLE CALLED CATHOLICISM.

One false religion of our time which claims over one billion adherent's world wide is the Roman Catholic Church. The beginnings of Roman Catholicism were set in place when the Roman Emperor Constantine supposedly became a Christian in A.D. 313, at a time when the Church that Jesus Christ had established in the first century, on the foundation of his apostles and prophets, had begun to drift into worldliness and false teachings. Conversion to Christianity was a clever political move for Constantine, who needed to solidify his rule, and for Christians it meant the end of persecution and torture. In 325 A.D. Constantine convened the Council of Nicea, Turkey, determined its agenda, gave the opening speech, and presided over it from an exalted position on a wrought gold throne. Out of this Council came the beginnings of the doctrine of the Trinity with which we have dealt extensively in this book. The historical record is clear that Constantine continued to officiate at pagan celebrations and support pagan temples, even as he was building Christian churches. As head of the pagans, he was *Pontifix Maximus*, but as leader of the Christians he called himself *Vicarius Christi*, Vicar of Christ. This meant that he was acting as "another Christ," and he surely is a prototype of the anti-christ *(in place of Christ),* that the world is soon to worship. Thus the church was wedded to Rome, Christianity to paganism, which developed during the Dark Ages into the Holy Roman Empire under the Pope (papa) of Rome. That the Roman Catholic Church is the harlot astride the scarlet colored beast of Revelation Chapters 17 & 18 has been believed and taught by men of God through the centuries. This fact has been acknowledged unashamedly by Catholic leaders and apologists in Catholic literature, and it is remarkable that all of the sins of that unholy system have been openly admitted to in the *Catholic Encyclopedia*, and other Catholic publications. These sins are many, from the outright purchase of the Papacy by money and favors, to the wars of rival claimants to the supposed "throne of saint Peter," to the sale of indulgences *(the right to sin),* to the deafening silence of Pope Pious XII while Hitler and the Nazis slaughtered some 6 million innocent Jews in concentration camps during WWII.

Let us see her as John saw her in Rev. Chapter 17:3-6:

> *"So he carried me away in the spirit into the wilderness: and I saw a woman sit upon a scarlet colored beast, full **of names of blasphemy,** having **seven heads** and ten horns. And the woman was arrayed in **purple and scarlet color,** and **decked with gold and precious stones and pearls,** having a golden cup in her hand full of abominations and filthiness of **her fornication:** And upon her forehead was a name written, MYSTERY, BABYLON THE GREAT, THE MOTHER OF HARLOTS AND ABOMINATIONS OF THE EARTH.* ***And I saw the woman drunken with the blood of the saints, and with the blood of the martyrs of Jesus:***

and when I saw her, I wondered with great admiration" (awe).

The angel begins to explain to John and us this awesome vision. Look at verse 18.

*"And the woman which thou sawest is that **great city**, which **reigneth over the kings of the earth"** (Rev. 17:18).* In John's day (A.D. 96) this could only refer to one city, **Rome.**

*"And saying, Alas, alas, that **great city**, that was clothed in fine linen, and purple, and scarlet, and decked with gold, and precious stones, and pearls" (18:16)!*

*"And cried when they saw the smoke of her burning, saying, What **city** is like unto this **great city"** (18:18).*

Bible Fact #1.

This harlot woman is **a city, a great city!** Now see Rev. 17:9:

*"And here is the mind which hath wisdom. The seven heads are **seven mountains**, on **which the woman** sitteth."*

Bible Fact #2.

This harlot woman, this great city sits on seven mountains. What great city in the world today was built on "seven mountains." It is none other than Rome, Italy, which legend says was built by Rumulus and Remus. It sits on **seven mountains** *(hills)* and is called, "the city of seven hills." *The Catholic Encyclopedia* says, "It is within the city of Rome, **called the city of seven hills**, that the entire area of Vatican State property is now confined." [1] This is Rome, the seat of the Papacy, home of Vatican City, which in 1929 was made a country of its own by an act of the Italian dictator Mussolini. Let's look further.

"And he (the angel) *saith unto me, The waters which thou sawest, where the whore sitteth, are peoples, and multitudes, and nations, and tongues" (Rev. 17:15).*

So the harlot woman, Rome, also sits on waters, representing peoples

253

(different races), multitudes *(masses)*, nations and tongues *(people of different languages)*. She had some other **shocking characteristics**. *"The woman was arrayed in purple and scarlet color" (17:4)*. These are the colors of the Roman Church, used by Bishops and Cardinals, **purple** being the color of the **Bishops** and other prelates and **scarlet** of the **Cardinals**. She was *"decked with gold and precious stones and pearls" (17:4)*. This woman is very rich. Is there a "richer" institution on earth than Vatican City, possessor of buildings and real estate holdings world wide, art treasures and paintings, gold, diamond encrusted crucifixes, etc., until it has shamed the name of Christ, who had no place to lay his head and was buried in a borrowed tomb? And to add to the farce, they have feigned poverty while chastising others, *(even the U.S.A.)* for not doing enough for the poor. Now look at verse 6 of Chapter 17:

> *"And I saw the woman drunken with the blood of the*
> *saints, and with the blood of the martyrs of Jesus."*

The fact that the Roman Catholic Church killed millions in her inquisitions against so called "heretics," through the centuries called the "Dark Ages," is a matter of history which I will not take time to document again in this book. One very good source of this information is a book written by John Foxe *(1516-1587)* an English Protestant Clergyman, called *"Foxe's Book of Martyrs,"* which contains full accounts of English Protestant martyrs. Foxe had been allowed access to official records and the horrors which he documents are painful to read. This book which has never been refuted was very popular in the colonial days of America, and helped to shape the thinking of our founding fathers, who gave us a government free from religious oppression. The Catholic Church opposed the founding of the United States of America, based on the freedom of the individual, a concept that she has opposed through the centuries of her existence. Mr. Foxe's book, along with other works, even Catholic materials that certify these horrors, are readily available in bookstores[20].

The current pope, Benedict XVI, the former Cardinal Joseph Ratzinger, was featured on the cover of *Newsweek* Magazine in an article entitled,

"Benedict XVI, What he means for American Catholics." Here are a few enlightening quotes, "Last week, after Ratzinger was elected to succeed John Paul II as heir to the throne of Saint Peter... ." *(If Peter had a throne it is a fact not hinted at in Scripture, and it is for sure that he did not and does not.)* "Today the 78-year-old pontiff presides over the much vaster empire of the 1.1 billion strong Roman Catholic Church - over its dogma and doctrine, charisma and communication, rituals and real estate, seminarians and aspiring Saints." *Newsweek* continues, "In 1981 John Paul II named him perfect of the congregation for the Doctrine of the Faith, a position that formerly went by the title Grand Inquisitor. **In Ratzinger's time**, of course, **torture wasn't part of the agenda**. But in the realm of ideas, **Ratzinger was ruthless**." [2] (emphasis mine) Note that the office of "Grand Inquisitor" has not been abolished, only the name has changed.

Another article from the same issue of *Newsweek*, titled, "The Real Benedict," begins with this shocking statement, "Judging from the hysteria in some quarters after his election, you might have thought Pope Benedict XVI was ordering boxes of freshly polished thumbscrews *(torture instruments)* to be brought to the papal apartments from the bowels of the congregation for the Doctrine of the Faith ("...formerly known as the Inquisition...." their quote) while concurrently issuing orders for the **rusty guillotine** that served the 19th century Papal States to be hauled out of storage and reassembled." [3] *(Remember John saw her "drunken with the blood of the saints, and with the blood of the martyrs of Jesus.")* May God have mercy on humanity if Rome ever gains absolute power again. This is not a Godly institution, and these are not Godly men. **This for sure is not the church that Jesus Christ built.**

> *"And he* (the angel) *cried mightily with a strong voice, saying, Babylon the great is fallen, is fallen, and is become the **habitation** of **devils**, and the hold of every **foul spirit**, and a cage of every **unclean** and **hateful bird**." (Rev. 18:2).*

The sins of the Roman Church are well documented in history but the angel cries out that she "is become" something more: *"the habitation of devils, and the hold* (a compartment) *of every foul spirit, and a cage of every unclean and hateful bird" (18:2).* This is demonic activity and unclean things are going on here that God **sees well**, but are only seen barely by you and me. But we have seen enough lately in the news to shock our minds and cause us to ask ourselves what is happening with the Catholic Church. For instance, an article appeared in our *The Tennessean* newspaper, with the large headline: *"Survey: 40% of nuns in U.S. suffer from sexual trauma."* "St. Louis - already shaken by a year-long sex abuse scandal involving priests and minors, the Roman Catholic Church has yet to face another critical challenge - how to help thousands of nuns who say they have been sexually victimized. A national survey, completed in 1996 **but intentionally never publicized**, estimates that a "minimum" of 34,000 Catholic nuns, or about 40% of all nuns in the U.S., have suffered some form of sexual trauma. Some of that sexual abuse...has come at the hands of priests and other nuns in the church, the report said." The article continued, "Many of the nuns said they were left with feelings of anger, shame, anxiety and depression. Some said it made them consider leaving religious life, and a few said they had attempted suicide." One of the study's researchers, Ann Wolfe said, "The bishops appear to be only looking at the issue of **child** sexual abuse, but the problem is bigger than that." These nuns were educated women, "more than 9 of 10 who returned questionnaires had at least a college education." [4] **What a shame!**

Consider this five column article in the *U.S.A. Today* newspaper with the large headline, *"Abuse Response varies by diocese."* The sub-headline reads, *"Catholic Church structure tends to complicate reform efforts."* "Boston - Year after year since 1985, Catholic dioceses across the nation have been forced to come forward with the same ugly confession. Some priests have committed acts of pedophilia. **Worse yet, church leaders knew but did little to prevent it."** The article continues, "Many of the nations 194 dioceses are struggling to come to terms with a cultural change from a time when **allegations of pedophilia were handled privately.** "[5]

An article from *The Tennessean* titled, *"Study puts more heat on bishops."* Sub-titled, *"Two-thirds kept accused priests on job."* The article read: "Dallas - **roughly two thirds of the top U.S. Catholic leaders have allowed priests accused of sexual abuse to keep working**, a practice that spans decades and **continues today**. Church spokesmen did not dispute the results of the study." One other statement, "Some representatives of the Vatican....are suggesting that U.S. church leaders **not cooperate fully** with secular authorities." [6]

Another huge article in the *U.S.A. Today* had this title, *"Can lawsuits dismantle Church?"* Quote, "American's legal system is shifting into high gear to punish the Catholic Church for the sexual misdeeds of its priests through multimillion dollar lawsuits." [7]

Time and *Newsweek* Magazines have covered the sex scandal extensively but I will cite only two issues. *Newsweek* featured a full cover picture of Cardinal Law of the Boston Diocese and large bold type, *"Sex, Shame, and the Catholic Church,"* then smaller print, *"80 Priests accused of child abuse in Boston and new soul searching across America."* From quite a large article, here are a few enlightening excerpts.

"The cases the church is grappling with now involve two phenomena that are psychologically distinct but are all lumped together for legal and moral consideration: pedophilia, defined as intense or recurrent sexual desire for prepubescent children; and sexual advances on sexually mature, but underage, boys and girls." It continues, "But some researchers think the priesthood may hold a dangerous attraction for pedophiles." Then this troubling question, "Is the failure of the Church to confront the problem of sex abuse **bred in its bones**?" *Newsweek* continues, "But secrecy and silence have always characterized the Catholic Church, and in many of these cases the Church does all it can to prevent the charges from coming to light - sometime to the point of **writing threatening letters to outspoken priests**, or advocating that incriminating documents be shipped out of U.S. jurisdiction." One authority on priests and sexual abuse is quoted as saying, "By Vatican light the worst thing a bishop can do is become **publically**

associated with a scandal." [8]

In *Time* Magazine an article titled, *"The Cost of Penance,"How do you put a price on sexual abuse?"* begins with this paragraph: "The Medieval Roman Catholic Church sold indulgences to sinners who **thought cash** could purchase exoneration in heaven. Today it's the church that is handing out money in hopes of **buying forgiveness** for itself. The surging scandal over sexual abuse by the priesthood is proving as financially damaging to the church as it is hurtful to the faith, as Catholic dioceses across the country dole out huge sums to victims to compensate them for their pain and to **keep them silent**." [9]

This harlot woman, with whom God says, *"The kings of the earth have committed fornication, and the inhabitants of the earth have been made drunk with the wine of her fornication,"* (she has prostituted herself spiritually in the name of Christ) was introduced to John thus in Rev. 17:3 :

> *"And I saw a woman sit upon a scarlet colored beast,*
> *full of the **names of blasphemy**."*

So John associated this woman with **"blasphemy."** Has she blasphemed? Yes, and continues to do so. It is blasphemy to proclaim that Mary the mother of Jesus is "co-redemptrix" *(redeemer)* with Christ, and that all of the grace of God which flows to man must come through Mary, as did the late John Paul II. *Soul Magazine*, Official publication of The Blue Army of our Lady of Fatima in the U.S. and Canada *(22 million strong)* declares: *"Mary is so perfectly united with the Holy Spirit **that He acts only through His spouse** (Mary)...all our life, every thought, word, and deed is in Her hands....at every moment, she Herself must instruct, guide, and transform each one of us into Herself, so that not we but She lives in us, as Jesus lives in Her, and the Father in the Son."* [10] To refer to Mary as the "**spouse**" of the Holy Spirit is blasphemy.

Mary is called in Catholic literature the "Queen of Heaven," and was referred to often using that title by the late John Paul II. *The Encyclopedia of Catholicism* says, "Queen of Heaven is a Marian title pertaining to the belief that, after her assumption, Mary was crowned Queen of Heaven" [11] (another Catholic fable). *Time* Magazine states that "*according to modern Popes*" Mary is "*the Queen of the Universe, Queen of Heaven, Seat of Wisdom...*" [12]

In John Paul II's September 1993 speech in Lithuania, he spoke of Mary as "Mother of the Church, Queen of the Apostles, dwelling place of the Trinity!" He told "priests and aspirants to the priestly life, men and women religious "to look to Mary...To Mary I entrust all of you." [13] The expression "queen of heaven" is found only one place in the Bible, Jeremiah Chapter 44, and refers to a pagan goddess to which the backslidden Israelites were burning incense. God condemned this worship through the prophet Jeremiah and said in verse 22:

> "*So that the Lord could no longer bear, because of the evil of your doings, and because of the abominations which ye have committed; therefore is your land a desolation, and an astonishment, and a curse, without an inhabitant, as at this day.*"

They call her "Queen of Heaven," but they try to make her God.

Look at the **titles** that the popes have appropriated for themselves and see the extent of their sacrilege. *(The word sacrilege means "appropriating to oneself what is consecrated to God," i.e.* **taking God's glory***)*. The pope is known by over one billion Catholics as "Holy Father," a title even used on T.V. by top Protestant and Full Gospel ministers in speaking of John Paul II at the time of his recent passing. The only time that "Holy Father" can be found in the pages of the Bible is in Jesus' great prayer to God the Father in John 17:11:

> "***Holy Father***, *keep through thine own name those whom thou hast given me, that they may be one, as we are.*"

Couple this with what Jesus said in Matthew 23:9, and you will see the extent of their blasphemy:

> "*And call **no man** your father upon the earth: for **one is your Father**, which is in heaven.*"

The Popes have at times called themselves, and been called by others **"God."**

Pope Innocent III *(AD 1198-1216)* declared "The Pope holds the place of **the true God**.". The Lateran Council *(AD 1123)* acclaimed the Pope as **"Prince of the Universe"** and Pope Nicholas *(AD 858-867)* boasted, "What can you make me **but God**?" Ferrar's *(Roman Catholic) AN ECCLESIASTICAL DICTIONARY* states:

"The Pope is of such dignity and highness that he is not simply a man but, **as it were, God** and the **vicar** *(representative)* **of God**...the Pope's excellence in power are not only above heaven, terrestrial and infernal things, but he is also above angels...He is of such great dignity and power that he occupies **one and the same tribunal with Christ**...The pope is, as it were, **God on earth**...the Pope is of so great authority and power that he can modify, declare or interpret the divine law." [14]

Pope Leo XIII, in his encyclical, The Reunion of Christendom (1885), declared that "the pope holds upon this earth the place of **God Almighty**."

The New York Catechism says:

The pope takes the place of Jesus Christ here on earth..... He is the infallible ruler, the founder of dogmas, the author of and the judge of councils; the universal ruler of truth, the arbiter of the world, the supreme judge of heaven and earth, the judge of all, being judged by no one, **God himself** on earth." [15]

Dear reader, all of this violence, debauchery, spiritual fornication and blasphemy which seeks to take from God Almighty the glory due **His holy name**, is built upon two main fables. One, that the apostle Peter, when he was given the keys to the kingdom by Jesus in Matt. 16:19, was given by Jesus absolute authority *("primacy")* over the other apostles and that he went to Rome and became its bishop, the first Pope of Rome. Thus the claim that the Pope sits on the throne of St. Peter. Vatican Council II states, "For God's only begotten Son...was a treasure for the militant church...he has entrusted it to blessed Peter, **the key - bearer of heaven**, and to his successors who are Christ's vicars on earth, so that they may distribute it to the faithful for their salvation." [16] **This is fiction, a fable**. First of all the "keys of the kingdom" of which Jesus spoke, pertained to the fact that Peter would preach the two sermons that God would use to open the door of salvation to the Jews, and also the Gentiles. On the day of Pentecost when the Holy Ghost was poured out on those who were waiting in the upper room, about 120 people were filled "and began to speak with tongues *(languages)*, as the Spirit gave them utterance."

> *"Now when this was noised abroad, the multitude came*
> *together, and were confounded, because that every man*
> *heard them speak in his own language" (Acts 2:6).*

"But Peter, standing up with the eleven, lifted up his voice" (Acts 2:14) and preached Jesus unto them and about three thousand new converts were added to their number that day *(v. 41)*. This was tremendous.

Several years later when it was time in God's plan to begin to add Gentiles to the Church, Cornelius, a Roman Centurion over a group of soldiers at Caesarea, was earnestly praying. And God sent an angel to tell him to send to Joppa for **Simon Peter**, and *"he shall tell thee what thou oughtest to do" (Acts. 10:6)*. Thus it was Peter who preached the message at Cornelius' house which God used to open the door of salvation to the Gentiles. The importance which the Lord placed on this was expressed by Peter at a gathering of apostles and elders in Jerusalem some years later.

> *"Peter rose up, and said unto them, Men and brethren,*
> *ye know how that a good while ago God made choice*
> *among us, that the Gentiles by my mouth should hear*
> *the word of the gospel and believe" (Acts 15:7).*

Since *"it pleased God by the foolishness of preaching to save them that believe" (I Cor. 1:21)*, Peter by preaching on these two important occasions used the "keys to the kingdom," **but this in no way created a "throne of St. Peter**."

The binding and looseing of sins, which Jesus spoke of also in Matt. 16:19, was not exclusive to Peter but was given to all of the twelve apostles

261

in Matt. 18:18 and John 20:23. In spite of the fact that the Catholic Church has claimed to have found Peter's bones under the Basilica of St. Peter in Rome, there is no good evidence in or out of the Bible to prove that he was ever in that city. Paul spent much time in Rome, in prison for the gospel, and though he mentions in his epistles the names of many brethren *(24 in Rom. 16)*, Peter is never alluded to. The record seems clear that he was not there.

The other main fable which Rome uses to hold power over her subjects is the **doctrine of purgatory**. The term "purgatory," taken from the word "purge" refers to a third realm of existence to which they teach the dead go, for an indeterminate period of time, to be "purged" by suffering from the sins for which they were not cleansed while on earth. This false doctrine arose in the fourteenth century and has been used to extract money from sorrowing loved ones on earth, who were fearful that the deceased were suffering in purgatory on one of its many levels. They were taught that the prayers of priests could aid the dead in transfer to a **less painful level**, or affect their **release into heaven**. The statements of Vatican Council II held in Rome in 1962-1965 prove that they still teach this heresy:

"The truth has been divinely revealed that sins are followed by punishments. God's holiness and justice inflict them. This **may be done on this earth through** the **sorrows, miseries,** and trials of this life and, above all, **through death. Otherwise the expiation** *(atonement)* **must be made** in the **next life** through fire and torments or **purifying punishments. The reasons for their imposition are that our souls need to be purified**, the holiness of the moral order needs to be strengthened and God's glory must be restored to its full majesty" [17]

"If anyone says that after the **reception of the grace of justification the guilt is so remitted and the debt of eternal punishment so blotted out** to every repentant sinner, **that no debt of temporal punishment remains to be discharged either in this world** or in **purgatory** before the gates of heaven can be opened, **let him be anathema** *(cursed)*" (The Council of Trent). [18]

Why do men persist in bowing under such grievous yokes when Jesus said:

> *"And ye shall find rest unto your souls, For my yoke is*
> *easy, and my burden is light" (Matt. 11:29-30).*

Catholicism teaches that there are two sources for truth and doctrines, the Bible and tradition. Some of the main Catholic apologists of our day admit that many of her primary doctrines are not found in the Bible; the **Trinity, prayers to Mary and Purgatory**. To defend the dogma of the assumption of Mary, Catholic scholar Graham Greene stated: "Our opponents sometimes claim that no belief should be held dogmatically which is not explicitly stated in Scripture...but the PROTESTANT CHURCHES have themselves accepted such dogmas as THE TRINITY, for which there is NO SUCH PRECISE AUTHORITY in the Gospels" [19] Jesus asked the scribes and Pharisees in Matt. 15:3, *"Why do ye also transgress the commandment of God by your tradition?"* God's word says in Mark 7:7, *"Howbeit in vain do they worship me, teaching for doctrines the commandments of men."*

The false church which taught for centuries that it was a mortal sin to eat meat on Friday, and told millions of travelers that St. Christopher was their patron saint and protector, and then removed these fallacies with the stroke of a pen, dare not give up the doctrine of purgatory. To do so would be to give up the **power through fear** by which Rome has held her subjects, even kings and emperors, who believed that their only hope of release from the horrors of purgatory lay in the hands of the church. Notice what the angel told John in Rev. 17:18, *"And the woman which thou sawest is that great city, which reigneth over the kings of the earth."* **Purgatory** is not mentioned once in the Bible, neither does it teach that there is any "purging" for sins **after** death. Hebrews 1:3 says of Jesus, *"when he had by himself purged our sins, sat down on the right hand of the Majesty on high."* John says in I John 1:7, *"And the blood of Jesus Christ his Son cleanseth us from all sin."* He says also in verse 9, *"If we confess our sins, he is faithful and just to forgive us our sins, and to cleanse us from all unrighteousness."* If

263

you depart from this world without receiving the blood of Jesus as **payment in full** for your sins, no amount of time spent in purgatory will bring atonement. God is not asking for "penance" but "repentance," and if we believe and repent, the blood of Jesus Christ is more than sufficient for our cleansing and purging. To teach otherwise is nothing short of blasphemy. There is not one example of prayers for the dead in the Bible, nor is that concept taught in its pages. **The doctrine of "purgatory" is another Catholic fable.**

These false doctrines are used by Rome for riches, power and prestige and to make "gods" of men. But God Almighty, "the only true God," has seen it all and spoken her destruction.

> *"For her sins have reached unto heaven, and God hath remember her iniquities" (Rev. 18:5).*
>
> *"Therefore shall her plagues come in one day, death, and mourning, and famine; and she shall be utterly burned with fire: for strong is the Lord God who judgeth her. And the kings of the earth, who have committed fornication and lived deliciously with her, shall bewail her, and lament for her, when they shall see the smoke of her burning" (Rev. 18:8-9).*

But our loving God makes one last strong appeal to those who have been deceived and taken in by her fables:

> *"And I heard another voice from heaven, saying, **Come out of her, my people**, that ye be not partakers of her sins, and that ye receive not of her plagues" (Rev. 18:4).*

God is not bashing Roman Catholics in Revelation Chapters 17 and 18, but is warning those **"my people"** who have perhaps unwittingly been partakers of this idolatrous deception, **to run to Him for true salvation and refuge**.

Chapter 14

The Fable Called Islam

While the fable of Roman Catholicism was taking form in the West, another fable called Islam was being birthed in the East. The story of its birth and growth has been well covered by many, including the news media, since the recent rise of Islamic terrorism, and especially after the horrors of 9-11. We will just briefly look at this story and then go into the Bible to try and make sense of what we are seeing.

Muhammad, its founder and prophet was born in Mecca, Saudi Arabia in the year 570 A.D. His father died before he was born and he was raised by his mother as her only child, until her death when he was six. He then went to live with his grandfather on his father's side, a man who was caretaker of the main place of worship in Mecca, called AL-Ka'ba, a temple filled with idols to various pagan deities. When Muhammad's grandfather died while he was still in his youth, the care of the temple and Muhammad passed to his uncle, Abu Talib. His family's care of this temple occasioned young Muhammad to be there often and see the people bowing down to idols, and the merchandising of the idols by those who made them for sale. Apparently Muhammad was repulsed by what he saw, and at some point decided that he would never bow down to idols.

There are two things that are told regarding Muhammad's childhood that may help shed light on his outcome.

One, a story mentioned often in Muslim sermons says that when Muhammad was a small boy, one day while playing with his friends, the angel Gabriel came and took hold of him, laid him on the ground and tore open his chest. The angel supposedly reached in and extracted a blood clot from his heart and said: "That was the part of Satan in thee." The angel then washed him and restored his chest. His frightened friends, thinking that he was being murdered, went running to his nurse and when they returned they found him shaken, but okay.

265

The second story concerns a trip that Muhammad took with his uncle Abu Talib in a caravan from Mecca to Syria, when he was 12 years old. While in Syria he came in contact with a monk of the Nestorian sect, a group who called themselves Christians, but denied that Jesus was the son of God. Islamic history claims that the monk took an interest in young Muhammad, and prophesied over him to his uncle that he "would be the final prophet for our world."

In young manhood Muhammad became the leader of a caravan to Syria and eventually at the age of 25 married a wealthy caravan owner, a woman of Mecca named Khadija, who was 15 years his senior. The wedding was performed by her cousin Waraqa bin Neufel, pastor of a large "Christian" church in Mecca, of the sect called Ebionites, who like the Nestorians denied that Jesus was the son of God. Thus Muhammad was exposed to Christian doctrine and teachings in the years immediately following, but it was a perverted message.

Mohammad continued leading caravans and would at times go to the caves around Mecca to meditate. In 610 A.D. at the age of forty, he had an experience that terrified him. While meditating in the Cave of Hira, he said that the angel Gabriel came to him and demanded that he, "Read!" Muhammad said, "I do not know how to read." The angel caught him and pressed him very forcefully and said again, "Read!" To which Muhammad replied again, "I do not know how to read." The angel then released him and said: "Read! In the name of your Lord who has created all. He has created you from a clot. Read! And your Lord is the most Generous." Thus were the first verses of the Quran revealed and they are recorded in Surah (Chapter) 96:1-3. Muhammad ran home to his wife Khadija in terror crying, "Cover me! Cover me!" They covered him until his fear subsided. Then he said to his wife, "O Khadija, what is wrong with me? What has happened to me? I am afraid for myself." He told her the story and she consoled him. [1] For a time the frightened Muhammad did not know if he had had an encounter with an angel of God **or with the devil**.

When Muhammad went to Khadija's cousin, the deluded Christian preacher Waraqa for advice, he swore over him and said, "In the name of God who is in control of my life, you are the prophet of this Arabic nation and you received the great signs from God who came to Moses in time past. People will deny you and persecute you and kick you out of your city and fight you, and if I am alive when that time comes, I will defend Allah in the way no one can know except Allah himself." Waraqa, this blinded false prophet would be of little help, for he died a short while later. [2]

In the following weeks, with the encouraging prophecy and support from his wife, Muhammad returned to the Cave of Hira again and again to receive the beginnings of his revelation that are now recorded in the Quran.

Since Muhammad could neither read nor write, the revelations were told to those around him who wrote them down on whatever was available, including stones and palm leaves. The revelations at first sounded friendly to Jews and Christians, but in the years to come, as they both rejected his new religion, the Surah's sounded increasingly hostile. The revelations came over a period of 16 years but were not compiled into a book until years after Muhammad's death. Muhammad married 12 other wives during his years in Mecca and Medina, the youngest of which, Aisha his favorite, was nine years old when the union was consummated. He died in 632 A.D., (the cause of his death is disputed) at the age of 62 after a life of sin, violence and delusion. He believed until the end that he had been visited by the one true God, which he, and a billion of his followers call Allah.

But had he? Jesus said in Matthew 7:15-20:

> *"**Beware of false prophets,** which come to you in sheep's clothing, but **inwardly they are ravening wolves. Ye shall know them by their fruits.** Do men gather grapes of thorns, or figs of thistles? Even so every good tree bringeth forth good fruit; but **a corrupt tree bringeth forth evil fruit.** A good tree cannot bring forth evil fruit, neither can a corrupt tree bring forth good fruit. **Every tree that bringeth not forth good fruit is hewn down, and cast into the fire.** Wherefore*

by their fruits ye shall know them."

Jesus said concerning **false prophets**, *"Ye shall know them by their fruits."* The writer of Hebrews says regarding those we follow, *"Considering the **end of their conversation.**"* Not just what they say, but what fruit their teaching produces. How can we know today, over 13 centuries after a spirit spoke to Muhammad, whether it was the Spirit of God or of the evil one. There are many voices in the world and how are we to know which ones are of God? One, by **what they say.**

> *"And when they shall say unto you,* Seek unto them
> that have familiar spirits, and unto wizards that peep,
> and that mutter: **should not a people seek unto their
> God? To the law and to the testimony: if they speak
> not according to this word, it is because there is no
> light in them"** (Isa. 8:19-20).

We must judge what is said by God's Holy Bible, and then as Jesus said, know them by the fruit that they and their message bear. What does the Quran, the word of Allah say? I bought one at a local bookstore for about $7.00, have read it extensively and I must say it is fascinating. It was definitely "inspired" by someone other than an illiterate, 7th century camel caravan driver from the Arabian desert. I found it also to be a book of falsehoods. The Bible and the Quran cannot both be right, for they are diametrically opposed in their messages and their spirits. The God of the Bible is kind, loving and approachable. The god of the Quran is hateful, capricious, and unpredictable. The God of the Bible is steadfast; the god of the Quran is unreliable. The God of the Bible used 40 holy men to record His book and there is not one contradiction in it. The god of the Quran used one very flawed man to convey his book, and its message does not go in a straight line, and it is full of contradictions. They simply cannot be the same being. The god Allah is not the most High God, Holy One of Israel.

There are many untruths in the Quran but let's deal with several of the most glaring.

1. The Bible says that Abraham offered his son Isaac on Mt. Moriah

to God *(Genesis 22:2,9)*.

The Quran says that Abraham (Ibrahim) offered his son Ishmael (Ismail) as a sacrifice, Surah 37:100-109. Verses 103-104 describe it thus: "so when they both submitted and he (Ibrahim) threw him (Ismail) down upon his forehead, and we called out to him saying: O Ibrahim!" [3]

So which one is right? The Holy Bible is right and the Quran spoke a falsehood.

2. The Bible says plainly that God has a son. *"For God so loved the world that He gave his only begotten son" (John 3:16). "Therefore also that holy thing which shall be born of thee shall be called the Son of God" (Luke 1:35). "A voice came from heaven which said, Thou art my beloved son" (Luke 3:22).*

The Quran very clearly says in several places that **Allah has no son.** Surah 112:2-3 says, "Allah is he on whom all depend, He **begets not**, nor is he begotten." "O followers of the Book *(Bible)!* do not exceed the limits of your religion, but *(speak)* the truth, The Messiah, Isa *(Jesus)* son of Marium *(Mary)* is only an apostle of Allah...Allah is only one God; **far be it from His glory that he should have a son"** (Surah 4:171).

"Nay! We have brought to them the truth, and most surely they are liars. **Never did Allah take to Himself a son"** (Surah 23:90-91).

"Certainly you made an abominable assertion: That they ascribe a son to the Beneficent God. And it is not worthy of the Beneficent God that He should take *(to Himself) (words in previous brackets are in the Quran)* a son" (Surah 19:89,91,92). There are many more examples but that should suffice to prove that the Quran is not speaking the truth.

3. God's Holy Bible says that Jesus died on the cross.

"Jesus, when he had cried again with a loud voice, yielded up the ghost" (Matt. 27:50).

"And Jesus cried with a loud voice, and gave up the ghost" (Mark 15:37).

"This man (Joseph of Arimathea) *went unto Pilate and begged the body of Jesus" (Luke 23:52).*

"I am he that liveth, and was dead" (Rev. 1:18).

The Quran says that Jesus did not die, that it only appeared so.

(Surah 4:157) "And their saying: Surely we have killed the Messiah, Isa *(Jesus)* son of Marium *(Mary)*, the apostle of Allah and they did not kill him nor did they crucify him, but it appeared to them so...And they killed him not for sure. Nay, Allah took him up to Himself." The Quran says that Jesus did not die, was not really crucified but that he was taken up directly to Allah. Surah 5:110 says that Jesus lived to "old age." This is a falsehood! And how many people believe this falsehood? **Over one billion!**

One more example of lying by the spirit that inspired the Quran.

4. God's Bible says that He made an irrevokable covenant with the descendants of Abraham, Isaac, and Jacob which includes a land, a throne and a Messiah.

> *"And I will remember their sin no more.* **Thus saith the Lord, which giveth the sun for a light by day, and the ordinances of the moon and of the stars for a light by** *night, which divideth the sea when the waves thereof roar; The Lord of hosts is his name:* **If those ordinances depart from before me, saith the Lord, then the seed of Israel also shall cease from being a nation before me for ever"** *(Jer. 31:34-36).*
>
> *"For it shall come to pass in that day, saith the Lord of hosts, that* **I will break his yoke from off thy neck,** *and* **will burst thy bonds, and strangers shall no more serve themselves of him:** *But they shall serve the Lord their God, and David their king, whom I will raise up unto them. Therefore fear thou not, O my servant Jacob, saith the Lord; neither be dismayed, O Israel: for, lo* **I will save thee from afar, and thy seed from the land of their captivity; and Jacob shall return, and shall be in rest, and be quiet, and none shall make him afraid.** *For I am with thee, saith the Lord, to save thee: though*

> *I make a full end of all nations whither I have scattered*
> *thee" (Jer. 30:8-11).*
>
> *"I say then, **Hath God cast away his people?** God*
> *forbid. For I also am an Israelite, of the seed of*
> *Abraham, of the tribe of Benjamin. **God hath not cast***
> ***away his people** which he foreknew...For I would not,*
> *brethren, that ye should be ignorant of this mystery, lest*
> *ye should be wise in your own conceits; **that blindness***
> ***in part is happened to Israel until the fulness of the***
> ***Gentiles be come in.** And so all Israel shall be saved:*
> *as it is written, There shall come out of Zion the*
> *Deliverer, and shall turn away ungodliness from Jacob"*
> *(Rom. 11:1-2, 25-26).*

Yes, Israel stumbled through unbelief but their failure was not final. Because the Jews did not recognize their promised Messiah and insisted that Rome crucify him, a door of mercy was opened to the Gentiles, "until the fulness of the Gentiles be come in." **Jesus is building his church**.

> *"And upon this rock **I will build my church**; and the*
> *gates of hell shall not prevail against it" (Matt. 16:18).*
> *"Husbands, love your wives, even as **Christ** also **loved***
> ***the church**, and gave himself for it; That he might*
> *present it to himself a glorious Church, not having spot,*
> *or wrinkle, or any such thing" (Eph. 5:25, 27).*

Yes, God has made promises to Israel and God has made promises to His Church, none of which will ever be broken.

> *"For the gifts and calling of God are without*
> *repentance" (irrevokable) (Rom. 11:29).*
> *"Hath he (God) said, and shall he not do it? Or hath he*
> *spoken, and shall he not make it good" (Num. 23:19).*

Soon God will bring these two streams together, *"one new man"* in Christ *(Eph. 2:15)*, to make a mighty rushing river that will wash all obstacles from its path.

But what does the Quran say?

Surah 5:12-14, "And certainly **Allah made a covenant** with the **children** of **Israel**, and we raised up among them twelve chieftains (tribes); and Allah said: Surely I am with you if you keep up prayer and pay the poor rate and believe in my apostles and assist them and offer to Allah a goodly gift, I will most certainly cover your evil deeds...**But on account of their breaking their covenant we cursed them** and made their hearts hard...and with **those who say, we are Christians, we made a covenant, but they neglected a portion of what they were reminded of, therefore we excited among them enmity and hatred to the day of resurrection;** and Allah will inform them of what they did."

Surah 5:78-80, "Those who disbelieved from among the children of Israel were cursed by the tongue of Dawood *(David)* and Isa *(Jesus)*, son of Marium *(Mary)*; this was because they disobeyed and used to exceed the limit. They used not to forbid each other the hateful things *(which)* they did; certainly evil was what they did...Allah became displeased with them **and in chastisement shall they abide.**"

Surah 5:51, "O you who believe: **do not take the Jews and the Christians for friends;** they are friends of each other; **and whoever amongst you takes them for a friend, then surely he is one of them; surely Allah does not guide the unjust people**.

Surah 23:41, "**So the punishment overtook them in justice**, and we made them as **rubbish; so away with the unjust people**." Verse 44, "So away with a people who do not believe."

Surah 9:30, "And the **Jews say: Uzair is the son of Allah;** and the **Christians say: The Messiah is the son of Allah; may Allah destroy them**."

There are many more such Surahs, including those that say the Jews became apes and swine (2:65, 5:60, 7:166), and are cursed (2:87, 4:46, 5:78, 9:30). Some of the Surah's are laughable, such as Surah 11:42-43, which says Noah had another son who refused to go on the ark and drowned in the flood. Or Surah 19:17-34 which says that Mary the mother of Jesus was

Moses and Aaron's sister and birthed Jesus under a palm tree. Surah 5:6, "O you who believe! When you rise up to prayer...and if you are sick or on a journey, or one of you come from the privy, or you have touched the women, and you cannot find water, betake yourselves to pure earth *(dirt)* and wipe your faces and your hands therewith." (A verse like this can not be found in the Holy Bible)

The spirit that inspired the Quran is not only a spirit that speaks falsehoods but a spirit that inspired violence, thievery and murder in the hearts of Muhammad and his followers. There are scores of Surah's that advocate fighting and violence to take Islam to the world. For example:

Surah 8:12 "I will cast terror into the hearts of those who disbelieve. Therefore strike off their heads and strike off every fingertip of them."

Surah 9:5 "So when the sacred months have passed away, then slay the idolaters wherever you find them, and take them captives and lie in wait for them in every ambush."

Surah 9:73, "O Prophet! Strike hard against the unbelievers and the hypocrites and be unyielding to them; and their abode is hell."

Surah 9:123, "O you who believe! Fight those of the unbelievers who are near to you."

Surah 8:65-67, "O Prophet! Urge the believers to war...It is not for any Prophet to have captives until he hath made slaughter in the land."

Muhammad's dying words were reported to have been, "May Allah curse the Christians and Jews!" [4]

History records that the Prophet of Islam financed the building of his religion through raids in which innocent people were slaughtered and their goods taken as spoils. Thus began a long history of violence in the spread of Islam, making converts at the edge of the sword with the cry "convert or die." Its violent history has been written well by others, even Muslim historians, so for now suffice it to say, it is a history of a sea of blood. As justification before the bar of public opinion they point to the Crusades as an example of horrible violence by Christians. There is one remarkable difference, those who maimed and slaughtered during the Crusades did it

273

totally **against** the example and teachings of our Lord Jesus, but those who have slaughtered down through the centuries in the name of Islam, did it as good Muslims, following the commands and example of their prophet Muhammad. The leader of the 9-11 attackers, Muhammad Atta attended a mosque in Hamburg, Germany, where the imam preached that "Christians and Jews should have their throats slit." [5]

These things are not inspired by the God of the Bible who says, *"The Lord trieth the righteous: but the wicked and **him that loveth violence his soul hateth**" (Ps. 11:5).*

Now the question with which we are most concerned in this chapter, "Who is Allah?" The answer may lie in asking another question. What **spirit being** would inspire a book of lies and motivate his prophet and followers to pillage, murder and violence? The answer seems clear: Lucifer, Satan, the devil. Allah can be none other than Satan. Let's look into the Bible for proof.

* The God of the Bible cannot lie *(Titus 1:2)*
* "It was impossible for God to lie" (Hebrews 6:18).

Who is the liar?

> *"Why do ye not understand my speech? even because ye cannot hear my word. Ye are of your father the devil...(He) **abode not in the truth, because there is no truth in him**. When he speaketh a lie, he speaketh of his own: **for he is a liar, and the father of it**" (Jesus speaking) (John 8:43-44).*

> *"No lie is of the truth. **Who is a liar** but he that denieth that **Jesus is the Christ**? He is anti-christ, that **denieth the Father and the Son**" (I John 2:21-22).*

Who is the thief?

> *"**The thief** (Satan) **cometh not, but for to steal**, and to **kill**, and to **destroy**: I am come that you might have life" (Jesus) (John 10:10).*

> *"All that ever came before me are thieves and robbers:*

274

but the sheep did not hear them" (Jesus) *(John 10:8).*

Who is the murderer?

*"**If ye were Abraham's children, ye would do the works of Abraham**. But ye seek to kill me...This did not Abraham. Ye do the deeds of your father. If God were your Father, ye would love me: Ye are of your father, the devil, and the lusts of your father ye will do. He was a murderer from the beginning"* (Jesus) *(John 8:39-44).*

Now, for one final Biblical proof that Allah the god of Islam is non other than Lucifer, or Satan, please look with me at Isaiah 14:12-13:

*"How art thou fallen from heaven, **O Lucifer**, son of the morning! How art thou cut down to the ground, which didst weaken the nations! For thou hast said in thine heart, I will ascend into heaven, I will exalt my throne above the stars of God."*

What do these verses picture? This is Lucifer, who says in his "heart," "I will unseat God, I will replace him in the heavenlys." Of course **this he will never do!** But look at the remainder of verse 13 and 14:

*"I will sit **also upon the mount of the congregation, in the sides of the north**: I will ascend above the heights of the clouds; I will be like the most High."*

Where is this **place**, "the mount of the congregation, in the sides of the north," on which Lucifer says, "I will sit also"? Look at Psalm 48:1-2:

*"Great is the Lord, and greatly to be praised **in the city of our God, in the mountain of his holiness**. Beautiful for situation, the joy of the whole earth, is mount Zion, **on the sides of the north, the city of the great King."***

This is a place on planet Earth where Lucifer said, "I will sit!" Psalm 48 is a Psalm of David, which is sung in many Christian churches today, regarding Jerusalem, called Mt. Zion on the north side of Mt. Moriah, *"the sides of the north."* Notice in verse 2 David called it *"the city of the great King."* Jesus said in *Matthew 5:34, "Swear not at all; neither by heaven; for it is God's throne;"* (remember Lucifer said, *"I will ascend into heaven, I will exalt my throne above the stars of God")* **"Neither by Jerusalem;** *for it is the* **city of the great King.***"* Who is this great King of Jerusalem?

> *"For the Lord most high...is a* **great King** *over all the earth" (Psalm 47:2).*

> *"For the Lord is a great God, and a* **great King** *above all gods" (Psalm 95:3).*

So the great King is the Lord God and Jerusalem is his chosen city. The Bible says over 50 times that Jerusalem, including the Temple Mount is **God's throne on earth**.

> *"Then Solomon sat on the throne of the Lord,"* (in Jerusalem) *(I Chron. 29:23).*

> *"At that time they shall call Jerusalem the throne of the Lord; and all the nations shall be gathered unto it, to the name of the Lord, to Jerusalem" (Jer. 3:17).*

> *"There is a river, the streams whereof shall make glad the city of God* (Jerusalem), *the holy place of the tabernacles of the most High.* **God is in the midst of her***" (Ps. 46:4-5).*

> *"Sing praises to the* **Lord which dwelleth in Zion***" (Ps. 9:11).*

> *"Mount* **Zion** *which* **He loved***" (Ps. 78:68).*

> *"For the* **Lord hath chosen Zion; he hath desired it for his habitation***" (Ps. 132:13).*

> *"In that time* **shall the present be brought unto the Lord..., to the place of the name of the Lord of hosts,** *the* **mount Zion***" (Isa. 18:7).*

> *"Arise ye, and let us go up* **to Zion unto the Lord our God***" (Jer. 31:6).*

Now go back to Psalm 48:9 and see that this Zion is the temple mount.

> *"We have thought of thy loving-kindness, O God, in the midst of thy temple."*

This is the place that God chose, after King David had sinned in numbering Israel and God spoke their punishment.

> *"So the Lord sent pestilence upon Israel: and there fell of Israel seventy thousand men.* ***And God sent an angel unto Jerusalem to destroy it: and as he was destroying, the Lord beheld,*** *and he repented him of the evil, and said to the angel that destroyed,* ***It is enough, stay now thine hand.*** *And the angel of the Lord stood by the* ***threshingfloor of Ornan the Jebusite.*** *Then the angel of the Lord commanded Gad to say to David, that David should* ***go up, and set up an altar unto the Lord in the threshingfloor of Ornan the Jebusite"*** *(I Chron. 21:14-15, 18).*

God stayed the destroying angel's hand at the threshing floor of Ornan and commanded David to build an altar of sacrifice there. So David purchased the land and threshing floor from Ornan:

> *"And David built there an altar unto the Lord, and offered burnt offerings and peace offerings,* ***and called upon the Lord; and he answered him from heaven by fire upon the altar of burnt offering.*** *And the Lord commanded the angel; and he put up his sword again into the sheath thereof.* ***At that time when David saw that the Lord had answered him in the threshingfloor of*** *Ornan the Jebusite, then* ***he sacrificed there"*** *(I Chron. 21:26-28).*

Up until that time, the place where the Lord received sacrifice from Israel, and where Moses' tabernacle and the altar were set up, was in Gibeon. Sacrifices could only be offered at the place of God's choice.

> *"Then David said,* ***This is the house of the Lord God, and this is the altar of the burnt offerings for Israel"*** *(I Chr. 22:1).*

277

From that time forward David and Israel worshiped and sacrificed to God at that location. That was the place of Solomon's temple and the second temple, called Zerubbabel's or Herod's temple, where Jesus and Paul worshiped.

But Lucifer had said, *"I will sit upon the mount of the congregation, in the sides of the north,"* **the temple mount** *(Isa. 14:13).* But why did he refer to it as "the mount of the congregation"? When David brought Solomon before Israel, **at the temple mount** to anoint him king, all the gathered people were called **"the congregation"** five times. *"All Israel, the* **congregation of the Lord"** *(I Chr. 28:8).* When Solomon dedicated the **temple on that mount** in II Chron. Chapters 5 & 6, when he prayed that wonderful prayer and the glory of the Lord descended, those who gathered and worshiped are called **"the congregation"** six times. So the **temple mount** is the **"mount of the congregation."** Lucifer said, around 700 years B.C., **"I will sit upon the mount of the congregation** *(the temple mount),* **in the sides of the north (Jerusalem)."** But how could this happen?

When Israel rejected Jesus their King Messiah, he prophesied the destruction of the temple.

> *"And Jesus went out, and departed from the temple; and his disciples came to him for to shew him the **buildings** of the temple. And Jesus said unto them, See ye not all these things? Verily I say unto you, **There shall not be left here one stone upon another, that shall not be thrown down"** (Matt. 24:1-2)*

And in 70 A.D. some 38 years after Jesus gave it, this prophecy was fulfilled when Titus the Roman general and his legions laid siege to Jerusalem and burned it, and completely destroyed the temple. God had warned Israel that because of their sins this would happen.

> *"Thus saith the Lord of hosts; **Zion shall be plowed like a field, and Jerusalem shall become heaps, and the mountain of the house** as the high places of a forest"* *(Jer. 26:18).*

278

This is Zion, "the mountain of the house (temple)"; and as the prophets had said some 600 years before it happened, **the temple mount was** *"plowed as a field"* *(Micah 3:12)*. At times, for the next 600 years after 70 A.D., it was farmed with oxen, several unsuccessful attempts were made to build a new temple, and a Christian church stood on this sight. But basically it lay waste. Control of it changed hands several times, until in 638 A.D. when under the rule of Byzantine Christians, Jerusalem was besieged by Caliph *(Islamic supreme ruler)* Umar and taken over. He cleaned off the temple mount and perhaps built a temporary mosque. But it was his successor caliph Abd al-Malik who built the Dome of the Rock in 691 A.D. His son, caliph al-Walid, built a mosque nearby called the al-Aqsa Mosque around 705 A.D.

The motives of these two men, Abd al-Malik and al-Walid, are still being debated by scholars, even Muslim scholars, today. Why was this conquest and construction so important? Jerusalem is not mentioned once in the Quran and it is likely that Muhammad was never in that city. There is an unfounded legend that in a night vision Muhammad went to a "distant mosque," on his horse al-Buraq *(Lightning)*, and ascended to heaven from the rock over which the Dome of the Rock is built. This is another Islamic fable.

The true motivation can be found in the inscription carved on the inside walls of the Dome, "Praise be to Allah, who begets no son and has no partner in *(his)* dominion." [6] There are also other inscriptions warning the Hebrews of errors in their beliefs. The Dome of the Rock sits there as a temple of Satan, by the name Allah, in **defiance** of the Lord God, the Holy One of Israel who called it, *"My holy mountain, Jerusalem" (Isa. 66:20)*. The master usurper has claimed God's chosen place for 1300 years in a profane building, which **declares to the world** and to the God who "so loved the world that He gave His only begotten Son," that **"God has no son!"**

This helps us understand the Middle East conflict a little better. It has

279

many layers like an onion and is very complex but:

1. At it simplest level it is a conflict between the Jews and Palestinians over land, a small piece of real estate that they both claim.

2. At another level it is a family feud, a war among brethren, Ishmael against Isaac. Pres. Clinton had a certain grasp of this fact in 1993, at the White House as the Oslo peace accords were signed. When Arafat and Rabin shook hands he said, "The Children of Abraham, the descendents of Isaac and Ishmael, have embarked together on a bold journey. Today, we bid them peace." Of course it was short lived.

3. At its most difficult level the conflict in the Middle East is a spiritual battle. Look at these facts.

    a. There are 47 Muslim nations in the world. Only 3 Muslim nations **recognize Israel's right to exist**. (Jordan, Egypt, Turkey)

    b. Forty-four Muslim nations **deny Israel's right to exist**. Of those 44 nations only 25% are Arab states.

    c. Seventy-five percent of the 44 are Muslim **but not Arab**. For example, Iran, Indonesia, Pakistan, and Afghanistan are Muslim but not Arab.

So Islam teaches that the Jews sinned and God gave the Muslims the Holy Land, their promises of blessing, and God's last prophet to the world, Muhammad. Does this sound familiar? It is the original "replacement theology." It seems like someone is always trying to replace Israel in God's plan, but it is not going to happen!

But for 1300 years after 638 A.D., **it looked as if Islam was right**. They had control of the Holy Land and **their temple** sat on the Temple Mount. By the early 1900's most of the world had forgotten that God's Bible says over 80 times, **the Jews will return** or that **over 200 times it says** that God is the **"God of Israel."** But they **were** beginning to return, and by a series of astonishing, God inspired events, Israel became a nation again on May 14, 1948, after over 2000 years. The Jews and their Christian friends who saw the Biblical significance, rejoiced, but much of the Muslim world went berserk. The rebirth of Israel as a nation spoke loudly that Muhammad was a **false prophet** and that Islam was a **false religion**. [7]

Osama Bin Laden and other radicals teach that **Israel** is Allah's punishment on Islam for their sins. They have become worldly. They have allowed the U.S. Army to come into, and defile their holy land Saudi Arabia, the place of Mecca and Medina. Thus the violence against the West. **And there is no human solution!** The Jews will never leave the Holy Land and the Muslim's will never admit that their prophet and Quran are false. The prophet Ezekiel tells of a coalition of nations, headed by Gog and Magog *(Russia?)*, and including "Persia *(Iran was called Persia until 1935)*, Ethiopia, Libya," perhaps Turkey and others coming against Israel in the last days. I believe we are beginning to see this take shape as Russia provides the know-how to Iran in the building of nuclear bombs. This hord of attackers will be decimated by God on the mountains of Israel *(Ezek. 38, 39)*.

The stage is now being set for the Man of Sin, the anti-christ to come out of Europe *(Dan. 9:26)* with a peace plan, **a plan from hell!**

> *"He shall magnify himself in his heart, and by peace*
> *shall destroy many" (Daniel 8:25).*

The Jewish temple will be rebuilt under this seven-year plan *(Dan. 9:27, II Thess. 2:4)*. But he will break the agreement and chaos will ensue *(Dan. 8:23-24, 9:27)*. And God has already written the last Chapter of this story.

To Lucifer (Allah) he says:

> *"Hell from beneath is moved for thee to meet thee at thy*
> *coming: it stirreth up the dead for thee, even, all the*
> *chief ones of the earth; it hath raised up from their*
> *thrones all the kings of the nations. All they shall speak*
> *and say unto thee, Art thou also become weak as we?*
> *Art thou become like unto us" (Isa. 14:9-10)?*
>
> *"Yet thou shalt be brought down to hell, to the sides of*
> *the pit. They that see thee shall narrowly look upon*
> *thee, and consider thee, saying, is this the man that*
> *made the earth to tremble, that did shake kingdoms;*

that made the world as a wilderness, and destroyed the cities thereof; that opened not the house of his prisoners" (Isa. 14:15-17)?

"Prepare slaughter for his children for the iniquity of their fathers; that they do not rise, nor possess the land, nor fill the face of the world with cities, **For I will rise up against them**, saith the Lord of hosts....The Lord of hosts hath sworn, saying, Surely as I have thought, so shall it come to pass; and as I have purposed, so shall it stand: **That I will break the Assyrian in my land, and upon my mountains tread him under foot; then shall his yoke depart from off them, and his burden depart from off their shoulders.** This is the purpose that is purposed upon the whole earth: and this is the hand that is stretched out upon all the nations. For the Lord of hosts hath purposed, and who shall disannul it? And his hand is stretched out, and who shall turn it back" (Isa. 14:21-22, 24-27)?*

How does God see this conflict?

*"For it is the day of the Lord's vengeance, and the year of recompenses **for the controversy of Zion**" (Isa. 34:8).*

*"Thus saith the Lord of hosts; **I am jealous for Jerusalem and for Zion with a great jealousy. And I am very sore displeased with the heathen that are at ease:** for I was but a little displeased, and **they helped forward the affliction.** Therefore thus saith the Lord; **I am returned to Jerusalem with mercies: my house shall be built in it**, saith the Lord of hosts, and a line shall be stretched forth upon Jerusalem. Cry yet, saying, Thus saith the Lord of hosts; My cities through prosperity shall yet be spread abroad; **and the Lord***

shall yet comfort Zion, and shall yet choose Jerusalem" (Zech. 1:14-17).

"And the Lord...shall choose Jerusalem again" (Zech. 2:12).

"And I said unto the angel that talked with me, What be these? And he answered me, These are the horns which have scattered Judah, Israel, and Jerusalem. Then said I, What come these to do? And he spake, saying, These are the horns which have scattered Judah, so that no man did lift up his head; but these are come to fray them, **to cast out the horns of the Gentiles,** *which lifted up their horn over the land of Judah* **to scatter it.** *Run, speak to this young man, saying,* **Jerusalem shall be inhabited as towns without walls** *for the multitude of men and cattle therein: For I, saith the Lord, will be unto her a wall of fire round about, and will be the glory in the midst of her" (Zech. 1:19, 21, 2:4-5).*

"Again the word of the Lord of hosts came to me, saying, Thus saith the Lord of hosts; I was jealous for Zion with **great jealousy,** *and I was jealous for her with* **great fury.** *Thus saith the Lord; I* **am returned unto Zion,** *and* **will dwell in the midst of Jerusalem:** *and Jerusalem shall be called a city of truth; and the mountain of the Lord of Hosts* **the holy mountain.** *Thus saith the Lord of hosts; Behold, I will save my people from the east country, and from the west country; And I will bring them, and they shall dwell in the midst of* **Jerusalem:** *and they shall be my people, and I will be their God in truth and in righteousness. Yea, many people and strong nations shall come to* **seek the Lord of hosts in Jerusalem,** *and to pray before the Lord. Thus saith the Lord of hosts; In those days it*

*shall come to pass that ten men shall take hold out of all languages of the nations, even shall take hold of the skirt of **him that is a Jew**, saying, We will go with you: **for we have heard that God is with you**" (Zech. 8:1-3, 7-8, 22-23).*

*"The Lord also shall roar out of Zion, and utter his voice from **Jerusalem**; and the heavens and the earth shall shake: but the Lord will be the hope of his people, and the strength of the children of Israel. So shall ye know that I am the Lord your God dwelling in **Zion, my holy mountain**: then shall Jerusalem be holy, and there shall **no strangers pass through her any more**" (Joel 3:16-17).*

*"And they shall fall by the edge of the sword, **and shall be led away captive into all nations; and Jerusalem shall be trodden down of the Gentiles, until the times of the Gentiles be fulfilled**" (Jesus) (Luke 21:24).*

So this is a conflict between the Lord God of the Bible, the Holy One of Israel and Allah the god of the Quran. But God is not against the Arab or Muslim people. He is against the false religion that has enslaved one billion Muslims in spiritual darkness. The West came out of the Dark Ages when the Bible began to be printed en mass and people saw the light of God's truth. The Muslim world is still in the Dark Ages because **Islam is darkness**. Spiritual darkness is the worst kind of darkness.

*"Woe unto them that call evil good, and good evil; that put **darkness for light**, and **light for darkness**" (Isa. 5:20).*

Franklin Graham was right when he recently called Islam an **"evil and wicked religion."** [8] Islam has brought unspeakable horror to our world and the worst is yet to come. President Bush said on October 6, 2005, "Islamic terrorism is the greatest threat to the free world today." *Time* magazine featured a cover story titled, "The Merchant of Menace," "How A.Q. Kahn became the world's most dangerous **Nuclear Trafficker**." The inside story was titled "**The Man Who Sold The Bomb**," "How Pakistan's A.Q. Khan outwitted Western intelligence to build a global nuclear smuggling ring that made the world a more dangerous place." This disturbing article told the story of Mr. Kahn, a Pakistani, who helped that country build its nuclear arsenal. He became a national hero and was twice awarded Pakistan's highest civilian honor, the Hilal -e- Imtiaz medal.

So what did he do with the knowledge he had acquired? He set up a network and spread nuclear bomb making knowhow and materials to such outlaw nations as Libya, Iran and North Korea. *Time* says, "Kahn offered a one-stop shop for regimes interested in producing **nuclear weapons**." And what was his motivation? *Time* says, "He became more religious after the successful nuclear test in 1998...Kahn claimed he was selling nuclear technology to **bolster the standing of Muslims**. 'We Muslims** have to be strong and equal to any other country, and therefore I want to help some countries be strong,' the source recalls Kahn saying." Colleagues say "he was driven by a devout faith and a **burning belief** that Muslim possession of nuclear weapons would **help return Islam to greatness**."

"Just how far Kahn was able to spread that vision is a question," says a former U.S. intelligence official, "**that still keeps a lot of us up nights**." *Time* concludes, "Although the man may fade into obscurity, the world is only beginning to reckon with his legacy." [9] **And Muhammad's legacy as well!**

"One sinner destroyeth much good" (Eccl. 9:18).

Let me close this by saying as Franklin Graham said also in *Newsweek*, I love the Arab and Muslim people. Through our music we have ministered to many Muslim people without conflict. We have seen numbers of that faith converted and come to know Jesus as Lord. I pray often for those who are blinded by Allah. There are many fine people among you, and I love you enough to tell you the truth. And I have hope! The God of Israel has spoken healing and restoration to Egypt and Assyria for these last days, when He will say, "Blessed be Egypt my people, and Assyria the work of my hands."

*"In that day shall five cities in the land of Egypt speak the language of Canaan, and swear to the Lord of hosts. In that day shall there be an altar to the Lord in the midst of the land of Egypt, and a pillar at the border thereof to the Lord. And it shall be for a sign and for a witness unto the Lord of hosts in the land of Egypt: for they shall cry unto the Lord because of the oppressors, and he shall send them a saviour, and a great one, and he shall deliver them. And the Lord shall be known to Egypt, and the Egyptians shall know the Lord in that day, and shall do sacrifice and oblation; yea, they shall vow a vow unto the Lord, and perform it. And the Lord shall smite Egypt: he shall smite and heal it: and they shall return even to the Lord, and he shall be entreated of them, and shall heal them. In that day shall Israel be the third with Egypt and with Assyria, even a blessing in the midst of the land: Whom the Lord of hosts shall bless, saying, Blessed be **Egypt** my people, and **Assyria** the work of my hands, and **Israel** mine inheritance"* (Isa. 19:18-25).

One Final Word from God's Holy Bible to Muslims.

"He that believeth on the Son of God hath the witness in himself: he that believeth not God hath made him a liar; because he believeth not the record that God gave of his Son. And this is the record, that God hath given to us eternal life, and this life is in his Son. He that hath not the Son of God hath not life" (I John 5:10-12).

Pray people pray!

Chapter 15

The Fable Called Mormonism

*"I marvel that ye are so soon removed from him that called you into the grace of Christ **unto another gospel**: Which is not another; but there be some that trouble you, and would pervert the gospel of Christ. But though **we, or an angel from heaven**, preach any other gospel unto you than that which we have preached unto you, **let him be accursed**. As we said before, so say I now again, If **any man** preach any other gospel unto you than that ye have received, **let him be accursed"** (Gal. 1:6-9).*

*"**For such are false apostles**, deceitful workers, transforming themselves into the apostles of Christ. And no marvel; for Satan himself is transformed into an angel of light. Therefore it is no great thing if **his minsters also** be transformed as the ministers of righteousness; whose end shall be according to their works" (II Cor. 11:13-15).*

he story is told of a man who was walking in a cemetery and came upon a large gravestone with this inscription: "Friend, where you are I once was, Where I am you shall be, So prepare to follow me." Someone had penciled in this reply, "To follow you I'm not content until I see which way you went."

It never ceases to amaze me that millions of people will follow strange men and false teaching and entrust to them the destiny of their eternal souls.

I have a newspaper article from the *U.S.A. Today*, August 28, 2002, which says that "more than 70,000 Australians, about *(.37%)* of the population, identify themselves as followers of the Jedi faith, based on the movies. Followers say they believe in the Force, the energy that empowers Jedi like Luke Skywalker and Yoda." The "Jedi movement" has started an "email campaign to get it recognized as an official religion."

In the U.S., fiction writer L. Ron Hubbard created another work of fiction, a fable called "Scientology," a new religion which claims to have millions of followers. Deluded celebrities can be seen on T.V., often, testifying to its benefits in their lives. This is gross heresy.

Our local newspaper reported recently that there is a growing Elvis religion, with at least one church called the First Presleyterian Church of Elvis the Divine. We have made a number of trips to Israel and one of the strangest things we have seen, in a nation where idols and images are strongly discouraged, is a shrine to Elvis. There is a tall statue of "the king" outside the large combination restaurant and museum. Inside are many photos, mementos, and life size statues of Elvis in various poses, and seated at a piano, with his music continually playing loudly. I must say it gives one a weird feeling to see a shrine to the "king of rock and roll" in Jerusalem, the city of Jesus, the King of kings.

Multiplied millions are falling into delusions and idolatry and the power of the delusion is multiplied greatly if the founder says that it was given to him in a visit by an angel. Look at Islam, whose prophet said that perverted message was given to him in a cave, by the angel Gabriel? And Mormonism, whose founder Joseph Smith said he was given his message by the angel Moroni.

The Apostle Paul, inspired by the Holy Ghost to write 13 great epistles in the N.T., was a very wise man. In the Scriptures cited at the beginning of this chapter he warns us of two main forms of deception. That taught by false teachers, *("false apostles")*, and that presented by demon's and angels. Notice what he says in Galatians 1:8:

*"But **though we**...preach any other gospel unto you*

288

> *than that which we have preached unto you, let him*
> (me) *be accursed."*

Paul put himself in that number. Here is a man so sure of his gospel message he says, *"If I come back to you preaching another gospel, let me be accursed."* Paul knew how insidious deception is. He also knew what the writer of the old poem knew:

The gray-haired saint may fall at last,

The surest guide a wanderer prove

Death only binds us fast

To that bright shore of love... [1]

Paul says:

> *"But I keep under my body and bring it into subjection: lest that **by any means**, when I have preached to others, I myself should be **a castaway"** (a reject) (I Cor. 9:27).*

Does this mean that Paul lived in constant fear of becoming a failure? No, it means that he had no confidence in the flesh, **even his own**. He says,

> *"For we...rejoice in Christ Jesus, and have no confidence in the flesh" (Phil. 3:3).*
>
> *"We have confidence in the Lord" (II Thess. 3:4).*
>
> *"For **I know whom I have believed**, and am persuaded that **he is able** to keep that which I have committed to him against that day" (II Tim. 1:12).*

We have confidence in God to keep our souls in Him until the day of final redemption. Paul also warns us strongly in the beginning verses regarding false or demonic angels that appear as "angels from heaven," or "angels of light." He said "Satan himself is transformed into an angel of light." How deceptive! And it has worked time and again, including A.D. 610 to Muhammad and in A.D. 1823 to Joseph Smith the founder and prophet of Mormonism. One thing that adds to the deception of Branhamism are the reports by some that while he ministered at various times until his death in 1965, a being in white *(an angel?)* was seen standing beside him.

Let's take a look at Joseph Smith and the church that he founded. In 1820 Joseph Smith Jr. was a 14 year old simple farm boy living in Palmyra, N.Y. It was a time of Protestant revivals and religious fervor, and a time of expectancy for young Joseph and his family. His grandfather had prophesied that one of their family members would revolutionize the world of religion. His father had had a series of "prophetic" dreams about his family's salvation and an aunt had become a local celebrity by claiming that she had been healed by Jesus himself. Joseph wondered if he should join one of the local churches as his mother had, or stay outside the mainline churches as his father did. One day Smith went into a grove of trees to pray and as he began, a dark force seized him until, he said, God himself intervened. "At this moment of great alarm," Smith later recalled, "I saw a pillar of light exactly over my head, above the brightness of the sun, which descended gradually until it fell upon me." He said both God and Jesus then appeared and gave a startling message: He shouldn't join any of the churches of the world, as they had all fallen away from Christ's true gospel. [2]

This experience is called by followers of Smith the First Vision, and marks the beginning of what is known to us today as Mormonism, or the Church of Jesus Christ of Latter-day Saints *(LDS)*. It has some 12 million members world wide and thanks to vigorous missionary efforts, begun by Smith himself, **it is one of the fastest growing religions in the U.S.** At present growth rates it is projected by Rodney Stark, a University of Washington sociologist, that in about 83 years worldwide Mormon membership should reach 260 million. [3]

Three years after this first vision Smith claimed that he was visited by an angel named Moroni, an ancient prophet from the Americas, who told him that God wanted him to bring forth new Scriptures. These new Scriptures were supposedly written on a set of gold plates in the unknown language called "reformed Egyptian," and were buried in a hill near Smith's house. He claimed to have translated these writings into English, the *Book of Mormon*, and accumulated some followers, but still did not have the "true church" that he yearned for. In 1829 Smith said he was visited by resurrected prophets and apostles including John the Baptist, Peter, James and John, who finally conferred on him the authority to re-establish Christ's church on earth. He officially founded his church in Fayette, N.Y. on April 6, 1830. The story of Smith and his growing church over the next 14 years, until his death, is a troubled one.

The missionaries that he sent out to surrounding areas made and baptized converts, including a Campbellite minister and some 100 of his congregation in Kirtland, Ohio. During 1831, Smith and his followers moved to Jackson County, Missouri which he said was the Biblical site of the Garden of Eden and the future land of Zion. 1831 is also the year when Smith claimed that he was commanded by God to take plural wives like Abraham and other O.T. figures. Over the next several years he would take some 30 wives. During the next 5 years, the Missouri "saints" were driven by mobs from Jackson County to Clay County, to Far West, MO. As prejudice against their strange doctrine and polygamous practices increased, Missouri's Gov. Lilburn Boggs issued an "extermination order" in 1838 and the Mormons fled to Nauvoo, IL. In Nauvoo, Smith, a political activist, was considered dangerous. Smith ordered the destruction of a printing press that was used against him and was jailed. On June 27, 1844, a mob stormed the jail, fatally shooting Smith and his brother Hyrum and injuring two other LDS men. Before dying, Smith shot and wounded three of his attackers. He was 38.

In a *Newsweek* Magazine article titled "The Making of the Mormons," subtitled "Beyond Prophecy and Polygamy: The Future of a Booming Faith," Elise Soukup, herself a Mormon makes some revealing statements. She says, "His church survived *(largely because follower Brigham Young led most of the remaining saints west to Utah)* and 161 years later, thrives - yet remains mysterious to many." "Central tenets of Mormonism seem confusing - even literally incredible - to those outside the faith. An Angel named Moroni? Plural marriage? A resurrected Jesus visiting the New

World?"

Soukup goes on to say "in Smith the record reveals a complicated man. The church's early coverts were sometimes shocked when they met Smith in person. He was uneducated, **he lost his temper, he enjoyed power**, and on occasion, his ventures failed. Simply put, he didn't always seem like a prophet. By the end of his life, he had accrued some 30 wives, massive debt and hundreds of enemies." "I never told you I was perfect," he told his followers. "But there is no error in the revelations which I have taught." (end of quote) [4]

Two things are very clear in reading the teachings of Joseph Smith and the story of his life and claims. This is not a thinking man's religion, nor is it a religion for a diligent reader of God's Holy Bible.

NOT A THINKING PERSON'S RELIGION.

Here are some examples of why it is necessary to check your mind at the door when you enter the world of Mormonism.

1.   Mormon leaders state that Joseph Smith's "first vision" is the foundation of the church, that the church stands or falls on the authenticity of the event, and that it validates all of Smith's subsequent work. But did this "vision" really occur? There are at least six varying accounts of this "first vision," as written and told by Smith up until his death. In some, God and Jesus are both present, in some only Jesus is present, and in others he was visited only by many spirits who "testified" of Jesus. Was it Jesus, God and Jesus, or a group of "spirits" who told Joseph to start a new church, because all of the others had become abominations? Why would thinking people accept the word of and follow, a fourteen year old boy, who said he was talked to by some unidentified "spirits," especially when he could not keep his story straight when telling it over the next twenty years?

2.   *The "Book of Mormon"* was suppose to have been divinely translated by Smith from "reformed Egyptian" words, written on "gold plates" into English and published in 1830. The Mormon

Church believes that the entire book is a "divine translation." If so the 1830 edition should have become God's word without need of subsequent changes. This is not the case. Lamoni Call in his 1898 work, *"2000 Changes in the Book of Mormon,"* documents **that number** of changes made up until his writing. [5] Jerald and Sandra Tanner, former Mormons, and authorities on the history and teachings of that church have documented over 3900 changes in the *Book of Mormon* since Smith published the original edition in 1830. Most of these are grammatical changes but many are changes in substance. [6] Another researcher found over 11,000 changes from the 1830 edition, including capitalization, punctuation, etc. [7] This book cannot be the Word of God, because God is the authority on grammar and immutable truth.

3.   *The Book of Mormon* claims to be the history of three groups of people who migrated from the near East to Central and South America. Two of the groups supposedly traveled on north to Mexico and North America. These people, the Nephites and the Lamanites were of Hebrew descent and the most important group, the Nephites were led by Lehi of Jerusalem. *The Book of Mormon* mainly deals with the history of the Nephites. Led by Lehi they supposedly left Jerusalem around 600 B.C. and eventually migrated to North America. The descendants of his sons Nephi, who was righteous and Laman, who was not, became two quarreling camps, the Nephites and Lamanites. Native American Indians are believed by Mormons to be descendants of Laman.

Mormons allege that when Jesus arose from the dead, he came to North America and preached to these tribes and they were converted. A few centuries later the Lamanites went into apostasy and went to war with the more righteous Nephites. The *Book of Mormon* teaches that from A.D. 380 to A.D. 420 the final battles were fought, and in one battle in A.D. 383, 230,000 Nephites died near the hill Cumorah in New York (Mormon 6:10-15, 8:2). By A.D. 421 all of the Nephites had been killed, leaving only the apostate Lamanites. Thus it was supposedly "Jewish Indians" that met Columbus in 1492. **That teaching has been proven false**. In 2004 molecular biologist and former Mormon bishop Simon G. Southerton published his book, *"Losing A Lost Tribe."* [8] Applying DNA studies he shows that Native Americans are descendants of Asians and not of Hebrews. He says, "Decades of serious and honest scholarship have failed to uncover creditable evidence that these Book of Mormon *(Israelite)* civilizations ever existed." [9]

Before the annihilation of the Nephites, their leader "Mormon," a historian - prophet gathered all the records of his predecessors and penned a history of his people on "gold plates" in "reformed Egyptian." This history was supposedly the story of his people from 600 B.C. to A.D. 385. He entrusted the plates to his son "Moroni," who allegedly finished the history and hid the plates in the hill Cumorah in New York in A.D. 421. Fourteen hundred years later Joseph Smith claimed he was led to this same hill by the spirit of the long-dead Moroni, and discovered the gold plates that Mormon had written. Translated into English by Smith, this became the *"Book of Mormon."*

If this book was truly history, there would be a great deal of archeological findings to verify it. According to the Book of Mormon, two entire nations, the Nephites and Lamanites *(the latter "exceedingly more numerous")* spread over the face of North America and became as numerous as "the sand of the sea." They built large cities *(The Book of Mormon* mentions thirty-eight)*, "nations developed" and they fought "great continent-wide wars." By A.D. 322, "the whole face of the land had become covered with buildings" (Mormon 1:7).

However, not one shred of evidence has ever been found to substantiate these claims, either by Mormon archeologists or others. The "gold plates" from which the *Book of Mormon* was allegedly translated are claimed to have been taken back to heaven, so they are not in evidence.

The book is known by credible researchers to be myth and historical invention. Dr. Walter Martin refers to "the hundreds of areas where this book defies reason or common sense." [10] Dr. Charles Crane, a professor knowledgeable on Mormon archeology, states, "I am led to believe from my research that this is not an actual story but is a fairy tale much like Alice in Wonderland" *(a fable).* [11] Dr. Gordon Fraser, asserts that the *Book of Mormon* in no way corresponds to the known facts of the ancient Americas.

"Both Mormon scientists and objective investigators have reconstructed the story of who lived where in ancient America, when they occupied certain territories, what their cultures were, and, to a large degree, what their writing methods were. Certainly these facts **were not known** when Joseph Smith wrote." Fraser continues, "If, for instance, the statements of history, geography, natural history, ethnology, and anthropology in the *Book of Mormon* **almost invariably prove to be untrue**, it is safe to assume that completely illogical statements in the rest of the book will follow the same pattern." [12]

Jerald and Sandra Tanner cite the case of Thomas Stuart Ferguson, who was recognized as a "great defender of the faith," and who wrote three books on Mormonism and archaeology. **He was head of the Mormon New World Archaeological Foundation**, which Brigham Young University supported with funds for several fruitless archeological expeditions. Ferguson truly believed archaeology would prove Mormonism right, but eventually became so disheartened that he repudiated the Mormon prophet Joseph Smith. On December 2, 1970, the Tanners received a surprise visit from Ferguson:

"He had come to the conclusion that Joseph Smith was not a prophet and that Mormonism was not true. He told us that he had spent 25 years trying to prove Mormonism, but had finally come to the conclusion that all his work in this regard had been in vain. He said that his training in law had taught him how to weigh evidence and that the case against Joseph Smith was absolutely devastating and could not be explained away." [13]

The massive amount of data accumulated by numerous archaeological excavations has failed to uncover a shred of evidence to support the *Book of Mormon's* claims. Whether we consider the purported cities, rivers, crops, fabrics, animals, metals, coins, kings, wars and war implements, palaces, and so on, no evidence at all supports their existence. [14]

As Marvin Cowan states in his work, "*Mormon Claims Answered,*" "Thus far, everything (Mormons) have pointed to as "proof" has turned out to be a forgery or else an exaggerated interpretation which cannot stand up under investigation. There has never yet been one (Book of Mormon) name, event, place or anything else verified through archaeological discoveries!....Dozens of **biblical sites** have been located by using the Bible as a guide - but not one has ever been found using the *Book of Mormon.*" [15]

Where are the plains of Nephaha? Or the valley of Nimrod? Where is the land of Zarahemla? Have we found coins such as the leah, shiblon, and shiblum? [16] They have never been found, because they never existed, except in the mind of Joseph Smith.

NOT A BIBLE READER'S RELIGION.

There is a more sure way of knowing that the *Book of Mormon* and its two companion "holy" books, *Doctrines & Covenants (1835)* and *Pearl of Great Price (1851)* are not divinely inspired Scripture, and that is to compare their teachings with that which is taught in God's Holy Bible. To do that is to assure ones' self that God the Father and Jesus did not appear to Joseph Smith in a grove in New York and that no **angel of God** led him to gold plates hidden in a hill.

The Bible is the **book of books**. It is the book by which every man will be judged at the final day *(Rev. 20:12).*

> *'To the law and to the testimony: if they speak not according to this word, it is because there is no light in them" (Isa. 8:20).*
>
> *'Thy testimonies are wonderful: therefore doth my soul*

296

> *keep them.* **The entrance of thy words giveth light;** *it*
> *giveth understanding unto the simple" (Ps. 119:129-*
> *130).*
>
> *"Sanctify them through thy truth:* **thy word is truth"**
> (Jesus speaking) *(John 17:17).*
>
> *"Yea, let God be true, but every man a liar" (Rom. 3:4).*

Fact #1

Though its identity and location might have been unknown to young Joseph Smith, the church that Jesus Christ founded in the first century was alive and well in 1820. **God has never been without a people!**

> *"Upon this rock I will build my church; and the gates of*
> *hell shall not prevail against it"* (Jesus speaking) *(Matt.*
> *16:18).*
>
> *"And are built upon the foundation of the apostles and*
> *prophets, Jesus Christ himself being the chief corner*
> *stone" (Eph. 2:20).*
>
> *For* **other foundation can no man lay** *than that is laid,*
> *which is Jesus Christ. Now if any man build upon this*
> *foundation gold, silver, precious stones, wood, hay,*
> *stubble; Every man's work shall be made manifest: for*
> *the day shall declare it,* **because it shall be revealed by**
> **fire;** *and the fire shall try every man's work of what sort*
> *it is" (I Cor. 3:11-13).*
>
> *Nevertheless* **the foundation of God standeth sure,**
> *having this seal, The Lord knoweth them that are his"*
> *(II Tim. 2:19).*

Imagine the ego of a man who thought that Jesus Christ failed in his mission to establish a lasting church and that he succeeded where Jesus failed. He said: "I have more to boast of than ever any man had. I am the only man that has ever been able to keep a whole church together since the days of Adam. A large majority of the whole have stood with me. Neither Paul, John, Peter, nor Jesus ever did it. I boast that no man ever did such a work as I. The followers of Jesus ran away from Him; but the Latter-day Saints never ran away from me yet." [17]

Fact #2

Joseph Smith and Brigham Young were not Godly men.

> *"To the saints and **faithful brethren in Christ** which are at Colosse: Grace be unto you" (Col. 1:2).*
>
> *"And the things that thou hast heard of me among many witnesses, the same **commit thou to faithful men**, who shall be able to teach others also" (II Tim. 2:2).*
>
> *"A bishop then must be blameless, **the husband of one wife**, vigilant, sober, **of good behavior" (I Tim. 3:2).**
>
> *"And ordain elders in every city, as I had appointed thee: **If any be blameless, the husband of one wife,** having faithful children **not accused of riot or unruly**. For a bishop must be blameless, as the steward of God; not selfwilled, not soon angry" (Titus 1:5-7).*
>
> *"Beware of false prophets, which come to you in sheep's clothing, but **inwardly they are ravening wolves. Ye shall know them by their fruits.** A good tree cannot bring forth evil fruit, neither can a corrupt tree bring forth good fruit. Wherefore by their fruits ye shall know them"* (Jesus speaking) *(Matt. 7:15-16, 18, 20).*

Look at the record regarding the first two prophets of Mormonism. Consider again, Elise Soukup (a Mormon) writing in *Newsweek* called Smith a "Prophet and polygamist, mesmerizor and rabble- rouser, saint and sinner." She says, "he lost his temper, he enjoyed power. Simply put, he didn't always seem like a prophet. Smith was involved in dozens of lawsuits. By the end of his life, he had accrued some 30 wives, massive debt and hundreds of enemies." She quotes Smith saying to his followers, "I never told you I was perfect, but there is no error in the revelation which I have taught." How do you separate the man from his message?

Newsweek continues: "Smith said he was commanded by God to take

298

plural wives like Abraham and other O.T. figures. Most historians agree that he married his first plural wife, a 16-year old who worked in his house, about 1833 - and some 30 more in the next decade. His associate Oliver Cowdery called the first plural marriage **"a dirty, nasty filthy affair**." Mark Scherer, Church historian for the Community of Christ, a branch of Mormonism that followed Smith's son Joseph III instead of Brigham Young after Smith's death says, "He committed ministerial abuse. He figured out a way to commit adultery and to do it sacramentally." [18]

And Brigham Young, who took up the torch upon the death by mob of Smith in 1844, and led some 30,000 Mormons from Illinois to Utah, followed Smith in this immoral martial confusion. In a *Time* Magazine article titled "Mormons, Inc.", *Time* says of Young's polygamy, "Young is thought to have had 27 wives and to have entered into ceremonies of **eternal** "sealing" with twice as many, as well as 150 women posthumously" *(after their deaths).* [19]

These acts and others by their prophet - founder and second prophet have proven embarrassing to the modern leaders of the Mormon church. In the late 1970's LDS leaders limited access to church records in an apparent effort to cover such history. Leonard Arrington, the then director of the Church's historical department wrote, "Some authorities apparently preferred that we have no history except that kept by public-relations writers." [20] In 1993 the Church excommunicated D. Michael Quinn, a leading historian, whose painstaking work documented Smith's involvement **with the occult** and also church leaders' misrepresentation of some continued polygamy in the early 1900's. [21] Such moral and marital confusion springs from the fact that Mormonism is a spiritual tower of Babel, a works based, man-made, demon inspired attempt to reach heaven and Godhood.

> *"Then Jesus said unto them, Take heed and beware of the leaven of the Pharisees and of the Sadducees. Then understood they how that he bade them...beware of the doctrine of the Pharisees and of the Sadducees" (Matt. 16:6, 12).*

"A little leaven leaveneth the whole lump" (Gal. 5:9).

The truth is that Smith and Young would not be qualified as **deacons** in the smallest **truly Christian** church in Utah, much less to found and shepherd a new Latter Day Church of Jesus Christ.

> *"Likewise, must the deacons be grave, not double-tongued, not given to much wine, not greedy of filthy lucre; Holding the mystery of the faith **in a pure conscience**. And let these also first be proved; then let them use the office of a deacon, **being found blameless...Let the deacons be the husbands of one wife**" (I Tim. 3:8-10, 12).*

Of course if you start your own church and write your own "holy books," why not have it the way you wish. But listen to what Jesus said of such:

> *"Woe unto you, scribes and Pharisees, hypocrites! For ye compass sea and land to make one proselyte, and when he is made, ye make him twofold more the child of hell than yourselves" (Matt. 23:15).* (Jesus loved spiritually blinded people enough to tell them the truth.)

The doctrinal errors of this church are too many to deal with in the scope of this book, but others have done a commendable job of exposing its myths. Their works are readily available. But I must close this chapter in our search for truth by pointing out one more false teaching of this church, which is of major proportions. That is their absolutely absurd concept of God. *Time* Magazine says, Mormons "believe that humans deal with only one God, yet they allow for other deities presiding over other worlds. Smith stated that God was once a humanlike being who **had a wife** and, in fact, still has a body of '**flesh and bone**.' Mormons also believe that men, in a process known as deification, may become God-like. Lorenzo Snow, an early Mormon President and prophet, famously said **'as man is now, God once was; as God now is, man may become.'** " (end of quote) [22] What heresy!

Here are Smith's own words on the subject of God.

"In the beginning, the head of the Gods called a council of Gods; and they came together and concocted a plan to create the world and people it...In all congregations when I have preached on the subject of the Deity, it has been the plurality of Gods". [23]

"God himself was one as we are now, and is an exalted man...He was once a man like us; yea, that God himself, the Father of us all, dwelt on an earth". [24]

"Here then is eternal life...you have got to learn how to be Gods yourselves, the same as all gods have done before you...To inherit the same power, the same glory and the same exaltation, until you arrive at the station of God". [25]

"Men can become gods." Bible readers know where that lie came from. That is the same lie that the serpent *(Satan)* told Eve in the Garden of Eden some 6000 years ago.

> *"And the serpent said unto the woman, Ye shall not surely die:* **For God doth know** *that in the day ye eat thereof, then your eyes shall be opened, and ye* **shall be as gods***, knowing good and evil" (Gen. 3:4-5).*

It amazes me that people still fall for this lie of Satan, but why should he use a new one, this old one has worked so well through the ages. Men cannot become Gods, **never have, never will!** But in Christ Jesus we can become **born again Sons of God**.

Mormons, God loves you and would not have you perish forever, but you must repent and have a book burning as the Christian converts in Ephesus did *(Acts 19:19)*. Without it you are lost, and one day soon **your condition will become eternal**.

301

Understanding Jesus' Authority

*The centurion sent friends to him, saying Lord, trouble not thyself;...but say in a word, and my servant shall be healed. For **I also am a man** set **under authority**, having under me soldiers, and I say unto one, Go, and he goeth; and to another, Come, and he cometh...When Jesus heard these things, he **marveled** at him, and said, I say unto you, I have not found so **great faith**, no, not in Israel.*

Luke 7:6-9

Chapter 16

Protestant Fables

*M*y wife LaBreeska and I were called upon recently to minister in a large mainline Protestant church, where I noticed on a wall in the educational department a sizeable multi-colored poster with the heading, "**Names of God**." Scattered over the obviously mass produced poster were about 16 names including Father, Jehovah, Creator, Almighty, Savior and Holy Spirit, with which I agreed. But also included to my amazement were Son, Messiah, Lamb of God, Jesus and Prince of Peace. I do not mean to be critical but this is very important to our understanding of God. Also to the understanding of countless youths who will be exposed to this poster throughout the land. Since when have "Son, Messiah, Lamb of God, Jesus, or Prince of Peace been **names of God?** Nowhere in the Bible is God called "Son," or "Messiah" *(which means **anointed of God**),* or "Prince of Peace." Nowhere in Scripture is God called "Prince" of anything, He is the Great King of Heaven and Earth and all else. The above mentioned are titles which are rightly given to God's Son Jesus, but never to Almighty God, Creator of the universe. To apply them to Him is at best doctrinal confusion and is possibly to insult Him with what someone has called "faint praise." Please give this serious consideration.

A few days later I was listening to Christian radio and heard a prayer which rather startled and saddened me. Let me say at this point that my favorite thing to do when I travel is to listen to good Gospel preaching on radio or C.D. I receive many wonderful scriptural insights from God's ministers, and they along with all T.V. preachers, pastors, evangelists, and missionaries are always in my prayers. While not agreeing with everything that I hear, I love them all with a sincere love. However, a person not grounded in the word of God could certainly become confused. Take the above mentioned prayer for example. It was prayed at the close of a program sponsored by a large internationally known ministry, headed by a well known, highly respected minister, and I ordered it for further study. It is quite long but here are excerpts:

-   "Heavenly Father, blessed Son, eternal Spirit"
-   "I adore thee as one Being, one Essence"
-   "One God in three distinct Persons"
-   "O Father, thou hast loved me and ......"
-   "O Jesus, thou hast loved me and......"
-   "O Holy Spirit, thou hast loved me and ......"
-   "Three Persons and one God, I bless and praise thee"
-   "O Father....O Jesus....O Holy Spirit......"
-   "O Father....O Jesus....O Holy Spirit......"
-   "O Triune God, who commandeth the universe......"
-   "Let me live and pray as one baptized into the threefold Name." [1]

Dear reader, I am being careful here as I realize that a prayer is a very intimate thing between the person praying and God, but Paul said *"Let the prophets speak two or three, and let the other(s) judge"* (i.e., weigh carefully what is said) *(I Cor. 14:29)*. The above prayer has no basis in Scripture. Nowhere in the Bible is God referred to as "three distinct persons," "three persons and one God," "Triune God" or as having a "threefold name." No place in Scripture are we as Christians commanded or encouraged to address prayers to Jesus or the Holy Spirit. There is no Bible example of an apostle or gospel writer doing so.

How did we reach a place of such utter confusion regarding who God is? There can be only one answer. The householder in Matthew Chapter 13, in whose field tares were sowed "while men slept," said to his servants, *"an enemy hath done this."* Seeds of confusion regarding the person of God were sowed by the enemy, through perhaps well-meaning men who brought in non-biblical concepts (Greek and Roman thinking), made orthodox in Church Councils of the fourth and fifth centuries *(Nicea 325 A.D. - Constantinople 381 A.D. - Chalcedon 451 A.D.)*.

Listen to the *Encyclopedia of Catholicism*:

"Trinitarian doctrine as such emerged in the fourth century, due largely to the efforts of Athanasius and the Cappadocians... . The doctrine of the Trinity formulated in the late fourth century thus affirms that the one God exists as three Persons. The purpose of this formulation was to profess that God, Christ, and the Spirit are equally responsible for our salvation, **thus each must be divine.**" [2]

The *New International Encylopedia* says:

"At the time of the Reformation, **the Protestant Churches took over the doctrine of the Trinity without serious examination.**" [3]

It is time to give this and all of the doctrines that we teach "**serious examination.**" We are not lemmings marching to death in the sea; we are people created in the image of God, with good minds and intellect, and with God given ability to look into the Holy Bible, with the help of the Holy Spirit, and **discover truth.** Especially the truth as to **who God is.** Jesus called the scribes and Pharisees *"blind guides"* who along with their many blind followers *"both shall fall into the ditch" (Matt. 15:14, 23:16).* God the Father has been patient with us in our ignorance of Him, but He is ready for us to open our eyes and see and acknowledge the truth.

Regarding following blind guides, many years ago some Protestants challenged the doctrine of the "assumption of Mary," because it is unbiblical. In answer to them, noted Catholic apologist Graham Greene said:

"Our opponents sometimes claim that no belief should be held dogmatically which is not explicitly stated in Scripture...but the **Protestant Churches** have themselves accepted such dogmas as **The Trinity**, for which there is **no such precise authority** in the Gospels." [4] And he of course is right!

THE FABLE CALLED "REPLACEMENT THEOLOGY."

Another erroneous doctrine, which a large segment of Protestant Christianity has borrowed from Catholicism "without serious examination," is the teaching called "Replacement Theology." That is the belief strongly taught by some noted ministers that the church, as the "New Israel," has replaced the Israel of the O.T. in all of God's covenants and promises of

305

future blessing. **That is gross error!**

Yes, there are many awesome promises from the Lord to the Church:

> *"Upon this rock I will build my church: and the gates of hell shall not prevail against it" (Matt. 16:18).*
>
> *"For if we be dead with him* (Christ), *we shall also live with him: If we suffer we shall also reign with him" (II Tim. 2:11-12).*
>
> *"Be thou faithful unto death, and I will give thee a crown of life" (Rev. 2:10).*

But my friend, there are many more promises in the Bible to God's chosen people Israel, the natural seed of Abraham, than there are to the Church. Have those who teach "Replacement Theology," *(that there is no future restoration for Israel)* not read the books of Isaiah, Jeremiah, Ezekiel, Daniel, Hosea, Joel, Amos, Zephaniah, Zechariah, Malachi, or the O.T. at all? For instance Jeremiah 31:35-37 says:

> *"Thus saith the Lord, which giveth the sun for a light by day, and the **ordinances of the moon and of the stars for a light by night,** which divideth the sea when the waves thereof roar; The Lord of hosts is his name: **If those ordinances depart from before me** saith the Lord, **then the seed of Israel also shall cease from being a nation before me** for ever. Thus saith the Lord; **If heaven above can be measured,** and the foundations of the earth searched out beneath, **I will also cast off all the seed of Israel for all that they have done,** saith the Lord."* (God is saying, **"It is not going to happen!** I will not cast off the seed of Israel!")

The promises of God are based on His faithfulness.

> *"Know therefore that the Lord thy God, he is God, the faithful God, which **keepeth covenant..." (Deut. 7:9).***

Yes, Israel has been unfaithful and so have we as Christians, but God's **gracious** covenants are not based on our performance but on His

306

faithfulness. To teach that God would break these covenants with Israel is a serious thing, for it is to ascribe unfaithfulness to God. Hebrews 6:10 says, *"For God is not unrighteous to forget your work and labor of love,"* and neither is He unrighteous to forget his everlasting covenants. If God would break His often stated promises to Israel, what's to say that He will not break His covenants with us? Shame on those who think so.

Please look again at Romans 11:25-29:

> *"For **I would not, brethren, that ye should be ignorant of this mystery,** lest ye should be wise in your own conceits; **that blindness in part is happened to Israel, until the fullness of the Gentiles be come in. And so all Israel shall be saved:** as it is written, There shall come out of Sion the Deliverer, and shall turn away ungodliness from Jacob: **For this is my covenant unto them,** when I shall take away their sins. **As concerning the gospel, they are enemies for your sakes: but as touching the election, they are beloved for the fathers' sakes. For the gifts and calling of God are without repentance."** God has not changed His mind!

<u>One note of caution.</u>

If you constantly find that you have negative feelings toward Israel and the Jewish people, you should examine yourself carefully before God. It could be with you as Jesus said of the disciples, *"Ye know not what manner of spirit ye are of" (Luke 9:55).* God has used the Jewish people to give to the world monotheism, the Ten Commandments, the Bible and the Messiah. Paul said to them pertain and belong the glory, the covenants, the promises and the *(O.T.)* fathers, and God yet has plans to use them to bless the world. Satan knows this and has tried to stop it through the centuries by putting anti-Semitism into the hearts of wicked men. At times it has cropped up in the Church to our shame. However, it is not necessary to agree with everything that the nation of Israel does to love the Jewish people and pray for the peace of Jerusalem *(Ps. 122:6).* Just know that anti-Semitism and all racial hatred are of Satan, and are sometimes disguised in the form of false teachings.

THE RAPTURE FABLE.

Another mistaken doctrine that has found its way into Protestant Christianity is the doctrine of the pre-tribulation rapture of the Church. May I humbly say that this teaching has no basis in Scripture and is a fabrication, **a fable**, though taught by many sincere ministers. Jesus is soon coming back to earth to reign for 1000 years with his saints, but if that coming is **before** the tribulation he did not know it. Look at Matthew 24:29-31:

> *"Immediately **after the tribulation of those days** shall the sun be darkened, and the moon shall not give her light, and the stars shall fall from heaven, and the powers of the heavens shall be shaken: And **then shall appear** the sign of the Son of man in heaven; and then shall all the tribes of the earth mourn, and **they shall see the Son of man coming in the clouds of heaven** with power and great glory. **And he shall send his angels** with a great sound of a trumpet, **and they shall gather together his elect from the four winds,** from one end of heaven to the other."*

Likewise the apostle Paul did not know it. Look at II Thess. 2:1, 3-4:

> *"Now we beseech you, brethren, by **the coming of our Lord Jesus Christ,** and by **our gathering together unto him** (the catching away), **Let no man deceive you by any means** (concerning the timing of Christ's return): **for that day shall not come,** except there come a falling away first, and **that man of sin be revealed,** the son of perdition; Who opposeth and exalteth himself above all that is called God, or that is worshiped; **so that he** as God **sitteth in the temple of God,** shewing himself that he is God."*

Paul says again:

> *"And to you who are troubled rest with us* (when will
> troubled saints rest?), **when the Lord Jesus shall be**
> **revealed from heaven with his mighty angels.** *In*
> *flaming fire taking vengeance on them that know not*
> *God, and that obey not the gospel of our Lord Jesus*
> *Christ: Who shall be punished with everlasting*
> *destruction from the presence of the Lord, and from the*
> *glory of his power;* **When he shall come to be glorified**
> **in his saints,** *and to be* **admired in all them that**
> **believe**...*in that day" (II Thess. 1:7-10).*

As a companion to the doctrine of the pre-tribulation rapture, another
mistaken doctrine is usually taught, the doctrine of the "imminent return of
Christ," the belief that Jesus could have returned to earth at any moment
after his ascension to the Father. **Please consider these facts**. The apostles
did not believe Jesus was coming back to earth in their lifetimes. He taught
them that certain things would happen before His return, including the
destruction of Jerusalem and the Temple *(A.D. 70) (Mark 13:2, Luke 19:43-
44, Luke 21:9)*. He told Peter plainly that he would grow old and be killed
for the Gospel *(John 21:19, II Peter 1:14-15)*. The disciples were shocked
when they misunderstood Jesus and thought he was saying that John would
live until his coming *(John 21:22-24)*. Paul knew that he would die, and
spoke of his "departure" and what would come after. He knew that the
rebuilt Temple would be defiled by the anti-christ *(Acts 20:29-31, II Tim.
3:1-6, II Thess. 2:1-8)*. They all understood that Jesus would come the
second time as He had the first, "when the fullness of time had come" and
not before *(Gal. 4:4, Rom. 11:25)*.

How did we get so far off in our understanding of basic Bible doctrines?
I am not saying that I have all of the answers to that tremendous question but
I do have some.

1. **Lack of prayer**. God, the Author of the awesome Bible, never
   intended for His intimate secrets to be known and understood by the
   casual reader, or those who only read it to get a sermon for next

Sunday morning. God's book must be approached prayerfully and with a real hunger to **know Him**. If you do not truly know the Author, you will never truly understand His book. God judges motives, and as in our giving, so in our Bible study, our motives must be right. Do we study the Scripture in order to argue doctrine, support our position, or because it helps produce our salary? **Only we and God know.**

2. **Blindly following others**. I began talking about my growing understanding of the Godhead with a very dear friend of mine, a wonderful minister who has pastored and evangelized for over 30 years in a mainline Pentecostal denomination. Not long into our discussion as to whether God is one person or three, whether God is in fact a Trinity, he said "I never thought about it. I just accepted what they told me when I got saved, without giving it much consideration." Thankfully he is now giving it serious thought and study. But I think this is symptomatic of where we are in Christianity. We have followed parents, grandparents, preachers and other well intentioned people who perhaps followed others in what they believed, without searching out these foundational truths for ourselves. Jesus said, *"Search the scriptures" (John 5:39).* He said some were, *"teaching for doctrines the commandments of men" (Mark 7:7).* Peter said, *"And be ready always to give an answer to every man that asketh you a reason of the hope that is in you" (I Peter 3:15).* **We need our doctrinal beliefs challenged.** Self examination is good.

> *"Let a man examine himself" (I. Cor. 11:28).*
>
> ***"Examine yourselves, whether you be in the faith;*** *prove your own selves" (II Cor. 13:5).*

3. **Departing from the Bible**. Walk into any religious bookstore these days and you will be overwhelmed by row upon row, shelf after shelf, full of books of "Christian fiction." These books have very little scriptural basis, with many based on false doctrinal

assumptions, which add to the confusion of people's minds as to what the truth really is. There are large books on Bible characters about which very little is said in Scripture: Joseph, the husband of Mary, Mary Magdalene, Timothy and others. Consider the *"Chronicles of Narnia"* series by C.S. Lewis which has sold over 100 million copies in 29 languages since it was first published in 1950. It is a seven book series, the first of which has just been made into a $150 million Disney movie, that tells the story of a lion named Aslan "who sang the world into existence," and was lord of Narnia. Our Nashville *Tennessean* paper quoted a local pastor who was using the story to preach a series of sermons, thus: "There is a clear parallel of Aslan and Jesus," and it helps "to explain a central belief among Christians that Jesus Christ was present at the creation of the universe, was with God and is God." [5] Children need to be entertained, and good Christian themes are the very best, but shouldn't it be based on sound doctrine? A small book written by Thomas Williams *(an authority on C.S. Lewis and Narnia)* and sold along with the "Narnia" series as a soul winning tool, titled *"Knowing Aslan,"* contains some interesting quotes. "To save us, God would have to die in our place." "Yet God died for each of these terrible sinners." "Dear God, thank you so much for loving me. Thank you for dying in my place. I pray this prayer through the name of your loving Son, Jesus Christ." [6] Now, one question. Did God die, or did *"God so love the world that He gave His only begotten son?"* **God cannot die,** He is immortal! His son, **"the man Christ Jesus"** died! I'm sure the intent is good, and much good is done, but to plant such non-biblical fundamental concepts about God in the minds of millions, young and old, is wrong without measure.

Consider the *"Left Behind"* series of books by Tim LaHaye and Jerry Jenkins ("60 million copies sold"), that is based on a non-scriptural concept, the pre-tribulation rapture of the Church and is totally fiction. Yes, it has made millions more aware of the soon coming of Jesus, and has warned countless millions regarding the anti-christ, the mark of the beast, and Armageddon, but at **what cost to the truth**? False concepts, ideas, events and dialogue have been planted deep in people's minds who will never look into the Bible to separate the wheat from the chaff.

Time Magazine did an article on Christian fiction called "*Father and Child*," which focused mostly on the spate of new books about Joseph, stepfather of Jesus, of whom very little is said in Scripture. *Time* interviewed Jerry Jenkins regarding his book *Holding Heaven*, a work of fiction on this subject. *Time* says Jenkins **"looks cautious, almost nervous"** discussing the **boldness** of *Holding Heaven*. Jenkins says, "If we get criticized for '*Left Behind*' its, **'Are you adding to Scripture?'** You're really on **more dangerous territory**, though, when you quote an entire chapter and a half of a novella *(short novel)* from a guy *(Joseph)* who is not quoted in Scripture, **ever**." *Time* says, "Jenkins sees a shift in even Conservative Evangelical preaching from stringent exegesis *(explaining the Bible)*, or analysis of text, **to more free-ranging storytelling**." While acknowledging that text preaching is "my favorite form of preaching," Jenkins says, "But there is a marketplace of ideas. People now have access to iPods and TV and movies." Christian fiction is booming, and "if you go to a good, big, Evangelical Church now, **you'll hear a guy weaving a story**." [7] To me, considering the warnings of Scripture for the last days, **this is a shocking admission**.

I saw an interview that was done recently with the young pastor of the largest Protestant Church in America *(Houston, TX)*, who has a huge T.V. and book ministry as well. He said with a smile that many *(perhaps most)* of the sermons he preaches do not include reading one verse of Scripture, but he gives a reference to Scripture that the hearers can read later if they wish. He was introduced by Paula Zahn recently at the beginning of an interview on CNN as "a young, New Age preacher, in whose Church you will never hear the words sinner or Satan." Who am I to argue with success, but his sermons that I have seen on T.V. are feel good, self help, positive thinking, spiritual Pablum. *("Let the prophets speak...and the others judge" - weigh carefully what is said).*

If this is where we are today in Protestant Christianity I fear for us. I know that little sermonettes produce little Christianettes that will not stand when the going gets rough. It seems to be with us as the famous London preacher, Dr. Joseph Parker, said it was with many religious teachers of his day: "Hell gone! Devil gone! And God going!" It is time to hear Paul's words to the young preacher Timothy again:

> *"I charge thee therefore before God, and the Lord Jesus Christ, who shall judge the quick and the dead at his appearing and his kingdom; Preach the word; be instant in season and out of season; reprove, rebuke, exhort with all longsuffering and doctrine. For the time will come when they will not endure sound doctrine; but after their own lusts shall they heap to themselves teachers, having itching ears; And they shall turn away their ears from the truth, and shall be turned unto fables" (II Tim. 4:1-4).*

My earnest prayer to God is, please send us more true Bible preachers. Preachers like Jonathan Edwards, D.L. Moody, John R. Rice, Clarence E. Macartney, Robert G. Lee, Adrian Rogers, Imon Ursery, Edward Kelley, Gale "Cyclone" Young and yes, W.T. Hemphill. Some, not widely known on earth, but well known in heaven. Preachers who greatly impacted lives and left the world better than they found it. They preached the love of God, **with** the love of God. They preached the **Word of God**, and with feet firmly planted on its solid rock foundation, declared sin despicable, hell hot, death sure and eternity long. They preached Jesus Christ and him crucified, and that his blood is sufficient to cleanse every sin-stain. That he is the only way to God, the only hope for this head dizzy, body weary, soul famished, hell-bound world in which we live. They preached that we are on a probationary sojourn here on earth and will all be called in one day to answer to God. They were preachers with whom I might not have agreed on every point, and who might not have immediately accepted the thesis of this book, *(until God opened their understanding),* but they preached the Word and **I salute their memories**.

I would like to say to my brethren, faithful ministers of Jesus Christ of every nation, race, and denomination, you are my heros! I love you. I pray for you, I weep for you. Though yours may sometimes seem to be a thankless job, **you have a high calling!** When asked to run for President a few years ago, Billy Graham, with no hint of pride but with clear understanding of a preacher's importance, reportedly said, "I would be stepping down." And I agree!

Preach the Word!
- Preach it though the doubters doubt it.
- Preach it though the deniers deny it.
- Preach it though the despisers despise it.
- Preach it though the gainsayers gainsay it.
- Preach it strongly though church boards meet and decide to soften it. The ground is hard - plow it fiercely!
- Preach it though the crowds be small and the offerings smaller.
- Preach it though the compliments be sparse, knowing that your Father in heaven seeth, and will reward you openly.
- Preach it with love and longsuffering.
- Preach it with fire.
- Preach it with zeal.
- Preach it with fervor.
- Preach it though hell rages.

Preach repentance necessary.
Whatever happened to that message? John the Baptist preached it. Jesus preached it as his first sermon (Matt. 4:17). Peter and Paul preached it.

"Repent ye: for the kingdom of heaven is at hand"

(John the Baptist) *(Matt. 3:2)*.

"But except ye repent, ye shall all likewise perish" (Jesus speaking) *(Luke 13:3)*.

*"And that **repentance** and remission of sins should be **preached in his name among all nations"** (Jesus) *(Luke 24:47)*.

"Repent ye therefore, and be converted, that your sins may be blotted out" (Peter speaking) *(Acts 3:19)*.

*"The Lord....is longsuffering to us-ward, not willing that any should perish, but that **all should come to repentance"** (II Peter 3:9)*. Notice, not just **to belief** but **"to repentance."**

*"And the times of this ignorance God winked at; but **now commandeth all men everywhere to repent"** (Paul on Mars Hill) *(Acts 17:30)*. Why must all men repent? *"Because* (God) *hath appointed a day, in which he will judge the world in righteousness by **that man** whom he hath **ordained**."* Paul was speaking to Greek Gentiles and God's commandment to them was the same as to the Jews, **"repent."**

*"Or despisest thou the riches of his goodness and forbearance and longsuffering; **not knowing that the goodness of God leadeth thee to repentance?"** (Paul) *(Rom. 2:4)*.

*"For godly sorrow worketh **repentance to salvation** not to be repented of"* (Paul) *(II Cor. 7:10)*. The Corinthians were Gentiles.

To accept people into the fellowship of our Churches who have not truly repented is to confirm them in their rebellion and comfort them **in their sins**. It is to go to the hog pen and give the Prodigal a ring, robe, sandals and a party without a washing first. *(John the Baptist refused to baptize those who came without true repentance - Luke 3:7-14)*.

315

If that message has changed, these great apostles never told us!

Preach water baptism in Jesus' name as important.

*"Repent and be **baptized** every one of you in **the name of Jesus Christ** for the remission of sins"* (Peter speaking) *(Acts 2:38).*

"They (the people of Samaria) *were baptized in **the name of the Lord Jesus"** (Acts 8:16).*

"And he (Peter) ***commanded them to be baptized** in **the name of the Lord"** (Acts 10:48).*

"When they heard this, they (the Ephesians) *were baptized in **the name of the Lord Jesus"** (Acts 19:5).*

*"And now why tarriest thou? Arise, **and be baptized, and wash away thy sins,** calling on **the name of the Lord"*** (Ananias to Paul) *(Acts 22:16).*

"Is Christ divided? was Paul crucified for you? or were ye baptized in the name of Paul (I Cor. 1:13)? No! The correct answer is **"Jesus."**

"And he (the Phillipian jailer) *took them* (Paul and Silas) *the same hour of the night* (midnight), *and washed their stripes; **and was baptized, he and all his*** (household), ***straightway"** (Acts 16:33).* Baptism is so important, **they were baptized that night, "straightway."**

*"He that believeth **and is baptized** shall be saved"* (Jesus speaking) *(Mark 16:16).*

Those who know, but neglect or rebel against water baptism and that in Jesus name, will come up short when they stand before God.

One final thought to close this chapter. Pastor Clarence E. Macartney told the story of a young minister who was called upon to fill the pulpit of an aged preacher who was nearing death. He went to his bedside before service to ask if there were any final instructions. The old minister lifted his feeble hand and said, "Put all of the word of God you can into it." That says it all!

Chapter 17

To God Be The Glory

*"They shall see **the glory** of the Lord, and **the***
***excellency** of our God" (Isa. 35:2)*

"And the glory of the Lord (God) *shall be revealed, and*
all flesh shall see it together: for the mouth of the Lord
hath spoken it" (Isa. 40:5).

"Our Father which art in heaven...thine is the kingdom,
*and the power, **and the glory, for ever**. Amen"* (Jesus'
prayer) *(Matt. 6:9, 13).*

"But my God shall supply all your need according to
*His riches in glory by Christ Jesus. Now **unto God and***
***our Father be glory** for ever and ever. Amen" (Phil.*
4:19-20).

*"For **the earth shall be filled with the knowledge of the***
glory of the Lord**, as the waters cover the sea. **God
*came from Teman, and the **Holy One** from mount*
*Paran. Selah. **His glory** covered the heavens, and **the***
***earth was full of his praise**. And His brightness was as*
the light" (Hab. 2:14, 3:3-4).

$\mathscr{S}$ince the day of restoration is fast approaching when the earth will not
only be filled with God's praise but also with *"the knowledge of the glory of*
the Lord, as the waters cover the sea," should not we His people begin to
seek to understand what is meant by the phrase "the glory of God"? I am
sorry to say, but millions of people who call themselves "Christian" do not
have a clear concept of who God is, much less what is meant by **His glory.**

Throughout the chapters of this book we have been on a search for Bible truths about the Lord God. In conclusion, we will review some facts and see what additional understanding we can gain.

God can be known and understood.

> *"But let him that glorieth glory in this, that he* **understandeth** *and* **knoweth me***, that I am the Lord"* (Jer. 9:24).

> *"That you may* **know** *and* **believe** *me, and* **understand** *that I am he: before me there was no God formed, neither shall there be after me" (Isa. 43:10).*

> *"The invisible things of him from the creation of the world are* **clearly seen, being understood** *by the things that are made, even his eternal power and Godhead"* (Rom. 1:20).

The Spirit of God fills the universe but He has a presence.

> Adam and Eve *"hid themselves from the presence of the Lord" (Gen. 3:8).*

> *"Cain went out from the presence of the Lord" (Gen. 4:16).*

> *"Cast me not away from thy presence"* (King David) *(Ps. 51:11).*

In the Bible God is a person ("having form, essence, and substance")

> *"Will ye accept his person? will ye contend for God?" (Job 13:8)*

> *"The express image of his* (God's) *person" (Heb. 1:3).*

God has a face.

> *"The Lord make his face shine upon thee" (Num. 6:25).*

> *"The face of my Father which is in heaven" (Matt. 18:10).*

> *"And they shall see his* (God's) *face" (Rev. 22:4)*

God has a right and left hand.

> *"I saw the Lord sitting on his throne, and all the host of*

heaven standing by him on his right hand and on his left" (I Kings 22:19).

"Behold, I see the heavens opened, and the Son of man standing on the right hand of God" (Acts 7:56).

"And he (Jesus) *came and took the book out of the right hand of him* (God) *that sat upon the throne" (Rev. 5:7).*

*"I will take away **mine hand**, and thou shalt see **my back parts**; but **my face** shall not be seen"* (God to Moses) *(Ex. 33:23).*

God in bodily form has the appearance of a man.

"I saw visions of God...upon the likeness of the throne was the likeness as the appearance of a man above upon it...Thus saith the Lord God" (Ezek. 1:1, 26, 2:4).

"So God created man in his own image,...in the likeness of God made he him. And Adam begat a son in his own likeness, after his image" (Gen. 1:27, 5:1, 3). (As Adam resembled God, so Seth resembled Adam).

"He (man) *is the image of God" (I Cor. 11:7).*

(Jesus) *"the image of him* (God) *that created him" (Col. 3:10).*

What does the word "glory" mean in Scripture?

It is the beauty, significance, worth, or goodness of a person, place or thing, and the esteem with which they should be regarded. God the Creator gave everything He made, a value of its own.

*"And God saw every thing that he had made, and behold, it was **very good**" (Gen. 1:31).* (Remember the popular song of several years ago, "Everything is beautiful, in its own way?").

*"Consider the lilies...Solomon in **all his glory** was not arrayed like one of these"* (Jesus) *(Luke 12:27).*

*"The **glory** of this latter house shall be greater than of the former" (Hag. 2:9).*

319

Everything in heaven and earth has its own **degree of glory.**

> *"There are also celestial* (heavenly) *bodies, and bodies terrestrial* (earthly)*: but the glory of the celestial is one, and the glory of the terrestrial is another. There is one glory of the sun, and another glory of the moon, and another glory of the stars; for one star differeth from another star in glory"* *(I Cor. 15:40-41).*

No man has seen God in the fullness of His Glory.

> *"And he* (Moses) *said, I beseech thee, **show me thy glory**...And he* (God) *said, Thou canst not see my face: for there shall **no man** see me, and live"* *(Ex. 33:18, 20).*
>
> *"No man hath seen God at any time"* *(John 1:18).*
>
> *"Blessed are the pure in heart: for they shall see God"* (Jesus speaking) *(Matt. 5:8).*
>
> *"Unto the King **eternal**, immortal, **invisible**, the **only wise God**, be honor and **glory**"* *(I Tim. 1:17).*

WHAT IS MEANT WHEN THE BIBLE SPEAKS OF GOD'S "GLORY"?

1. **The Shekinah** *(sha-ke-na).* The awesome radiance of God's seldom seen presence.

> *"And the glory of the Lord abode upon Mount Sinai...and the sight of the glory of the Lord was like devouring fire on the top of the mount in the eyes of the children of Israel"* *(Ex. 24:16-17).*
>
> *"And the glory of the Lord appeared in the tabernacle...before all the children of Israel. As I* (God) *live, all the earth shall be filled with the glory of the Lord"* *(Num. 14:10, 21).*
>
> *"The priests could not stand to minister by reason of the cloud: for the glory of the Lord had filled the house* (temple) *of God"* *(II Chron. 5:14).*

320

"And behold, the glory of the God of Israel came from the way of the east: and the earth shined with his glory" (Ezek. 43:2).

"And I looked, and behold, the glory of the Lord filled the house of the Lord (the millennium temple)*: And I fell upon my face" (Ezek. 44:4).*

"And the glory of the Lord shone round about them (the shepherds)*; and they were sore afraid" (Luke 2:9).*

"And the city had no need for the sun, neither of the moon, to shine in it: for the glory of God did lighten it" (Rev. 21:23).

God has given Jesus radiant glory of his own.

"And (Jesus) *was transfigured before them: And **his face did shine as the sun**, and his raiment was white as the light" (Matt. 17:2).*

*"But Peter and they that were with him were heavy with sleep: and when they were awake, they saw **his** glory" (Luke 9:32).*

*"Ought not Christ to have suffered these things, and to enter into **his** glory"* (Jesus speaking) *(Luke 24:26).*

*"Of him shall the Son of man be ashamed, when he shall come in **his own** glory" (Luke 9:26).*

"His (Jesus) *head and his hairs were white like wool, as white as snow; and his eyes were as a flame of fire; And his feet like unto fine brass, as if they burned in a furnace" (Rev. 1:14-15).*

"God that raised him (Christ) *up from the dead and **gave him glory**; that your faith and hope **might be in God**" (I Peter 1:21).*

"But (we) *were eyewitnesses of **his** (Jesus') **majesty**. For **he received from God the Father** honor and **glory**...and this voice which came from heaven we*

321

heard, when we were with him in the holy mount" (II
Peter 1:16-18).

God the Father's glory is far greater than Jesus' glory for Peter says, *"he*
(Jesus) *received from God the Father...glory."* God's glory is innate and
underived and Jesus' glory is a "given" glory. Also Peter says that from the
cloud that was overhead on the Mt. of Transfiguration *"a voice came to him*
(Jesus) *from **the excellent*** ("exceedingly great") ***glory" (Mark 9:7, II Peter
1:17).* Peter, James and John saw Jesus' glory, but the voice from above
came from the "excellent glory."

2. **The Bible also speaks of God's glory in the sense of His total
   goodness, and awesome majesty, splendor, beauty, wisdom,
   magnificence, wealth, weightiness, greatness and moral
   perfection.**

When Moses asked to see God's glory, God said:

> *"I will make **all my goodness** pass before thee, and I
> will proclaim **the name of the Lord** before thee" (Ex.
> 33:19).*

And the next morning with Moses hidden in the cleft of the rock:

> *"The Lord descended in the cloud, and **stood with him
> there**, and proclaimed the name of the Lord. And the
> Lord passed by before him, and proclaimed, The Lord,
> The Lord God, **merciful** and **gracious, long-suffering,**
> and **abundant in goodness** and **truth**, Keeping **mercy**
> for thousands, forgiving iniquity and transgression and
> sin" (Ex. 34:5-7).*

King David says of God's glory:

> *"Thine, O Lord is the greatness, and the **power**, and the
> **glory**, and the **victory**, and the **majesty**: for all that is in
> the heaven and in the earth is thine; **thine is the
> kingdom**, O Lord, and thou art exalted as **head above
> all**"* (King David) *(I Chron. 29:11).*

That David was speaking of God the Father, Jesus confirms in Matt. 6:9,

13:

> *"After this manner therefore pray ye: Our Father* (God)
> *which art in heaven...for **thine is the kingdom**, and the*
> ***power**, and the **glory**, for ever. Amen."*

David says again:

> *"O Lord our Lord, how excellent is thy name in all the*
> *earth! who hast set **thy glory** above the heavens" (Ps.*
> *8:1).*

> *"One thing have I desired of the Lord, that will I seek*
> *after; that I may dwell in the house of the Lord...to*
> *behold the **beauty of the Lord" (Ps. 27:4).*** This is my prayer

God is Majesty! for all my family.

> *"He* (Jesus) *was received up into heaven, and sat on the*
> ***right hand of God" (Mark 16:19).***

> *"Jesus sat down on the right hand of **the Majesty** on*
> *high" (Heb. 1:3).*

God's glory, His goodness, His majesty, His greatness, His moral perfection is seen in Creation. We just have to open our eyes

> *"The heavens declare the glory of God; and the* and really see with our
> *firmament showeth his handiwork" (Ps. 19:1).* eyes + our heart,

In fact the theme of the Bible throughout proves that the ultimate reason why God made all of Creation is as a display of **His** glory.

> *"For I have created him* (Israel) *for my glory, I have*
> *formed him, yea I have made him" (Isa. 43:7).*

> *"The branch of my planting, the work of my hands, that*
> *I may be glorified" (Isa. 60:21).*

> *"That they might be called trees of righteousness, the*
> *planting of the Lord, that he might be glorified" (Isa.*
> *61:3).*

> *"Unto him* (God) *be glory in the church by Christ Jesus*
> *throughout all ages, world without end. Amen" (Eph.*
> *3:21).*

323

*"Fear God, **and give glory to him**; and worship him that made heaven, and earth, and the sea, and the fountains of waters" (Rev. 14:7).*

"The Lord hath made all things for himself" (Pro. 16:4) Lest we become too self - centered,

God's glory, His "goodness" is seen in His character (divine nature).

"God is love" (I John 4:8).

*"I will place **salvation** in Zion for Israel my glory" (Isa. 46:13).*

*"According to the good pleasure of his will, to the praise of the **glory of his grace**" (Eph. 1:5-6).*

*"Remember not the sins of my youth, nor my transgressions: according to thy **mercy** remember thou me for **thy goodness** sake, O Lord" (Ps. 25:7).*

*"The Lord is gracious and **full of compassion, slow to anger**, and of great mercy" (Ps. 145:8).*

God's glory is seen even when His righteousness demands that He judge the wicked.

*"What if God, willing to show his wrath, and to make his power known, endured with much long-suffering the **vessels** of **wrath** fitted to destruction: And that he might make known **the riches of his glory** on the vessels of mercy" (Rom. 9:22-23).*

*"For the Lord is **good**; his **mercy** is everlasting; and his **truth** endureth to all generations" (Ps. 100:5).*

God's glory is seen in Christ and his redemptive work.

*"For **God**, who commanded the light to shine out of darkness, hath shined in our hearts, to give the light of the knowledge of **the glory of God** in the face of Jesus Christ" (II Cor. 4:6).*

"Now is my soul troubled; Father, save me from this hour (the crucifixion)*: but for this cause came I unto*

this hour. **Father, glorify thy name***. Then came there a voice from heaven, saying, I have both glorified it, and will glorify it again" (John 12:27-28).*

"And whatsoever ye shall ask in my name, that will I do, **that the Father may be glorified in the Son"** *(John 14:13).*

"Father the hour is come; glorify thy Son, **that thy Son may glorify thee"** *(John 17:1).*

We have been given glory in Christ.

"And the glory which thou gavest me I have given them: that they may be one, even as we are one" (John 17:22).

"In bringing **many sons** *unto glory" (Heb. 2:10).*

"The glory which shall be **revealed in us***" (Rom. 8:18).*

"But we all, with open face beholding as in a glass (mirror) *the glory of the Lord, are changed into the* **same image** *from glory to glory, even as by the Spirit of the Lord" (II Cor. 3:18).*

"Our light affliction...worketh for us a far more exceeding and **eternal weight of glory***" (II Cor. 4:17).*

We desperately need this "eternal weight of glory" in Christ, for without him the glory of man is temporary and worthless.

"For all flesh is as grass, and all the **glory of man** *as the flower of grass. The grass withereth, and the flower thereof falleth away" (I Peter 1:24).*

3. **The Bible speaks of God's Glory in regard to the praise, honor, esteem, adoration and worship that we His creatures give to Him**.

Now would be a good time to look back over item #2 and reflect on God's precious and wonderful Divine nature and praise Him with a heart full of thanksgiving for this reason: If God was a tyrant, you could do absolutely nothing about it. You were born into His world, breathing His air, totally

325

dependent on all He has provided. But I hope you have awakened in awesome wonderment to the realization that He is kind and compassionate, patient and forgiving, full of grace and tender mercy. What if He delighted in creating only to destroy, or took pleasure in our pain! What if He had created hell for **all of humanity,** instead of "for the Devil and his angels." But Hallelujah, let us shout it again, **God is love and loveable!** He cares about our heartache.

> *"In all their* (Israel's) *affliction **he** (God) **was afflicted,***
> *and the angel of His presence saved them: in **His love***
> *and in **His pity** He saved them; and He bare them, and*
> *carried them all the days of old" (Isa. 63:9).*

God is approachable and can be entreated. He is light and in Him is no darkness. He is truth and in Him is no error. He is stability and in Him is no variableness nor shadow of turning. God is a good God. God is a happy God and He enjoys being God. He delights in **His perfect** majesty, power, beauty, righteousness and glory. God also delights in His creatures and creation.

> *"The Lord thy God in the midst of thee is mighty; he*
> *will save, **he will rejoice over thee with joy; he will rest***
> ***in his love, he will joy over thee with singing" (Zeph.***
> *3:17).*

And likewise God wants us to delight in Him and give Him the honor, esteem and adoration that is due to **Him only.** The greatest fulfilment a human can have on earth is to get a glimpse of God's glory and reflect that glory in **living, giving** and **praise.**

> *"O sing unto the Lord a new song; Sing unto the Lord,*
> *bless his name; Declare his glory among the heathen,*
> *For the Lord is great, and greatly to be praised: Honor*
> *and majesty are before him: Strength and beauty are in*
> *his sanctuary. **Give unto the Lord the glory due unto***
> ***his name:** O worship the Lord in the beauty of*
> *holiness" (Ps. 96:1-9).*

God is jealous of His Glory.

Yes, God the Father has given His only begotten Son "great glory," his "own glory," but the Lord God will not give **His glory** *(honor, esteem and worship)* to another.

> *"I am the Lord; that is my name: and my glory will I not give to another" (Isa. 42:8)*
>
> *"As for our redeemer, the Lord of hosts is his name, the Holy One of Israel. I will not give my glory unto another" (Isa. 47:4, 48:11).*

God is the source of all that is good.

The grace by which we are saved is **God's grace**. Calvary was a display of **God's love** *("For God so loved")*. If you have ever had a prayer answered, **God answered it!** He is the source!

> *"Do not err, my beloved brethren. Every **good gift** and every **perfect gift** is from above, and cometh down from **the Father** of lights" (James 1:16-17).*
>
> *"The **grace of God**, and **the gift by grace**, which is **by one man**, Jesus Christ" (Rom. 5:15).*
>
> *"**Thanks be unto God** for his unspeakable gift" (II Cor. 9:15).*
>
> *"By grace are ye saved through faith; it is **the gift of God**" (Eph. 2:8).*

When I was a small boy about the age of four, my Dad took the pastorate of a Church some fifty miles from our hometown, where most of our family lived. My older brother Dub bought me a pop gun and sent it to me by my brother-in-law who was coming down to visit us. Since Buck brought the pop gun, in my childish mind, I thought the gift was from him. I kept calling it *"the gun that Buck gave me."* My Mother had a hard time making me understand that although my brother-in-law delivered it, the gift was from my brother. Let us not be children in our understanding. God the Father is the source of everything that has been brought to us by Jesus.

> *"**The gift of God is eternal life** through Jesus Christ*

our Lord" (Rom. 6:23).

*"That **God** in all things may be glorified through Jesus Christ" (I Peter 4:11).*

Please understand this truth: God is our Savior but He has used faithful men as saviors. Look at Hebrews 11:7:

*"By faith Noah, being warned of God of things not seen as yet, moved with fear, prepared an ark **to the saving of his house.**"*

Noah not only became the savior of his household but of **the entire human race** as well. Genesis Chapter six tells the story.

*"And God saw that the wickedness of man was great in the earth...And the Lord said, I will destroy man whom I have created from the face of the earth; both man, and beast, and the creeping thing, and the fowls of the air; for it repenteth me that I have made them. **The end of all flesh is come before me**; for the earth is filled with violence through them; And, behold, I will destroy them with the earth" (Gen. 6:5, 7, 13).*

*"**But Noah found grace in the eyes of the Lord.** Noah was a just man...and Noah walked with God" (Gen. 6:8-9).*

God made a great deposit of grace in His man Noah. He became God's exclusive agent in salvation. He alone understood God's **purpose**, knew God's **plan**, and had God's **power** to deliver. The one and only way to be saved from destruction was to heed Noah, for he spoke God's words. He became *"Noah...a preacher of righteousness" (II Peter 2:5).*

All those on board the Ark, as the storm beat on the boat and the waters covered the mountain tops, were thankful to Noah for his obedience, faithfulness and sacrifice, but **they worshiped God** who had saved them! Ponder this: Everyone in heaven **from the flood on** will owe Noah a debt of gratitude, for we are all his descendants and **he saved us all!**

But the **greater salvation** *(eternal salvation)* that God wrought through

328

Christ goes back past Noah to the first Adam.

> *"For since **by man** came death, **by man** came also the resurrection from the dead. For as in **Adam** all die, even so in **Christ** shall all be made alive" (I Cor. 15:21-22).*

> *"For as by one man's disobedience many were made sinners, so by the obedience of one shall many be made righteous" (Rom. 5:19).*

Yes, Jesus is the only way to God, His exclusive agent in salvation, but **the object is to get to God.**

> *"No man **cometh unto the Father** but by me" (John 14:6).*

> *"For Christ also hath once suffered for sins...that he might **bring us to God** "(I Peter 3:18).*

> *"**All things are of God**, who hath reconciled us **to himself** by Jesus Christ...God was in Christ, reconciling the world **unto himself**...as though God did beseech you by us...be ye reconciled **to God**" (II Cor. 5:18-20).*

> Jesus *"is able to save them to the uttermost **that come unto God by him**" (Heb. 7:25).*

Jesus is the door but we have stopped at the door. Beyond the door is an ocean of grace, acceptance, forgiveness and unconditional love. Love to swim in. **The love of God!**

God our Creator is the one against whom we have sinned.

> *"Against thee, **thee only**, have I sinned, and done this evil in thy sight"* (King David speaking) *(Ps. 51:4).*

> *"I have sinned against heaven, and in thy sight, and am no more worthy to be called thy son"* (the prodigal) *(Luke 15:21).*

But God has made a great deposit of grace in Jesus *(often called the grace of Christ)*, and through him offers forgiveness and cleansing.

> *"Even as God for Christ's sake hath forgiven you" (Eph.*

4:32).

Thank you Jesus! But praise and glory be to God! For almost 1700 years Christianity has put the spotlight on Jesus, and that is okay, but we have made him God, and **that is not okay.** God the Father who sent Jesus to be our savior, never intended that he would replace Him in our hearts, esteem and worship. Every father wants his son to excel, but no father wants to be completely replaced by his son, or see him receive credit for what he himself has done. Give glory to Jesus as Messiah, Son of God, but give glory to God the Father as God alone. As Jesus said in regard to charitable acts, *"These ought ye to have done, and not to leave the other undone" (Matt. 23:23).*

God does not exist because Jesus does, but rather Jesus is derived from God, the "I Am" *(the self existent one)*, who told humanity for thousands of years B.C. that Christ was coming *(Gen. 3:15, Deut. 18:18, Isa. 53:2-3, 11).*

How should the Lord God be regarded?

To understand the degree of esteem with which the Creator of the universe should be regarded, just imagine a balance scale with the Supreme God on one side and the whole of creation on the other. The proportion by which one outweighs the other determines the share of the regard. **Be assured that compared to the Creator, all of creation will weigh no more than the dust of the scales, even as nothing and vanity.** As the Creator is infinite in excellence, perfection and significance, so He must have **all** possible regard. As He is in every way the first and Supreme, and His is in all respects ultimate beauty and glory *(the original good and the fountain of all that is good)*, so He must at all times have the supreme regard. As He is God over all, and worthy to reign as Supreme Head, so it is fitting that He should be thus esteemed and honored by all. [1]

> *"O Lord our Lord, how excellent is thy name in all the earth! Who hast set **thy glory** above the heavens. When I consider thy heavens, **the work of thy fingers,** the moon and the stars, which thou hast ordained; **What is man,** that thou art mindful of him? **And the son of man,** that thou visitest him"* (King David) *(Ps. 8:1, 3-*

330

4)?

*"Behold, the nations are as a drop of a bucket, and are counted as **the small dust of the balance**: all nations before **him** are as nothing; and they are counted to him less than nothing and vanity" (Isa. 40:15-17).*

"My Father...is greater than all" (Jesus speaking) *(John 10:29).*

Creation is about God.

"The heavens declare the glory of God; and the firmament showeth his handiwork" (Ps. 19:1).

Salvation is about God.

*"The **grace of God** that bringeth salvation" (Titus 2:11).*

The Bible is about God.

*"Almost the whole city came together to hear the **word of God**" (Acts 13:44).*

Heaven is about God.

"And (God) *will dwell with them, and they shall be his people, and **God himself** shall be with them, and be their God. And his servants shall serve him" (Rev. 21:3, 22:3).*

Our very existence and all we do is about God and His glory.

*"Whether therefore ye eat, or drink, or **whatsoever ye do, do all** to the **glory of God**" (I Cor. 10:31).*

*"**The God** and Father of our Lord Jesus Christ... having predestinated us unto the adoption of children by Jesus Christ **to himself**... To the praise of the glory of his grace" (Eph. 1:3, 5, 6).*

*"Whoso offereth praise **glorifieth me** (God)" (Ps. 50:23).*

*"And the shepherds returned, **glorifying** and praising **God**" (Luke 2:20).*

*"That they may see your good works, and **glorify your Father** which is in heaven"* (Jesus speaking) *(Matt. 5:16).*

*"That ye may with one mind and one mouth **glorify God, even the Father** of our Lord Jesus Christ"* *(Rom. 15:6).*

*"Therefore **glorify God** in your body, and in your spirit, which are God's"* *(I Cor. 6:20).*

*"Fear **God**, and give **glory to him**"* *(Rev. 14:7).*

*"**Lord God Almighty**, just and true are thy ways, thou King of saints. Who shall not fear thee, O Lord, and **glorify thy name**"* *(Rev. 15:3-4)?*

*"To **God** only wise, be **glory** through Jesus Christ for ever. Amen"* *(Rom. 16:27).*

*"To the only wise **God** our Savior, be **glory** and majesty, dominion and power, both now and ever. Amen"* *(Jude 25).*

*"Now unto the **King eternal**, **immortal**, **invisible**, the only wise **God**, be honor and **glory** for ever and ever. Amen"* *(I Tim. 1:17).*

To God be the Glory!

Appendix A - A Message From God

Early in 1986 God spoke to me through prophetic utterances and delivered me from a troubling personal situation. It was an awesome experience and *Charisma* Magazine told the story of our visitation in the July 1988 issue, in an article titled "A Family In Revival."

The Lord told me at that time to study the Scripture as He was going to reveal Himself to me in His word. He said that I would "write a book or books" about His glory. Though I had written, published and recorded over 200 gospel songs, I had never written a book, and what I knew regarding His glory could have perhaps been written on one page.

In addition to what God said pertaining to our personal situation, He gave me four specific messages to others.

To Our Large Christian Family

God said that many are careless and foolish, and their hearts are not turned toward Him, but they are turned toward the world and they are playing near the darkness. God said, **"Return to me and seek my face** and I will stretch forth my healing hand and heal your wounds, for if you do not **return** to me I will soon stretch forth my hand in **wrath.**"

<u>My Comment:</u> This was before the church experienced the wounds of preacher failure that made the news in early 1987. Of course God knew in advance of these wounds to "His Body," as well as our individual wounds which He so desires to heal. Again God says, **"return to me"** as He said through the prophets Isaiah, Jeremiah, and Hosea. **Wake up church!**

To Preachers

God said that many preachers had tried to package Him, and merchandise Him as the healer, or the solver of financial problems, or as the quick and easy way to success and prosperity. He had been

333

portrayed as "someone to whom you could beckon to come do this or do that" and God said, "It is not so." God said, "I do heal, and I do meet financial needs, but I am the Lord God of the Mighty Hosts, the Great King, soon coming back in majesty as a Bridegroom to receive a bride that has made herself ready," and He wanted to be presented in that manner.

My Comment: This seems to speak to the doctrine of "prosperity" or "name it and claim it," which is spreading in some Christian circles. Again, this was spoken in 1986 when this doctrine wasn't as popular as it is today.

To Gospel Singers

God said that many singers had said in their hearts, "We get paid and the people get blessed, so it doesn't matter how we live." God said, "It's not so." He said if we make our living by singing and testifying His name we are as the Levites, and we must offer an acceptable sacrifice of our lives to Him. He said that His **anger had come up in His face** because His body had been wounded by His people seeing that some of the singers sang one thing and lived another. He said if we do this we are "as money changers in the temple or as foolish children who take up a pretty serpent to their bosom to play with it" and we would be bitten by it.

My Comment: God answered once and for all the famous question, "Is Gospel music ministry or entertainment?" God said **ministry**. There is certainly nothing wrong with preachers or gospel singers being as entertaining as possible, within the bounds of taste and "what seems good to the Holy Spirit," but God said it is a serious thing when someone is given permission to use another's name and that "He had permitted us to use His name to make a living."

A Warning To All

God said, "I am soon going to **shake the nations** with a demonstration of the power of my wrath." He said, "Many will think that it is the end but it is not," it is just to show His power to the nations. God said that He did not want His church stirred by the shaking, but He wants us stirred by the Word, now, so that we will have strength to reap the harvest of souls that the shaking will bring. **My Comment:** We later found Scriptural references to this shaking in Ezekiel 38:20, Haggai 2:6-7, Hebrews 12:26-27, Joel 2:31 and 3:16 where the prophet says it happens "before....the day of the Lord comes." Jesus said in Luke 17:26 and Matthew 24:37 "*As it was in the days of Noah, so shall it be also in the days of the coming of the Son of man.*" Genesis 6:13 says, "*And God said unto Noah, the end of all flesh is come before me, for the earth is filled with violence and I will destroy them.*" We must be getting very close to that point again. **Pray people pray!** God told the prophet Habakkuk 2:2-3, "*Write the vision make it plain...that he may run that readeth it. For the vision is yet for an appointed time, but at the end it shall speak, and not lie: though it tarry, wait for it; because it will surely come.*"

Appendix B - Questionable Verses

It has never been a practice of mine to support a doctrine which I hold, by casting doubt on the anthenticity of Bible verses that seem to disagree with it. God is the custodian of His word and I believe He has given us all we need of Holy Writ for salvation and service. You will notice that I have used the authorized King James Version and have not gone from translation to translation to try to prove a point. Some of the modern translations are good, and I use them for study, but my preaching and writing are done from the KJV, which I believe is the best we have.

However, in my studies pertaining to this book I have found some things in this area that should be addressed. The men who translated the KJV, first published in 1611, though well intentioned and under strict orders from King James I of England, were nevertheless Trinitarian in belief and this is reflected in words supplied in certain verses. In the front of many KJV Bibles you will see a disclaimer printed which reads something similar to this:

"It should be borne in mind that the use of *italics* in the English Bible text indicates that **these specific words are not present in the original languages of the Bible**...*(Hebrew and Greek)*. They were **inserted** by the translators of the King James Version for the purpose of clarification."

Also please bear in mind the warning that my Dad, a faithful minister of the Gospel for 68 years, gave me when I was a young minister: "Son, be aware that Hebrew and Greek scholars will **bend** the Hebrew and Greek to fit their doctrine."

Here are some examples of words supplied by the translators that do not fit what the inspired text teaches.

- "Hereby, perceive we the love of *God*, because he laid down his life for us" *(I John 3:16)*. Of course "*God*," did not lay down his life for us, God is immortal (deathless) and cannot die. His Son Jesus died for us.

- "Whosoever denieth the Son, the same hath not the Father: *but he that acknowledgeth the Son hath the Father also*" *(I John 2:23)*. Half of this verse was not in the original but added, and may or may not be true. Many people acknowledge the Son but exclude or ignore the Father.

- "Gird thy sword upon thy thigh *most* mighty, with thy Glory and thy majesty" *(Ps. 45:3)*. Again, an attempt to make the Messiah, God, by calling him "*most*" mighty. He is "mighty" but only His Father is "most mighty" the "most High God."

The original texts of the O.T. and N.T. as breathed by the Holy Spirit are infallible and inerrant. However there has possibly been some tampering with the original text in the ensuing centuries to support the doctrine of the Trinity. The following is mostly from Trinitarian sources.

I John 5:7

Author Lee Strobel in his book, *"The Case for Christ" (over 2 million copies sold)* interviewed Bruce M. Metzger, PH.D., an 84 year old authority on the authenticity of the N.T., who has authored or edited fifty books relating to the subject. He puts the "grand total of *(early)* Greek manuscripts at 5,664." Metzger tells Strobel that if someone challenges the authenticity of I John 5:7: *"For there are three that bear record in heaven, the Father, the Word, and the Holy Ghost: and these three are one,"* saying "That's not in the earliest manuscripts," his answer would be, **"And that's true enough**. I think that these words are found in only about seven or eight copies *(manuscripts)*, all from the fifteenth or sixteenth century. **I acknowledge that is not what the author of I John was inspired to write.**" [1] Strobel and Metzger are both Trinitarians but they have cast doubt on one of the main scriptures Trinitarians use to support their mistaken doctrine.

The NIV quotes in its text **notes** the words "the Father, the Word and the Holy Spirit, and these three are one. And there are three that testify on earth:" and then explains why they are not in the **text** of the NIV. They say, **"the addition is not found in any Greek manuscript or N.T. translation**

prior to the 16th century.[2] These words are also not found in the New Revised Standard Version, the New American Standard Bible, the English Standard Version, or the New Living Translation.

Matthew 28:19

Now to Matt. 28:19, another mainstay of those who hold the Trinitarian view of God.

- *"Go ye therefore, and teach all nations, baptizing them in the name of the Father, and of the Son, and of the Holy Ghost."*

  The Interpreters Dictionary of the Bible says: "There is grave doubt whether they (the traditional words Father, Son and Holy Ghost) may be regarded as the actual words of Jesus."[3]

  Encyclopedia Britannica says: "Elsewhere in the New Testament the triune formula is not used. Some scholars thus doubt the accuracy of the quotation in Matthew."[4]

  Encyclopedia Britannica says: "In the **oldest sources** it is stated that baptism takes place in the name of Jesus."[5]

Hastings' Dictionary of the Bible says:

"It has been customary to trace the institution of the practice *(Christian baptism)* to the words of Christ recorded in Matt. 28:19. But the authenticity of this passage has been challenged on historical as well as on textual grounds. **It must be acknowledged** that the formula of the threefold name, which is here enjoined, does not appear to have been employed by the primitive church, which, so far as our information goes, baptized 'in' or 'into the name of Jesus' *(or "Jesus Christ" or 'the Lord Jesus': AC. 2:38, 8:16, 10:49, 19:5; of I Co. 1:13, 15)* without reference to the Father or the Spirit."[6]

Hastings elsewhere holds up for the doctrine of the Trinity but must admit here that it cannot be supported by Matthew 28:19.

Regarding baptism as mandated by the Lord in Matt. 28:19-20 and Mark 16:15-16, The Encyclopedia of Catholicism says, "Both passages contain the commission to baptize. While the explicit **formula in Matthew may come from the liturgy of the Church,** the command to baptize and the central meaning of baptism **comes from Jesus**." [7] *(We should not follow "the liturgy of the Church" that is not backed up by Holy Scripture)*

You be the judge as to whether we should teach the doctrine of the Trinity, and base it on scriptures which even Trinitarian scholars say are not authentic.

I Timothy 3:16

The apostle Paul in his 13 epistles makes a clear distinction between God and Jesus over 500 times. However I Timothy 3:16 in the King James Version seems to blur this distinction.

> *"And without controversy great is the mystery of godliness: God was manifest in the flesh, justified in the Spirit, seen of angels, preached unto the Gentiles, believed on in the world, received up into glory."*

Did Paul actually write that *"God was manifest"* in Jesus' flesh? It is possible for he said in II Cor. 4:11:

> *"That the life also of **Jesus might be made manifest in our mortal flesh**."*

We of course are not Jesus and Jesus is not God. Look at how Paul opens this same epistle of I Timothy:

> *"Paul, an apostle of Jesus Christ by the commandment of **God our Savior*** (God is our Savior but He used His Son Jesus to save us), *and **Lord Jesus Christ**, which is our hope; Grace, mercy, and peace, from **God** our Father **and Jesus** Christ our Lord"* (I Tim. 1:1-2).

To Paul they are not the same and only one is God. See verse 17:

> *"Now unto the King **eternal, immortal*** ("deathless"), ***invisible**, the only wise God, be honor and glory for ever and ever."* (The "*only wise God*" is the one who is "*eternal, immortal, invisible*").

Many of the best Bible scholars of today, even those of the Trinitarian persuasion, based on the most reliable manuscripts, have been forced to admit that Paul probably did not include the word "God" in this verse. The NIV says:

> *"Beyond all question, the mystery of godliness is great:*
>
> ***He appeared in a body."***

The NASB, *The New English Bible*, *The Holman CSB*, *The English Standard Version* and *The Message* all agree using "He" or "He who" instead of "God." The New Living Translation renders it thus:

> *"Without question, this is the great mystery of our faith.*
>
> *Christ was revealed in a human body."*

Did Paul call Jesus "God"? Listen to James Hastings, noted Trinitarian Bible Scholar, writing in *Hastings' Dictionary of the Bible*:

> "It may be that St. Paul nowhere names Christ 'God'." To a Jew the idea that a man might come to be God would have been an intolerable blasphemy" [8] (end of quote).

Please note also that the Godhead is not Paul's subject in I Tim. 3:16. The subject is the "mystery of godliness." This word "godliness" is the Greek word "eusebeia" *(Strongs #2150)* and means "piety" or "holiness." *"Great is the mystery of piety or holiness, Christ who was manifest in the flesh."*

"It may be that St. Paul nowhere names Christ 'God.' To a Jew the idea that a man might come to be God would have been an intolerable blasphemy"

James Hastings – Noted Trinitarian Bible Scholar [8]

Appendix C - 101 Bible Reasons Why Jesus Cannot Be God or the Second Person of a Triune God

Jesus Christ *(Messiah)* is our Saviour and Redeemer, the anointed, appointed, approved, highly exalted, virgin born, sinless Son of God *(Luke 1:27, I Pet. 2:22, Matt. 16:16).* He is the only way to God *(John 14:6).* *"There is none other name under heaven given among men, whereby we must be saved" (Acts 4:12).* **But we can say on the authority of God's Holy Bible that he is not the Supreme God.** *(He always pointed beyond himself to another!)* Here are 101 Bible facts to prove it.

1. He is the virgin born, sinless Son of God, the *"one mediator between God and men, the man Christ Jesus" (I Tim. 2:5).*

2. "Son of God" is not a synonym for God, and in the Bibles **does not mean God.** *"Adam, which was the son of God" (Luke 3:38).* (When "Son" of God is written with a capital "S" it is a choice made by the editor or publisher and does not affect the meaning of the word "son").

3. The angels, Adam, Solomon, and Jesus were all **created** "sons of God," (Jesus was created in the womb of Mary), but were not **kin** to God *(Gen. 1:27 & 31, I Chron. 17:13, Matt. 1:18, Luke 1:35, Rev. 3:14, Col. 1:15).*

4. God is a unique being ("one of a kind, having no like or equal"). *"I am God, and there is none else; I am God, and there is none like me" (Isa. 46:9).* *"I am he and there is no god with me" (Deut. 32:39).* *"Thou art God alone" (Ps. 86:10).* (What does **alone** mean?)

5. Jesus is *"the beginning of the Creation of God" (Rev. 3:14),* "the firstborn of every **creature**" *(Col. 1:15),* and is *"after the image of him* (God) *that created him" (Col. 3:10).*

6. In Jesus' own statements and those of the sacred writers, he is seen as

343

a distinct being from God as one man is distinct from another. *"It is written in your law, that the testimony of two men is true. I am one that bear witness of myself, and the Father that sent me beareth witness of me" (John 8:17-18).* "Ye believe *in God*, believe *also in me (John 14:1).* (Remember, in scripture God is a "person" *(Job 13:8, Heb. 1:3)*, which means having "a **face**, **form**, **essence** and **substance**"). *"Saith the Lord God, my fury shall come up in **my face" (Ezek. 38:18).** "The similitude* (form) *of the Lord* (God) *shall he* (Moses) *behold" (Num. 12:8).*

7. The apostle Paul who said that the fullness of God dwells in Jesus, said that Christians likewise should be "filled with all the fullness of God." *"It pleased the Father that in him should all fullness dwell" (Col. 1:19). "That ye might be filled with all the fullness of God" (Eph. 3:19).* Being "filled with the fullness of God" does not make a person "God." How was God in Christ? The same way that Christ is in us *(John 14:10; 17:21-23).*

8. God is omnipotent ("having unlimited power") and Jesus is not. *"The Son can do nothing of himself, but what he seeth the Father do...I can of mine own self do nothing" (John 5:19, 30).*

9. God is omniscient ("having infinite knowledge") and Jesus is not. *"But of that day and that hour knoweth no man, no, not the angels, which are in heaven, **neither the Son**, but the Father"* (Jesus speaking) *(Mark 13:32).*

10. God is omnipresent ("in all places at the same time") and Jesus is not. Jesus said he was not in Bethany when Lazarus died: *"I am glad for your sakes that I was not there" (John 11:15).*

11. Jesus died, and God is immortal ("**deathless**") and cannot die. *"Now unto the King eternal, **immortal, invisible, the only wise God"** (I Tim. 1:17).*

12. Jesus was tempted and God cannot be tempted. *(Luke 4:2, James 1:13).*

13. Jesus was made lower than the angels and God cannot be lower than

344

His creatures *(Heb. 2:9)*.

14. Jesus is **one in substance with us** his brethren *(Heb. 2:11)*. **God is not our brother**, He is our Father. *"That he* (Jesus) *might be the firstborn among many brethren" (Rom. 8:29). "That ye might be partakers of the divine nature" (II Pet. 1:4)*.

15. It was necessary for Jesus *"in all things to be made like unto his brethren" (Heb. 2:17)*.

16. Jesus **increased in favor** with God. *"And Jesus increased in wisdom and stature, and in favor with God and man" (Luke 2:52)*.

17. Jesus **learned obedience**. *"Though he were a Son yet learned he obedience by the things which he suffered" (Heb. 5:8)*.

18. Jesus suffered being tempted. *"He hath suffered being tempted" (Heb. 2:18)*.

19. Jesus was made perfect through sufferings. *"To make the captain of their salvation perfect through sufferings" (Heb. 2:10)*.

20. The life of Jesus, as told in the scriptures, was a life in the flesh which moved within the normal lines of a human mind and will. He asks questions to get information, he feels and expresses surprise, he looks on the fig tree to find fruit and there is none. He is the Savior but **can this be God?**

21. Jesus is the Son of God and the **perfect man** but he went through life like every man does, with fears, doubts and pain, and with the possibility of sin. (Without the possibility of sin the accounts of his temptation would be just a charade.) *(see Isa. 53:3, Mark 14:33-35, Luke 22:43-44, John 12:27)*.

22. Jesus is the second Adam. Adam was created from the dust as told in Genesis one, and Jesus was created in the womb of Mary as told in Matthew one and Luke one. *"The first man Adam was made a living soul; the last Adam was made a quickening spirit. The first man...the second man" (I Cor. 15:45, 47)*.

23. Adam was made with a sinless nature, but as an act of his will **he sinned anyway**. Jesus was made with a sinless nature and as an act

of his will **he did not sin**. *"That ye should follow his steps: Who did no sin, neither was guile found in his mouth" (I Pet. 2:21-22).*

24. Jesus Christ, begotten from the womb of a virgin as "the Son of God," was genetically equal to the first **Adam** *"which was the son of God" (Luke 3:38),* but without the inherent sin that Adam passed to all of his descendants. *"The gift of grace which is by **one man**, Jesus Christ...as by one man's disobedience many were made sinners, so by the **obedience of one** shall many be made righteous" (Rom. 5:15, 19).*

25. As the only man ever **born** without inherent sin Jesus was a unique (one of a kind) human being, the **only man** equipped to be the Savior and Redeemer of mankind. *"As by the **offense of one** judgement came upon all men to condemnation; even so by the **righteousness of one** the free gift came upon all men" (Rom. 5:18).*

26. Jesus was begotten ("brought into being") on **a certain day**. *"Thou art my Son, **today** have I begotten thee" (Ps. 2:7, Heb. 5:5).*

27. God is the God of Jesus, just as He is of Christians. *"I ascend unto my Father, and your Father; and to **my God,** and your God" (John 20:17).*

28. Jesus never one time in scripture said he was God. **If it was true he would have told us.**

29. Jesus denied being God. *"Why callest thou me good? There is none good but **one**, that is, God" (Matt. 19:17).*

30. Jesus denied saying he was God. *"Because thou, being a man, makest thyself God (the Pharisees speaking)."* Jesus answered, *"I said I am the Son of God" (John 10:33, 36).*

31. Jesus said he and the Father are one (one in love - unity - fellowship), **just like** he wants Christians to be one *(John 10:30, 17:22). "That they may be one, **even as we are one**."*

32. *"He (Jesus) went out into a mountain to pray, and continued **all night** in prayer to God" (Luke 6:12).* If Jesus is God, why would he need to pray to God?

33. Jesus had a will of his own. He was not a robot, pre-programmed to do the Father's will, but he always submitted his will to God's *(John 4:34, 5:30, 6:39)*.

34. For a short time **Jesus' will** was not the same as **God's will**. *"Nevertheless, not as I will, but as thou wilt...And prayed the **third time**, saying the same words" (Matt. 26:39, 44)*.

35. Jesus prayed in Luke 22:42, *"Saying, Father, if thou be willing, remove this cup from me: nevertheless, not my will, but thine, be done."* How could one who is deity pray to another who is deity without **undeifying** himself?

36. Every Christian in the world testifies that Jesus is not God, for we all say that Jesus died on the cross, and therefore he is not God, for God is immortal ("deathless"). **God cannot die!** *(I Tim. 1:17, 6:16)*.

37. Death for a man is the separation of his human spirit from his human body. Jesus died as **a man**, not just as a body. *"Jesus....yielded up the ghost"* (his human spirit) *(Matt. 27:50)*.

38. The death of one who is **deity** could not redeem fallen men, for we are not **deity**. It took the sacrificial death of a sinless **man**. *"By man came death, **by man** came also the resurrection of the dead"* (Paul) *(I Cor. 15:21)*. In Rev. 5:3 a search was made for a **"man"** worthy to open the 7 sealed book. Jesus is that **man!**

39. Jesus never once said he was God, but he did say he was **a man**. *"A man that hath told you the truth" (John 8:40)*.

40. *"God is not **a man"** (I Sam. 15:29), "neither **the son of man"** (Num. 23:19)*.

41. The prophet Isaiah said Messiah (Christ) would be **a man**. *"A man of sorrows and acquainted with grief" (Isa. 53:3)*.

42. The prophet Jeremiah said it would be "a man" who would sit upon the throne of Israel as David's heir, Messiah **a man** *(Jer. 33:17)*.

43. The prophet Zechariah said that Israel's coming "shepherd" would be a **"man"** *(Zech. 13:7, Matt. 26:31)*.

44. The prophet Micah said the Messiah born in "Bethlehem" would be a

"**man**." *"And this man shall be the peace" (Micah 5:2, 5).*

45. The prophet John the Baptist said Jesus was **a man**. *"After me cometh **a man**" (John 1:30). "All things that John spoke of **this man** were true" (John 10:41).*

46. The apostle Peter said Jesus is *"**a man** approved of God" (Acts 2:22).*

47. The apostle Peter said Jesus' heart rejoiced and his flesh rested in hope because he knew that God would not **leave his soul in hell**, or allow his body to decay in the grave *(Acts 2:24-27, 31, I Pet. 3:18-20).*

48. Peter knew that Jesus is not God, but said that **God was with Jesus**. *"How God anointed Jesus of Nazareth with the Holy Ghost...for God was with him" (Acts. 10:38).*

49. Jesus had a soul as all men do. *"**My soul** is exceeding sorrowful, unto death" (Mark 14:34).*

50. *"God is a Spirit" (John 4:24).* The resurrected Jesus said he was **not a spirit**. *"A spirit hath not flesh and bones; as ye see me have" (Luke 24:39).*

51. The apostle Paul said Jesus is **a man**. *"Through **this man** (not this God) is preached unto you the forgiveness of sins" (Acts 13:38). "The gift by grace, which is by **one man**, Jesus Christ" (Rom. 5:15).*

52. The inspired writer of Hebrews called Jesus Christ "**this man**" four times *(Heb. 3:3, 7:24, 8:3, 10:12).*

53. Jesus is called "Son of man" (a human being) 84 times in the gospels. Ezekiel is called "Son of Man" 90 times by God in the book of Ezekiel. Jesus and Ezekiel were both human beings.

54. When Jesus arose from the grave **he was still** "the son of man." *"Tell the vision to no man, until the son of man be risen again from the dead" (Matt. 17:9).*

55. Acting as **God's agent in resurrection**, Jesus raised up his body, "this temple" from the grave. *"**I have power** to lay it down, and I have power to take it again. This **commandment** have I received of*

348

my Father" (John 10:18). (Almighty God can empower anyone to do anything).

56. When Jesus forgave a man's sins and healed him of palsy, rather than proving him to be God, it proved he was **a man** with God-given power and authority. *"That ye may know that the Son of **man** hath **power on earth** to forgive sin...arise" (Matt. 9:6).* The witnesses understood what they had seen for they *"**glorified God**, which had given **such power** unto **men**" (v. 8).* (Jesus later gave this **power** to his apostles - *John 20:23*).

57. After **Jesus** had been on earth for 33 years and seen by thousands of people, his apostle John said twice, *"**no man hath seen God** at any time" (John 1:18, I John 4:12).*

58. Jesus said *"My Father...is greater than all"* and *"my Father is greater than I" (John 10:29, 14:28).* How can one who is God be greater than another who is God?

59. Jesus said his Father is **the only true God.** *"And this is life eternal, that they might know **thee**, the only true God" (John 17:3).*

60. Jesus said there were positions of honor in **his own** coming kingdom that he did not have authority to fill. *"But to sit on my right hand and on my left hand is not mine to give" (Mark 10:40).*

61. Jesus was limited in his miracle power by the unbelief of his own countrymen. *"And he **could** there **do no mighty work**" (Mark 6:5).*

62. The apostle Paul speaks of *"Christ, who is **the image of God**" (II Cor. 4:4).* An image is not the original but *"**a representative likeness.**"*

63. Paul says that just as *"the head of every man is Christ; and the head of the woman is the man; **the head of Christ is God**" (I Cor. 11:3).*

64. Paul says just as we belong to Christ, Christ belongs to God. *"And ye are Christ's; and **Christ is God's**" (I Cor. 3:23).*

65. The Bible calls Jesus the **servant of God**, just as Abraham, Moses, Daniel, James and John are called servants of God *(Isa. 52:13, 53:11, Zech. 3:8).* *"Behold **my servant**, whom I have chosen; my*

*beloved, in whom my soul is well-pleased: I will put **my Spirit upon***
him" (God speaking) *(Matt. 12:18).*

66. Paul uses the word "God" over 500 times in thirteen epistles and not once can it be proven that he is talking about Jesus. *"For there is **one God**, and **one mediator** between God and men, **the man** Christ Jesus" (I Tim. 2:5).* (He never contradicted that statement).

67. In the N.T. the word "God" is used over 1300 times and it is not speaking of Jesus.

68. After Jesus' ascension Paul prayed 34 prayers as recorded in Acts and his epistles, and they were all offered to God and not to Jesus.

69. Not once in Paul's writings did he say for Christians to pray to Jesus. *"Strive together with me in your prayers to God" (Rom. 15:30).* *"Let your requests be made known unto God" (Phil. 4:6).*

70. Paul said in six different scriptures that he prayed to God, (not Jesus). *(Eph. 3:14, Phil., 1:3-4, Col. 1:3, I Thess. 3:9, II Cor. 9:11, Phm. 1:4). "I bow my knees unto the Father of our Lord Jesus Christ " (Eph. 3:14).* (There is no record in the Bible of any apostle or gospel writer praying to Jesus after his ascension). *"Let him ask of God" (James 1:5).*

71. Jesus said that after he went to the Father we would not pray to him. *"And **in that day ye shall ask me nothing**. Verily, verily, I say unto you, Whatsoever ye shall **ask the Father** in my name, **he will give it you**" (John 16:23).*

72. The words "worship" or "worshiped" are not used in regard to Jesus after his ascension. There are many mentions of "worship" to God but none to Jesus. *(Acts 18:13, 24:14, I Cor. 14:25, Phil. 3:3, Rev. 19:10, 22:9).*

73. "Hallelujah" or "Alleluia" mean "praise be to God" and in scripture are never spoken to Jesus but only to the Lord God. *(Rev. 19:1, 3, 4, 6).*

74. Paul said that the one and only God to Christians is "the Father." *"But to us there is but one God, **the Father**" (I Cor. 8:6). "One God*

and **Father** *of all" (Eph. 4:6).* Paul was consistent!

75. Our Lord's half brother Jude said that *"God the Father"* was the *"only Lord God,"* as separate from our *"Lord Jesus Christ" (Jude, vs. 1 and 4).*

76. There are seventeen verses in the N.T. where the Father is referred to as **"one"** or **"only"** God, and not a single verse in which the Son is referred to in this manner.

77. Jesus had a reverential **fear of God**. *"And the Spirit of the Lord* (God) *shall rest upon him* (Messiah), *the spirit of knowledge and of the **fear** of the Lord; And shall make him of quick understanding in the **fear** of the Lord" (Isa. 11:2-3).* (Christ) *"was heard in that **he** feared" (Heb. 5:7).*

78. Only God the Father is the great "I Am," **underived** the "self existent one." All that Jesus the Son **was, had,** and **did** were **derived** from God. *"As the living Father hath sent me, and I live by the Father" (John 6:57).*

79. Jesus said his life came from the Father. *"As the Father hath life in himself; **so hath he given** to the Son to have life in himself" (John 5:26).*

80. Jesus claimed **no power** of his own. *"I can of mine own self do nothing" (John 5:30).*

81. Jesus said that after his crucifixion they would understand his total dependance on God the Father. *"When ye have lifted up the Son of man, then shall ye know that I am he* (the Messiah), *and that I do nothing of myself; but as my Father hath taught me, I speak these things" (John 8:28).*

82. Jesus denied that he was the source of his miraculous works. *"The Father that dwelleth in me, he doeth the works (John 14:10). "If I cast out devils by the Spirit of God" (Matt. 12:28).*

83. Jesus denied that his doctrine was his own. *"My doctrine is not mine, but his that sent me" (John 7:16).*

84. Jesus acknowledged his dependence on the Father for his witness.

"If I bear witness of myself, my witness is not true" (John 5:31).

85. Jesus states repeatedly that his authority **derived** from God the Father. *"He hath given to the Son to have life in himself, and hath **given him authority**" (John 5:26-27).*

86. Jesus acknowledged his dependence on the Father for **example** and **direction** in all he did. *"The Son can do nothing of himself, but what he seeth the Father do. ...the Father loveth the Son, and showeth him all things that himself doeth" (John 5:19-20).*

87. Jesus is called several times in Hebrews a priest. *"So also Christ glorified not himself to be made a high priest...Thou art a priest **for ever**...called of God an high priest" (Heb. 5:5, 6, 10).* The work of a priest is to **minister to God**, therefore Christ as a priest **cannot be God**. *"Jesus, made an high priest **for ever**...Thou art a priest **for ever**...We have such an high priest, who is set on the right hand of the throne of the Majesty in the heavens" (Heb. 6:20, 7:17, 8:1).*

88. Jesus is an apostle appointed by God. *"Consider the Apostle and High Priest of our profession, Christ Jesus; Who was faithful to him that **appointed** him" (Heb. 3:1-2).*

89. Jesus is equal to God in sinlessness but inferior to God in power, knowledge and Glory. *"All power is **given unto me**..." (Matt. 28:18). "Which the Father hath put in **His own power**" (Acts 1:7). "The glory which thou **gavest** me" (John 17:22).* God who **gave** the power and glory has greater power and glory.

90. God, who put all things under His Son Jesus, **is not under him**. *"But when he saith, all things are put under him...he (God) is excepted, which did put all things under him" (I Cor. 15:27).*

91. When the **kingdom** is completed Jesus will deliver it up to God, and then shall himself be subject to the Father. *"Then cometh the end, when he (Jesus) shall have delivered up the kingdom to God, even the Father...then shall the Son also himself **be subject unto him** (God) that put all things under him, **that God may be all in all**" (I Cor. 15:24, 28).*

92. We have made **Jesus "all"** in our hearts and worship and given God the Father's glory to the Son, but the inspired apostle Paul said that **God is "all"** *(I Cor. 15:28).*

93. The ascended Jesus was in heaven, perhaps for several years, before God revealed to him the events of Revelation. *"The Revelation of Jesus Christ **which God gave unto him**, to show unto his servants things which must shortly come to pass" (Rev. 1:1).* (Jesus ascended around 32-33 A.D. and Revelation was written around 96 A.D.).

94. **Nowhere** in scripture is Jesus pictured as sitting on the **throne of God**. *"But this man...sat down on the right hand of God" (Heb. 10:12). "Jesus...is sat down at the right hand of the throne of God" (Heb. 12:2).*

95. Jesus **overcame** and therefore sits with the Father in **His throne**, just as we as overcomers will sit with Jesus in his throne. *"To him that overcometh will I grant to sit with me in **my throne**, even as I also overcame, and am set down with my Father in **his throne**" (Rev. 3:21).*

96. Even though he was seated at the right hand of God in heaven when the Book of Revelation was written, Jesus still calls God *"my God"* four times in one verse *(Rev. 3:12).*

97. The purpose for Jesus being seated at the right hand of God is to act as our intercessor, our advocate, our go-between. *"We **have an advocate** with the Father, Jesus Christ the righteous" (I John 2:1). "He is able to save them to the uttermost that come **unto God by him**, seeing he ever liveth to make **intercession** for them" (Heb. 7:25).* The object is to get to God the Father. *"No man cometh **unto the** Father, but by me" (John 14:6). "Christ also hath once suffered for sins...that he might bring us **to God**" (I Pet. 3:18).*

98. Jesus never instructed his disciples to worship or pray to himself or the Holy Ghost, but to the Father, and the Father only. *"When ye pray, say, Our Father which art in heaven" (Luke 11:2). "The hour cometh and now is, when the true worshippers shall **worship the**

Father in spirit and in truth: for the *Father* seeketh such to *worship him*" *(John 4:23)*. "The Father himself...ye have neither heard his voice at any time, nor seen his shape" *(John 5:37)*. (They had been blessed to **see** and **hear Jesus**).

99. Both God and the Lamb (Jesus) will light the new Jerusalem *(Rev. 21:23, 22:5)*. Jesus' "light" *(Gk. luchnos - #3088 Strongs Concordance)* is "a candle or portable lamp" and God's "light" *(Gk. photizo - #5461 Strongs)* is "shed rays." There is a tremendous difference between "shed rays" of glory and a "candle" or "portable oil lamp."

100. After Jesus has reigned on earth for 1000 years *"Satan shall be loosed out of his prison" (Rev. 20:7)*, and will come with the hordes of Gog and Magog against Christ and the saints at Jerusalem *(Rev. 20:8-9)*. And **God** who is still in heaven **will come to the rescue!** *"And fire came down from God out of heaven, and devoured them,"* and Satan is cast into hell forever *(Rev. 20:8-10)*.

101. **God Himself is coming!** God Almighty, the Most High God, the Creator is coming to earth to **live with** and **reign over** us. *"And I heard a great voice out of heaven saying, Behold, the tabernacle (habitation) of God is with men, and he will dwell with them, and they shall be his people, and God himself shall be with them, and be their God. And God shall wipe away all tears from their eyes" (Rev. 21:3-4). "And they shall see his face" (Rev. 22:4).* "Blessed are the pure in heart, for they shall **see God**" (Jesus was speaking and they had already seen him) *(Matt. 5:8)*. *"Which is, which was, and which is to come, the Almighty" (Rev. 1:8)*.

Appendix D - To My Jewish Brethren

May I take this opportunity to thank you for holding on tenaciously to your God-given Torah down through the centuries; and for giving to the world its greatest truth, *monotheism,* as stated so clearly in your *Shema, "Hear O Israel, the Lord our God is one Lord."* May I also take this opportunity to apologize to you as a Christian, for the efforts of **some** misguided Christians over most of the last two millennia to force on you the non-biblical doctrine of God as three persons, a trinity. You have suffered much at their hands to our shame. You know, what we did not understand, that a man though perfect and sinless **cannot be God**. The inspired book that we call the New Testament, though written by Hebrew writers, was taken and made a Greek book, and interpreted with a Western perspective. But the scales are beginning to fall from our eyes.

May I hasten to add that we do have a great Biblical truth to share with you in love and that is; the Messiah came in Bethlehem about 2 or 3 B.C.E. At God's direction they named him Yeshua, and he is all that your inspired Scriptures say he would be, the anointed, appointed, empowered son of God, a man.

PLEASE TAKE ANOTHER LOOK AT YESHUA.

Your Messiah was to be a prophet like Moses from among your brethren, speaking God's words in God's name *(Deut. 18:15-19).* Yeshua was. He was to be of the seed of David and the "son" of God *(II Sam. 7:11-14; I Chron. 17:7-14).* Yeshua was. He was to be born of a virgin *(Isa. 7:14).* Yeshua was. Born in Bethlehem *(Micah 5:2-5).* Yeshua was. Messiah was to come 69 weeks (sevens) (483 years) from the going forth of the decree to rebuild Jerusalem in Nehemiah's day (445 B.C.E.) which would have been 32 C.E. *(Dan. 9:25).* Yeshua began his three year ministry to you about 29 C.E. and presented himself to you as your Messiah at the beginning of Passover Week in the spring of 32 C.E. He was rejected and slain as the Lamb on that Passover. Hear the prophet Daniel:

"Messiah (shall) be cut off, but not for himself" (Dan. 9:26).

He was to be a suffering servant; despised, rejected, wounded, bruised, chastised, striped and crucified *(Isa. 53:2-12, Ps. 22:1, 7, 8, 14-22)*. Yeshua was! Saul of Tarsus *(Paul)* wept over you. Yeshua wept over you. He knew that because you are the people chosen by God through whom He has and will bless the entire world, **you have enemies**. Yeshua warned you of these enemies. Hear him as recorded in Luke 19:41-44:

> *"And when he was come near, he beheld the city* (Jerusalem), *and wept over it, saying, If thou hadst known, even thou, at least in this thy day, the things which belong unto thy peace! But now they are hid from thine eyes. For the days shall come upon thee, that **thine enemies** shall cast a trench about thee, and compass thee round, and keep thee in on every side, and shall lay thee even with the ground, and thy children within thee; and they shall not leave in thee one stone upon another; because thou knewest not the time of thy visitation."*

Sadly this happened in 70 A.D., some 38 years after Yeshua spoke it. I regret to say it, but you still have enemies. **You also have many friends!** Bible believing Christians are the best friends that you have in this world. And you need Messiah Yeshua now more than ever before. Cry out to God as many of you are doing, for He has promised to send him again. Listen to your prophet Malachi:

> *"But unto you that fear my name shall the Sun of righteousness arise with healing in his wings; and ye*

*shall go forth, and grow up as calves of the stall. And ye shall tread down the wicked; for they shall be ashes under the soles of your feet in the day that I shall do this, saith the Lord of hosts. Remember ye the law of Moses my servant, which I commanded unto him in Horeb **for all Israel**, with the statutes and judgements. Behold, I will send you Elijah the prophet before the coming of the great and dreadful day of the Lord: And he shall turn the heart of the fathers to the children, and the heart of the children to their fathers, lest I come and smite the earth with a curse" (Mal. 4:2-6).*

"Behold, I will send my messenger, and he shall prepare the way before me: And the Lord (Messiah, Ps. 110:1) *whom ye seek, shall suddenly come to his temple, even the messenger of the covenant, whom ye delight in: **behold he shall come, saith** the Lord of hosts" (Mal. 3:1).*

Notes

Chapter 1 - Ye Shall Know The Truth

1. Hunting, Charles & Buzzard, Anthony; *The Doctrine of the Trinity*; International Scholars Publications; Lanham, Maryland; 1998; p.17.

Chapter 2 - The Godhead 101

1. The first use of the Latin word "trinitas" (trinity) with reference to God is found in Tertullians's writings (about 213 A.D.). He was the first to use the term "persons" (plural) in a Trinitarian context (*New Catholic Encyclopedia*; 1997 Ed.; Vol. 13; p. 1012).

2. Wilson, Ian; *Jesus: The Evidence*; Harper & Row Publishing; 1984; p. 165.

3. *A Summary of Christian History*; Baker & Landers Broadman & Holman Publishing; p. 65.

4. Johnson, Paul; *A History of Christianity*; Atheneum, NY; 1976; p.141; Doctrine of the Trinity.

5. Schaff, Philip; *History of the Christian Church*; Grand Rapids: Eerdmans Publishing; 1907-1910.

6. McBrien, Richard P.; Gen. Ed.; *The Harper Collins Encyclopedia of Catholicism*; p. 916.

7. *Newsweek* Magazine; March 28, 2005; p. 48.

8. Wilson, Ian; *Jesus: The Evidence*; Harper & Row Publishing; 1984; p. 168.

9. Baker, Robert & Roberts, John; *A Summary of Christian History*; Broadman & Holman Publishing; p. 66.

10. McBrien, Richard P.; Gen. Ed.; *The Harper Collins Encyclopedia of Catholicism*; p. 564-565.

11. Hagee, John; *Jerusalem Countdown*; Frontline Publishing; Lake Mary, FL; 2006; p. 72-79.

12. Boyle, Isaac, translator; *Eusebius Eccl. History*; 1995; p. 52.

13. Chrysostom, St. John; 344 A.D. - 407 A.D.

14. Hunting, Charles & Buzzard, Anthony; *The Doctrine of the Trinity;* International Scholars Pub.; Lanham, Maryland; 1998; p.143.

15. Encyclopedia Americana; 1992 Edition; Vol. 21; p. 635.

Chapter 3 - God Has A Son

1. *New International Encyclopedia*; 1916 Edition; Vol. 23; p. 47, 477.

2. McBrien, Richard P.; Gen. Ed.; *The Harper Collins Encyclopedia of Catholicism*; p. 564-565.

3. *Encyclopedia International*; University of Glasgow; 1982 Edition; Vol. 18; p. 226.

4. *Hastings' Dictionary of the Bible*; Hendrickson Publishing; 1994; p. 707.

5. *Hastings' Dictionary of the Bible*; Hendrickson Publishing; 1994; p. 708.

6. Hunting, Charles & Buzzard, Anthony; *The Doctrine of the Trinity*; International Scholars Publications; Lanham, Maryland; 1998; p. 60.

Chapter 4 - The Man Christ Jesus

1. *The Truth About One God* (pamphlet); Know The Truth Literature; Huntsville, AL; p. 6.

2. *New International Encyclopedia*; 1916 Edition; Vol. 22; p. 47, 477.

3. *Newsweek* Magazine; November 28, 2005.

Chapter 5 - What Is God's Name

1. *Encyclopedia Britannica*; Eleventh Edition; Vol. 3; p. 365, 366.

2. *The New International Encyclopedia*; 1916 Edition; Vol. 22; p. 47, 477.

3. *Hastings' Dictionary of the Bible*; Hendrickson Publishers; 1994; p. 702-703.

Chapter 6 - Where Is Jesus Now?

1. Hay, David M.; *Glory At The Right Hand*; Society of Biblical Literature; Atlanta, GA; 1989.

2. Know The Truth Literature; P.O. Box 6565; Huntsville, AL.

Chapter 9 - When Jesus Received Worship.

1. Snobelen, Stephen D.; cited in *"God of Gods, and Lords of Lords:"* *The* Theology of Isaac Newton's General Scholium to the *Principia*; University of Cambridge; 2001

Chapter 10 - How Paul Prayed

1. I an indebted to David Bordon and Rick Killian for their fine work *Discover the Power in the Prayers of Paul*; Harrison House Publishers; 2005; Tulsa, OK. However, they did not dwell on to whom Paul prayed.

Chapter 11 - Another Jesus

1. Goudge, H.L.; *The Calling of the Jews*; Shears and Sons; 1939.
2. The New York Catechism
3. Boettner, L.; *Roman Catholicism*; The Presbyterian and Reformed Publishing Co.; Philadelphia., PA; 1962; p. 127.

Chapter 13 - Fables (Catholicism)

1. *The Catholic Ency.* Thomas Nelson Publishing; 1976; s.v. "Rome."
2. *Newsweek* Magazine; May 2, 2005.
3. *Newsweek* Magazine; May 2, 2005.
4. *The Tennessean* Newspaper; January 6, 2003.
5. *U.S.A. Today* Newspaper; February 25, 2002.
6. *The Tennessean*; June 12, 2002.
7. *U.S.A. Today*; May 28, 2002.
8. *Newsweek*; March 4, 2002.
9. *Time* Magazine; March 25, 2002.
10. *Soul Magazine*; November-December; 1984; p. 4.
11. McBrien, Richard; *The Harper Collins Encyclopedia of Catholicism*; p. 1075.
12. *Time* Magazine; Dec. 30, 1991; p. 62.
13. *The Pope Speaks*; March -April; Vol. 39; No. 2; 1994; p. 105.
14. Ferrar, John; *AN ECCLESIASTICAL DICTIONARY*; London; John Mason; 1858.
15. Boettner, Loraine; *Roman Catholicism*; The Presbyterian and Reformed Publishing Co.; Philadelphia, PA; 1967; p. 127.

16. Flannery, Austin; Gen. Ed.; *Apostolic Constitution on the Revision of Indulgences*; Vatican Council II: *The Conciliar and Post Conciliar Documents*; Rev. Ed.; Costello Publishing; 1988; Vol. 1; p. 63.

17. Flannery, Austin; Gen. Ed.; *Apostolic Constitution on the Revision of Indulgences*; Vatican Council II: *The Conciliar and Post Conciliar Documents*; Rev. Ed; Costello Publishing; 1988; Vol. 1; p. 66-70.

18. Flannery, Austin; cit.; Vol. 2; p. 394.

19. *Life* Magazine; October 30, 1950; Vol. 29; No. 18; p.51.

20. For example *A Woman Rides the Beast* by Dave Hunt, Harvest House Publishers, 1994.

Chapter 14 - The Fable Called Islam

1. Gabriel, Mark A.; *Jesus and Muhammad*; Charisma House; Lake Mary, FL; Notes p. 241.

2. Gabriel, Mark A.; *Jesus and Muhammad*; Charisma House; Lake Mary, FL; p. 34-35.

3. *The Quran*; Tahrike Tarsile Quran Inc.; Elmhurst, NY; 2003; p. 298

4. Hunt, Dave; *Judgement Day*; The Berean Call; Bend, OR; p. 178.

5. *The New York Times*; July 16, 2002.

6. Cline, Eric H.; *Jerusalem Besieged*; University of Michigan Press; Ann Arbor, MI; 2004; p. 154.

7. I obtained some of my understanding of the Mid-East conflict from an excellent address given by Eric Morey at the Southwest Radio Church, East Coast Prophecy Conference; October 2004; www.swrc.com; Bethany, OK.

8. *Newsweek* Magazine; December 27, 2004/January 3, 2005.

9. *Time* Magazine; February 14, 2005.

Chapter 15 - The Fable Called Mormonism

1. Author Unknown

2. *Newsweek*; October 17, 2005; p. 54.

3. *Time* Magazine; August 4, 1997; p. 52.

4. *Newsweek*; October 17, 2005; p. 56.

5. Ankerberg, John & Weldon, John; cited in *"What Mormons Believe"*;

Harvest House; 2002; p. 312.

6. Tanner, Jerald & Sandra; *3913 Changes in the Book of Mormon*; Lighthouse Ministry; Salt Lake City, UT.

7. Free, Jack; *Mormonism and Inspiration*; 111; cited in Arthur Budvarson *Changes in Mormonism*; 5 (pamphlet).

8. Southerton, Simon G.; *Losing A Lost Tribe*; Signature Books; Salt Lake City, UT; 2004.

9. *Newsweek*; October 17, 2005; p. 57.

10. Martin, Walter; *The Maze of Mormonism*; Revised Edition; Santa Ana, CA; Vision House Publishers; 1978.

11. Ankerberg, John & Weldon, John; *What Mormons Really Believe*; Harvest House; 2002; p. 177.

12. Fraser, Gordon H.; *Is Mormonism Christian?*; Chicago, IL; Moody Press; 1977; p. 135.

13. Tanner, Jerald & Sandra; *The Changing World of Mormonism*; Rev. Edition; Chicago, IL; Moody Press; 1981; p. 140-141.

14. Cowan, Marvin W.; *Mormon Claims Answered*; Marvin W. Cowan Publishers; 1975; Revised in 1989.

15. Cowan, Marvin W.; *Mormon Claims Answered*; Marvin W. Cowan Publishers; 1975; Revised in 1989.

16. Ankerberg, John & Weldon, John; *What Mormons Really Believe*; Harvest House; 2002; p. 179.

17. Smith, Joseph; *History of the Church*; Volume 6; p. 408-409.

18. *Newsweek* Magazine; October 17, 2005; p. 60.

19. *Time* Magazine; August 4, 1997; p. 53.

20. *Newsweek* Magazine; October 17, 2005; p. 58.

21. *Time* Magazine; August 4, 1997; p. 57.

22. *Time* Magazine; August 4, 1997; p. 56.

23. Smith, Joseph; *History of the Church*; Vol. 6; p. 308, 474.

24. Smith, Joseph; *History of the Church*; Vol. 6; p. 305.

25. Smith, Joseph; *History of the Church*; Vol. 6; p. 306.

Chapter 16 - Protestant Fables

1. Bennett, Arthur; The prayer titled "The Trinity"; *The Valley of Vision*; The Banner of Truth Trust; Carlisle, PA; 1975; p. 2-3.

2. McBrien, Richard P.; *Harper Collins Encyclopedia of Catholicism*; 1995 Edition, p. 1271.

3. *New International Encyclopedia*; 1916 Edition; Vol. 22; p. 476-477.

4. *Life* Magazine; October 20, 1950; Volume 29; No. 18; p. 51.

5. *The Tennessean*; December 5, 2005; Section B; p. 1, 3.

6. Williams, Thomas; *Knowing Aslan*; W. Publishing Group; Nashville, TN; p. 30, 33, 56.

7. *Time* Magazine; December 19, 2005; p. 73-74.

Chapter 17 - To God Be The Glory

1. I am indebted to John Piper and his work *God's Passion for His Glory* for the thought behind and some of the content of this paragraph. Crossway Books; Wheaton, IL; 1998; p. 143.

Appendix B

1. Strobel, Lee; *The Case for Christ*; Zondervan Publishing; 1998; p. 65.

2. *The NIV Study Bible*; Zondervan; 1973, 1978, 1984; p. 1913.

3. *The Interpreters Dictionary of the Bible*; 1980 Edition; Volume 1; p. 35.

4. *Encyclopedia Britannica*; 1987 Edition; Volume 1; p. 877.

5. *Encyclopedia Britannica*; 1937 Edition; Volume 3; p. 82.

6. *Hastings' Dictionary of the Bible*; Hendrickson Publishers; 1994 Edition; p. 83.

7. McBrien, Richard; Gen. Ed.; *Harper Collins Encyclopedia of Catholicism*; 1995; p. 134.

8. *Hastings' Dictionary of the Bible*; Hendrickson Publishers; 1994; p. 707-708.

Scripture Index

Advertisement of CDs and Books

For more inspirational material from Joel and LaBreeska Hemphill:

Books
CDs *(Music and Preaching)*
DVDs
Songbooks

P.O. Box 656
Joelton, Tennessee 37080
Phone: 615/299-0848
Fax: 615/299-0849
Email: thehemphills@bellsouth.net
www.thehemphills.com

"Partners In Emotion"
By LaBreeska Hemphill
Trumpet Call Books

"To God Be The Glory"
(Examining The Bible View Of God)
By Joel W. Hemphill
Trumpet Call Books

Books available from the above address
or wherever fine books are sold.

The Hemphills: Partners In Emotion

LaBreeska Rogers Hemphill has spent her life ministering through gospel music. In the early 1950's, she traveled as a member of The Happy Goodman Family and later for twenty-five years with her immediate family, The Hemphills. The Hemphill family, LaBreeska, Joel, and their three children, has received a total of eight Dove awards from the Gospel Music Association.

Drawing from her life and ministry experiences, LaBreeska has done an outstanding job of writing her story. This is a life changing book that has ministered hope, encouragement and comfort to many thousands of people. She is very transparent in speaking of their martial problems and the healing, as well as Joel's two year bout with severe clinical depression, and restoration.

Joel says, of *"Partners In Emotion"*, "This book is a story of divine intervention and restoration, how God brought joy out of our pain, hope out of our despair and turned our test into a testimony. Thank you, Darling, for telling our story."

Bill Gaither says, "Someone has said, 'If you're going to make the journey, you might as well enjoy the trip.' I don't know two people who are enjoying the trip any more than Joel and LaBreeska Hemphill. I think you'll enjoy the journey also as you experience their emotions in the pages of this book."

Zig Ziglar says, "*Partners In Emotion* is a book about faith, love and hope. It's also about overcoming adversity, patiently pursuing your dream, honoring Christ as Lord and fulfilling your commitment through obedience to Him and His calling...You'll laugh, cry, rejoice and get downright enthusiastic as you share the experiences that LaBreeska makes so personal."

Pat Boone says, "The Hemphills have been glorious staples in gospel music for decades now--and it's no wonder that the enemy of our souls would target them in vicious ways. But Jesus promised to be with us even through 'the valley of the shadow of death.'...Read this wonderful testimony and be encouraged as I have been."

This book is a must for your Christian library.
Available from The Hemphills, Lightning Source, Inc., or wherever fine books are sold.

ISBN 0-9671756-1-5 - Price $12.99 US

About The Author

Joel Hemphill was saved at the age of ten in the church that his father pastored in West Monroe, Louisiana. He answered the call to Christian ministry at the age of nineteen and has pastored and evangelized since that time. His pastoral work included the pastorate of Pentecostal Temple in Bastrop, LA from 1961-1971 and Peytonsville Baptist Church of Thompson Station, TN for thirteen months in 1993-1994. His evangelistic work, along with his wife LaBreeska, whom he married in 1957 at the age of seventeen, has taken him around the world to minister in Israel, South Africa, Scotland, England, N. Ireland, Egypt, Mexico, Honduras, and throughout the U.S.A. and Canada.

Joel has written and recorded over 300 Gospel songs and has received Dove nominations ten different years from the Gospel Music Association as songwriter of the year. His songs include Pity The Man, Consider The Lilies, He's Still Workin' On Me, Master Of The Wind, I Claim The Blood and Let's Have A Revival. He has written scores of inspirational magazine and newspaper articles. Joel and his wife LaBreeska, along with their children have received eight Dove Awards (Gospel Music's highest), in various categories and he has received three BMI Awards of Excellence.

They have two sons, a daughter and six grandchildren. Since 1972 they have made their home in Nashville, Tennessee.

Notes

Pg. 189 – Worship God only!